S S E C E R K O E L R L S

THE BLACK DRAGON OF DEARTH

JASON D. MCINTOSH

WWW.JASONDMCINTOSH.COM

Information about the author, sales, illustrations and more may be obtained by visiting www.jasondmcintosh.com.

First printing: February 2020

ISBN (hc): 978-1-7346626-0-3
ISBN (pb): 978-1-7346626-1-0
ISBN (ebook fixed layout): 978-1-7346626-2-7
ISBN (ebook reflowable): 978-1-7346626-3-4

For my wife and children.
You are the story of my life.
— JDM

And I saw an angel coming down out of heaven, having the key to the Abyss
and holding in his hand a great chain. He seized the dragon, that ancient serpent,
who is the devil, or Satan, and bound him for a thousand years.

He threw him into the Abyss, and locked and sealed it over him, to keep him from
deceiving the nations anymore until the thousand years were ended.

After that, he must be set free for a short time.

The Bible, Revelation 20:1-3

Part I: The Gift

"GRAYVYKS!" THOMAS GROANED. A cold dread turned his stomach. And from the sound of it, there were *hundreds* of them. Each guttural shriek and heavy footfall of their talon-laden claws all bent in one ominous direction—*His*. Stopping to catch his breath atop the ravine, Thomas tracked the converging paths of crashing underbrush and tree rattling below.

They were closing in fast.

Without armor-piercing rounds, the weapon holstered at his side was all but useless against their tightly woven scales. Firing off a half dozen short-range shells at one of these ancient serpents was almost surely a death sentence, and he was not eager to shake hands with death tonight. He chided himself for not preparing for this mission better, then quickly excused the oversight. *How could I possibly have known?* He thought they had all been destroyed years ago in the Logarthiym war, yet here, panting in the pale blue and green moonlight of Haizorr's dual moons, he had more than his share of them to deal with. On any other night, the moons with their halos of blue and green would have been breathtakingly beautiful. The kind of spectacle that caused starstruck lovers to reach out, as if magnetically, to clasp hands with each other in a heart-hammering silence. Like he and Jillian had shared all those years ago…

A splintering crack sounded as one of his rhino-sized pursuers, consumed with blind rage, ran headlong into a small nearby tree. Thomas' breath caught ragged in his chest at the ground-shaking impact. They were closer than he thought! His hopes that the creature had smashed its own brains in, or at least knocked itself senseless, were dashed as the dark silhouette of the offending tree rocked and then fell to the earth with a sickening thud. Shaking its serpentine head side to side as if merely swatting an annoying insect, the beast ran onward unfazed—if not a little angrier than before. A bone-chilling call shot out from its throat.

The entire wood flooded with the curling echoes of dozens of answering snarls and shrill replies. The call of a grayvyk, the Book had said, is so potent that it can be heard for *years*. Surpassing the physical laws of sound, it is told that the echo can reverberate within the very soul of any who are so unlucky as to be within earshot.

That *Book*. The one possession Thomas both loved and lamented. It had set him free, unlocking his spirit from the gravelly gray of his ordinary life. It had also bound him to this mission, luring the very hounds of Hades to his own doorstep. Indeed, for that is exactly where he was heading. Home. He had tried all night to evade the beasts, and once he even thought he had succeeded. But the scent of the artifact he had stolen had proven stronger than his stealth. Evil is simply drawn to itself.

Perhaps *stolen* is not the best way to describe Thomas' actions of this particular evening. He preferred to think of these tasks simply as academic adventures aimed at collecting remarkable relics. The one he now carried was perhaps one of the most powerful artifacts ever recorded, and judging by the creatures pursuing him, had nearly fallen into the hands of a purely evil force with foul intentions. By those standards, Thomas judged his deed as right and just. But a grayvyk knows neither righteousness nor justice, and right now, in their eyes Thomas was a down-and-dirty thief. And a tired thief at that. Lack of sleep and an endless night of ducking and weaving beneath the shadows were beginning to take a toll on him. Not nearly as much as it would have on Earth where his strength was lessened, but nonetheless, if he did not cross over soon, it could be the end of his journeys altogether.

For a brief moment he entertained the idea of hiding high in the boughs of one of the *trabalisk* trees that lined the rim of the northern forest. They were easy enough to climb and had a staggering height—nearly double that of the tallest redwoods of Earth. Their fruit could sustain him for days if need be. Grayvyks could not climb, having only two legs, however the thought of being treed and driven mad by the mind-splintering shrieks of the serpents quickly drove the notion from him. He fought the urge to panic.

The Gate was at least three or four more miles from here. He was not worried about his strength failing, since this realm added a robustness to his body that did not exist anywhere else. It was the tenacious speed of his pursuers that troubled him. At this pace, and in this terrain, his hopes of ever crossing over were beginning to fade. He began considering his options. There was a stream down the valley just ahead beside a trabalisk grove; perhaps the huge trees would provide some cover while he tried switching his trail from bank to bank over the running river. Like a crafty raccoon attempting to outwit coonhounds. He dismissed the foolish strategy; these beasts could *feel* his cargo. Thomas would simply be making their hunt easier. Perhaps he could devise a trap? *There is no time!* he thought. *Even a bear trap wouldn't stop one of them, much less dozens!* Thomas knew he had to simply continue this mad sprint through the night. In the end, he decided that he was sick of crashing through the bushes. He could run along the bank of the stream and have less underbrush to tangle up his legs. It would also be less noisy. Alternating between prayers and gasping for great lungfuls of air, he plodded on toward the river.

Being pack animals, grayvyks seldom hunt alone. Bred by the hundreds for their simple minds and odd sort of loyalty that drives them to blindly obey their master's every command, they make a formidable and expendable army. Yet, once in a great while, one of the dark brood hatches with a blend of keen and cunning setting it apart from its mindless companions. This strain of grayvyk is slightly larger than the others with talons a shade of light blue, as opposed to the usual steel gray. The mutation, referred to as a *keen grayvyk,* is also deadly silent. Where the rest of the pack seems content to fill the wind with vicious howls, a keen grayvyk will utter no sound at all when hunting. Other than those factors, there is virtually no way to distinguish a keen grayvyk from the rest of the group.

Normally, a keen grayvyk would be weeded out and destroyed by its master, as most of the fiendish folk who prefer grayvyks as pets are vicious themselves and cannot bear the thought of an intelligent minion. But as fate, or luck, or some evil plan would have it, this particular grayvyk-master had not noticed one of the blue-clawed menaces living among the pack. With a will of its own, a dark, and silent shadow broke off from the main group and began a snaking descent toward the river valley. The keen grayvyk had picked up a fresh trail and began hunting Thomas. Alone.

Thomas' plan to run along the river was not going as well as he had hoped. For one, the mud kept sucking at his boots, nearly pulling them off twice now. Then, there were the insects. Swarming in dense clouds, the fat-bodied flies lazily hovered just even with his head. They were not a biting species nor did they seem to be curious about him, but their position in the air was more than troubling for someone gasping for breath while running through their mid-air meetings. Thomas was sure he had dozens of them stuck in his nose by now.

When he stopped to spit out another mouthful of the horrible tasting brownish bugs, something pricked his senses. He pulled up sharply to listen. He was almost sure that the echoing calls of his pursuers sounded just slightly off course. He willed his breath to still in his chest so he could listen. Yes! There it was! The sound of the crashing and howling seemed to be falling away and to the left behind him. But why? Thomas was not an overly prideful man and so was not quick to think that he had the ability to outrun such swift creatures. Reasoning that the dense forest nearby must be obscuring his trail he abandoned the riverbank, altering his course into the trees.

After a moment he paused to rest and listen. Content that the grayvyk pack must be having difficulty tracking him, he took stock of his surroundings. The tree trunks about him were huge and he marveled at their thickness. *They must be over a thousand years old!* he thought. He was about to restart his journey forward when he noticed a subtle movement out of the corner of his eye. It was about twenty feet or more off the ground and swayed like a tree in the breeze. But there was no breeze. The moment he turned to stare at it directly, however, it vanished behind one of the huge trunks. Then, just as suddenly, he noticed another swaying motion appear in the periphery of his other side. It too, vanished when confronted by Thomas' searching eyes. A chill trickled down his spine. He was being watched. But more than that—his watchers *knew that he knew* they were watching!

Thomas was unsure if this new discovery was friend or foe, but one thing was certain: many foes were already nipping at his heels and home was still a long way off. His knowledge of the grayvyks was not much, but it was enough to propel him forward and take his chances with these new creatures in the wood. The fact that they had not attacked him outright gave him a small measure of hope, and he continued onward, threading his way in between the watcher-filled trees.

After nearly a half-hour of jogging through the thick woods, Thomas began to find his hope strengthening. In fact, he could barely hear the grayvyks any longer and the dual full moons cast a perfect light into the majestic forest so that finding his way through it was quite easy. Only the eerie presence of the watchers kept his hope from returning fully. They were so good at remaining in his peripheral vision that Thomas had given up trying to catch a full view of one. Every step of the way, they had been there. From time to time he would also feel a subtle *thump* that shook the ground nearby. It felt as if something very heavy yet soft, had fallen onto the forest floor from high above. He had stopped whenever he felt the vibrations to figure out where it was coming from, but it stopped as soon as he did. As usual, his curious followers would avoid his probing stares into the trees.

It began to feel like a frightening sort of game. For what felt like the hundredth time Thomas stopped to scan the trees, always about twenty or thirty feet above ground. And for the hundredth time the onlookers dodged away from him just before he could catch a glimpse of one. It was maddening! In a fit of frustration, he bent down, snatched up a fist-sized stone and hurled it where he was sure one of the watchers had been just seconds before. A hollow knock, and he knew he had simply hit the trunk of an ancient tree. But, now just to the right of the same tree, Thomas was able to make out a distant clearing ahead. The Gate was now only a few hundred yards away! Recognizing the terrain, he picked up the pace.

Whump! The ground beneath his feet trembled.

Thump! Thumph! Thummmp! The tree trunk nearest Thomas groaned heavily as if something very tall, and very large had just leaned against it. Without bothering to look, Thomas took off on a wild dash toward the moonlit clearing.

Thump! Whump! Thump! The watchers in the woods were no longer just watching. Now at least one of them was matching pace with Thomas' mad scramble through the trees. To his left, and of course remaining out of his clear view, he could just decipher a very tall, thin figure taking enormous steps as it passed through the pale beams of moonlight falling between the trees. It was huge. Standing at least two stories high it appeared to have long pale arms and legs that took massive strides hurtling it through the forest at incredible speed. The only sound it made came from the heavy *thump, thump* of its footfalls.

I'm going to be eaten by a giant! I never should have thrown that rock at it, thought Thomas. He tried zigzagging through the trabalisk grove to shake its pursuit. *Thump! Thump!* It was closing the distance, angling through the dense growth directly toward him. His only hope now was getting to the clearing and reaching the Gate. With a rush of terror that surprised him, Thomas pushed his body to its limit and ran for his life. His shirt tore on a broken branch. He felt his right boot loosen as the laces began to unravel after catching on a gnarled root. Every twig, vine, rock and log seemed determined to prevent his escape! Finally, like a wild animal freed from its cage, Thomas burst through a cluster of low bushes and suddenly found himself knee-high within the grasses of the clearing.

Bathed in bright moonlight, he was now exposed in full view. Realizing this new danger, he did not slow his step. If he had taken but a half a breath to survey the new terrain, he would have noticed the odd pile of fallen branches that lay tangled in the weeds before him. With a grunt, his leg sunk deep between the space of two twisted trunks and down he went. A sickening *snap* followed, but Thomas was so stricken with fear that he was not sure if it were his ankle bones or the offending branch that had given way. *Thump! Whump!* It did not seem to matter either way. The giant had followed him out of the woods and was rushing toward him.

In seconds it would all be over.

What happened next could only be described as one of the most incredible moments of his life. The beast that emerged from the woods was of a colossal size, but it was not nearly as frightening as Thomas imagined it would be. It had a form that could be described as human-like, but at the same time, appeared almost *tree-like*. Long, sinewy limbs and torso met a thick neck. But what was most striking about it was its face. His imaginations of this creature eating him earlier had filled his mind with thoughts of a beast that had jaws simply filled with dripping teeth and long, angry claws. This could not be further from the truth. It possessed a sort of kind, yet sad face. Grim and sober. Like the face of someone who had been thinking the most serious and responsible of thoughts for a thousand years. Its stout chin met a flat, firmly set mouth that followed high cheekbones into deep-set diamond blue eyes. There were no ears to speak of, or hair, except its skin looked rough in patches, like a thick, living tree bark. The only parts of the creature that looked truly menacing were its enormous hands and feet. And right now, both hands were balled into fists the size of small cars and the *thump, thump* of its feet looked more like angry, determined stomping than pursuing strides. The kind of steps a bull takes just before making ready a devastating charge at an intruder.

Thomas kicked and struggled against the tangled knots of branches beneath him. Thankfully it *had* been the branch and not his ankle that had broken. The logs rolled awkwardly beneath him and he stumbled again, losing his footing. *Whump, thump, thumph!* He fell flat on his stomach; knocking what little wind he had left out of his lungs. Rolling to his back, he saw the giant's foot—which looked much more like a mass of branches and dirt clods than an actual foot—lift above him. *Like an annoying insect!* he thought. *I'm going to be squashed like a cockroach!* He squeezed his eyes tight, bracing for the impact that would end his days.

When the crushing blow did not come, he looked up to find that the twenty-five-foot beast had simply stepped over him and appeared to be fixed on a different target altogether. It stood in the bright, pale moonlight breathing heavily. Thomas rolled over to get a better look at the creature, which now had its back to him. Steamy breath curled out of its nostrils as it turned its massive upper body side to side. It was searching the bushes and

15

trees ahead for something. Thomas nearly choked when it spun quickly and glanced over its shoulder back at him. The piercing blue eyes studied his own. Thomas swallowed hard. Such eyes! They looked so bright. Intelligent. Almost human. And then the realization struck Thomas. This was no mindless forest giant, but an honest-to-goodness *darchlyte!*

THOMAS ALMOST LET OUT A WHOOP OF JOY. If he was right and this was indeed one of the ancients of the darchlyte race, then Thomas was in good company. Darchlytes have no love for evil things that lurk in dark shadows. He then realized that this was precisely why he was able to evade the grayvyks. Thomas reasoned the good-natured presence of the darchlyte must have obscured his scent, throwing them off his trail!

The disdain possessed of the darchlytes for injustice runs deep in their bloodline, and could be traced back to a single, nearly forgotten legend. The Book in the secret study back on the Earth side of the Gate held an entire chapter dedicated to the sad story. When the planet was new, and its creator had barely finished hanging both moons in the sky, the darchlytes—known simply then as *lytes*—were charged with the glorious task of maintaining fair dominion and rule over the planet. The trees, plants, animals—virtually all of Haizorr—fell under the careful watch of the noble, powerful race of lytes. All of that changed, however, when a black-scaled, jealous serpent from the void-land of Dearth convinced several of them that ruling just one planet was not enough for such lofty beings.

The devious old Dragon convinced them that their creator was keeping secrets from them all. The beast promised to grant the race of lytes dominion over the great sun in addition to their planet. Fooled by the forked tongue of the coal-black serpent, the earliest of the lytes pledged their allegiance to the dark beast. In exchange, the black Dragon granted the lytes an immense measure of physical strength. Overnight, their stature and speed grew, so that it seemed that they would be able to indeed rule the sun! But they were all deceived. For in the very moment the oath was sworn, they also bound themselves to a terrible curse. The lytes could no longer stand to be in any sort of darkness. As soon as the sun would begin its daily downward path to the horizon, they found themselves drawn to travel with it, like a magnet tugging at them from the sky. So began their new cursed existence. A life suddenly filled with a daily, endless pursuit of the sun, circling the planet each day on foot. The sun, ever before them, yet always just beyond reach. It was this hated curse born of dark and light that gained them the name *darchlyte*.

The curse of the Black Dragon of Dearth had achieved exactly what it wanted. With every part of the planet left virtually unguarded by the darchlytes during the night, evil grew unchecked throughout the lands. The darchlytes would find their homes destroyed daily, as they returned with the rising sun. The only time the darchlytes could withstand a full nightfall was when the dual moons of Haizorr hung full and bright in the clear night sky. The full moons seemed to serve as a sort of loophole in the curse. Though its occurrence was rare, it was a rest that generations of these giants grew to revere as a holy time. Theirs had become a life of endless hiding, running and searching: Hiding from darkness. Running after the sun. Searching for a way to break the curse. Longing for a way to destroy the Black Dragon and his servants. At some point in their history they had combined their strength against the beast and succeeded in blocking the Dragon's further advances on the planet by banishing it back to Dearth, but that is another tale entirely.

The fate of the darchlytes is a story not unlike that of many other ancient and noble races. Haizorr was but one planet of thousands where the venom of that wicked black snake had all but snuffed out the light of hope.

Thomas breathed a prayer of thanks that the moons hung so bold and bright in the sky tonight. The blue-green light made the darchlyte's shadow stretch across the clearing. Then the beast began huffing and snorting heavily, as if it had caught an offensive whiff of something on the wind. Thomas had barely enough time to cover his ears before the giant darchlyte drew an enormous gulp of air and let out the most angry, earth-shattering battle cry he had ever thought possible. The force of the shout shook the ground and Thomas' teeth chattered together in his head. The tall grasses parted before the lumbering creature and the bushes in front of it shook violently as if they had been shot with a hot cannon blast. Then all fell silent. Thomas lay still as a dead man, his heart hammering his ears. In reply came a low, throaty *hissssss* from beyond the bushes that had just been decimated by the behemoth's yell.

A silvery shadow snaked out from the darkness, its blue claws raking the tall grass as it strode forward. Thomas felt his own heart freeze like a chunk of ice in his chest. The keen grayvyk opened its jaws showing row upon row of steel-sharp teeth, answering the challenge to do battle. There was no standoff or delay. Neither foe sized up the other. The blue-taloned grayvyk simply charged without any display or warning and the towering giant did the same. Thomas felt his eyes widen in his head as he watched. He had to admit, that despite his terror, he was feeling a little excited at the prospect of watching his attacker get pummeled by an angry darchlyte.

But then a frightening thought entered his mind; *What if the grayvyk wins?* The grayvyk was certainly the faster of the two, and this proved true as it crossed most of the open space between them before the giant had hardly taken a forward stride. In a great bowing motion, the darchlyte lunged forward to snatch up an enormous fallen log. It snapped the waist-thick branch in two, which left one of the broken ends tapered to a sharp point. Thomas could only assume that it was creating a weapon of sorts. The towering creature was just straightening back up, when the grayvyk pounced. In an impossibly high bound it hurled itself toward the unguarded shoulder of the darchlyte. Thomas saw the blue talons rake across its hard flesh and then run straight down its back. The wicked lizard had simply leapt over its challenger and now fixed its fiery eyes on Thomas! Scrambling to get off of the cumbersome log pile, he stumble-stepped backwards in a sort of crazy crab walk, trying to put distance between himself and the charging serpent. It was useless. The grayvyk was already on top of him, drawing its head back to strike the final blow.

Like lightning, the great neck snapped forward like a whip, teeth clashing together a mere six inches away from the man's sweaty face. The deadly bite had fallen short! Rancid breath and clammy drool smacked against Thomas, and he nearly vomited. The grayvyk's eyes widened suddenly in shock and it let out a short, high shriek of surprise. The beast threw itself into a rage then, snapping and clawing at the mound of logs and earth, straining forward to devour the shaking man before it. Thomas took his chance to get clear of the beast, yet when he did, it did not advance after him. And then he saw why it could not. The great tree-trunk spear that the darchlyte had fashioned stuck straight through the meaty part of the keen grayvyk's tail and was driven deep into the ground on the other side. The enormous darchlyte had pinned it to the earth like a dog on a chain. The grayvyk was angrier than anything Thomas had ever seen in his life. The mad frenzy of thrashing, hissing and clawing was a frightful thing to watch yet all the while, its evil eyes remained trained on Thomas. The display was so violent that he was sure it was going to rip its own tail in half.

Thomas had nearly forgotten all about the darchlyte until it took a quick half step toward the trapped grayvyk. Without so much as a whisper, the towering hero balled up both enormous fists and raised them high into the air above its head. With a deep moan it heaved its full strength, bringing them down square onto the neck of the grayvyk. The crash was tremendous. The nearby trees rattled, and several dead branches were shaken loose from their ancient trunks. Thomas was thrown backward off his feet. When he staggered back up, his ears were still buzzing from the shockwave. A cloud of dust slowly settled around the broken grayvyk. The darchlyte's savage blow had done its work. The force had made a crater large enough to hide a pickup truck and had driven the beast several feet down into the dirt. A grave fit for a grayvyk.

"Not so *keen* now, are you?" said Thomas, a slight grin turning up the corners of his stubbled chin. He kicked a clod of dirt onto the crumpled serpentine corpse in the crater below. Leaning back to look up at the looming savior above him he said, "Thank you," and then awkwardly added, "friend." He raised an arm in order to greet the giant with a handshake.

Sapphire blue eyes, as deep and mysterious as the darkest caverns of the deepest oceans stared back at him. There was no expression, or hint that it even acknowledged him, but one look into those deep eyes said otherwise. Somehow Thomas felt that his new friend understood more about the cargo he carried than he himself realized. He lowered his hand back to his side.

The giant stooped down into the crater and wrapped a thick hand around the fallen grayvyk, picking it up by a clawed leg as though it were a freshly hunted turkey. The darchlyte's strength was incredible! With the same effort it took for a child to snap a pencil, it removed one of the blue-taloned toes from the foot of the keen grayvyk. Black liquid oozed from the wound like sticky syrup. The plump flies that had plagued Thomas near the river-bed were already starting to swarm near the lizard's reeking body. Thomas swatted several of them away, afraid they might somehow end up in his nose again. Dropping the scaly carcass to the ground like a sack of wet rags, the darchlyte turned its serious face back toward Thomas. Leaning its massive head down low to the ground where Thomas stood, it gingerly laid the blue claw next to the toe of his right boot.

Thomas blinked in surprise at the gesture. He was unsure what to do with the sticky gift lying at his feet. Was he supposed to take a bite of it to show his approval? Should he bow? Before he could respond, the darchlyte quickly spun and sniffed the air. Almost at the same time, the distant wails of grayvyks crept into the field. Whether they had followed the path of the keen grayvyk, or had heard the colossal battle in this meadow, Thomas could not tell but the fact that they could be heard once again meant that they were most certainly on their way to this very spot. The immense darchlyte glanced again at Thomas, and then to the talon in the grass at his feet. The message in its fathom-deep eyes was clear: *Take it!*

He bent down to grasp the five-inch long claw, when he stood back up the darchlyte was gone. Movement from the corner of his eye at the tree-line told him where it had most likely retreated. The woods again started filling with the cries of pursuing grayvyks. Stuffing the claw into his satchel, Thomas took a deep breath and resumed his dash toward freedom.

The clearing where the Gate was located opened further before him and Thomas nearly cried out at the sight. To the untrained eye, the Gate looked like little more than an oddly gnarled tree. Two twisted limbs reaching East and West gave it the appearance of a man whose arms were being stretched wide. Other than that, there was nothing very interesting about the tree unless, of course, one had read and understood the Book. By now, Thomas was running so hard that he nearly collided full force with the Tree Gate.

With a practiced motion he wrapped both arms wide around the rough bark of its trunk, uttering the ancient phrase he had memorized.

His dry throat made his words hoarse. *"From East to West the span is wide, with love cross to the other side. Should the Harm descend across the land, may Death's own sting be in thy hand."*

He was always a little nervous about saying the last part. Though no harm had ever come to him, it still gave him goose bumps to utter the words that he did not yet fully understand. With a low *rip* the trunk began to buck and twist. Its heavy bark and dense wood taking on the look and feel of cloth as the center of the trunk began to unroll like a giant scroll. Thomas stepped back a few paces to gaze at the Gate finishing its opening process. He never got over just how magnificent this part of the journey was.

Suddenly, the trees and forest around him exploded in a flurry of scales, teeth and shrieks. The pack of grayvyks had caught up with him! Row after row of the hard-scaled beasts began pouring through the bushes and thick undergrowth. He dashed back to dive through the Tree Gate but stopped short. It was not yet open. The folds of the tree trunk were still un-curling layer by layer. He could just begin to make out the familiar shapes of his secret study on the other side, but it was still closed to him.

Out of instinct, and mostly fear, Thomas snatched the revolver from the holster at his hip. Though he knew it to be useless against the armored grayvyks, just holding a weapon of any kind helped him feel like he could at least do *something* to defend himself.

The shrieking howls rose up like a storm. The grayvyk pack had cornered its prey and seemed to be enjoying the moment. Thomas took aim at the face of the nearest charging beast and gripped the trigger, firing off three shots. *Ting! Ta-ting!* The bullets glanced off the armored head with a spray of sparks, nothing more. Enraged, it howled with a pitch so painfully sharp, Thomas was sure his ears must be bleeding by now. He suddenly felt queasy and could feel his legs wobbling, the scene around him began to tip. His nose felt wet. Blood? The howls were shaking his senses to the breaking point.

In a last effort to regain control, Thomas fired the remaining rounds at the rushing mob of snapping jaws. The gun belched fire and he felt the recoil against his palm, but he heard nothing. The gunshots drowned by the shrieks and the throbbing in his head.

The first beast had reached him and launched itself into the air, mouth open wide. Thomas staggered back, caught his heel on a root and fell through the Gate just as the last layer had peeled open. In an instant, the howling vanished. Thomas blinked in shock. He had made it through! He sat once again on the floor of his study, his limbs trembling. His satchel had fallen open when he had collapsed backward, strewing its contents across the marble floor. The precious scroll he had redeemed had stopped rolling and lay near the blue talon, still sticky with blood from the keen grayvyk.

Thomas was scooting across the floor to retrieve them when a dread knotted his stomach. He had left the Gate open! He glanced up at the rough stone wall that he had just fallen through. From this side of the Gate, one could not see or hear the awaiting realm that existed just a breath away on the other side. Crossing over was simply a matter of trusting the guidance of the Book, and, in this case, also walking headfirst though solid blocks of stone. But, with the Gate wide open, the view from the other side was clear for whoever, or whatever, happened to be watching.

Thomas jumped to his feet, lunging for the glowing crystal shard affixed to the surface of the ancient stone wall. By twisting it in a sunwise semicircle and speaking the correct words, the Gate would instantly block any access between worlds. He had to close it now! Just as his fingers reached the crystal dial, a shriek shattered the silence. A grayvyk! Thomas jumped in shock, away from the massive head full of teeth now sticking through his wall like some kind of living hunting trophy.

Its head wagged wildly from side to side. The dark eyes darting around the room, then landing on the prize it had come for. If it had seen Thomas, it made no hint that it noticed him at all. All focus seemed trained on the scroll that lay on the cold floor just inches from its snapping jaws. Another scream tore from its throat. The serpent's head lunged forward in a frenzy to seize the scroll, but then it seemed to panic. Thomas could now clearly see that the beast was stuck fast. Fortunately, it was one of the larger of the grayvyk herd. Too large to fully fit through the Gate, it was wedged tightly in the portal between worlds.

Seeing his chance, Thomas dove across the floor at the scroll, coming face to face once again with a nightmarish mouth. Hot, acrid breath assaulted his senses. With the scroll, claw and his satchel in hand he began inching backward on his seat, just as the beast managed to get part of its leg through. In seconds the creature would force its way fully through into his own home!

"Oh no you don't!" Thomas cried as he hefted the dagger-like blue talon above his head and slashed it across the face of the grayvyk. Shockingly, a spray of black blood and a deep, ragged wound appeared across the forehead and left eye of the monster. He had expected the blow to have very little effect, but the keen-grayvyk claw had cut through the armor-scaled hide of its comrade as if it were made of butter! The animal let out a wounded howl and pulled its leg back through the portal.

Thomas slashed again and again, landing blows directly on the snout and between the eyes of the lizard. It punctured deeply. Black blood began pooling on the floor. With one final, hate-filled gurgling hiss, the head disappeared as the beast retreated fully. Thomas jumped up and spun the ancient amulet-dial.

"*Signate portæ!*", he shouted. A faint green glow of the dial signaled its closure. Thomas collapsed to his knees and pressed his head against the solid cold stone, catching his breath. He closed his eyes and stood there, frozen in shock and relief for several long moments.

The low, scraping sound of a door opening behind him bolted him upright. His nerves still taught from the tussle with the grayvyk, he drew back the blood-blackened claw ready for another strike.

"What's all the horrible noise in here, Thomas?" came the voice of Jillian as she entered the room. Her long, auburn hair swept back in a braid, fastened with a simple yellow ribbon. She wore the light blue flowered dress that always made Thomas smile like a schoolboy when she wore it. Her perfect sea-blue eyes landed on the black stain spreading across the floor at her husband's feet.

"Ah, I see you've been playing again. Well, I'm not sure if a cleaner exists that could lift a stain like that one." She sniffed. "What a stench! You've outdone yourself." Holding her nose against the foul odor she smiled playfully at him.

Thomas staggered backward with a sigh of relief. "Jillian! I got it! And I met a darchlyte—it gave me this!" He held the talon forward for her to see but noticing how filthy it was, began to clean it off with his already tattered shirt. "I just killed a grayvyk with it…well almost, I think. Its head was coming through the portal wall—" Thomas sputtered the words. He was excited, relieved, and utterly exhausted all at once. He could feel his legs trembling, and he gripped the nearby table to steady himself. "Whoa. I think I need to sit down." He tottered unsteadily across his study and flopped onto the thick leather couch, dropping the claw onto the mahogany writing desk nearby.

Jillian walked lightly on bare feet and stood beside him. Bending down she tenderly kissed his tired forehead. The key pendant necklace she wore dangled forward from her neck, bumping him lightly on the nose as she leaned in close. "Don't stay up too late, love. You have church and we have the competition in the morning," she whispered.

But Thomas did not hear a word. He had entered a deep and satisfying sleep. After a moment the rhythm of his slow, deep breathing was the only sound as Jillian stood surveying the room. Her eyes traveled a worried trail from the black smear on the floor to the bluish talon resting on the smooth wood of the desk.

Did she just hear him say that a *grayvyk* had poked its head into the room?

With all her heart, she desperately hoped not.

PART II: THE LIE

"I JUST WISH I WAS IN CHURCH," Heidyl breathed to herself, trying to clear her head and steady her nerves. It was bad enough that she had to wear this ridiculous uniform that practically bared her soul, but to parade in it before hundreds of sets of eyes was unnerving. She much preferred performing her gymnastics routines wearing her own leggings and t-shirt in the empty meadow behind her home. Alone. Her mom always wondered how she managed getting those clothes so "unearthly filthy." Heidyl simply told her that she falls a lot while playing with Jayce in the woods. Which was not entirely untrue, but she knew that if her mother suspected her of vaulting through routines of backward handsprings through the tall grass and uneven ground of the meadow, she would have a fit.

Out of old habit, she had popped a few sugar candies in her mouth several minutes before, to help ensure her blood sugar would not drop dangerously low somewhere in the middle of her performance. The music of her floor routine began on hollow notes through the aging speaker system of the gymnasium and Heidyl felt her pulse quicken. She cast a quick, searching glance across the bleacher stands to find her mom. Jillian was sitting where she always sat, two rows from the top, center section. Hands clasped in her lap with her back straight as a pin. She smiled, winked back and spread her arms as wide as she could in a sort of air-hug. That was their own shared routine and it gave Heidyl just enough courage to take the first step into her first big move on the open floor.

Heidyl was built for speed and power. Even as a toddler, she had a low center of gravity that gave her terrific balance. In many heart-stopping instances, Thomas and Jillian would turn their backs for but a second, and in the next moment find her balancing along the back of the sofa or the kitchen bar top. They suspected from the start that she would most likely have a promising future in some sort of ballet or dance.

Entering her into gymnastics had not even been considered until one day her second grade teacher called home to inform them that Heidyl had been performing what she described as "Olympic level uneven-bar routines" on the playground and that they should probably discourage their daughter from doing so. Thomas and Jillian, however, did quite the opposite and enrolled her in a local gymnastics school that very week. This proved to be one of the best parenting decisions they ever made for her. Heidyl rose to the top quicker than any child in the school's history. The trophy case at home was stuffed to bursting with medals and honors that she had won over the years.

For a dark year, the family thought that her career might have been at an end when she was diagnosed with type-one diabetes. The auto-immune disease that attacked her pancreas required multiple daily insulin injections and countless finger pokes to check her blood sugar levels. It was very unpredictable, even maddening at times, often requiring her to force-feed herself juice, maple syrup—anything that could quickly get her blood sugar up to a safe level. There were often many sleepless nights as they battled the disease together. Other days her blood was so full of sugar it took several injections to get it back to a normal range. Heidyl was forever feeling as though she was walking a balance beam while riding a roller coaster. The complication certainly did strain her resolve and challenged her always, but Heidyl proved to be no quitter. And today, she was poised to win yet another competition. She was so far ahead in her scores that all she needed to do was finish this floor routine. She did not even need to finish it cleanly. Just waltz out there, fumble through it if she wanted—maybe even fall—and walk away with the highest score in the Chattan Regional Conference. Again.

Heidyl closed her eyes, breathed deep, then coiled herself like a spring. Music erupted from the loudspeakers with a sudden burst of drums and a racing guitar solo. She purposely chose music that was not the usual classical numbers that much of her stuffy competition preferred. She exploded into her routine with all the ferocity of a caged lion, bare feet pounding the spring floor in time with the heavy beat. With top speed achieved, she flung her arms forward, vaulted into a perfect handspring, and with a half twist in mid-air tucked her body into a tight ball. She seemed to sail into orbit. After turning head over heels twice, Heidyl planted her feet and stuck a perfect landing to the double-back maneuver just as the bass drum in her music hit a heavy, hollow beat. The audience was on its feet with whoops of stunned approval. She was captivating. But Heidyl was just warming up.

In between these power moves, Heidyl and her coach had wisely woven in some more restful ones so that she could catch her breath. To the average person, they looked anything but restful. Tumbling, turning and leaping she held the rapt attention of the entire room. Jillian, hands still tightly clasped in her lap, had been holding her breath for nearly sixty seconds as she watched her daughter. With taut nerves, she glanced at the device in her hand. The glucose monitor screen showed her daughter's blood sugar as relatively normal if not a little high, and she breathed a mother's relief. Dropping blood sugar levels were her greatest worry. Her respite was cut short, however, when the music took a turn, signaling the end of the routine was coming. Jillian had a hard time allowing herself to breathe normally, then absently she reached up to her neck and began worrying at the odd shaped key pendant she always wore on a green ribbon about her neck. Over the years, she had all but worn off its strange markings as she rubbed the key's metal surface between her slender fingers. Thomas was always telling her to get a new habit.

Just three more moves and I can go home and get out of this stupid getup, Heidyl thought. She was getting tired, but not from the routine. She loved performing her routine, but the thought of the judges and the staring crowd whittling away at her with their thoughts and words made her soul weary and her skin crawl. She was ever conscious of the small bump under her uniform made by the glucose sensor device she wore on her stomach. On one hand, she knew the injected device had likely saved her life on more than one occasion; simultaneously she hated it and wished she could tear it out and throw it across the ocean. Gymnastics routines always made her feel like she stood under a thousand microscopes. She could perform feats of aerial beauty that most people could only dream of, but those same people critiqued her every move while sitting on their ever-widening rear ends eating hot dogs and fries. It never felt very fair. And that fueled her inner competitive fire.

From the eastern corner of the mat, she took a deep breath to begin the next series. Sprinting across the open space she lofted once again into the air, preparing for the following leap that would propel her into a backward twist and find her ending the maneuver by landing in a split. The move always made her brother cringe in mock horror when she performed it in front of him, and she smirked at the thought of his agonized face in her mind's eye.

Halfway through her midair twist, however, everything went utterly and instantly black. To Heidyl, the room had simply disappeared. The ceiling, the floor, the lights were all swallowed into a black hole of sudden darkness. The heavy music stopped dead. Heidyl was flying blind. With her bearings lost, she flailed out with all four limbs for a footing as if floating through deep space. For a split second, she was unsure if she had lost consciousness. The room spun. Or was that her own mind? There was a loud popping sound followed by a knife-sharp scream slicing through the darkened room. When the lights came back on a few seconds later, she found herself lying on her side cradling her lower right leg. To her astonishment, she realized the scream had come from her own mouth. She clenched her jaw shut against the pain and shock, forcing her cries into one long sobbing groan. One look at her swelling ankle told the whole story. Heidyl would not be finishing her routine today. The thundering music was now replaced by a low hiss of static over the speakers. A swirl of murmuring voices joined the chaotic chorus that surrounded her.

Jillian was on her feet the second the lights vanished and was taking the descent down the bleacher steps two at a time. A concerned crowd was already stirring, and she nearly knocked two spectators back on their seats trying to shoulder past them. One of them grunted a curse.

No! This could not be happening. Not to her Heidyl. Jillian struggled to push away the wash of fear and dread racing up her spine. Normally, Jillian was a picture of poise and grace, measuring each word and action with equal seasonings of dignity and disarming kindness. But hearing the cry of pain from her daughter had vaulted her mothering instincts into overdrive. Right now, she would stop at nothing to get to Heidyl's side.

An elderly gentleman stepped into the aisle directly in front of her and she collided with him mid-stride. The parcel he was holding skittered to the ground, its contents rattling and rolling under the metal framing of the bleacher stands. Under normal conditions, Jillian would have been appalled at her lack of awareness and would have dropped what she was doing to practically dive under the seats to retrieve all of the odds and ends for him. But these were not normal conditions.

"Oh, sorry," was all she managed to say, and surged forward without looking back. The gentleman, certain that the apology was not genuine, angrily stooped down with a groan to gather up his scattered belongings.

By the time Jillian had reached her side, Heidyl's coach, several teammates and her trainer had all gathered around her in a messy semi-circle. Each face registered grim concern. An ice pack had been applied to the injury, held steady by the reassuring hand of Janice, the team trainer. Jillian knelt beside her daughter to wrap her arms around her heaving shoulders. Heidyl was making no sound, but the steady stream of tears told her mother that the pain was going beyond her ankle and into her hopeful future. They were both already wondering if the injury was the kind that ended promising sports careers.

A heavy man with a bulbous nose and a hairline that had marched backward toward the top of his head many years ago came waddling up to the scene. His black shoes left dusty footprints on the spring-floor. An impossibly large ring of keys hung below his protruding belly, threatening to pull his pants down with each jangling step. He was sweating profusely through a white button-down shirt with a yellowed pin on it that read: JAMES STILTER - MAINTENANCE.

"She gawn be okay?" the sweaty man panted, pulling up his trousers for what seemed the twelfth time in as many steps.

"It doesn't look broken, but we need to get her to a doctor." Janice looked up at the large man looming over them. "What happened to the lights, Jim?"

"Ah think th' wind finally took out the ol' pine in th' front. Probably knocked out th' transformer. Musta blacked out b'fore th' genny-rator could kick in." Jim replied with a heavy drawl. "I seen th' telly-phone r'pair trucks jus' the other day havin' a look-see at it. They knew 'twas trouble. Poor kid. She gawn be OK?" Jim looked sadly down at Heidyl's form huddled against her mother.

"We need to get that ankle stabilized and get her out of here." The voice of Janice was calm and professional. Turning her focus back to Heidyl, she asked, "Can you hold the ice in place while I get the wrap ready?"

Heidyl nodded through her tears and clutched the ice pack. She winced, grunting at the slight change in pressure. *This is bad*, she thought.

Janice dove well-trained hands deftly into the red duffel bag at her side producing a thick roll of athletic tape and pre-wrap. She stretched a length of it between her hands, ready to apply. "Okay, now drop the ice, slowly pick up your leg and press your heel against my knee if you can. I won't lie to you; this is probably going to hurt."

Heidyl let the dripping pack of ice plop to the floor. Both mother and daughter could see the rapid swelling clearly now. It *was* bad. The area looked to have enlarged to nearly twice its normal size becoming discolored with purples and blues. The thought of moving it was daunting to Heidyl.

"It hurts already!" She replied through clenched teeth, and then turned to Jillian, "Mom? Can you help me lift my leg? I'm not sure that I can do it."

"Sure thing, sweetheart." Jillian shuffled around on her knees until she was on the other side of the shaking girl. Jillian could feel her own stomach knotting. The glucose monitor that she wore on her belt gave two sharp beeps, indicating that the stress of the trauma was already causing her daughter's blood sugar to spike. She drove away the fear that only a mother could know, and gingerly eased her arms under her daughter's wounded limb. Heidyl drew in a sharp breath between her clenched teeth.

Jillian looked to her daughter, "I'm so sorry."

She leaned forward, readying herself for the lift. At the same moment, the key pendant she wore swung loosely away from her neck, brushing the bare skin just above Heidyl's swelling ankle. There was a blinding flash. Jillian gasped. The timeworn key had emitted a brilliant blue stream of light, like the sudden piercing flash of a camera in a blackened room. Jillian snatched her hands back to cover the key and tuck it back into her shirt. Heidyl's foot thudded to the floor. The sudden movement caused her face to twist, but more out of surprise than pain.

Jillian cautiously glanced from side to side, waiting for the rest of the onlookers to exclaim their surprise at the dazzling light. No one said a word. It was as if time had stopped. They all stood still, eagerly waiting for Jillian to lift her daughter's leg again. She looked over to Heidyl. But her large, round eyes told her that she had seen it, too. The small crowd around them seemed oblivious to what had just happened.

"Mom? What was *that*?" Heidyl's voice was trembling.

"It was...Uh...I'm not..." Jillian was grasping for words.

Janice cut in matter-of-factly, "That's odd. I've never seen anything quite like that before."

Jillian looked at her, eyes wide. "You saw it, too?"

"Sure did! That's unbelievable," she gestured toward Heidyl's ankle. "Take a look."

Jillian, a little confused, turned to look toward her daughter's foot. Like the crowd, the trainer had not seen the light either but had witnessed a miraculous change. The swelling around Heidyl's ankle had subsided almost completely and much of the bruising had vanished. All that remained was a dark purplish line, rapidly forming into the shape of a rough, two-inch spiral. The mark traveled as if being drawn in ink from an invisible pen and resembled something more like a birthmark than bruising. Jillian swallowed hard. Her hands shook. Out of habit, she reached up toward the antique key pendant to steady them, but then stopped herself, afraid to touch it now. The color had drained from her face. Her eyes held a vacant stare.

"Mom? You okay?—Mom?" Heidyl's voice reached into the fog of her mind snapping her back to the moment.

Jillian's eyes had misted over. "It'll be OK, baby," she said, and stroked back a stray tendril of her daughter's hair, more to help collect herself and steady her own trembling fingers.

"What's happening, Mom? Your necklace—Wait. The pain is totally gone." Heidyl wiggled her toes and slowly rotated her ankle in a careful circle.

Janice cut in again, "Amazing. The swelling has just about disappeared. The bruising is localizing itself into one small area!" Her hands were still holding the pre-wrap taut, ready to administer the stabilizing athletic tape. She turned to Jillian, "Have you seen anything like that before?"

"I have…" Jillian looked deliberately at her daughter and exhaled a breath, "Not."

"Well, swelling or no swelling, let's get this wrapped and go get you checked out." Janice was back to being all business, which is what made her such a good team trainer.

The group surrounding them parted, allowing the trio through.

The keys on Jim's belt jangled as he pulled up his retreating trousers. "That's gawn be one heckuva bruise!" he said.

He had no idea just how true that was.

SLEEP HAD CLAIMED THOMAS YET AGAIN. The hushed voice of the boy beside him poked through his engulfing shroud of sleep. "—hate this. Oh, jeez. Really, Dad? Again?" Thomas felt an elbow in his ribs, making him jump in his seat.

"Dad! Stop it! You're snoring!" The boy whispered harshly as he slid down in the chair trying to avoid being spotted by anyone else in the room who happened to be within earshot of the stuttering snores.

Thomas looked up, startled to find that he was in an enormous room simply packed with people. A lone female figure stood in the front reading a long list of announcements. Ah, yes. Church. It all came back to him again and the fog lifted from his eyes—for the moment. For about the twelfth time that morning, Thomas had dozed off during the service. Why they insisted people stay wide awake while sitting in a warmly lit room, filled with soft music and comfy chairs was beyond him. Especially after the kind of night he had just had.

His son, Jayce, slouched beside him hoping no one was looking. He sighed heavily, lost in his own thoughts. *I wish I could be anyplace but here. Even Heidyl's stupid gymnastics meet would be better than this.*

Jayce, who was fairly tall for his age, had entered that odd part of life where a boy feels as strong as an ox one minute, and as awkward and obvious as a three-legged penguin the next. But the trouble is, one could never be sure which minute they were in until that moment was long past. Most boys his age spent many hours trying to avoid the penguin-minutes. Which is precisely why Jayce was anxiously wishing himself away from this place. Now that he was old enough to participate in the church youth ministry program, it was his turn to do the scripture reading for the service; in front of hundreds of sets of eyes. Normally, Thomas and Jayce would not have missed Heidyl's regional competition today, but Thomas had insisted that this was an important responsibility for Jayce, and that he needed to learn to follow through with his commitments.

It would not have been so bad, if not for the black eye that adorned his face above his left cheekbone. Jayce had earned it honorably, in his opinion. He had rounded the corner at school just in time to hear Shawn Dhoule, a school bully with a reputation for making anyone around him uncomfortable, concoct the dirtiest, most untruthful comment he had ever heard anyone ever make. This in itself was not unusual for Shawn, but Jayce saw red when he heard his sister's name become the punch line of the big oaf's disgusting lie. In a fit of rage, Jayce had launched himself at the boy to defend his sister's good name.

Despite having the element of total surprise in his favor, his attack did little good and was a bit like watching a grasshopper trying to take down a tractor. In the end, the bully still walked away laughing leaving Jayce to limp his way to the nurse's office. Yes, this was definitely shaping up to be another one of those penguin-minutes for Jayce. In fact, lately it felt like *The Journey of the Three-Legged Penguin* would become the title of Jayce's life story.

Thomas had once again fallen asleep and was slowly starting to droop forward in a heavier slumber than before. Jayce was about to nudge him yet again but stopped when he realized that what might happen next could actually be quite entertaining. A mischievous grin spread across his face and he hunched lower in his seat to watch his father's large frame slowly inch ever forward with each deep breath.

Finally, the laws of gravity and momentum took over and Thomas spilled forward out of his seat and onto his knees. In his sudden startled panic, he threw his arms forward to catch himself, but instead succeeded in knocking the large yellow hat off of the head of the elderly woman in front of him. It flew through the air like a floppy Frisbee, finally sliding to a stop three rows ahead of them, right in the middle of the main aisle. Jayce could hardly control himself any longer and let out a hog-snort of laughter.

The elderly woman had stood to her feet in a huff and tromped up to retrieve her hat by the time Thomas had regained his seat. Stuffing it roughly back onto her head she stormed right past them and out the back doors before Thomas could apologize. It was then that he noticed the room had gone silent with every eye turned on him. Awkwardly, Thomas half-stood and waved a hand.

"I'm sorry", he mouthed out breathlessly to the crowd, and sat back down, hanging his head, feeling very much like his own version of a three-legged penguin. The young woman who had been reading the string of announcements finished her task, and the service continued. The church band, which consisted of a longish-haired guitarist, a drummer who barely looked twelve years old, and a keyboard player who reminded Thomas of his mother all took their places and began playing the next song in the worship music set. Despite their differences, they actually sounded quite good. As if on some unspoken cue, the entire congregation stood and began singing along.

Jayce had been laughing so hard that hot tears were streaming down his face so quickly he could scarcely wipe one away before another took its place. He gave his father a sideways glance, catching his eye.

Thomas was giving his son 'the look'. This was the very same one that he had honed to perfection during his years as a father. 'The look' had become quite effective, especially in church, and it was now telling Jayce it was time to stop—immediately. Jayce stifled his laughter, but then noticed that his father was wearing a necklace of some sort. Jayce had not seen it before and figured that it must have swung out of his shirt when he had tumbled to the floor in his sleep. The thought of the scene with the flying hat almost made him begin laughing all over again. But then he got a good look at what it was that his father actually wore.

There, fastened around his neck with a heavy strip of worn leather was the largest claw that Jayce had ever seen. It actually looked foolishly huge and he wished his dad would put the thing away so as not to draw even more attention to himself. But curiosity drew him to lean closer to his father for a better look.

Thomas followed the motion and tracked Jayce's gaze, noticing that he was staring directly at his chest. He looked down to see what his son was so focused on and to his horror, saw the keen grayvyk claw dangling on top of his shirt like a gaudy piece of primitive jewelry. In his excitement at receiving it from the darchlyte, Thomas wanted to keep it with him. Since it was too large and sharp to fit in his pocket, he had fashioned it into a crude necklace of sorts. It still smelled a bit like grayvyk. He grasped the curved talon so quickly that his son jumped back. Thomas' hand barely covered the huge hook and he struggled to tuck it nonchalantly back into his clothing. Feeling a sudden sharp pain on the inside of his hand he opened his palm to reveal a neat cut running across the fleshy part of three of his fingers. Blood was already trickling down the creases of his palm like a small red river.

Jayce's eyes widened at the sight. "Dad, are you okay?" he whispered.

"Yeah. Sharper than it looks, I guess."

"What is that from, anyway?" asked Jayce, "A bear?"

"Sure," was all the reply that Thomas gave. He was feeling uncomfortable and did not want to speak untruthfully to his son.

Jayce was not easily put off. "But...*it's blue!*"

"Mmhm," Thomas grunted.

"What kind of bear has blue claws? Is it from a polar bear?"

Thomas grunted again, half-nodded, and shifted in his seat.

"Where on earth did you get a polar bear claw?" Jayce pressed.

Thomas averted his eyes. "One of my clients took a research expedition to Antarctica. Brought a gift back for me once. Now, *hush!*"

Jayce pulled back and folded his arms, letting out a long, perturbed sigh. Why was his father behaving so strange?

After a few more minutes, the church band music had trailed off and the congregation resumed a seated position. This was Jayce's cue and he stood woodenly to his feet. His face went pale when he realized he had left his Bible for the scripture reading on the counter at home. He spun around.

"Dad—I completely forgot…" he started.

Thomas was already holding up his own black, leather bound copy of the scriptures toward his son. With his thumb he held the place for the chapter and verse assigned to Jayce for today's reading.

"Here, use mine," Thomas smiled.

"Thanks."

Jayce made his way up the hushed aisle to take his place behind the podium. He felt his face grow hot and flushed. He suddenly felt as if his black eye was glowing bright red for all to see. Jayce flipped open his father's large, worn Bible, knocking his knuckles against the microphone stand. The resulting *pop* that crashed through the speakers caused a few of the elderly in the crowd to startle in their seats. Several people snickered.

Jayce cleared his throat and began to read:

"Then war broke out in heaven. Michael and his angels fought against the dragon, and the dragon and his angels fought back. But he was not strong enough, and they lost their place in heaven. The great dragon was hurled down—that ancient serpent called the devil, or Satan who leads the whole world astray. He was hurled to the earth, and his angels with him. Revelation chapter twelve, verses seven through nine.*"*

Thomas had been listening eagerly and proudly as his son read. But something about the ancient passage caused his eyes to grow wide and his breath to stick dryly in his throat. An uneasy feeling overcame him, and his pulse began pummeling his eardrums as his mind replayed portions of his last excursion to Haizorr. A host of suspicions and questions surrounding the scroll he had just retrieved sprung up at once and he felt a sudden, overwhelming urge to get back to his hidden study and review his most recent discovery. Inwardly he prayed that he was wrong about the strange dread he felt inside, but he had learned over the years not to ignore this feeling.

Thomas was already on his feet before Jayce had even returned to his spot next to him.

"How'd I do, Dad?"

"We need to go," he whispered and turned toward the back of the room, too distracted to even notice if Jayce was following him out the door.

Thomas stalked out of the church without a backward glance.

The pastor had taken his place behind the podium and was beginning his sermon, his clear voice trailing them out the door. "As you can see, to make war against a dragon," he began, "takes a special blend of faith and courage. And I'm here to tell you, that war rages on today—" The southern twang in his voice was cut off as the door swung closed behind them.

THE SOUND OF SCUFFLING FEET on the dusty gray gravel driveway behind him reminded Thomas that he was not alone as he walked toward the pickup truck. Shaking himself from the niggling worry, he turned his cell phone back on and reached for the door handle. His phone chirped several times at him. Four texts from Jill, five missed calls, and two voicemail alerts stopped him halfway through his climb into the extended cab's roomy leather interior. This could not be good.

Jayce had already buckled himself in and was anxious to get home and away from this place. He still felt pretty embarrassed, even though his reading was over. Thomas stood motionless, half in and half out of the truck, staring at the shiny screen of his phone.

"Dad?" Jayce's voice sounded frustrated; especially after his father had just brushed him off a few moments ago. But one look at Thomas' face and it melted into concern. "Dad...? What is it? Dad!" His voice was just shy of a shout.

Thomas snapped out of the phone induced trance and hopped into the seat, stuffing the key into the ignition and slamming the door closed in the same motion. He popped in the earbuds and said, "Call Jill." The voice recognition feature on his phone did the rest. While waiting for the call to go through he realized he had quite ignored his son.

"Heidyl's had an accident," he said.

"A car accident? Is she OK? What happened to—?"

"She's at the hospital with Mom—"

Thomas held up a hand and cut off the conversation as the phone relayed Jill's voice through the receiver.

"Jill? Hello? Hang on. You're breaking up. I can hardly hear you. Jill? JILL? Agh! I lost her!" In frustration, Thomas roughly tossed the phone onto the console beside him. It skittered across the smooth surface and bounced out, landing on the floor beneath Jayce's feet. He glanced up at the high mountain peaks rimming his line of sight. Normally he would utter praise for their majestic beauty, but right now Thomas was stifling a curse over how perfectly they were blocking cell phone reception.

Reaching to retrieve his father's phone, Jayce tentatively broke the hot silence with a nervous tremor in his voice.

"Dad? Is Heidyl okay?"

Thomas's eyes were riveted to the road. He had begun working his jaw pretty hard, too. His thoughts were taking him places far beyond the mountains and his son's question seemed to evaporate into the dry air between them. Jayce looked at the screen of the phone in his hand and swallowed hard. The text messages from his mother still glowing on the touchscreen:

Heidyl had an accident during her routine. Meet us at the hospital. Pray.

--

Call me.

--

We need to talk tonight.

--

It's happening all over again. Heidyl may be marked!

Carefully, Jayce placed the phone back in the console after switching off the screen. *Marked?* What that meant, he could only imagine, but he did not dare ask his father. The look in those eyes was fierce enough to melt steel, and Jayce could already feel the tension flooding the air like a thick fog.

He noticed a reddish-brown stain had started spreading on the right leg of his father's blue jeans. At first, Jayce thought that it must have been from a muddy spot on the driver's side of the truck, but then he looked up at the steering wheel. It was slick with blood. Thomas was gripping the steering wheel so tightly with his fist that the gash caused from the grayvyk claw had reopened.

Another drip. Thomas didn't even notice.

"Uh...Dad? You're bleeding."

"Mhm?"

"Blood, Dad. You're getting it all over your pants." Jayce handed him a wrinkled coffee shop napkin he found in the glove compartment.

Thomas vaguely came out of his trance and began wiping the blood from the steering wheel and pressed the napkin into his bloodied palm to stanch the wound.

Jayce tried to lighten the mood by changing the subject. "That bear claw sure must be sharp. How did your friend ever get that thing through airport security?"

"What friend?" Thomas seemed genuinely puzzled.

"The one from the Antarctic expedition."

But Thomas had already resumed his previous focus and didn't seem to hear his son. His nerves were frayed, and it was all he could do to concentrate on the road in front of them.

Jayce puffed out a sigh and leaned back in his seat. "That must have come from one heckuva bear."

HEIDYL HEARD THE MUFFLED VOICES of her mother and father as they said goodnight to Jayce in his room down the hall. It had been a long day and she was anxious to put it behind her. She had more people stare and poke at her ankle today than she could even count. After several injections of insulin, they finally got her blood sugar back under control, too. At one point it made her feel like an animal in a zoo, on display for the amusement of the masses.

Each of the doctors and nurses had walked away scratching their heads at how she had healed so quickly. The word 'miracle' had even slipped out of the mouth of one of the doctors. But the way he had said it, low and under his breath, made Heidyl feel that he had broken some sort of medical oath by admitting to something so unscientific as a miracle. Heidyl thought people shrugging and scratching their heads seemed just as unscientific. She had settled in her heart long ago that the miraculous was just as possible as the mundane and were so entwined with each other that the two could easily be confused.

The sound of footsteps coming down the hall signaled that her parents had finished saying goodnight to her brother and were coming to her door next. But she was too tired to talk anymore. And she did not want anyone to have another 'quick look' at her ankle or another drop of blood squeezed from her sore fingers. Quickly, she pulled the covers up and turned over in bed, pretending to have fallen asleep already.

There came a light knock on her door. Heidyl caught her breath to steady herself, and tried to mimic the deep, content breathing of one who is fast asleep. The light from the hallway streamed into her room, traveling across the bed as her parents gingerly pushed open the door. She lay in a motionless pile of blankets and pillows, just the top of her auburn hair visible.

"Heidyl? Are you still awake, honey?" Jillian's voice was a pleading whisper. Filled with a mother's worry.

"Poor girl, she's had such a long day. She's out. Let's just let her sleep," whispered Thomas.

Yes, please! Heidyl thought.

"But, what does this mean, Thomas?"

"It means we are a family and keep things as they are."

Jillian could feel a hot tear forming in her eye. "You saw it, too. She's marked. Just like us. I'm afraid for her safety now. And I've never heard of a mark appearing like this before." She tugged at the key dangling on her necklace. "I think the key might have something to do with it."

"Perhaps it's hereditary," whispered Thomas.

"Then why doesn't Jayce have it? He's older, and it probably would have appeared long before now. This burden is too heavy for her, she carries enough already!"

Thomas wrapped his arms around his wife as silent tears splashed into his shirt collar. Their shadowed silhouette could have easily been mistaken for a romantic moment, had the topic been any different.

Their hushed conversation made Heidyl's ears burn and her heart freeze. What on earth were they talking about? Marks? Her safety? She was about to roll over and ask at least a dozen questions that were bouncing across her mind like flies against a window screen.

Thomas drew back and held his wife by her shoulders. Her beauty always caught him off guard and he smiled. "Hey. I love you. *This big.*" Thomas then spread his arms as wide as he could from left to right in a gesture to his wife.

Despite the confusing torrent of emotions she was feeling, Heidyl smiled as she pictured her dad in that pose. It was their family's *thing.* Whenever one of them was hurt or in doubt, or even after a family squabble, it was a reassuring message that they reserved for one another. Arms wide open, heart exposed, vulnerable. An expression of unwavering and unconditional love reserved for the other person. Jillian took the invitation and wrapped her arms tightly around her husband in a bear hug. This was always the appropriate response, although, lately her brother seemed less likely to participate in the gesture.

"Okay. But we can't tell her, though. Not yet," whispered Jillian.

And with that, they pulled away from the door, gently drawing it closed. The room once again became shrouded in the deep, cool dark of colorless night. With nothing else for Heidyl to listen to, however, the wheels of her mind began spinning into overdrive from what she had overheard. It was going to be a long night.

THE MOTH AT HIS WINDOW was driving Jayce nuts. At first it was a welcome distraction from the day, and the fluttering wings were even a bit mesmerizing. That all changed when it got caught in an abandoned spider web and was now thrashing mindlessly against the glass pane making the most annoying tapping sounds. Jayce began to wonder how long it would take for the poor thing to knock itself unconscious.

He decided it was taking too long. In a fit of frustration, he threw back his covers and went to the window, whether to free the creature or finish it off was yet to be decided. His computer desk was positioned in front of it, and he had to strain across to free the window latch. He then began prying at the base of the window, but it was stuck fast, probably from the glass of orange juice he had spilled last week over the back edge of his desk. With an angry shove, the window shot upward, and Jayce fell flat across his desk. The computer keyboard tumbling to the floor popped his monitor screen back to life after its several hours of digital slumber. The moth was gone. Jayce angrily blew a shot of air from his nose as he inspected various parts of the computer for any signs of damage. Slumping into the chair in front of the monitor he stared with sleepy eyes at the illuminated screen before him. A highly detailed digital painting of superheroes and villains locked in explosive combat stared back at him.

Placing the keyboard back on the desk, he tapped a hotkey he had programmed to bring up his favorite search engine for a bit of research. Sleep was out of the question at this point anyhow, and several questions had been needling his mind since this morning. The cursor hovered in the text field awaiting his query. With a few quick strokes, Jayce typed what had been on his mind much of that day: *"polar bear claws"*.

IT DIDN'T EVEN HURT to walk on her tiptoes! Heidyl made this surprising discovery early in the day and had stopped sneaking halfway down the hallway to test it for the hundredth time. She marveled at the complete recovery her ankle had made in just a few moments. Or, rather, in just a few *seconds*. The moonlight streaming through the high arched hall window illuminated her every step. Looking down once again at her bare ankle, her eyes rested on the spiral 'mark' that had mysteriously appeared that morning. She felt a wave of anxiety rise up inside her stomach and tried to brush it aside. *It'll go away on its own,* she thought. But her mother's cryptic words were still fresh in her mind. Heidyl swallowed hard and silently glided toward Jayce's door.

The bluish glow from his computer screen was leaking through the door crack. Good. He was awake. Heidyl turned the knob and stole into her brother's domain. She needed to talk to him.

Jayce and Heidyl were closer than most brothers and sisters. While an intrusion like this might have started a sibling war in other families, in the case of these two, it was usually welcomed. They had shared a room for most of their earlier years and had begged to stay together as long as their parents allowed them. They read stories, wrote stories, acted, built, decorated and pretended their way into adolescence together and the bond between them had grown strong.

Jayce heard the door thump and knew who it was without looking away from his research. "Hey, Superstar," he said.

He had started calling her that when she won her very first gold medal and the nickname had stuck. Given how many times she had won over the years, it was also a very fitting description. Even though Jayce was not very prone to winning medals, he never allowed himself to feel jealous of her. On the contrary, he was quite proud of her, even if he did not express it often.

Heidyl flopped down onto his rumpled bed and let out a great big sigh. Jayce smiled to himself. He knew this drill well. Something was bugging her, and she needed to get it out.

"Jayce," she began, "do you think Mom and Dad keep secrets from us?"

"I sure do." He replied with no hesitation.

Heidyl bolted upright on the bed, eyes wide in surprise. She was not expecting such a response so quickly. She had thought for sure that he would need some convincing.

"Really?" she asked.

"Yeah. Just last week I overheard them talking about how we found you in the woods when you were a baby. You were being raised by a pack of coyotes." The grin spread wider across his face.

His jest was rewarded with a pillow being launched at the back of his head, pitching him forward. Jayce chuckled.

"Knock it off! I'm serious." Heidyl did not feel like playing games at the moment.

Sensing that his sister was truly troubled, Jayce turned in his swivel chair to face her. Her eyes were moist, and she looked tired, and a little scared. He came over and sat on the edge of the bed next to her.

"Did it hurt?" he asked, pointing toward her right foot.

"Did that?" she retorted, pointing toward his bruised face.

He laughed and gingerly touched his eye. "Still does."

"Mine doesn't. But I know it should."

Heidyl lay back down and stared at the ceiling, her thoughts turning inward and confused again. Jayce had once been given several sheets of glow-in-the-dark star stickers as a birthday gift and had done his best to accurately reconstruct some of the more recognizable star constellations. Their soft green light drew her eyes around the room.

If he were to be honest, Jayce had been wondering the same thing lately. Secrets. Recently, nearly every time he asked his parents about their antique dealing business, the answers he received seemed to become increasingly vague. He wanted to get more involved with it, maybe even help out someday. But he could only ever get so far in conversations with them about it. He still was left wondering what his own father did for work! Other kids at school had dads and moms who were electricians, shop owners, or teachers. When asked what his dad did for work, Jayce most often just shrugged. The response made him feel foolish in front of his friends, but he really did not know what else to tell them.

Heidyl broke the silence. "What are you working on?"

Jayce gave her a confused look and she pointed over his shoulder toward his computer. Jayce nodded. "Oh, that. Yeah. Funny you should mention secrets. Look at this." He stood up and plopped back into his desk chair. Heidyl followed, and peered over his shoulder, squinting at the bright screen. After scrolling through a few pages of a document, he paused when he reached what looked like a nature picture gallery.

"This. Right here."

"So, you're doing a school report about bear feet?"

"Well, no. Look at their claws." He zoomed in the pictures to show row after galleried row of razor-sharp curved claws.

Heidyl teased, "Oooh. Scary!"

Now it was Jayce's turn to be serious. "Quit joking around. Haven't you noticed that ridiculous necklace Dad has been wearing this week?"

Surprised at his sudden sour tone Heidyl just shrugged, a vacant stare crossing her face. She was beginning to wonder what was bothering her brother so much, and perhaps it was he who needed to talk more than she.

He was growing irritated with her. "How could you not see it? It's as big as a bicycle!" He blew out a frustrated sigh. "OK, since you must have recently gone blind, the thing is huge, blue, and sharp enough to slice human flesh with just a touch. He told me it was from a polar bear."

"Odd. Where would he even get a polar bear claw?" asked Heidyl.

"That's what I wondered, too. He said it was from Antarctica." Jayce leaned back and crossed his arms. "He's such a liar."

"What do you mean? Don't say that about him!"

"I'm telling you, sis, he lied right to my face. First of all, polar bears don't even live in Antarctica! They are native to the *Arctic,* as in, the direct *opposite* part of the earth!" He clicked a button to zoom in on a habitat range map of the creature to make his point.

"So what? Maybe he got his words mixed up."

Jayce raised an eyebrow at her with a doubtful look. They both knew that their father had a reputation of having a memory like a steel trap. He never seemed to forget anything. Obscure facts were his specialty. Heidyl was trying to defend their dad, but she had to concede that point. For several moments, Jayce pored through his data to prove his suspicion. They were both so engrossed in the conversation that neither of them noticed the doorknob twist behind them. Or the door silently slide open. Or a large, dark figure slip behind them into the bedroom.

With another tap, Jayce illuminated some more close-up imagery. They were all pictures of polar bear claws this time. "See? Black. Not a blue one in the bunch." He was on a roll now. He scrolled deeper into the photo set to find one showing a tape measure stretched across one of the claws in the frame. "See, that? Less than three inches."

"I don't get it, Jayce. What's your point?"

"The one he has on his neck is humongous! It couldn't have come from a polar bear or *any* bear! It's blue, for Pete's sake. It looks like it came from a velociraptor's big brother! I'll say it again, Dad's a liar."

The dark figure behind them stepped forward and broke into the conversation so abruptly that it sent ice into the veins of both children.

"That will be quite enough of that, young master!" A deep, voice tinged with a Scottish brogue rumbled through the darkness.

It was Samuel, the long-time caretaker of their family estate. He had been taking his nightly security rounds about the property and noticed the light coming from the bedroom.

The relief that washed over both Heidyl and Jayce could almost be seen as the hair on their necks and arms settled back down, and the fearful chill bumps went flat once again.

Samuel spoke again, "In all my years, I've not met a couple as loving or giving as the parents you now speak ill of." The reproach in his strong, gentle voice struck the children in their hearts. "Protective? Yes. Mysterious? Absolutely. But none should dare call them liars while I still draw breath, for that, young man, would itself be a falsehood."

With that, he walked to where the power cord to the computer stuck out of the wall like a shiny black snake and gave it a sharp yank. The screen went dark and so did the room. Jayce felt his face go hot with anger, but he knew not to cross Samuel, whose legendary wisdom and patience over the years had earned him the deepest respect of every family member.

The aging caretaker clicked on the desk lamp beside the bed. The soft yellowish light streamed up across his tanned leathery face and played in his short-cropped white hair. He was very tall with broad shoulders. His hands looked strong enough to break raw lumber. He had enough boxing trophies in his living quarters to prove that they could at least break noses. Jayce had spent a good deal of time admiring the golden memoirs of the man's fighting days. When asked how he had earned the curious nickname "Counter-punch Champ", the gentleman had simply shrugged with a smile, "That's a long story, lad. I just do what I do."

But he was not smiling now.

With a tired sigh he turned to address the surprised children.

"Don't you realize they love the both of you more than anything else in these worlds?" It was a rhetorical question, with no answer needed. Samuel's words were often like that. Both question and answer tightly wrapped into one.

Jayce wondered what he meant by the expression "these worlds" and was about to say so, but Samuel cut him short.

"Off to bed with you now. And especially you, young miss. It's been a frightfully adventuresome day." Ever the gentleman, Samuel bowed, offering Heidyl his arm and she slipped her hand through it. She seemed to have all but forgotten her worries in his assuring presence.

Jayce watched them go back through the doorway down the hall, the moonlight illuminating their silhouettes as they passed each window. Heidyl embraced the tall gentleman with a goodnight hug and disappeared into her room. Samuel drew her door closed and looked back at Jayce to give him an almost imperceptible nod before disappearing down the dark corridor.

As he closed his door, Jayce made a vow to himself.

Liars or not, they were hiding things, and he was going to find out the truth.

PART III: THE BOOK

THE DRUMMING OF HIS FINGERS ON THE TABLE was the only sound in the kitchen now. Thomas had been awake for hours. He figured he may have drifted off to sleep for short time during the night, but it certainly did not feel like it had done him any good. He poured himself another cup of black coffee from the steaming carafe on the table, however his body was beyond the help of the caffeine. The only thing keeping him from slumping over into a snoring mess right here on the table was the constant drip of adrenaline that his brain was receiving.

It had been nearly a week since that last trip through the portal. His mind had been frantically working for days now striving to make sense of what he had experienced. Try as he might, Thomas could not shake the feeling that something was not quite right with the scroll he had found—and how he had found it. Then there was the question of the timing of Heidyl's marking. It seemed to go beyond coincidence. Or was he imagining things? He simply could not stop thinking, and the lack of sleep was making him irritable. The rest of the family seemed to have moved on from the encounter to continue with normal life. Of course, he had caught Heidyl peeking at her ankle mark several times when she thought no one was looking, but that was to be expected. He could recall doing the same thing with his own mark. Jayce seemed a little more aloof than usual, but Thomas chalked that up to teen hormones. Jillian, ever the rock, had kept her usual cheerful demeanor, but Thomas thought it looked a little forced the past few days. He knew she had been silently working the situation in her mind as well.

It was a quarter to five in the morning. Thomas listened as the birds began rousing to gather bits of nesting or insects for their spring brood. Staring through the large picture window beside the table, he rested his tired head on the palm of his hand. He could feel his vision begin to blur from exhaustion, but he was too weary to try to refocus his eyes. Two-day old stubble from his chin chafed against the slow-healing angry gash he had received from the grayvyk claw and the pain brought him back.

"How'd this happen?" He breathed out a tired sigh.

"Maybe 'why' is the question we should be asking." Jillian could not sleep either. Her soft voice floated through the cool stillness as she glided over to her husband, resting her head on his shoulder as he sat.

Thomas inhaled deeply through his nostrils. He loved the scent of her. A musky, floral essence always seemed to flow from his bride, and it drove him wild for her. He lifted a hand and caressed the soft skin on the back of her neck. He stopped when his fingers traced an area of her skin that was slightly raised from the surrounding tissue. It felt vaguely like a scar.

"Can I see it? So I can compare, I mean."

"You're killing the mood, my dear," she joked, but then swinging her hair forward, she leaned into him and tucked her chin down so the base of her skull was exposed to the light.

As he gently brushed his fingers through her hairline, a purplish rough spiral was revealed on her soft skin. It was nearly identical to the one on the ankle of their daughter, although perhaps a bit more faded. Thomas sighed, and then kissed the spot gently. Jillian slid into the seat beside him and tousled her hair back into place.

"It's the same. And the same as mine, too," he declared as he patted the area just above his left hip, indicating the location of his own spiral marking.

"Yes, I know. And now we need to ask, *why*?"

Thomas always hated asking that question. It simply seemed selfish to him to ask the *why* of things. Did it ever really change the outcome of anything? When did knowing why things happen ever serve anyone other than the asker? Would knowing why something was stolen bring it back, or would knowing why an ailing friend perished do the same? In his mind, it was God's job to know why, and man's job was to trust God. It always felt like an internal assault on his faith. Would it be any different with Heidyl?

For Jillian's sake he would play along.

"It's hereditary, that's why," he said flatly.

Her eyebrows went up. "We've already ruled that out. If it were tied to our genes, then why not Jayce? And why would it have appeared like it did? Thomas, you should have seen the flash of light. That wasn't genetic, it was simply unbelievable."

He had to admit, she was good at this game. While he was happy to steam ahead toward the next venture, she was just as happy to pause and think things through. Often just long enough to drive him crazy, but also long enough to keep him from doing something crazy.

"Thomas," she continued her point gently, "what are the odds that two people with nearly identical birthmarks would find each other and fall in love?"

He swallowed. She had him cornered. Sensing that he was backpedaling mentally, she reached across the table lacing her soft fingers with his. Her touch was as disarming as her sea-glass eyes.

"And what are the odds that this couple would be able to pull back the thin veil of this world to see the dangers and wonders that lie just beneath its shallow skin?"

Thomas closed his eyes, knowing what she'd say next.

"There *is* a why to us. And when we find the answer to that, then we will have the answer to everything."

He hated to believe it, but the logic and pure line of thought in her words could not be argued against. He let her statement stand. His silence was proof enough of his agreement with her.

Thomas sat and drank in the private, vulnerable moment with his wife. Streams of pale sunlight were now just visible through the cool morning mists rising from the tree line at the far edge of the manicured property. A tall, lone figure pushing a wheelbarrow loaded with yard waste crossed his line of sight. Samuel had gotten an early start at trying to keep the endless onslaught of weeds and brambles at bay. He did a terrific job keeping the old mansion grounds looking tiptop, and Thomas was genuinely proud of the older man, whom he considered more of a confidant than hired help. Watching him work in his signature long-sleeved button down, neatly tucked into khaki work pants he could not help but admire the man's work ethic and attention to detail. Samuel had served the family for years in so many ways. He had become like an uncle to the children, filling a vacant role in their life that desperately needed attention. Thomas had a hard time imagining their lives without his steady presence.

He let his eyes wander around the room as the pale morning light grew in strength. The seating area of the kitchen was positioned beside an expansive receiving room with high arched ceilings. The warm toned marble floors covered with oriental rugs spread beneath mahogany and ironwood tables met an impressive stone fireplace that boasted a hand-carved rendition of the family crest above the mantle. Artifacts, antiques and rarities from around the world filled the shelves and adorned a few carefully placed pedestals.

Dealing in antiques—or, more precisely, ancient artifacts—had started years ago as a simple hobby. That all changed when, as a young man, he had stumbled across an ancient samurai sword that he had bought in an online auction for hundreds of dollars from an unwary owner in Tennessee. Then, after verifying its authenticity, sold it for nearly twenty times that amount to a desperate collector in Japan. He was shocked by his good fortune. Immediately he became a fervent student of archaeology and learned that relics and rare fragments from the ancient past can be bought and sold for very large sums of money. If you can find them.

That is where Thomas seemed to have an advantage. Even from childhood he was gifted in this regard. He always seemed to know just where in the woods to look to see a perfectly camouflaged deer or find an obscure game trail. He was always finding lost coins. Once his mother had even lost her wedding ring and had set him on a mission to find it. In less than ten minutes he returned to her, covered in mud and mosquito bites, with the ring in his hand. It had been in the storm drain at the end of their driveway.

As he grew a little older, he knew he had more than just a knack for finding things and began to recognize his skill as something special. It was an ability that ran deeper than mere talent. More than instinct. It was endowment. He learned this as a young man when he had walked into the old second-hand bookstore on his hometown Main Street without really knowing why. His left side began aching as he was drawn down the aisles of dusty leather books. Then it began to itch. Still he walked past the rows of ancient pages, feeling a frantic and overwhelming sensation come over him. His mind just said '*seek*' over and over, the word bouncing around in his head like an angry hornet. A throbbing and burning started in the area just above his left hip as he finally stood before the last wooden bookcase in the far corner of the musty old bookstore. Ripping back the corner of his shirt to look at his birthmark, he expected to see it glowing red or his skin bubbling, but only saw the same purplish spiral that had been there all his life. The pain felt like a searing iron! He clenched his jaws to keep from screaming out.

And then his eyes saw it. A heavy, leather-laden collection of hundreds and hundreds of pages lay leaning inward against the shelf. The Book. In that instant the pain stopped as quickly as if someone had turned off an electrical switch. Thomas blinked. His mind said '*found*'. With trembling hands, he grasped the sturdy leather binding and unsheathed the great tome from its resting place. He did not even open it, but simply paid the shopkeeper for the hefty manuscript and went straight home.

When he had finally worked up the courage to open its ornate bindings, he was sadly disappointed. Expecting to find the answers to some ancient mystery, or at least a series of treasure maps, he only found endless pages of obscure writings and scribbles. Some pages were legible, other he could scarcely make out every third word or so. There were even entire pages blotted out with gobs of black ink, and others with crude drawings ringed with some sort of hieroglyphics that made no sense to him at all. If it had not been for the odd feelings surrounding his finding the Book, he would have thought himself a fool for buying it. He considered trying to sell it back, but the burning sensation he experienced around his birthmark drove that thought from his mind. At a loss, he packaged it into a box under his bed and all but forgot about his dubious purchase at the bookstore.

Until Christmas Eve, six months later.

He was going up the stairs from the first floor of the mall. She was going down. Both were loaded with last minute gift packages for distant cousins or forgotten co-workers. When they accidentally brushed elbows while passing one another, each let out a short shriek of pain. Thomas clasped his free hand over his burning left side. She instantly pressed her fingers against the base of her neck. When she stooped to recover the packages she had dropped, her foot slipped, and she began to fall. Thomas reached out, catching her in his arm. When their eyes locked, the electrical switch of pain was instantly shut off for each of them and they stared at each other, catching their breath. *Found.*

Thomas always felt that in that moment, Jillian had been his most precious discovery, and always would be. Once again, he was right. As gifted as Thomas was in the art of seeking, Jillian possessed an unparalleled ability to *understand.* She probed and pondered the deep meanings. Patience and clear thought enabled her to solve troublesome puzzles or riddles and mysteries of word play. Sudoku, crosswords and foreign languages were food that her mind feasted upon regularly. When they had first met, Thomas had found it intriguing. When he had first shown her the Book, he found it utterly amazing.

Before ever opening the cover, she had uncovered a hidden word key, etched in the gold bindings. She read it aloud to him.

"From East to West the span is wide, with love cross to the other side. Should the Harm descend across the land, may Death's own sting be in thy hand." Her voice trembled as she read.

"What's the matter?"

"I don't know. But I have the feeling that this Book has a great deal of power between its pages. I'm actually a bit frightened by what we may find." She was rubbing the base of her neck again.

The truth of it was, it did more than scare them. The Book terrified them both. It infuriated them. It filled them with wonder. With hope. In short, it thrust them on a lifelong journey of danger and sheer joy that bound them together with the tightest of bonds.

And now it brought them to this very point in their family. Thomas had often wondered how many others were out there who might share these gifts. If Heidyl possessed some special ability, it remained yet to be discovered. Three people in the same family tree sharing such a unique mark was beyond what he ever expected. Though Thomas' path had once crossed with another marked person long ago, he kept that memory buried.

Jill had fallen asleep against his shoulder. His coffee had grown cold where it sat on the table.

Thomas cleared his throat, "I need to consult the Book, Jill."

She stirred and sighed sleepily. "Now?"

"Yes. And I need your eyes on it with me. Something feels strange about this last scroll."

"You say that every time," she yawned. "You're right. They're all weird."

"Not this one. It's not just weird. There's more to it than that." His hard gaze into the morning sunrise told her his mind was set.

"Okay, but please have Samuel come in and keep working on the lovely stain you left by the Gate. The room still smells like rotting grayvyk."

She meant it as a half joke to lighten his mood, but he barely heard her as he stood and gulped down the cold coffee. Without a word he began stalking off toward the secret study. Jill felt a sudden chill creep up her spine. Truthfully, she wanted answers just as much as her husband and she eagerly trotted after him to catch up.

FINGERS DRUMMED THE GARGOYLE HEAD that served as a black armrest to the enormous iron chair. The room was totally dark, save for a dull purple glow coming from the low burning fires beneath five black, bubbling cauldrons. The indigo flames danced lazily, sending uneven shadows to play along the slick black walls of the cavernous room. The effect made the walls appear to be writhing and oozing like worms in a prehistoric tar pit.

Clickety-click. Clickety-click. Clickety-click. The lone figure's large bony fingers continued the endless drumming. He was waiting.

Always waiting.

A smile twisted the man's thin lips at the thought. *That's okay. I'm the patient one. Patience always wins.* He lifted his hooded head to gaze upon the swirling mass before him. The five massive cauldrons were arranged pentagonal around a large maroon circle crudely painted on the floor. The surface within the center of the circle no longer appeared to be made of stone as the rest of the surrounding floor. It shifted and moved like water: peaceful and tranquil one moment then churning and stretching the next, as if something beneath were straining against it trying to burst through a thinly stretched veil. *Soon. Patience, dear one. Patience. I've found you. I will open the door soon.*

A hollow thud thundered into the dark silence. At the end of the room a huge iron door groaned and was pushed open. The light from two waxing moons streamed in but was instantly swallowed by the living darkness of the black lair. Lord Drayven stood from his iron perch and smiled. *You see? Patience wins.* The floor within the cauldron circle began thrashing wildly.

The large visitor stood unmoving in the doorway.

"Come! Quickly, bring it here!" The commanding voice of the dark cloaked lord spurred the creature forward. But the labored, hesitant steps it took as it entered the chamber to ascend up to the dais spoke of defeat.

A black, oily liquid spurted from its drooping head with each stride. The putrid scent of grayvyk blood flooded Lord Drayven's nostrils as the beast finally stood before him. Heavy, rancid breath dragged in and out between its teeth in ragged gasps. The grayvyk swayed unsteadily. It was dying before his very eyes. The dark master lifted a hand to the seeping gash, guessing at what happened to his minion. Then, in a sudden fit of rage, he balled his fist and punched the open wound savagely. "How dare you return to me with nothing?" he thundered.

The shriek of pain from the wounded grayvyk nearly cracked the cavern walls, as it buckled beneath the blow. But the beast did not retreat, ever loyal to the cruel master. The tall man shrugged, "It is no matter. I will send others to retrieve what is needed." Lord Drayven again lifted his hand, now slick with inky blood, and pointed to the center of the maroon circle on the floor.

"Serve your last purpose. I need you no longer."

The pale eyes of the creature widened in understanding. And fear. Obediently turning a drooping head, it stumbled forward. Lord Drayven spun away in disgust and stalked up the five stone steps to return to his cold metal throne.

The floor within the stone circle lay still as the grayvyk limped toward its center. The hollow *clack-click-clack* of talons against cold stone echoed its own death march throughout the room.

Drayven took in the scene with hate-filled eyes.

The floor rippled along the outer rim of the cauldron circle. The grayvyk tilted its head nervously at the movement. A second ripple on the far side of the circle but edging closer to the center gave the impression of a shark swimming beneath dark waters closing in on its prey. The huge reptile in the middle began turning in circles, frantically trying to prepare for an attack. Its black blood spattering all around, painting crude patterns in the dust.

In a rush of panic, the beast tried to make a run for it. But it was too late. In the space of half a second, the ground beneath it bolted straight up with such force that the grayvyk was flung high into the air. Then, a colossal *thud* shook Lord Drayven's throne as several tons of reptilian body landed with crushing force back against hard stone.

The grayvyk lay still. Only the rhythmic rising and falling of its massive ribcage gave proof that it was still alive and breathing. The once liquid-like floor was firm as bedrock again. It raised its head cautiously. The dark lord's scowl deepened. The blow had not been fatal. He would have to punish the failure personally. Rising again from his seat, and pulling a curved, blackened blade from the sheath at his side, he descended the stone steps.

But the second his foot brushed across the circle's edge, the center of it erupted like a volcano. Lord Drayven jerked back as inky smoke shot upward and a black claw as big around as a tree trunk ripped through the floor. The earsplitting scream of the grayvyk was clipped short as the claw clamped across its middle, pulling it back against the rift. There was a brief struggle and then total silence as the once colossal beast was effectively folded in half and yanked through a hole many times smaller than itself. The floor bobbed up and down several times like the surface of water returning to calm after being disturbed by a stone.

A smattering of scales, black blood and a length of scraped off skin was all that remained of the grayvyk. Somewhere in the excitement, Lord Drayven had dropped his blade. Bending to retrieve it, he noticed a change in the room. A thick odor like grease and sulfur now filled the air around him. His dark eyes rested their gaze on the new hole in the center of the cauldron circle. Lazy wisps of smoke rose toward the domed ceiling high above.

He could not help but smile. "So. The veil is thinning I see. Perhaps we are not as far away as we once thought." He stared hard into the center of the hole and was almost certain he could feel it staring back at him. An area above his left hip began to itch. Smiling, he patted the spot with his hand. With a turn, he climbed the dais to his dark roost and sat. The tiny hole in the portal before him made him feel as if he had an old friend in the room with him now.

"It looks like you and I *both* have found a doorway in. Now that I know where they keep the key, we shall send for them again soon." A raspy cackle escaped his throat and he pointed to the hole. "See? I told you. Patience!" Looking down, he noticed the pool of black grayvyk blood beneath his boots. But he was so elated he no longer cared about the stains it would leave, and absently dropped his hand back onto the gargoyle armrest.

Clickety-click. Clickety-click. Clickety-click.

"THIS STAIN WILL NEVER COME OUT," Samuel grumbled to himself. He had tried tackling it several times this week with very minimal success. Today he was determined to be rid of it once and for all. He had already changed the water in three buckets and gone through a half-gallon of bleach. Though the stench had lessened somewhat, the stain only seemed to spread from a single black spot, to a growing gray smear as he tried scrubbing it from the stone floor. Sweat made his aged brow shine and his apron and rubber gloves were smeared with the black ooze. Pausing to rest his aching knees, the old caretaker eased back and blew out a long slow breath. He had needed a rest from the morning's yard work and so gladly accepted Thomas' invitation into the secret study to continue 'cleaning up that little stain'. Now he longed to get outdoors once more to escape the infuriating grayvyk stain and attend to less odious messes.

Thomas and Jillian sat at the large oak table across the room. The scroll from the previous week's excursion had been unrolled and pinned to the wood surface. Jill carefully examined the ancient script, scribbling notes in her leather journal beside it as she uncovered one clue after another. Thomas had been hunched over the Book, scanning its pages for any additional signals that might match the scroll to help decipher it. After all, the Book had pinpointed the scroll's location for him, so it seemed logical to expect a few more answers. Although, he had to admit he was not nearly as good as his wife at decoding.

Hearing his old friend's sigh, he sat up and smiled. Samuel was the closest thing to family that Thomas had. "Need a break, Sam?"

"Aye. And a new set of knees wouldn't hurt either," he replied, then marveled, "What sort of diet does a creature have to ingest that would make its blood turn black as pitch?"

"I don't even want to know, but I was nearly on that menu," said Thomas as he shook his head.

"You probably would have been the healthiest meal it had ever eaten in its sad life. Like a walking stalk of broccoli!" Samuel laughed, returning to his work on the stain.

Jillian cleared her throat, "Could you two please talk about any subject other than that of my husband being digested?"

Thomas laughed and leaned back in his chair, rubbing his tired eyes. The secret study naturally had no windows, and the stark lighting from the buzzing bulbs overhead was giving him a headache.

Originally, he had built this room as a hidden survival vault for his family. Thomas had a growing distrust of the world around him, so had it fully equipped with a hidden entrance, separate plumbing system and a solar powered battery bank that supplied more than enough electricity to run it year-round. It was completely off the grid, off the radar and the only three people that knew of its existence were in the room at this very moment. He and Jillian often debated about when they should tell the kids about it but had agreed to wait until they were older.

The survival shelter became the default location of a sort of secret headquarters where they could work in solitude with minimal risk to those around them. The nature of their work proved too dangerous to be public knowledge. One incident made this evidently clear shortly after Thomas and Jillian were married.

Long before their children were born, they had accidentally discovered how the Book worked. Or, as it seemed most times, how the Book worked *them*. Jillian would spend hours deciphering hidden riddles and messages within its pages. Often, they were directions and phrases that referred to various geographical regions of Earth. She found that as she neared the completion of a set of directions, the mark behind her head would buzz and throb. Desperate for relief, she spurred herself onward until it stopped.

The moment Thomas reviewed the deciphered messages passed on to him from Jillian, the buzzing and throbbing would take up residence in the mark above his left hip. The experience both thrilled and scared them at once. But nothing could have prepared them for the discovery of their first truly remarkable find.

After months of code breaking and chasing dead ends, the young couple found themselves in the Painted Desert of Arizona, surrounded by remnants of petrified wood. Armed with little more than shovels and a bad case of the butterflies, they dug holes all day until they thought their palms would bleed. Near sundown Thomas' shovel collided with something metallic. The sensation above his hip stopped abruptly.

Found.

They dug up the oblong container and immediately pried open the dusty lid. Entombed in the metal box lay a rolled parchment tied neatly with a leather strip. Afraid to contaminate their prize further, the elated couple resealed it in the box and took the next flight home where they could more closely, and more safely, examine it.

As they carefully unrolled it the next morning on the kitchen table, they found that a crystal shard neatly wrapped in black cloth had been concealed in the core of the scroll. They carefully laid it on the table. It pulsed slowly through a colorful spectrum of light. Jillian's skull began to buzz, as she scanned the cryptic writings for words and patterns.

As if she were reading an instruction manual for a recent purchase, she looked up from the directions in the scroll and reached over to the crystal giving it a ninety-degree twist as if it were a dial. The spectrum pulse stopped, and then glowed red steadily. She squinted again at the parchment in her hand and said, *"Dissere portas!"*

For a moment, nothing happened. Then the tabletop beside the scroll rippled as if it were suddenly made of Jell-O. Thomas' coffee mug that had once sat there steaming simply sank into it like water. Expecting to hear the mug crash to the floor on the other side, he ducked beneath the oak table to try to catch it. But it was gone. Vanished before their eyes. Goose flesh rippled up their arms and legs. Thomas reached into his pocket, pulled out a quarter and dropped it onto the surface of the table. It too disappeared through the wooden tabletop.

Jillian had been holding her breath and was feeling lightheaded. Thomas, ever the thrill seeker did the unthinkable. He rolled up his sleeves and thrust both arms into the middle of the table, plunging them beneath the surface. They vanished as if he had stuck them into a bucket of thick mud.

"Thomas! No!" Jillian shouted.

Her husband fueled by blind curiosity leaned too far forward and lost his balance. When his head and torso vanished through the tabletop, Jillian screamed and wrapped her arms around his legs to pull him back up. Instead, his weight proved too much for her and she was dragged across the terrifying threshold.

They tumbled together through a split second of breathless void and landed face down in a heap. Something was tickling Jillian's nose. Grass? They were outside! Speechless they sat up and found themselves beneath the most massive tree trunk either of them had ever seen. Two thick branches stretched straight out from its middle. The bark of the trunk appeared to have been peeled back, and as she looked closer, Jillian could vaguely see her own kitchen ceiling and dome light. It was as if she were looking upward at them through a cloth screen. The couple rose to their feet unsteadily as adrenaline raced through their veins. Jillian took a shaky step backward and kicked something. The coffee mug. A metal glint in the grass revealed the shiny quarter beside it. She bent down to pick them up.

"Thomas, where are we?"

"Maybe the better question is *when* are we?"

Jillian looked at him, confused.

"Look at your watch, Jill. It's still morning. But why is it dark?"

Slowly, his wife turned around, taking in the dimly lit scene surrounding them both. They were standing at the edge of a clearing near the middle of some sort of wooded forest. She inhaled sharply and grasped Thomas' hand.

"My love, I think my first question is still the more important."

"What do you mean?" he asked.

Jillian simply pointed upward through the darkly silhouetted trees. Two full moons hung suspended in the night sky. One was sapphire blue, the other shone green as if made of polished emeralds.

Thomas looked up and his eyes widened at the sight. "Why do you always have to be right?" He grasped her trembling hand and they stood for a moment, wrapped in wonder.

That magical night long ago was the first of their many excursions to Haizorr. Soon they began finding a number of powerful scrolls and artifacts that were referenced in the Book. Some were on the Earth side of the portal, others on the Haizorr side. The couple realized that they needed someplace safe to hide the things they found. Some items, like the portal summon scroll they found, might simply be too powerful to exist anyplace other than in secret. If they fell into the wrong hands, there could be terrible consequences. People would stop at nothing to attain this level of power. The survival shelter became that hiding place. Its secrecy, and self-sustaining nature were encased behind walls of stone two feet thick. A private hidden vault of ancient secrets.

In time, they developed a system. Jillian would decipher the hidden powers of the items outlined in the Book. Together, they would decide whether or not it was a relic worth hunting for and hiding, Thomas would then seek out and find it to bring it under lock and key. They found there were times it seemed that the Book allowed them to make the choice, and other times their marks irritated them so badly that it was impossible to ignore until found.

The industrial shelves running the lengths of each wall in the room were lined with sealed metal boxes, each containing a scroll or some other ancient object of power. Some had been tested. Most had not. But all were categorized, and then stored according to class.

An open space on each box was labeled with terms like *teleport, transfer,* and *stealth.* Others sounded less innocent: *pestilence, fear,* and *mind control.*

Long ago, Thomas had decided to permanently affix the portal opening to Haizorr to the adjacent wall, along with the crystal dial that controlled it like a sort of doorknob. He had fashioned a clear case for the crystal and held it to the wall using magnets. Quickly they learned that the portal could not be opened by using the crystal alone but that it served as an agent to *thin* the gateway enough for the commanding words to open it fully when spoken. The Book alluded that there were other ways to thin the veil between worlds, but the crystal was by far the purest and fastest method. Thus, it became a locked door of sorts allowing them to more easily come and go as they pleased as well as provide a safe fixed point of entry on the other side. That scroll had then been stored in a box labeled *portal summon* and placed among the others.

It was beginning to appear to Jillian that the new scroll pinned to the table in front of her would fall under the same sort of *summon* category. She rose from the table to retrieve the portal summon scroll from its latched container on the nearby shelf so she could compare the two. Carefully laying the second scroll beside the first she pinned it to the table as well.

The familiar buzzing throb on her head grew more intense as she perused both documents side by side. She was getting closer now. Jillian's eyes flashed back and forth between the two, scanning for similarities. Then she found it. About halfway down each scroll on the left-hand side a small symbol had been drawn; a circular arrangement with five evenly spaced dots and an object in the center of it. On the portal summon scroll the symbol had a dark rectangle, presumably a door, in the middle of the circle. The new scroll they had just acquired had a squiggled line with two small dots drawn on one end of it, and four tiny segments sticking out from the middle. It was hard to tell for sure, but it looked vaguely like an animal.

That seemed to make some sense. The scroll did have names of animals haphazardly written throughout its length. Some she recognized as common Earth creatures while others were native residents of Haizorr: *Logarthiym, Justhynial, Eyquuariu*. The rest of the arrangement made less sense to her for in between were lists of adjectives, colors, plants, even common structures. At one point she chuckled, as one of the words seemed to indicate *waste*. Not the kitchen trash variety, but something far less sanitary.

Thomas looked up from scanning the Book. "Did we actually find a scroll with some comic relief this time?"

"That would be a switch, wouldn't it?" Then Jillian's laugh quickly faded. She rubbed her throbbing head.

"What's wrong?"

"I think this is a summon scroll." She looked down at it again.

"Another one?"

"This one isn't like our beloved doorway here," she said gesturing to the portal wall. "I think it can be used to command living things. Perhaps even objects."

"Seriously? That's amazing!" Thomas stood up and shuffled over to where she stood to gain a better view.

"Don't you dare say anything out loud," she warned. "You know as well as I do that there's always a catch with these things. If I hadn't shoved you back through the portal before it re-sealed itself, we'd still be stuck in Haizorr, remember?"

He remembered. The bark of the Tree Gate had started to close behind them the first time they crossed over. They learned that portals remain open only for a time before closing of their own accord. And that length of time seemed to vary greatly each instance. They had conducted experiments to measure how long they had between openings until the point it would begin to close again and discovered sometimes it was a mere two minutes, other times much longer. Jillian had noticed the change just in time and hurried them back through. They had been incredibly fortunate.

Thomas was feverishly reading what he could on the parchment. The fades and cracks made it hard to decipher in some places. But much of it was very clear to him. *Bovine, Orange, Wave, Trabalisk, Dark, Worm, Nine.* There were hundreds of lines of gibberish text with no detectable pattern, which was making this one quite difficult to interpret.

"Well, at least you get to read something that's interesting," he declared. "I just keep coming back to a page in the Book that has words and images clipped out of it. It looks like someone was cutting holes in it with a razor blade. Look!" He flipped back several pages to show her.

Small rectangles, circles and slits had been neatly cut throughout the page. Entire words were missing, as were parts of diagrams. It appeared as if someone had intentionally destroyed this page of the Book in order to hide something. Suddenly, the spot on the back of Jillian's head sent a bolt of pain into her brain. She gasped and slapped her hand over the spot as if a wasp had stung her.

"Jill! Are you okay?" Thomas could not hide the alarm in his voice. He put his arm around her waist to steady her. Samuel, who was still in the room scrubbing the stain all this time, stood up from his work. Alarm spreading over his features he strode across the room to face them on the opposite side of the table, ready to assist if needed.

She could not answer. With shaky hands she silently unpinned the scroll with the rambling list of random objects. It crackled audibly as the edges curled inward, attempting to return to its original rolled-up position. Jillian's face scrunched up with tension as she braced against the stabbing pain in her head. Carefully she transferred the delicate document over to the Book and laid it beneath the page with the holes.

"It's a key," she whispered. The pain switched off, and she exhaled in relief. *Found.* Suddenly exhausted, she flopped backward into her chair and closed her eyes.

Thomas stood frozen in place. His wide eyes were fixed on the scene in front of him. If he understood correctly, and if this indeed were a summon scroll, then the holes in the Book's page would highlight a phrase on the parchment beneath it to command each element individually. Eagerly he began to slide the parchment beneath the page, trying to line up the cutouts with phrases and words that made sense to him.

True red whistle four. No.

Grave-hound triplet. That sounded unpleasant.

Logarthiym scout green one. Thomas scanned the rest of the page trying to find more word combinations that appeared similar to some of the other phrases they had found in times past. He traced his finger across the spot so he would not lose his place in the jumbled mess of words.

"Jill?"

Her sleepy reply came from behind him, "Mhmm?"

He squinted as he read. "What does, *veni ad meam vocant*, mean?"

"Thomas!" Jillian bolted up from her chair. "I told you not to say anything you read from there!"

"I'm just asking! Please, calm down. I'm not commanding anything. It was phrased as a question. Commands need to be forceful."

She brought her hands to her face and rubbed her eyes. "Sorry, love. I'm a bit jumpy. I've never had it hurt like that before. This one just feels different."

"I'll say! I think I can actually call for the *Logarthiym!* Do you remember them? This is incredible." Thomas could feel the excitement coursing through his veins. He moved the page back and forth highlighting a huge variety of combinations. There were tens of thousands of possibilities. Then, one word in particular froze him in his search: *darchlyte*. Could it actually be possible to rouse one of these giants? If so, would this scroll give him the power to control one of them? He was beginning to understand his wife's concern, but feverishly pressed on through the manuscript. He was nearing the bottom margin of the scroll now. The top of it had flopped over the edge of the table down to the floor and rolled a bit, bumping against the front of Samuel's shoe. He looked down at the parchment, and then frowned.

"Jill, look at this here. What do you think this code means?" Thomas pointed to a tiny word code scribbled down low on the long brown paper: *uo6bvp.*

"Thomas." It was Samuel's voice this time. "Perhaps we all could do with a rest. I'll put on some tea if you wish."

Thomas did not seem to hear him. "Do you think it's some sort of a pass code?" he asked his wife.

Jillian leaned in and squinted. "I'm not sure. It certainly looks like an alpha-numeric combination, but it's removed from the rest."

The page-key from the Book had holes lining up with other words all across the page. As with most of the combinations, they appeared to be senseless. But two words stood alone on the left and right margins and had been written vertically. The tiny words appeared to be *Black* and *Dearth*.

Samuel cleared his throat, speaking a little louder this time. "It says *dragon*."

"Huh? Where do you see that? I've scanned every combination on this page," Thomas dropped his nose closer to the page.

"I don't see it either, Samuel." Jillian sounded apologetic.

"That's because you two are not standing where I am." He thumped a large finger at the mix of letters and numbers at the bottom of the page: *uo6bvp*. "It's been written upside down."

Both tilted their heads. Then they all saw it. Thomas swallowed hard. A hush fell over them for a moment. Slowly, Thomas slid the documents apart from one another and began to reroll the scroll. He bound it with the leather strip and laid it to rest on the table before them. Lost in a swirl of new thoughts, he turned away and walked quickly out of the room without another word. The others followed close on his heels.

Samuel was right; it was indeed time for a rest.

JAYCE'S STOMACH WAS GROWLING. Usually his mother or Samuel would have prepared their favorite Saturday pancake breakfast for them long ago. Wandering through the hallways and around the edges of the yard, he had spent the past fifteen minutes looking for her. But now it seemed he could not find anyone. Not even Samuel who was usually buzzing about the property fixing or cleaning something. He passed through the kitchen and sniffed. That smell certainly was not pancakes. It smelled like something had died.

Sniffing and peering around the trashcan and behind corners, he half expected to find a dead mouse any moment now. Looking down the adjoining corridor, Jayce saw nothing but a lone wash bucket against the wall outside the pantry. The scent grew stronger in that direction, so he headed into the hallway. Drawing nearer to the bucket he had to hold his nose. The rancid smell was coming from the frothy black mess inside it. As he leaned closer to see what on earth it could be, his father suddenly burst around the corner with his mother and Samuel following closely behind. Thomas' knee accidentally caught Jayce in the bottom, pitching him forward. The startled boy lost his balance and thrust his arms forward to catch himself, plunging his left arm deep into the bucket. He sank up to his elbow in black ooze. In horror he recoiled and then dry heaved from the awful stink.

In between gags, Jayce shot out, "Ugh! What *is* that?"

Samuel was there in an instant, wrapping Jayce's arm in one of the rare clean spots of his work apron. "It's utterly wretched, is what."

Stunned, Jayce was having a hard time not being angry. "Dad, you pushed me right into that stuff! Didn't you even see me there?"

Thomas looked apologetically at his son. The truth was he had been so focused on what they had just discovered that he had not been paying any attention at all. It also occurred to him that they had nearly given away the hidden entrance to the secret study. He swallowed and was about to speak, when Samuel interrupted.

"The fault is all mine, young master," he said with his kindest smile. "I had left the bucket there and was shoving your father down the hallway to keep him from interfering with my cleaning. I'm so sorry."

Jayce relaxed a little, but his eyes were watering from the stench, and he was gasping over his shoulder for cleaner air. "It smells like a skunk died in a trash compactor!"

"That's it!" Samuel practically shouted.

Jillian jumped. "What is it, Sam?"

"He needs a skunk bath."

Jayce groaned, "That sounds like a horrible idea! No way, I smell bad enough already!"

Thomas laughed, "No, Jayce. It's a remedy sometimes used to deodorize dogs when a skunk sprays them. It's just a mixture of peroxide, baking soda and dish soap."

Samuel was already ushering Jayce down to the utility room at the far end of the house to start the process. He called over his shoulder, "If this works, I'll use it to finish off that beastly stain in your study!"

Thomas' eyes went wide, and he raised a finger to his lips to caution the caretaker on his choice of words. Samuel stiffened as he realized his blunder. Their excitement was making them all careless. The old caretaker quickened his pace to escort Jayce from the room.

"Since when does Dad have a study?" came Heidyl's voice from the other end of the kitchen. In all the commotion, no one had seen the sleepy-eyed girl enter the room in her pajamas. Thomas and Jillian held their breath and let the question dangle in the air, unsure of how to respond. Heidyl yawned and rubbed her eyes, "We having pancakes today, Mom? I can help if you'd like."

"Sure, sweetheart. That would be wonderful, thank you." Jillian smiled at her, relieved that her daughter had already seemed to forget she asked anything concerning the secret study. The two of them began to gather the griddle and ingredients, filling the air with clattering and banging.

But standing in the dank utility room, the question was not yet lost on Jayce.

His mind began drifting as Samuel mumbled and scrubbed his smelly arm for him in the slop sink. *The only thing at the end of that hallway is an old pantry, which is barely large enough for one person to fit into, much less three. And why are they acting so weird?* Jayce had never seen his usually calm mother rush around for anything unless it was an emergency. He thought again about his sister's question.

Since when does Dad have a study?

To Jayce, the answer was clear.

He doesn't.

PART IV: THE SCROLL

"IT ALL MAKES SENSE NOW!" Thomas was trying to whisper, but excitement had elevated his voice so much that whispering was proving to be a pointless exercise. Now he just sounded like he was yelling hoarsely. Jillian pressed a finger to her lips to warn him to keep it down.

"Sorry. I just can't believe this is happening. It's got me all fired up inside!" Thomas was pacing the room.

The Saturday morning breakfast routine had ended an hour ago. By the time Jillian and Heidyl had finished preparing breakfast, Samuel had won the battle with the stench on Jayce's arm. The concoction had worked so well that the old caretaker could barely wait to try using it in the hidden room. Jayce watched him mix another large batch.

"What are you making more of that stuff for?" he asked.

"Because I need a miracle," came Samuel's hurried reply as he marched out of the room and around the corner, carrying the sloshing bucket.

Jayce tried to follow him, but his mother pulled him into the dining room, effectively distracting him with a tall tower of steaming pancakes. Immediately following the meal, the rest of the family dispersed to tackle their own various weekend tasks. Heidyl said she had homework to finish as she tromped up the stairs. Jayce left the table with a grunt and wandered upstairs as well, which usually meant he would be playing a video game or building an invention of some sort. Thomas and Jillian were alone. Which was good, because they *really* needed to talk about this latest development.

Quietly they had crept up the stairs to their own bedroom, trying to avoid the known creaky spots in the floor so as not to alert the children of their presence.

Thomas always paced in wild circles when his mind was swirling. It reminded Jillian of watching a puppy slowly chase its own tail. She could not help but smile a bit at him.

"So, what's got your brain in a twister, Thomas?" Jillian lay back on the bed and closed her eyes.

"Okay. It's a summon scroll, right?"

"Apparently."

"But, not just any summon scroll. It's, like, the mother of all summon scrolls. It's a summon scroll, but with a *menu* for crying out loud!" Thomas was making large gestures with his hands to help drive his point.

"Yes. If used with the key-code page from the Book, it looks like you can summon almost anything you'd like. If you know how to read them together."

"Exactly!"

"Thomas, I'm not following you." Jillian did not have her husband's boundless energy. Her head still ached a little, too.

"On my last trip to Haizorr, remember how I told you I met a darchlyte?" Thomas smiled as he remembered the amazing encounter.

"You've only told me a hundred times so far, love, yes."

"Right. But why *this* visit?"

"What do you mean?"

"We've been to Haizorr more times than we can count. We've seen dozens of creatures, but not once have we encountered even a trace of the darchlytes."

"That's because they don't like to be seen. Even in perfect sunlight or full moonlight they can make themselves nearly invisible."

"That's my point, Jill. Not only did I see one, it escorted me, protected me. Heck—it even gave me a present!" He patted the area above his chest where the grayvyk claw still hung under his shirt. "I think it knew that this particular scroll could call forth its arch enemy."

Jillian propped herself up on one elbow, "A dragon?"

"No, Jill. Not just *any* dragon. *The* dragon. That page in the Book had the words *Black* and *Dearth* highlighted in the margins of that page for a reason."

"But that may just be an old Haizorr legend, Thomas."

"I don't think it is. I think someone is trying to summon the Black Dragon of Dearth and we just stopped him!"

Jillian tilted her head to look up at her husband. "Who?"

Thomas' expression quickly changed from excitement to melancholy. He huffed out an enormous sigh and plopped on the bed beside his wife. "It's got to be him."

"My love, I don't know what you mean. Who are you talking about?" She was genuinely perplexed, if not a little alarmed.

"There are others out there like us, you know."

"I've always suspected there were, yes. But we've never met any of them before. We've both searched the world over and came up empty. You remember, don't you?"

Thomas rubbed his tired eyes and lay back on the bed, staring at the ceiling. "That's my point. We only ever searched *this* world for those kinds of people, Jill."

Her eyes widened in understanding. "Haizorr?"

Thomas rolled over on his side and faced the bedroom windows. The view of the distant hills and trees began drawing him into deep thought.

"That night, the Book led me to a black stone structure to collect that infernal scroll. The second I crested the hill and saw the place, my heart seized up like a rock in my chest. I could almost taste the evil in the air. The building was huge, Jill. Like a castle or some sort of compound. It was the most frightening place I've ever seen." His heart began beating faster as the vivid picture replayed in his mind. "I could *feel* the evil everywhere. The Book calls the place *Blackynspyre.*" He swallowed hard and sighed heavily again at the thought.

Jillian rested her hand on her husband's shoulder to steady him. She could sense he was pained somehow by the experience. She wished to help him but was unsure how. "Why didn't you tell me this before?"

A pause.

"Because, I—I was afraid." His voice cracked.

"Shhh. Hey, it's okay—"

"No. It's not like that. I'm afraid because of—", his voice trailed off and a distant stare glazed his eyes.

"What is it, Thomas?"

He blinked, rubbed his eyes and smiled, "It's nothing. Just wondering what sort of person would hide a scroll like this, that's all."

Jillian cocked her head in disbelief. "Have you forgotten that *we* are the sort of people who hide scrolls like this?"

Her point had cornered him, and he licked his lips. "No, what I mean to say is that this proves we aren't the only ones with the drive or ability to find and keep these artifacts." He sounded a bit disappointed.

"And that's a bad thing? We've longed to connect with others like us for years!" Jillian could not believe what she had just heard. The burden they carried together felt so heavy at times, to her it would be a relief to know they were not alone.

"Yeah, you may be right." Thomas sighed, but not for relief. "But I'm the one who just took that scroll from that horrible place. And the worst part may be that now its previous owner knows our address, too."

"I HATE THIS LEVEL!" Jayce pounded his fist on the desk in frustration. The computer monitor was alive with animated explosions, gunfire and hordes of vicious looking creatures attacking a fortress. Jayce was frantically pushing buttons and combinations, but it was too late. His online fortress had been overrun. He toggled a key on his keyboard to exit the battle. Large red letters appeared on the screen: *Are you sure you want to quit?* Jayce sighed and clicked a button. The images disappeared.

"Oh yeah. I'm sure." He leaned back in his chair and rubbed his eyes. The hand that he had plunged into the bucket of black slime still smelled slightly, and he jerked it away from his face in further annoyance. "I never should have let that stupid spy past the gate! What was I thinking?" Jayce opened a nearby drawer and rummaged for a notebook and pencil. He kept notes about his gaming strategies and wanted to make sure he did not make this mistake twice.

Like many boys his age, he both loved and hated video games. As long as his quests were successful, he felt confident inside but when the game went sour, like today, it made him sullen. Either way, he always felt a bit empty knowing that none of his other world was real, no matter how many times he leveled up his characters. Hours of successful gaming still left him with a gnawing feeling in his gut that he had wasted his time.

Now, he felt utterly bored. Jayce pushed back from the desk, stood up and stretched his aching neck. Slowly he scanned his room, looking for something, *anything,* to catch his interest. The pile of textbooks and home-work near his bed was not appealing. His rumpled bed could use some atten-tion, but it was Saturday, and he was allowed to skip making his bed on the weekend. Several flies were buzzing around something in his wastebasket. Wadded papers, a soda can, and a dried-up food wrapper had tumbled from the top of the mound of trash to the floor. He decided that was a good place to start, and after crushing the overflowing garbage back down, he scooped up the trashcan and headed downstairs.

Jayce could hear the muffled voices drifting from his parents' bed-room as he walked past their door. They stopped abruptly when he stepped on a creaky floorboard. *They must be talking about something pretty important,* he thought. He lingered for a minute, hoping to capture snatches of their con-versation, but when the talking resumed it was just the soft buzzing of whis-pers and he could not make out what they were saying.

Downstairs, the kitchen had been cleaned up and was empty. Every-one had retreated to his or her own place in the house for some quiet time. Saturdays were like that sometimes in this family. The busy week of school and work would give way to a slow-paced day as a sort of personal reward. Jayce began dumping his small wastebasket into the large kitchen trash bin by the hall. He noticed that Samuel had removed the stinking bucket of black slime and had scrubbed the floor where the day's catastrophe had happened earlier.

Clank! Jayce had not been paying attention to his task and the aluminum soda can bounced off the edge of the bin to go tumbling down the pantry hallway. As he retrieved the wayward container, he peered into the dark pantry where his parents and Samuel had all been huddled earlier. *What in the world could they possibly have been doing in here?* The tiny room was dark and impossibly small, holding little more than narrow shelves filled with dried herbs from his mother's garden and some obscure canned foods. He picked up the most grotesque looking of the jars. The contents were a tangle of some sort of thin green plant that formed a tight coil on one end. He could not help but think they looked like a variety of earthworm. He read the label: *Pickled Fiddleheads.* A wave of nausea hit his stomach as he put the jar back in its place on the shelf.

Turning to leave, something caught his peripheral vision, like a drifting spider web reflecting sunlight. Slowly, Jayce backed up and moved his head from side to side, trying to recreate what had captured his attention. There it was! A tiny crack of light appeared where the end of the shelf met the corner of the wall. He inched his face closer to get a better look. A razor-thin slice of light played across his face and he felt a slight draft of cool air brushing his cheek as he pressed in close. Squinting, Jayce tried to make out the source of the light but ended up shrugging it off. *The house is pretty old, it's probably just an old crack,* he thought. But behind another jar of the gross looking pickled vegetable, he noticed the glint of a square, metallic object mounted to the wall. He slid the jars to one side revealing what looked like a telephone number pad. It was similar to the kind he saw in a phone booth of an old movie once.

He looked further but could see no phone. There were no wires either. Just a numbered keypad stuck to the wall. He wondered if it was a hidden lockbox or a safe. Cautiously he tapped one of the buttons. Nothing. Not even a beep. Just for kicks, he pressed 9-1-1.

Suddenly, the jars rattled ever so slightly. Jayce jumped back. He could hear a soft, rhythmic thumping from the other side of the wall that grew louder, as if someone were coming up a stairway. He pressed his face to the crack once again. The thumping stopped. He gasped as something passed by the small slit, blocking the light. The jars rattled again, and the entire wall began to move toward him. Too startled to run, Jayce simply backed up as the wall swung inward, pressing him against the far side of the little pantry. He was trapped! Tiny fingers of fear closed around his throat, and he was just about to cry out when he heard Samuel's muffled voice.

"Don't know why I didn't think of that before! Nearly broke my back trying to scrub the death off that floor!" He was again carrying a bucket of blackened water.

Jayce noticed tiny shards of light begin playing off the glass jars in the corner of his little prison. He leaned against the wall and was able to see a larger crack and something like hinges. Jayce realized with great relief that he was merely caught in the empty space behind a door that Samuel had opened. All at once, a hundred questions and suspicions popped into his mind. *A secret door in the pantry? Why didn't I know about this? Something strange is happening here. What's hidden down there?*

He thought about how good it might feel confronting Samuel and his parents about this secret entrance later, but a second, more enticing thought entered his mind at the same instant. Quickly, he grabbed a small metal measuring spoon from the spice rack beside him. The door began to swing away from him, back toward its locked position. He could hear Samuel's strong steps moving down the hallway and knew he only had a few seconds to make his move. Carefully, Jayce wedged the spoon into the opening next to the hinges, slowing down the door's automatic closing mechanism just long enough for him to scoot around to the other side of the door.

The heavy door groaned and creaked against the foreign object preventing it from closing. But the spoon shifted, slipped and fell. The glass jars rattled gently as the door finally latched closed. Hearing the spoon clatter to the floor Samuel paused to set down the bucket and returned to the pantry to place the spoon back in its home on the spice rack. He studied the object a moment. It had a black, greasy smear and was oddly bent at the handle. As he wiped it off and began straightening it with his strong fingers, he noticed the shelf with the glass jars slid to the side and the exposed keypad. He felt a sick feeling creep through his stomach.

"Samuel," he chided himself, "you are getting too forgetful in your old age!" Carefully, he returned the spoon and the jars to their rightful places. He shook his head, still upset with himself. "Someone might have seen this!" The large man strode back to the smelly bucket of water and continued down the hall.

Inside the hidden stairway, Jayce listened with his ear pressed against the smooth, metal surface of the secret door. He was not totally sure, but he thought he heard the sound of Samuel's footsteps moving away from where he stood. He did not realize that he had been holding his breath the whole time and exhaled loudly. Turning around, he rested his back against the cold door. He stood in complete darkness. Gingerly he slid his foot forward across the floor and ran his fingers along the smooth wall beside him. His toes met the lip of a stair at the same time his wrist knocked against the end of a wooden railing. With great care, he descended the stairway—more curious now than afraid, but his heart still pounded hard in his chest.

Upon reaching the bottom, his echoing footsteps gave him the feeling that he stood in a large room. Slowly he started turning in a complete circle to get his bearings. The stinging scent of bleach hung in the air.

A faintly glowing light pulsated on the far wall to his left. It shimmered randomly through a spectrum of rainbow colors. Jayce moved toward the light source, struck with a new sense of curious wonder. Expecting it to be sort of nightlight, he was amazed to find that it was actually a variety of stone, like quartz. It hung in a Plexiglas tube affixed to the wall with strong neodymium magnets. A few feet away, he saw the dim outline of a light switch and flipped it on. The low hum and click of a string of industrial lighting came to life, bathing the room in a wash of bright light. Jayce squinted his eyes, then felt them widen as the room came into full view.

His mouth hung open at the sprawling scene of shelving, boxes, desks, chairs and artifacts that filled the room. His eyes eventually came to rest on a large wooden desk in the center of it all. A scroll bound with a strip of material lay next to the thickest book Jayce had ever seen. He crept forward, feeling very much like an intruder but adventurous curiosity spurred him further on. He did not dare to touch anything. Especially the scroll, as it looked so delicate and ancient. As he rounded the desk his eyes began to drink in the ancient words and cryptic pictures penned across the pages of the mountainous book sitting beside the tattered parchment.

Beside it lay a smaller scroll, neatly pinned open. He squinted as he tried reading the faded words. At first, the symbols and phrases made absolutely no sense to him, but he found the more he stared at the markings the more he seemed to understand. He did not want to linger long, for fear of discovery, but neither could he stop himself from reading. It was all so fascinating! His eyes flew over the lengthy document, paused, then grew wide. He looked up again at the glowing crystal mounted to the wall before him. His eyes flashed back to the parchment describing the very same shard. *No way! That's amazing!* he thought. But in the same instant the instructions and descriptions of the summon portal scroll seemed too fantastic to fully believe. Both doubt and intrigue fought a silent war in his mind. After a moment's pause, he shrugged. *Why would they keep this hidden if there wasn't something to it all?* In the end curiosity won the battle and following the directions in the scroll, Jayce walked over to the crystal dial on the wall and gave it a sharp turn. The glowing spectrum stopped pulsing then held a steady red glow.

"Whoa! Cool!" he exclaimed, but then clapped his hand over his mouth. He was being too loud. He ran back to the parchment and then stated the phrase he had just read, *"Dissere portas."*

For a moment, nothing happened. Then a section of the stone wall wobbled like it had suddenly become a stiff liquid. Jayce felt the blood in his limbs run cold and his heart begin to race. He stepped toward the wall and reached out an unsteady hand to touch it. When his fingers vanished from sight, he snatched his arm back, expecting them to be injured. Seeing no sign of harm, he ventured a second more probing touch. The wall simply felt like nothing at all. Not cold, not liquid, and certainly not stone. Just nothing. Reaching his arm all the way up to the shoulder, he expected to feel studs or wires, or maybe insulation, but came up empty.

Jayce held his breath and pressed his face into the portal. He closed his eyes tightly and held his nose with his other hand, thinking it would be a good idea in case the wall really had become liquid. Opening his eyes very slowly, the scene that met them made him forget he was holding his breath.

He gasped sharply. Rich earthy scents poured into his nose and the air filling his lungs felt both strong and clean. A dense forest surrounded him. Trees taller than redwoods stretched to the heavens and a lush meadow spread out before him. Looking down where his feet should have been was the trunk of an enormous tree. When he looked up to the scene again, a very stout creature stood no less than six feet in front of him.

It had two legs and arms and stood upright like a human, but that was as far as the resemblance went. Jayce stifled a yelp and would have retreated if not for the kind features of the little man's face. A grin tugged at the corners of its wide mouth. He looked like he was about to tell the funniest joke and was holding back laughter. The wide set eyes were kind and the deepest green Jayce had ever seen. He wore a simple green tunic lashed together in the front, and brown hide leather pants that were tucked into the top of a pair of dark green boots. The creature had enormous feet. In his large, three-fingered hand he held a sort of bamboo staff with a black stone affixed to the top of it. It looked like it could be either a weapon or a walking stick, Jayce could not tell which.

The small man spoke. "Wista calls back long time. Was worth it! You pokes out like this!" Then he grabbed his own little nose, scrunched his eyes shut and puffed out his cheeks. Howling laughter erupted from him and he fell on the ground while pointing at Jayce, giggling like he was being tickled.

Jayce then realized how foolish he must have looked when he first came through the portal, holding his breath like a snorkeler. He could not help but chuckle, too. The small man had the most infectious laugh, punctuated by two tufted rabbit-like ears that stuck straight out from the sides of his head. They flapped wildly as he lay cackling on the ground. A shock of golden curly hair covered the top of his broad head. Jayce could not believe what he was seeing.

He ventured a reply, "I guess I do look pretty weird hanging halfway out of a tree like a monkey!"

The man stopped laughing and hopped to his feet. He kicked his staff up from the ground with the toe of his boot and caught it with such speed that Jayce flinched. Before he had scarcely reopened his eyes from blinking, the little man was beside him, sniffing at his arm.

"Monkey? No. Thomaseed, betchya."

Jayce withdrew his arm; frightened at the blinding speed this creature was capable of. "Thomas-what? You know my father? How?"

The green eyes narrowed a bit and a proud smirk creased his face. He thumped his own chest heartily, "Mine Logarth green scout! Itsum eyes knows lots." He bolted back to his original spot on the grass and began twirling his staff faster than a boat propeller. Jayce could actually feel the wind created by the spinning stick. Jayce decided then that it most definitely had to be a weapon.

The Logarth gave one final spin behind his back before ramming the base of the rod into the ground beside him. He pointed to the shiny black stone on the staff, "Big Tom-Tom gives us this. Shatter shield, scale buster!" The little man looked pleased with his gift. Then he cocked his head giving Jayce a puzzled look, "Tommy Big holding your tiny feet?" He was squinting now as if trying to see past Jayce and into the opening in the Tree Gate.

Jayce laughed, "What are you talking about?"

"Hims rang the Caller bell. Wista calls back long time. Biggy Tom still monkeying in your tree? Hims always likings to be hidden ups in them."

"Huh?" Jayce looked puzzled, trying to decipher the funny creature's meaning. He then looked down and realized that he was still sticking half in and half out of the trunk of the Tree Gate like a worm poking through a hole in an apple. He must have looked ridiculous. "Um, no. It's just me. I accidentally opened—"

"Crank down! Hush that!" The Logarth suddenly spun to face the line of massive trees, brandishing his war-staff. His ears twitched.

Jayce whispered, "What's the matter?"

Wista pointed a stubby finger at the boy, "Thomaseed strong stink. Shush it!"

A sharp crack in the nearby woods set them both on alert. A dense row of bushes shook violently followed by a loud snap.

The little man again poked a thick finger toward Jayce's face. "Gravehounds make you food! Me thoughts they was all goneaway gones, but nopedy nope! They's back. Now Wista goes! And you close it!" Then, with a blast of speed, the Logarth was gone faster than if he had been shot from the barrel of a cannon.

Jayce scanned the trees and bushes but could find no further trace of him. Instead, what he saw froze his blood. The flat, metallic head of a giant reptile rose above the underbrush. A black tongue lashed in and out from the tip of its pointed snout. The dense thicket shook again as a second, and then a third beast emerged near the first.

Jayce eased his arms slowly back into the portal, gently inching his way backward into the secret study behind him. When all but his head was back through, Jayce saw the first reptile open its mouth wide, gaping at the sky. Dark drool dripped from the steel colored teeth that stuck out from the beast's mouth like a thousand daggers. It belched a terrifying scream that instantly sent knife-stabbing pains into Jayce's ears. He snapped his head backward through the portal into the hidden room and the painful noise abruptly cut off.

He staggered back and found the stairs, holding his throbbing head in his hands he stumbled his way up them. The steel door was magnetically sealed, but fortunately had a crash-bar release on the inside for an easy return into the pantry. Too afraid to care about secrecy, he burst back into his home, spun around and slammed the door behind him, violently rattling every spice canister and jar on the shelves.

He walked on unsteady feet back into the kitchen and sat down hard at the table. He was breathing heavily, trying his best to calm down. What had he just seen? His head suddenly felt heavy. The fearful sight and splintering shriek from the—what did Wista call them, *grave-hounds?*—had rattled his nerves. *Am I dreaming?* Jayce wondered, but his ears were still ringing from the assault on his eardrums. He pinched his arm and looked around the room. *No, this is real.* Holding his head between trembling hands, he slowly eased his face down to rest against the cool surface of the kitchen table. It felt familiar and real. It felt good.

"Hey there sleeping beauty!" Heidyl burst into the room.

Jayce jumped backward in his chair. "Don't do that!"

She noticed that he had gone pale and was visibly shaking. "Big brother, you don't look so good. You feeling okay?"

"Are Mom and Dad around?"

She pointed toward the side windows. Thomas, Jillian, and Samuel were gathered outside near the vegetable garden. Their father was pacing in circles as he talked with the others. "Looks like something's got Dad all riled up again."

When she looked back, Jayce was holding his trembling hands in front of himself. "I think I need to go talk—" then he stopped.

"What?"

"Shh. Listen!"

A low vibration could be felt through the floor of the kitchen, like someone had dropped a heavy load in a nearby room.

"Did you feel that?" Jayce's eyes were wide.

"Yeah. What is that? What's going on?"

"There it is again!" This time it was stronger, rattling a few plates together in the kitchen cupboards.

"Do you think it's an earthquake?" Heidyl's voice began to register some concern. "But we don't get those in this part of the country."

Jayce got on his hands and knees and pressed his ear to the floor, straining to listen. He heard some muffled thumps, and then an unmistakable short shriek that sounded like metal nails being raked across a dirty chalkboard.

He bolted upright, terrified.

"Oh no! Now I know what he meant when he told me to close it!"

WE'VE GOT TO HURRY! Jayce's grip on his sister's wrist was starting to hurt as he half-dragged her through the house and out the back door. Ordinarily she would have kicked him in the shins to get him to stop, but he seemed genuinely afraid, and even concerned for her safety. His alarming behavior compelled her to tumble out the back door with him.

"Run! Don't stop! Let's get to the tree house."

"Okay, but I can run a lot faster if you'll let my arm go!"

The two siblings dashed across the back yard and disappeared into the woods at the outskirts of their property. Long ago, their father had built them a fabulous tree house that offered them hours of fun as young children. It even had a slide and a secret trap door. Years of weather had rotted the rope bridge that led to their lookout tower addition, and they vowed to fix it every summer, but always ended up remembering to do it in the dead of winter.

They climbed the uneven wooden-slat ladder and squeezed into the hidden room at the back of the fort where they kept their childhood treasures of old deer bones, bullet casings and large slabs of shiny mica they had found in the woods over the years.

Jayce sat on the rough plank floor and huddled his knees to his chest to steady himself. Heidyl found her usual stump chair that their father had carved for them with his chainsaw. She did not remember it being this small. Slowly her eyes adjusted to the dim light. She swatted a mosquito away while she waited for Jayce to speak. He looked frightened and though he had just been running, his face was still a bit pale. When he did not speak for several minutes, she nudged him with her toe.

"Hey. What's wrong with you?"

He was staring into nothing. When he spoke, his voice was a croaking whisper, "I saw something. I don't even know what I saw." His eyes were moist, and a tear was beginning to form at the corner of his bruised eye.

Heidyl could tell he was shaken up. She loved her big brother, and compassion swelled within her. "It's okay, Jayce. You can tell me, I promise I'll just listen." Awkwardly, she touched his arm to reassure him. "Okay?"

The kind gesture seemed to snap him out of his shocked state, and he blinked. Swallowing hard he said, "You're not going to believe one ounce of what I'm about to tell you." Then, all at once the words began to tumble out of him. For several minutes he painted the entire picture telling her of the hidden door in the pantry, the secret room, the scroll, and the portal. When he mentioned the part about meeting the little man, she giggled, and he glared at her. "See? I told you. Not one ounce."

"I'm sorry. But c'mon Jayce, a troll in our basement?"

He held up a hand to stop her. "Not a troll, a Logarth—or maybe it was a Wista, he kept saying something like that. And not in our basement, well, not really, he was at the tree with me. But I was only half in the basement, he was still outside. Wow, that little guy could run!" Jayce paused and scratched his head. He was not making any sense, and he knew it. None of this made sense.

Heidyl raised her eyebrows at him. "Well if it wasn't a little troll in our basement, then what did you hear down there that made you run like a madman out here dragging me with you?"

Jayce swallowed hard. "I don't know, but I think it was something very bad." Suddenly, he shot upright and scrambled to his feet. Forgetting the low ceiling, he crashed his head against a beam.

"Ouch!" He felt the lump and his fingers came away moist with blood. "The house! It might have come upstairs by now!"

A look of startled confusion crossed Heidyl's face.

"What? The little troll?"

"No! Something worse!"

He jerked her roughly back toward the tree fort ladder. "Mom and Dad and Samuel are there! We need to warn them! C'mon!"

"We're seriously doing this crazy run again?" She pulled her arm away from his grasp and shot him a look.

Jayce did not respond, he just kept urging her toward the ladder hurrying her out of their secret hideout. Heidyl was the faster runner, but she was getting a little tired of her brother's game and she lagged behind. Jayce, on the other hand, sprinted as fast as he could. He would never forgive himself if anything happened to them.

"YOU LEFT IT OPEN!" Thomas' voice boomed through the open window. As he ran across the yard, Jayce could see his mother standing against the refrigerator with her fingers over her mouth. She looked very pale. Samuel was seated at the table looking down at his lap while Thomas loomed over him.

"You were the last one to go down there! I warned you just this morning about this very thing!" Thomas was shouting at the older man and pointing his finger angrily.

"Sir, I assure you. The Gate, the scrolls, that blasted Book, all of the items were untouched when I left the room. I latched and secured the door myself."

"Then how else did this happen? Don't you see what you've done? Now I've got to try to take that scroll—for the second time!"

Jillian's voice quivered, "Are we certain that was all that was taken? There are so many—"

"I accounted for them all. The room is in shambles, but just the one is missing," Samuel replied, his calloused hands fidgeting in his lap.

"It might as well be all of them! Those scrolls are dangerous! There's no telling how much damage could be done if even one of them lands in the wrong hands!" Thomas pounded the table with his fist. Samuel flinched, but still did not look up.

The screen door creaked as Jayce gingerly stepped into the room, panting from his run. Thomas glared at him and then glanced at Jillian.

"Take him out of here while I deal with this."

Jayce protested, "But, Dad! I have to say something!"

"Go!" Thomas' voice thundered.

Jillian rested a hand on Jayce's shoulder and steered him into the next room. Heidyl was just walking in through the back door as they were sitting down together on the sofa.

Sensing the thick layer of tension in the room, she asked, "Is everything okay in here?"

Her mother patted the cushion beside her. "Have a seat beside me, Heidyl. There's a storm brewing in the kitchen."

At that, Thomas drew the door closed that separated the rooms and the tense conversation erupted once more, although greatly muffled by the heavy door.

Jayce could not wait another second. "Mom, I have something to tell you. There's something dangerous in the house."

Heidyl interrupted, not wanting her brother to say anything foolish. "We heard an animal or something under the floorboards and got worried."

Jayce was about to say more, but his mother chuckled.

"Oh, that. Yes, we know all about that already. It's just what your father and Samuel are discussing right now."

"Really?" Jayce's eyes went wide.

His mother nodded. "Some wild animal got in and did a bit of damage to the under parts of the house, but Samuel and your father plugged the hole after it left."

"It sure made a ruckus. What was it?" Heidyl asked.

"I'm not totally sure. We didn't really see it. Don't worry, love, it's gone now." She pressed a hand to her daughter's knee, but Heidyl thought it felt clammy and noticed that she was trembling.

They sat in silent tension for a long moment. The argument in the next room rose and fell like muted waves—most of the waves belonging to Thomas. Jayce was still visibly shaken from his experience and forced himself to stare intently at certain objects in the great room to steady his nerves. His eyes flew about his surroundings before landing on one of his favorite corners of the house. It contained a floor-to-ceiling bookshelf, intricately built into the stonework of the room. The shelves were each made of a solid slab of green marble and mortared in between angular joints of cut granite. There were six tiers in all, the topmost ending in a carved arch where a lone sculpture of The Thinker sat staring blankly into nothing. The bottom two had held much of Jayce's attention as a young boy as they were simply stuffed with full volumes of wildlife encyclopedias. There was also an impressive hand-illustrated collector set of books built entirely around imaginary space travel vehicles and their proposed history. The creators had included exploded views of each vessel in fascinating detail. The books' cracked spines and torn pages revealed just how much he loved them.

Jayce's eyes traveled further up the shelves and stopped to rest at a small photograph in a simple frame half hidden in shadow. He had seen the picture perhaps hundreds of times, but now found himself really studying the figures in it this time. It was an old picture of his father standing together with another couple. Jayce did not recognize the surroundings. They were holding a young child. The other man in the photo beside his father stood stoic-faced and his half-turned body suggested that he had missed the cue to smile for the picture. *Dad's brother,* thought Jayce. To his knowledge this was the only picture he had ever seen of his uncle, aunt, and cousin. He could just barely recall meeting them during a handful of family occasions long ago. Being very young at the time, Jayce's memories of the encounters were little more than wispy mental cobwebs. *What ever happened to them?* Jayce wondered. He knew they had fallen on hard times and the little family had split up years ago. Jayce thought he remembered something about his aunt winning custody of the child but that was as far as he could recall. Heidyl had been too young to remember their uncle at all, and he never came up in conversation or even when Thomas told stories to the children of his own family upbringing.

The voices in the kitchen were dwindling to the faint drones of serious conversation now. Jayce was still feeling very uncertain about his mother's reassurance of the "wild animal" being gone. He was about to say as much to her, when she suddenly patted both of their knees and stood. "I'm going to go take a shower and then get some food ready." She turned a serious face to her children still seated on the couch, "You two should go upstairs to wash up. It looks like I'm going to need some help tonight."

She looked very tired. Stress lines spread like tiny fingers across her lovely face. Jayce and Heidyl watched her leave and then stared at each other.

"What in the world is going on?" asked Heidyl.

IN THE KITCHEN, Thomas took a deep breath to steady himself. There were times he hated being so very passionate about everything. He knew it could be good if applied correctly, but when that passion spark hit his anger fuse, he became a powder keg. He needed to try calming down. Knowing the children were within earshot now, he lowered his voice to just above a whisper.

"Samuel, I've known you for a long time. You're more than my groundskeeper. You are a true friend and I don't believe you would ever lie to me."

The older man shifted uncomfortably in his seat but did not say a word in reply. He guessed at what may be coming next.

"I don't know how it happened, and maybe you don't know either. But we both do know that you have been too careless lately. This is catastrophic," then added, "and it cannot happen again."

Samuel nodded and slowly stood up. Even at his age, his strong body cast a powerful shadow. His kind, moist eyes told Thomas that he felt the depth and guilt of his mistake, though he could not recall ever making it. Perhaps he was getting too old for this. He reached out to shake his friend's hand. "It's been an honor serving you and your family, sir. I'll go pack my belongings."

Thomas frowned and awkwardly accepted the hand shake. He had not expected such an abrupt reaction. He opened his mouth to say more, perhaps even something to stop the man, but Samuel had already turned his back and disappeared down the long hallway to his bedroom. Thomas knew his friend was just as stubborn as he, and that his mind was already made up. Still, a spasm of frustration squeezed him from the inside because he knew friendship should never end in this manner.

SUNDAY BROUGHT A DREARY RAIN. The air felt unseasonably cold, forcing the two children to rummage through their closets for warmer clothing to wear to church. Heidyl was the first one dressed and had come downstairs for breakfast. She was surprised to see her mother preparing the meal. The mountain of dishes from last night's dinner was still heaped in the sink. She looked around the corner. "Where's Samuel? He usually makes the eggs on Sundays."

Thomas bustled into the room, tucking in his shirt. "He resigned last night," he said flatly. "I thought he'd at least come to church with us one last time, but he left without even saying goodbye." He dropped a folded paper on the table in front of his daughter before walking to the coffee pot. "I found this note on his bed and that was all."

Carefully she studied the folded letter. The graceful script of Samuel's impeccable handwriting left no doubt. Heidyl felt like the air had been sucked out of the room. Dropping the note, she sat as stinging hot tears of confused sadness burned at the corners of her eyes. "He didn't even say why?" Jillian rounded the table and draped her arms over her daughter to comfort her.

Jayce had come down a moment before and had been standing in the doorway long enough to piece together the conversation. Silently he reached across the table and picked up Samuel's note to read it:

My dear family,

It is with such ponderous sorrow that I pen this letter.
The events that have led up to this point are the fault of no one but me.
As every great race has a finish line and every great day has its sunset,
I believe my time here with you is at an end.

My heart and soul will ever remain steadfast to this family. Though my many errors and shortcomings may mark my record, please know that all I have done up to this point, and my future deeds, I do for the benefit of this family that I have served these past years.

I remain ever your friend in this world and beyond,
~Samuel

Jayce lowered the letter, dropping it back to the table. He had to ask. "Dad, did you fire Samuel?"

Thomas looked up from his coffee. "The thought had crossed my mind, but no, I didn't actually say 'you're fired'. I don't think I could ever really do that." He scrunched his eyebrows trying to remember the conversation. He had been pretty heated when speaking to the man. "I confronted him about a mistake he made, and he simply resigned on the spot. Truthfully, I didn't think he'd actually leave. I thought he just needed to cool off."

Jayce felt flush with frustration. "What did he do that made him feel he had to just take off like this? And why were you yelling at him like that last night?"

Thomas clenched his jaw. He knew he must choose his next words carefully.

"He had a duty to perform and neglected to do it."

Jayce pointed at the dishes in the sink and crossed his arms. "What, like scrub the pots better? Was the floor not clean enough?"

Thomas did not like his son's tone, but also understood his frustration. "No. It's more than that. His neglect endangered our family," a look of sadness darkened his features, "and maybe many others."

Jayce knew there was much more under the surface and he knew that he was now directly involved. A pang of guilt had nagged him all night, robbing him of sleep. He looked at his sobbing sister and the tired lines on his mother's face. His own understanding of this world had been unraveled in a single afternoon and he had no choice but to be truthful about it.

"Dad. This is my fault."

Thomas set his mug down. Shaking his head, he said, "No, son, it isn't. There's much—"

Jayce held up a hand to cut him off. "Dad, stop. Please." He was not sure where to begin exactly, so he just blurted the details. "I—I found the secret door in the pantry. I was wondering why you all had been in there before. I saw light and found a keypad."

Thomas' mouth fell open. Heidyl had stopped crying for the moment and Jillian stood, staring at him with wide eyes. Jayce suddenly felt like he was on a stage. Perspiration began to trickle down his back.

Pressing on he said, "Samuel opened the door while I was in the room and I hid. I snuck in behind him and then he latched the door." Jayce lowered his eyes. He felt so ashamed, and worse, now Samuel was gone all because of his own childish curiosity. His face went flush, and his ears burned. He felt like such a foolish little boy.

Thomas sat heavily in the chair beside him. He could scarcely believe what he was hearing. They had always been so careful to shield their children from this until they came to the day where they were ready to handle it. It looked like today would be that day, ready or not.

"I'm the one who let the animal in, too," Jayce mumbled.

Thomas looked up, shocked. His words began to come out in spurts. "What? How did you even—? You lied and let Samuel take the fall?" He was pointing now.

"Please, don't talk to me about lies, Dad." Jayce was defensive, pointing his own finger back at Thomas. "I know that thing around your neck isn't from a polar bear. You've probably been hiding all this from us for years!"

He had a good point, and Thomas visibly softened. Maybe Jayce was right. Perhaps it would have been better if they had never hidden this from them in the first place. He took a deep, calming breath before continuing. "Your mom and I always planned on telling you and Heidyl about this. We just never knew when that time would come," Thomas smiled at his son. Despite his frustration at their predicament, he still could not help feeling a little proud of his boy. "Looks like there is a bit of explorer in you, too. How did you ever figure out how to open that Gate?"

"I saw a scroll on a table and just gave the words a try. I didn't really think it would work. I mean, I thought it would be pretty cool if it did, but I didn't really believe it. I should have closed it behind me like he told me to, but I was too scared to remember. I thought he was just telling me to shut up."

Jillian's eyebrows shot up, "Who told you to close it?"

"A really funny little man. He said he was a...Logarth?"

"You met one of the Logarthiym?" Thomas stood back up so fast he bumped the table with his hip and knocked his coffee over.

Heidyl began sopping up the mess with a handful of crumpled tissues and looked up at her brother, "Wait a second. This is all real? I thought you were just having a nervous breakdown or something."

"Just one ounce of faith in me is all I wanted," he shot back.

Thomas kept vacillating between excitement and dread. On the one hand, he thought it was the most marvelous thing on Earth to share a secret like this with his own children, but on the other, it put them in a world of peril that required the utmost respect and care.

"You could have been lost forever, that Gate only stays open for a few minutes at a time." Thomas' tone had turned grave. "Or worse. If you passed through as it closed, the portal could have cut you in half!"

Jayce swallowed hard, remembering how he had been partially hanging out of the Tree Gate. The thought made him shudder.

Jillian's mind had been swirling with a set of questions and fears of her own, as well. "Did you enact any other scrolls while you were down there?" The one that had gone missing was dangerous enough, but there were plenty of others down there that could be downright deadly.

"Well, there was another one beside that huge book, but it was rolled up, so I skipped it."

Jillian sighed with relief, but then another thought entered her mind. A curious smile crossed her face, "Was the little man you met named Wista, by any chance?"

"Yeah! I think he said that. You know him too, Mom?"

"Yes. And let me guess, he wore green and said he was a scout?"

"Uh huh. And holy cow, I've never seen anything move so fast!"

Jillian cocked her head and gave Thomas a look. He caught her glance and knew he was in trouble.

She cleared her throat, "Tom, I told you not to read anything out loud from that scroll!"

He looked guilty and blew out a puff of air. "I didn't think anything of it! The words were jumbled." He was sputtering out excuses now. "They were helter-skelter all over the page; *Logarthiym scout green one*. That doesn't make any sense! How was I supposed to know it was going to call Wista?"

Jayce laughed. "So that's what he meant when he said that Big Tom-Tom rang a caller bell! He seemed to be looking for you, Dad."

"He actually said that?"

"Well, something like that. He sort of talked in riddles, which is why I guess I didn't understand him when he freaked out and told me to close the Gate. After I saw the teeth on that lizard, I ran, too!"

The pieces to the puzzle were all starting to fit together. Jillian could see now who the real culprit may be. She narrowed her eyes at her husband, "Thomas, what other 'random jumbles' did you happen to notice on that page?"

He gulped. *"Grave-hound triplet"*.

The room went silent. Heidyl was still in shock that her family was talking about fairy tales, but due to their conviction she decided it was best to remain quiet for now. Thomas, Jillian and Jayce all sat down at the table together with her.

Thomas was the first to speak after a long moment.

He rested his large hand on his son's shoulder, "Like I said before,

Jayce. This is not all your fault."

THEY HAD BEEN DRIVING FOR HOURS. After the lively family discussion at the table, Thomas decided they needed to try to find Samuel and explain what had really happened. And apologize.

Since Samuel never used a cell phone, and left no clue as to where he may have gone, they tried narrowing down the options. He had left his ring of keys on his old dresser, which was to be expected, and his old truck was still parked in the detached garage. Wherever he had gone, he had gone on foot. He may have used his bicycle, but no one thought to check the shed to see if it was missing.

They thought he may have headed to the bus station, but this was Sunday. The local bus depot was not even open today. Their small town did not have a train station or local airport, and Samuel was too sensible to take up hitchhiking. One of the hotel managers in town had said he saw an older gentleman come in this morning very early looking for breakfast in their attached diner. His description seemed to match Samuel fairly well. This gave the family a brief glimmer of hope, until they realized that a lot of men in this town take an early breakfast at the diner and many of them were older.

As the four dejected family members climbed back into the family car, the mood became as dismal as the rain outside. They were tired and out of ideas. Thomas rested his hands on the wheel and stared at the gray sky.

"Any more thoughts, love?" Jill rested a hand on his knee.

Thomas sighed and slid the key into the ignition. The vehicle roared to life. "Just one."

A few minutes later they pulled into the church parking lot. The Sunday services had ended some time ago, but the doors were still open. The tired family walked into the large room and filed into their usual section. Someone had left a Bible behind by mistake in the row in front of them. A few Cheerios lay scattered on the floor, remnants of a parent trying to keep a toddler quiet during the sermon. Thomas smiled, remembering how he and Jill would do the very same thing with their own children. He missed those days. Things sure seemed much simpler then.

Leaning forward he bowed his weary head. Jill and the kids noticed his posture and imitated him.

"Lord, we need your help," he started. His voice wavered as soon as the words left his lips. A tear escaped his eye.

It was all he could manage to say.

It was all he needed to say.

INCENSE SMOKE CURLED UPWARD. The glowing embers cast a soft glow, etching deep shadows into the large man's face.

A low, rumbling chant poured from his cracked lips.

Kneeling on the stone floor he threw off his robe. His bare chest was covered in deep cuts where he had sliced the flesh in order to please the beast that strained against the portal door before him. The Dragon was quiet today. *The calm before the storm,* Drayven thought as he reached to pick up the curled scroll between his knees. It was still slick with drool from the grayvyk that had brought it back.

Earlier, when the three grayvyks had left the herd of their own accord he was quite curious. When he later learned that they had gone on a hunt to retrieve this scroll, he was actually a bit impressed. Normally only a keen grayvyk exhibited a sense of initiative. The behavior was strange for other members of the grave-hound pack to act of their own free will, but he was sure it was because his power over them had given them greater cunning and observance to his plans. Lord Drayven considered himself a fair master, and so had rewarded the first beast, but had slain the other two for returning from their errand with nothing.

His pale eyes had hungrily pored over the jumbled words and crude hieroglyphics many times. There were only snatches of phrases he could actually read. He suspected there must be dangers of uttering them without full knowledge, so had remained silent. The more he read, the more apparent the solution became to him. The scroll was but a piece to bringing forth the dark minion beneath, but it was not intended to function alone, he felt certain of that now. He was missing something.

He needed understanding.

Grayvyks were good for simple tasks, but this required more than basic retrieval skills. Much more.

"Come," he croaked. When nothing happened, he shook his head and rolled his eyes at his own forgetfulness. *They're deaf you fool! How could you forget?* He picked up the bowl of burning incense beside him and hurled it at a black corner of the room. A shower of sparks exploded in every direction, illuminating three hunched figures huddled together like huge bats. Instantly, they whirled around to face him. Their large, lidless eyes shone back from the darkness like six green lanterns.

When their dark lord motioned for them to come to him, they burst into startled flight on black, leathery wings. Circling around the cavernous room once, they descended in front of him and knelt, but kept their huge eyes riveted toward his face.

The grotesque trio awaited Lord Drayven's orders. Eagerly leaning their faces in an unnerving huddle, crowding their master. Mucus leaked from their noses, which were little more than two black nostrils atop a short snout. Small pale gray faces pockmarked with black and brown met a hairless scalp and an impossibly skinny neck. They had no ears at all, but made up for it with their enormous, unblinking eyes. With long purple tongues they licked their faces and dripping nose holes constantly. One of them licked a speck of dirt from its eyeball.

Large bat wings stuck out from their possum-like bodies, wrapping each other in a half embrace. Their long, pink hairless tails twitched back and forth behind them as they waited.

They stood face to face with their kneeling owner, breathing in short wheezing gasps, their noses leaking torrents of slime. The sound began to annoy him, and he waved an arm to shoo them backward. The trio hopped back a step as one.

Drayven slipped a bone-handled knife from the folds of his cloak beside him and sliced open his palm. The blood pooled in his open hand. One of the winged creatures caught a whiff of the scent and chirped in excitement. It hopped forward impatiently but was rebuked with a sharp swat to the side of its face.

"I said stay back!" Drayven thundered angrily. The minion cowered behind a wing and returned to the others.

Still kneeling, the man closed his eyes. He thought of the Dragon. The scroll. His plan. The enemy. He left out no detail. He had been clenching his fist so tightly that the blood began dripping between each finger, running from the base of his palm to the floor below. Slowly raising his fist into the dark space before him, he opened his eyes and nodded.

In a rush, the three lunged upon his hand. Long purple tongues lashed against his fist, lapping up each drop of blood. Like a brood of nursing puppies, they whined and grunted, shoving each other to get the best angle for the feast. When he opened his palm, they yelped in renewed excitement, now able to get to the source. Lord Drayven smiled as he felt their sticky tongues probing the cut. In a moment, the bleeding ceased, and he withdrew his hand to observe it. Their saliva had completely mended the wound. It was a property these beasts possessed that still amazed him.

As Drayven rose up before them his strong frame stood in contrast to their diminutive stature, making them appear as sickly children in comparison. He looked into their expectant green eyes.

"Now you know," he said simply. "She must cross over. She is the key to his freedom. Do not fail me."

Though their ears heard nothing, the new blood-bond they had formed with their master tangled their minds with his for a time. They chittered and croaked, looking at one another as if to discuss their master's plan.

All at once, they struck their tails together.

The center beast shivered once in a full body spasm. Like an old television screen that had lost a signal, its entire frame was covered in a jumbled mass of black and white dots that shook and bounced against each other violently. A moment later its color reappeared and the creature reformed itself into the image of a young maiden with red hair and deep green eyes. Freckles dotted her face. She wore a simple dress with a flowered pattern.

The second and third creature convulsed in similar fashion. One became a white dove that fluttered and perched on one shoulder of the girl. The other twisted itself into a polished wooden staff to be grasped by the girl in the other hand. The trio that had once looked so wretched had created a scene completely shrouded in innocent beauty. With their transformation complete, they stood together as one, expectant before their dark lord. He examined them for a long moment. His angry expression softened as he reached a hand toward the face of the fair skinned girl.

Drayven inhaled deeply and sighed. "I do miss you."

He softly brushed a finger against the cheek of the young girl before him. Fearing another blow, the transformed beast nervously glanced about before slowly recoiling from his touch.

A curse shot from Drayven's lips. Anger swelled within him. He knew the truth and it both soothed and pained him to see it once again. The hard edge returned to his stare and he clenched his fist. The creatures hopped backward in a panic, separating from one another. In a flash the mirage vanished, and the ghastly trio returned to their true, hideous forms.

"Away from me you filthy carrion feeders! Bring her to me! I need the key!" Drayven's voice boomed, filling the dark room with rage and thunder. He swung at them once again but being bonded to his thoughts they saw his intent and easily dodged the blow. Like a flock of startled turkeys, they erupted into flight snapping their twisted wings out from their bodies like sails in a storm. Soaring upward into the dark rafters, they escaped through a thin window high above.

HEIDYL WAS STARING THROUGH THE GLASS. The rain tapped against the kitchen window, driven by a cold northern wind. The noise was annoying, making it hard to think. Things seemed to be moving too fast. Just yesterday the biggest concern on her mind was if they had enough syrup for pancakes. Today, everything was covered in a thick layer of uncertain fear.

After hours of searching for Samuel, they were no closer to finding him. The time in prayer together at the church felt more like a cop out to Heidyl. Were they giving up the search so quickly? She could feel the stinging tears starting at the corners of her eyes again. Her father sat beside her at the table to slide his arm across her shoulder for comfort, but she shrugged it off. She was still angry with him for driving Samuel away so harshly.

"He still has our phone number and all of our online contacts. He'll reach out to us when he's ready to talk again." Thomas tried to make his voice sound hopeful, but a hint of sadness betrayed his tone. He felt more and more terrible about being so abrupt with Samuel. He turned to look at his son, but Jayce's eyes were downcast, and he seemed even more sullen than usual.

Silence seeped into the room, swallowing the moment. Heaviness clung to the air and Thomas felt the tingles of uncertainty toying at his mind. *What do I do now?* A moment later, he felt the tender touch of his wife's hand at his elbow.

"Thomas," she whispered, "I think this is probably the time."

He paused to think a moment and then nodded. It *was* time to come clean. *But where do I start?*

"I guess the best place for me to start is at the beginning of this whole tangled mess." Thomas began unbuckling his belt.

Heidyl and Jayce both registered a look of bewilderment. What was their crazy father up to now?

Thomas pulled the waistband of his pants ever so slightly down and to the left to expose a purplish mark on his hip. "My whole life went completely topsy-turvy the day this birthmark began to burn. And I've been chasing things ever since." He straightened his pants back up and refastened them in place. Turning to Jill, he smiled. "Your turn, my dear."

Jillian leaned over the table and dropped her head so that her hair tumbled forward, exposing the purple spiral on the back of her scalp. Jayce and Heidyl leaned in to get a better view.

"The same holds true for me," she said, though her voice was muffled a bit by the table at her face.

Jayce blew out a laugh, "Oh, that's cute. Matching tattoos."

Jill snapped her head back up and shot him a look.

Heidyl, however, had gone very pale and was scratching a spot on her ankle. "No. I don't think those are tattoos, Jayce."

"You're right," said Thomas, "Tattoos hurt once and then leave you alone, but these things, well, they hurt all the time." He patted his hip as if clapping the back of an old friend.

"But, mine doesn't hurt right now," Heidyl sounded anxious.

Jayce furrowed his brow, "Your what?"

His sister turned on him, and angrily lifted her ankle to show the mark to him. "Where in the world have you been these past couple of days? Look! It's the exact same mark!"

Jayce leaned in to inspect the pattern. He could not resist making another joke. "That's so adorable! When did you all have time to go to the tattoo parlor together?"

Heidyl's emotions were still very raw and she angrily snapped her foot forward at him, just missing a kick to his blackened eye. "Shut your mouth!" she spat.

Jayce's eyes went wide. He had never seen his sister so angry. He pulled away, glowering at her.

"That's enough, both of you!" Thomas' voice was firm. "There's no need to make things worse by fighting like stray cats! We need to be on the same team."

Jillian's calm voice lightened the tone; "Perhaps it would be best if we simply showed them."

PART V: THE GATE

TAP—TAP—TAP, TAP—TAP. Jayce distinctly heard the rapid keystrokes as his father entered the secret code on the number pad in the pantry. Thomas had shielded the console from view with his other hand, but Jayce could not help but notice that his finger had been low on the keypad when entering the first number. *Probably a zero,* he thought.

With barely a whisper, the secret door slowly swung inward. Heidyl gasped and gripped her mother's hand beside her. Thomas plunged into the dark mouth of the doorway. A second later, light illuminated a set of stairs. One by one, they descended into the long-hidden study.

The room was in complete disarray. Heidyl's eyes went wide as she took in the scene of overturned chairs and tables, shattered lamps, and an impossible number of scrolls scattered across the stone floor. Something that looked like it had once been a leather couch was little more than a pile of splinters and fabric. Heidyl could hear the blood pumping in her ears. Her mouth hung open, suddenly feeling very dry.

Thomas stood in the center of the mess, silently working his jaw while surveying the damage. For years this room had been a haven of safe-keeping and to have it invaded like this was unsettling.

Jill was the first to speak, "They certainly were thorough."

"Who was?" Heidyl asked.

Before her mother could answer, Thomas declared, "Yep. Left open." He was pointing to the crystal dial fixed to the portal wall. Jayce looked up and noticed that it was in the same open position he had left it the other day. He swallowed hard, looking away.

"It's a good thing the Gate closes by itself after a time. Who knows how many more could have gotten in here!" Thomas was starting to fume, his anger at himself for being so hard on Samuel was rekindled. Speaking ancient words, he roughly spun the dial to its proper position and the glowing red light of the crystal turned solid green followed by a slow pulsing spectrum of color, indicating that the portal was no longer thinned.

Jillian scanned the room with probing eyes. "It's an even better thing that one of them didn't get trapped on the Earth side of our beloved study."

Heidyl was starting to feel panicky inside. "Someone, please tell me what we are talking about!" She did not mean to yell, but her voice had risen steadily with each word. She felt herself trembling. "Who—*what* did this?"

Jillian shot a glance toward Thomas as she picked her way across the debris toward her daughter. Picking up two toppled chairs she motioned for Heidyl to sit down, and then eased herself beside the quaking girl. Her soft hand began smoothing Heidyl's hair.

"It was a grave-hound."

"A what?"

Thomas removed the claw necklace from under his shirt and tossed the ragged talon across the debris and into a tattered pile of papers at his daughter's feet. "That's one of the names it has been given. On the other side they also call it a grayvyk." He nodded toward his necklace on the floor. "That talon belonged to one of them."

Heidyl leaned forward to grasp the bluish claw.

"Careful. It's very sharp," cautioned her father.

She hesitated and then leaned back, content to just stare at it on the floor. The curved hook looked more like a sickle than a claw. Jayce strode over to the spot and snatched it up. He began turning it over in his hands thoughtfully.

"You said it was a polar bear claw, Dad. Why would you lie to me about something like this?" His voice sounded more disappointed than angry.

Thomas lowered his eyes. Shame swelled in his chest and he sighed heavily through his nostrils. "Would you have believed me if you hadn't seen for yourself first? I couldn't have just told you I killed a monster in the basement, could I?"

Jayce pondered that for a moment. "No. You're right. I would have thought you'd gone nuts."

"Still, I never should have been misleading, and I am sorry. We've kept this secret from both of you to try to keep you safe." He gazed around the ransacked room, feeling defeated. "And yet, here we are."

This was certainly not how Thomas had envisioned letting his kids in on the family secret. He looked at the wall of toppled shelves and was struck with an idea. Positioning himself behind the nearest one, he asked, "Jayce, can you help me lift this?"

"Sure," he said taking the opposite end. Together they righted the heavy shelf and began working their way down the line of shelving that had fallen like a row of dominoes.

Jillian and Heidyl had struck up their own conversation and the air in the room started to grow a bit lighter.

After the fourth shelf had been lifted, Jayce's tongue was loosened, and he began asking questions about their family situation. Thomas was so glad that he had remembered this quality about his son. Years ago, while building a small boat dock together at the pond behind their house, Thomas had found that the manual labor seemed to disarm the boy's inner defenses. Jayce opened up about some of his fears and a long and meaningful talk ensued as they drove nails together that day. It was still a good memory that both of them shared.

Thomas decided to let Jayce guide the conversation with his own questions rather than lecturing him about what he thought was important. He was surprised at how much easier this method worked. Jayce peppered his father with one query after another: *Is the crystal magic? What's the name of the other world again? Where did that lizard thing come from? Can I go back with you sometime?*

Thomas did his best to answer them all as clearly as he could without giving away too many details too soon, but he had to think about that last question. Haizorr at one time had been more peaceful. Most of the creatures he and Jillian had encountered were placid, even friendly. But over the past several years, darkness and dread have been seeping across the land like an ill wind.

"Maybe I'll take you sometime, son. There's something I have to take care of first." His voice became distant and he could not help but feel his mind start constructing a plan for his next move.

Jayce had seen this look come over his father before and knew their talk was most likely over. He said nothing, nodding slowly. His reticence had suddenly returned, Thomas noticed. Jayce picked up the grayvyk talon from the table where he had set it down before and pressed it back into his father's hand. "Thanks for telling me about this stuff, Dad. I'm sorry that everything is happening this way." He averted his eyes to the floor.

"Jayce, look at me." Thomas stood with his arms stretched out as wide as he could. "I love you—*this big.*"

Jayce nodded and cleared his throat. He came closer to his father giving him a half embrace. With that, the two of them resumed their heavy work in silence.

Jillian and Heidyl were still talking while they organized the scrolls and strewn debris. Dust was everywhere and Jill had taken to wiping the shelves with a cloth. Since Heidyl had not yet experienced the sights and sounds of Haizorr as Jayce had, her questions revolved more around what she was feeling. And right now, she was feeling very confused.

"Mom, I need to know about the mark on my ankle. It's really been bugging me."

"Really? Does it hurt or burn?"

"No, not like that. I mean, it looks the same as the one that you and Dad have. But the way it appeared wasn't just weird; it was scary. Am I going to be okay?"

Jillian smiled at her daughter. She remembered feeling the exact same way long ago about her own experience. "You're going to be more than okay, sweetheart. This mark is a phenomenon I can't clearly explain. All

I've come to know is that it is a sign of greatness and purpose. Some sort of ability has been released and I think that something special is waiting to be unleashed in you."

Jayce began listening more intently to their conversation now. A dark twinge of jealousy flashed inside, giving rise to a strange feeling of disconnection with his family. The emotion surprised him at how quickly it arose. Like someone who had just stumbled into a room full of laughing people but was left wondering what the joke was about. It stung and frustrated him. *Why don't I have a mark, too?* He knew it was a selfish question even as he thought it, but he somehow felt less special than he had just a few moments ago. And it irritated him.

Jillian reached up behind her neck and slipped her necklace off. The strangely carved key she always wore twirled at the end of the silky green ribbon as she held it outstretched to her daughter.

"I want you to have this. It seems like it might have been meant more for you than for me."

Heidyl hesitated. Her mind recalled what happened the last time she touched the key, and she eyed it a moment as if it might explode. Slowly she lifted her hand to receive the gift, closing her eyes tight and bracing herself as the cool metal met her open palm. When nothing happened, she ventured a peek with one eye. The key sat lifeless in her hand. Except for the strange markings etched along its edges, it appeared as if it were just an ordinary skeleton key.

"Mom, you've had this key for years. Why now? Why me?"

"It was a gift from a wise and noble winged creature I met while on mission to Haizorr with your father. Perhaps you'll meet him one day, too. He told me that I would know what to do with the key when the time came."

Heidyl let her fingertips trace the intricate carvings and the etched runes. "What does this writing say?"

"That one took me a while to decipher," her mother responded, "but basically it reads, *Any lock may be opened, should motive be true. If the eye contain darkness; forever closed to you.*"

"What does that mean?" Heidyl asked.

"I think it indicates that the key will open any door or lock you wish, but it somehow has the ability to measure your intentions. It seems to be both a promise, and a warning."

"Have you ever tried it?"

"I've certainly been tempted to, but I always came to the conclusion that mere curiosity might not be a pure motive. At core, my own curiosity would be a selfish reason. So, I never have." Then she added, "Do be careful with it. Know what is in your heart before trying to use it."

Heidyl circled the ribbon over her head and down to her neck, allowing the key to slip beneath the neckline of her shirt. "I promise," she said, with her hand over her heart.

Thomas and Jayce had finished with all of the shelves and the family started working together now, sweeping and straightening until the room gradually resembled its former self once again. They kept talking with one another as they all worked, and the questions kept coming, but more from Heidyl. Her brother had seemed to become somber and was even sulking a bit. She guessed he might be feeling a bit left out.

Finally, Heidyl asked the one question that had been on her mind since first laying eyes on the scroll-filled room. "What made you guys start doing this in the first place?"

Thomas leaned his broom against the wall and motioned for everyone to meet him at the table with the Book. He pointed to the huge tome. "This," he stated.

"A book?" Heidyl was puzzled.

"When my mark first appeared, it would burn like crazy whenever I was near something of value. Like a compass, it led me to the Book—and even to your mother, as a matter of fact!" He winked at his wife.

"See? It proves I am something of rare value," Jillian teased.

Thomas slipped his arm around her waist and kissed her cheek, "More than you'll ever know, my love!"

Jayce rolled his eyes. "So, what does this thing do?"

Thomas turned to his son, "On its own, nothing. But somehow your mother's mark has made her something of a whiz with breaking codes." He gestured to the Book. "Show them how we began, Jill."

Jillian came around to face the Book and pulled the huge pages back to a section in the beginning of the large volume.

"This page is where we first learned about the portal summon scroll," she said as she pointed to the empty place where the open parchment had once been pinned to the table beside the Book. There were corners of torn parchment still stuck in place by thumbtacks, left behind by the thieving grayvyk. "My mark buzzed and burned as I read the page until suddenly all of these markings began to come together and make sense. The second I scribbled the translation down, the pain stopped."

Heidyl squinted at the brown page. It was covered in dark lines and scratches of a language that mostly made no sense to her. She could understand snatches of words here and there, but none of it seemed very clear. She secretly hoped that her own mark would start to burn, like her mother's, but so far, nothing. "What was the translation?" she asked.

"Much of it contains rules and warnings, but this section here," she traced a line with her finger, "gives an actual longitude and latitude and describes the region where the scroll could be found."

Thomas was waiting for this part, "And that's where I come in. Almost to the minute of her pain ending, my mark started to tingle prompting me to action."

Heidyl's eyes went wide as she started to realize the incredible ability her parents had. It was as if she were seeing them for the first time. "Wow. A perfect team."

Jillian blushed as she smirked, "I like to think so."

Thomas continued, "Once we found the scroll and the crystal, we followed the instructions and discovered that it would open a door to the other side. The land we now know as Haizorr."

A nagging thought prompted Jayce to speak up, "But you said the Gate closes by itself after a few minutes, right? Then how do you get back home?"

His mother responded, "We almost didn't the first time. We actually were very fortunate. As we dove deeper into the secrets of the Book, it led us to another scroll."

Thomas opened one of the other labeled containers nearby and produced a parchment, bound with a thin leather strap. "This one," he said as he held it up for them to see, "gave us the instructions to open the portal from the Haizorr side." He returned it into the container and sealed the lid before sliding it back to its place on the shelf. "If it ever gets into the wrong hands, on either world, who knows what could happen. Portal scrolls are unpredictable. You could open one up on Earth and come out a mile in the air on Haizorr." He swallowed hard, looking down. A strange sadness crossed his features. "I've seen it happen."

Jillian noted his odd discomfort and decided to take over the conversation, "This is why we do what we do," she said. "We find and hide away these artifacts to protect the worlds from harm. It's the highest responsibility. And it must remain the most secret of secrets." She paused to look each child in the eyes and cautioned, "All could be lost, or great peril unleashed if we slack but for one moment."

The heaviness of her words and their family mission sunk in then. Both children could see that their life was never going to be quite the same again knowing what they knew now.

After a moment, Jayce spoke up, "Was the scroll that was stolen from us very powerful?"

Thomas nodded. "Yes, but not as powerful as the other summon scroll I discovered most recently. *That* one is one of the most powerful scrolls we've found yet. Here, I'll show it to you." He began to turn in a slow circle, looking for it. "Now, where did I put that thing?"

Her curiosity piqued, Heidyl asked, "What does it do?"

Thomas' voice came from under the table now, "It's a summon scroll that can be used to control and call other creatures. I accidentally enacted it, which is how Jayce met Wista."

Jillian interjected, "And the three grayvyks."

Thomas rolled his eyes, "Yes, and those. I should have been more careful." Then he asked, "Jill? Did you see where I put the creature summon scroll?"

"Did you try one of the shelves?" she replied, pointing.

Heidyl frowned, "But isn't he friendly?"

Thomas had straightened and was rummaging through the scroll containers now. "Who, Wista?" he asked, then blew out a laugh, "He sure is!

The Logarthiym are the most loving creatures imaginable. But there are other beasts on Haizorr that are not so friendly. Given how hard I was chased and to what lengths they went to get that scroll back, my guess is that whoever wants it has nothing but evil plans."

Thomas' search through the room was beginning to take on a bit of a fevered pace. He had dropped several canisters clanging to the floor and had been scrambling on hands and knees looking under each shelf several times.

Jillian watched him, concern growing on her face. "Thomas, are you okay?"

"Did you see where that thing went?" he asked, his face pressed against the floor as he squinted under the same shelf for what seemed like the tenth time.

"Samuel told us it was accounted for. I trust him."

Thomas stood, "I do, too. But he has been a little absentminded lately." He thumped the wooden desk with his finger. "It was right here when we left the room. Maybe he missed it."

Before joining the hunt, Jillian rose and instructed the children to help their father search the room over. It had to be here someplace. It just *had to be.*

The family turned the hidden room upside down together, effectively undoing all of their hard work in search for the missing creature summon scroll. Thomas had even left the secret study several times to rummage through every room in the house, only to return as empty-handed as before. Every possible corner of the study had been thoroughly searched.

Finally, out of breath and out of ideas he threw up his hands in defeat, "It's gone. They stole that one, too!" He rubbed his face in frustration and sat down hard on a nearby chair. The others stood in a semi-circle around him, tired and at a loss. Thomas gave a knowing look to his wife and asked, "Anything?"

"No, not so much as an itch." She shook her head and nervously rubbed the mark at the base of her skull.

"Me neither," he sighed, inwardly wishing that one of their special abilities would kick in and help solve the mystery.

After a few quiet seconds Jayce asked, "So, now what do we do, Dad?" He could not hide the nervousness in his voice.

Worry was starting to gnaw at his sister as well, "What if they come back?" Heidyl cast a fretful glance at the portal wall as if a host of monsters might come tumbling out any moment.

"The Gate is fully locked now, and we have the re-entry scroll, so we are safe," Thomas assured her. "But now they know where this opening is, so we will have to be extra cautious if we ever cross over."

Jillian turned and patted her hand on the Book, "Plus, they cannot enact the creature summon scroll without this."

Relief washed over Thomas and he eased back in his chair. "That's right!" he exclaimed. "I guess we are not as worse off as I had thought. Thank goodness!"

"What do you mean, Mom?" asked Heidyl.

"Let me show you." Jillian began flipping back through the massive pages. "The Book contains a key code page that enables…" she faltered. "If I can find it, I'll show you here—" her hands were flipping the pages back and forth now, faster and faster. "Where is that page?"

Suddenly she froze, her face going pale as frost.

Thomas noticed and stood. "Jill? Are you all right?"

"It's gone."

Thomas could see the jagged edges near the spine where the code page had been ripped from the Book. The shock of it hit him like a punch to the gut.

"God, help us," he whispered, "They got the code, too."

"I NEED TO GET OUT OF HERE." Jayce opened his backpack and began stuffing in a change of clothes, a flashlight and some toiletries. After watching the family situation deteriorate from bad to worse, and then flirt with the catastrophic, he felt like his heart was in a vise.

"I'm so stupid," he said to himself, angrily jamming a pair of socks deep into the pack. "Wista told you to close hit. But did you listen? No. Do you ever listen? No." He could feel burning tears of frustration threatening to spill down his cheeks. He roughly fought them back with a crumpled shirt before cramming it down by the socks. By leaving the portal open he had foolishly opened their home, and the world, to dangers he did not fully comprehend. After seeing the defeated look on his parents' faces and with no clear solution to be found, the guilt started gnawing at him like a caged rat in his chest. What made it worse was his father's demand that they search every inch of the room again, and then the house "just to be sure." Coming up empty handed for the second time only poured salt in the wound. Jayce needed a break.

After the fruitless searching he slipped away and immediately called his friend Davey to see if he could sleep over. They had been closest buddies since the fourth grade and shared nearly identical interests. The plan concocted by two boys at this point consisted of playing video games and eating Doritos until they could no longer keep their eyes open. It sounded like the perfect diversion to Jayce. He then pleaded with his parents to let him go.

After sternly warning their son that he must not whisper a word of their situation to his friend, they had no objections to his request. The next day was a teaching staff development day at their local school, so there were no classes. They agreed it was probably best for the children to learn to go on with life as normal in order to keep suspicions at a minimum.

Life as normal. That was something Jayce was sure would never happen for him again. Right now, nothing was even remotely normal. He was not even sure what that phrase meant anymore. All he wished for was the ability to turn back the clock and pretend none of this had ever happened. Heidyl seemed to accept their parents' advice a little more readily than Jayce, but she had not seen what he had. To her, it was still a bit of a fairy tale. He envied her ignorance as she lightly stepped up to her room to read and do homework.

Thomas and Jillian encouraged Jayce to go and enjoy himself saying they had some very "important work" to do anyhow. The family had decided together that this would be their sort of code phrase for entering the secret room. Jayce imagined his parents would likely bury themselves in that big Book and be talking for hours about how to solve their dilemma. After checking to be sure her son had finished his homework, Jillian called Davey's mother to verify she would be there and to let her know that she would pick Jayce up in the morning. The distance between their homes was only several blocks, but she guessed her son would be too tired to walk home since it was likely that he would be up all night with his pal. Selfishly, it was also a welcome excuse to get Jillian out of the house, if only for a scant few minutes. The atmosphere at home had become very heavy these past few days and she thought even the briefest change of scenery might do her some good.

Jayce gave his mom a light peck on the cheek and gave a backwards wave over his shoulder to his father as he walked down the long driveway to the sidewalk. Looking up, he saw his sister's bedroom light on in her window. For some unknown reason, he hoped to see her face peer out at him so he could wave to her, too. However, Heidyl was too consumed with her homework to notice his departure. Turning back to the concrete path he felt his heart grow lighter with each step and by the time he reached Davey's house he was whistling to himself. He bounded up the steps of the front porch and rapped a beat on the door with his knuckles.

In a moment, Davey threw wide the door and smiled. "Hey man! You ready to take back some stolen artifacts?"

Jayce froze and his dry mouth sprung open. He stared blankly at his friend.

"You know, in *Treasure-X*...I just bought it last night and I'm dying to play it!" Davey gave him a puzzled look.

Jayce exhaled. "Oh. Yeah. Of course!" Feeling relieved, he awkwardly hugged his friend. Davey pulled back a little, unsure of what had just come over his companion.

Davey was the most likeable person Jayce had ever met. He was shorter, and a little round in the middle. His thick glasses and enormous smile somehow put everyone at ease who spoke with him. Easygoing and incredibly witty, Davey had an uncanny ability to get along with most people, simply because he was masterful at deflecting negativity. His choice of clothing provided additional firepower to his friendly arsenal. Today he wore a neon traffic green tee shirt with the imprint of a bear riding a unicycle.

Laughing nervously, he slugged Jayce on the shoulder, "OK, easy there big fella, I missed you, too. A few days *is* a bit long to go without seeing the likes of me, I guess. C'mon, let's go to my room."

The two friends raced upstairs to the game console, ready to dive into an imaginary world of digital heroes and monsters.

HIS PACK WAS GROWING HEAVY. Thomas figured he might need enough food and gear to last him a week at least, but he also required enough room to carry a number of scrolls that may need to be activated if things should go badly.

Checking and rechecking the weight of the pack every few minutes, Thomas had to be sure it would not weigh him down too much. Even though his physical stamina and strength were increased on the other side of the Gate, so too were those of the creatures he may encounter. Achieving the perfect balance between speed and fatigue could very well mean the difference between life and death on Haizorr.

The plan was simple. Trek to the dark fortress and take back the scrolls and missing page from the Book. The details from that point on would have to develop on their own, he reasoned. He doubted that this would be like the previous mission, however. When he had first discovered the scroll, it had simply been enclosed in a small stone vault on the property near the large structure. There had been no need to enter any buildings or kick down doors to retrieve it. It had been so easy he nearly laughed to himself. However, the moment he hefted the stone lid that covered the scroll, the howling grayvyks informed him that he had been caught in the act.

On this trip, Thomas knew he might very well have to knock on the front door of that same brooding castle. After his returning with the scroll, the Book revealed the name of the fortress; *Blackynspyre*. Either Thomas had missed it before, or the name had inscribed itself into the ancient pages of its own accord. At times like that the Book felt alive. It seemed to change and subtly alter the vast contents of its pages from time to time, as if driven by some force or will. Sometimes new pages appeared, other times entire paragraphs or sections would simply disappear. It had happened several times before, each maddening instance renewing the fearful awe he and Jillian shared for the Book's contents.

While thoughtfully placing the necessary items in his pack, Thomas began to wonder if perhaps this time, his return to Blackynspyre would be expected. That thought unnerved him most. There was the very real possibility that the ruler of the castle was just a maniac bent on destruction. What if he were indeed the sum of all of Thomas and Jillian's fears during their quests? What then? He did not want to think about what might happen next.

Then the darkest thought he had been pushing away rose like an unbidden specter once again to his mind. He shuddered to imagine it, but there was the very real possibility that the owner of the castle might be someone he knew. Someone from a past he had desperately tried to forget.

JAYCE'S EYES FELT HEAVY. The day's endless hours of playing video games with his friend had taken a toll on them. After reaching a level that neither boy could defeat, they decided to take a break. Empty chip bags and a half empty bottle of orange juice sat in a semi-circle of crumbs on the rug around them. The sun, that seemed to have been brightly shining just moments ago, had long since retreated leaving a pale moon to dangle in its place in the night sky. It always amazed Jayce how time seemed to vanish when he immersed himself in a game. The world would simply stop spinning for him, fading all worries into distant fog. It was a chance to run away, without actually going anywhere. The feeling was so addicting at times. But now, with the flashing video screen turned off, he could feel his chest tightening while the weighted dread of the events at home began to creep back into focus and squeeze his insides.

Davey had groggily stumbled over to his own bed and dropped onto it. He mumbled something, but his pillow badly muffled the words. Jayce thought he heard him say the word "light", so he flipped the switch. The room became bathed with the dull blue haze of moonbeams streaming through the windows. Sometime during their gaming marathon, Davey's mother had set up a cot for their guest in a corner of the room. She had graciously fitted it with sheets, a pillow and several blankets for Jayce to use. *How did we not hear her come in and do all of this?* Jayce wondered as he crawled between the cool sheets.

He was so tired he did not bother to change into the sweatpants he had brought to sleep in, but his brain did not seem to want to power down. He simply could not stop wondering what might be going on at home. A wave of sunken feelings began growing from the pit of his stomach. He blew out a big sigh in an attempt to ease the swelling tension within.

"You thinking of her, too?" Davey's voice punctured the silence, startling Jayce.

"Huh? I thought you were asleep!"

"How can I sleep when visions of beauty run through my mind?"

Despite his heavy heart, Jayce could not help but smile and play along. "What on Earth are you talking about?" he asked.

"Not a what. A *who*." Davey stifled a yawn.

"Okay. *Who* then?"

"Haven't you seen the new girl in Algebra class?"

"I'm usually asleep in that class," Jayce laughed.

"Well, you might want to open your eyes, buddy. I don't know her name yet, but she sits near the back window. She has curly hair and a tattoo on her shoulder."

Jayce tried to remember but came up blank. "I'm not sure who you mean. Is it that new exchange student from France?"

"No, she's not nearly as pretty as who I'm talking about. How could you have missed her, man? I tell you, when the sunlight hits her hair it looks like fire. I can't even think straight." Davey's voice began to trail off.

Now it was Jayce's turn to tease. "So, you mean to tell me that a flaming redhead with a biker tattoo is the reason you're getting a C-minus in Algebra class?"

"Who cares? If I marry her someday, it'll be worth it."

Both boys laughed together at the thought. Through sporadic yawns and a variety of topics, the friends talked long into the night. After a while yawning increased and conversation died away. Jayce could now hear slow, rhythmic breathing as Davey slipped into heavy sleep. Alone again with his thoughts, Jayce turned over on the squeaky cot and tried forcing his mind to quiet down. The effort was useless. The more he reminded himself to forget about home, the more about home he thought. Finally, he could take it no longer. He reasoned that it would do no good to lie awake all night in guilt and sorrow. Action alone is what would remedy the situation. He lay there a while as a plan slowly began to form from the fog of his mind.

Throwing the blankets back, he reached for his sneakers on the floor and slipped them on. Rummaging through his pack, he found the flashlight and scribbled a note for Davey, letting him know he went for a walk and forgot to take care of something at home and would be back soon. He did not quite feel like he was lying, but still, he could not help but feel deceptive. *It's probably the same thing,* he thought. Careful not to bump into things, Jayce crept out of his friend's room and into the chilly darkness of the house. His heart began pounding harder; as he realized that waking Davey's parents now would make him look very suspicious, sneaking through their home with a backpack and a flashlight.

He reached the front door and slid the deadbolt back with a *click*. The stark silence of night seemed to amplify the tiny noise a hundred times over. Inhaling sharply, he twisted the knob and jerked the door open, disappearing into the cool air outside. Summer was not quite in full force, and Jayce was thankful he had remembered to wear something with sleeves. Bounding down the steps he broke into a run. But thinking better of the idea, he paused after a hundred feet or so. It would look even more suspicious if a nosy neighbor happened to be awake at this hour and witnessed a young man running down the street with a loaded bag and flashlight. He forced himself to walk casually the rest of the way home. This would also allow him a few more minutes to formulate the rest of his plan.

He too had "important work" to do.

SNEAKING OUT HAD BEEN THE EASY PART. Breaking into his own home without detection was another feat entirely. With so many precious relics and antiques on the premises, Jayce knew that his father did not take chances concerning security. Thomas had entrusted the system to Samuel's careful eye, and the old caretaker had personally overseen the installation of each part of the anti-burglary devices. There were cameras, sensors and alarms all over the place. Fortunately, Jayce did not need to worry about Samuel doing his rounds tonight since he was gone. But he had to be very cautious nonetheless. One misstep and his plan was shot.

Grateful that he paid attention when his father had shown him the alarm codes and sight lines for the cameras, Jayce timed each step and planned his entry accordingly. It was a slow and tedious process and by the time he reached the front door, heavy beads of perspiration gleamed across his forehead. He slipped his key into the locks, turning the deadbolts one by one to open the side door. Almost immediately, a sequence of short, chirping beeps pierced the perfect quiet inside. Jayce flew to the console on the far wall, punched in the alarm code and held his breath. Silence once again engulfed the room. Jayce stood rigid, listening for the telltale *thump* of someone stepping out of bed upstairs to investigate.

When no sound came, he relaxed and proceeded to wind his way through the house toward the pantry. *The pantry.* Jayce shook his head at the thought that all along, that tiny room dotted with spices and canned vegetables also housed the mysteries of the universe. He was still having a hard time shaking off the sour feeling that his parents had not trusted him with the secret. He also tried to ignore the small voice in his head telling him that it was precisely the course of action he was taking at this very moment that had contributed to their hesitancy in telling him.

It did not matter what they thought of him anyway. *After tonight they will think of me as a hero.*

The pale LED glow from his flashlight glittered and bounced off the various glass and metal surfaces of the jars in the dim pantry as he scanned the shelves for the one tin he needed. A well-worn red container on the bottom shelf bore the word *FLOUR,* scrawled in black permanent marker. He hefted the tin to peel back the lid. The stubborn top came loose with a sudden *pop* and tumbled from his fingers, skittering to the hardwood floor like a clanging cymbal. He stomped his foot on it to silence the noise. This was not going as well as he imagined it might.

Carefully he reached to the upper shelf and slid several jars aside, revealing the hidden number pad. Dipping his fingers into the dented tin still cradled in his arm, he retrieved a pinch of flour. Leaning forward he lifted his fingers to his lips and gently blew the white powder onto the shiny buttons above the shelf.

A cloud of dust rolled and danced through the light beam of his flashlight, curling through the air around him like a miniature fog storm. His heavy breathing had drawn some flour particles into his nose, and he stifled a sneeze into the crook of his elbow.

When he looked up again, a fine layer of flour had coated just about every surface of the numeric console. Jayce frowned. He had expected that only the number keys used in the code sequence would be covered due to oils from his parents' fingers that remained on the keys when pressed. At least that is how it seemed to work in crime stories. Frustrated, Jayce replaced the lid to the flour tin and shoved it back in place. Being no closer to getting in than before, he decided to clean up and avoid further suspicion. He began blowing away the dust from the shelf and the code lock above. Suddenly he stopped. Tiny amounts of white powder remained stuck to five of the keys! Jayce smiled. *All those secret agent movies are finally paying off,* he thought.

He had guessed correctly about one of the numbers from his observation of his father before. The *zero* key at the bottom of the series was clearly highlighted in flour. Jayce wondered at the full combination his spy trick had revealed; *zero, one, seven, eight.* Flour had also adhered to a fifth, unlabeled key to the top right of the console. It was circular and smooth and did not resemble any of the other keys. Jayce wrinkled his brow. He had not remembered his father punching five keys. Perhaps that was something like a *delete* button?

All that was needed now was a correct guess at the combination. He tried to figure in his head how many possibilities it could be, but then gave up on the math and began to punch in random sequences. He was fairly certain that the zero should be pressed first from what he remembered, but after a few unsuccessful attempts he began to doubt what he thought he had seen. And then there was the unexpected problem of that fifth button. Where did that fit into this? Were any of the numbers entered more than once? He did not think so, but doubt was crowding its way into his mind with the press of every button. The folly of his plan began to worm its way into his gut.

Suddenly the hair at the base of his neck tingled. He was not sure, but he thought he felt a faint stirring of the air around him. The room felt different somehow. The odd sensation confused him for a moment until he realized what it was. He was no longer alone. He half turned toward the pantry opening when Heidyl popped her head around the corner and hissed a whisper at him. He nearly jumped out of his skin.

"Hey! What are you doing?" Her tone was at once accusing and genuinely curious.

Jayce was instantly defensive, and now flooded with adrenaline he hissed back, "None of your business! Go back to bed, snooper!"

Heidyl laughed. "Me? A snooper? I'm not the one sneaking through the house with a flashlight and poking at secret buttons. I'm only down here because I thought I heard something fall." A confused looked crossed her face. "Wait. Aren't you supposed to be at Davey's tonight?"

Her brother shrugged. "You wouldn't understand."

"Aw. Did he beat you again in a video game?" Heidyl teased.

Jayce shot her a look that told her not to push any further. Even in the ghostly luminance of the flashlight, she could tell he was angry. But she also sensed there was something more he was wrestling with inside.

"C'mon, big brother. What's going on?" Her tone had softened.

Jayce scratched his head and blew out a heavy sigh, as if trying to weigh if he could trust his sister with the crippling weight of his next words. In the end, he decided he could. After all, he had already spilled his heart to her in the tree house earlier, so he could not possibly sound any crazier to her now. Jayce lowered his eyes and settled into a sad, resolved tone of voice. He told her how guilty he felt about how it was his fault that the scrolls and code page were both stolen. How it was he, and not Samuel, who had left the Gate open in the first place. Which also meant that it was his fault that Samuel was gone because Dad had accused him and then fired him for something he not even done. Or even known about. Jayce reasoned that it was up to him to at least try to fix his blunder and set things right.

"I'm going to get those scrolls back."

Heidyl's mouth hung open. "Are you *insane?* You don't even know what's on the other side! It's too dangerous, Jayce."

"Haven't you been listening? Look around you. Dad and Mom have finally opened up to us! We're part of this now. They showed us everything!"

"Not everything," she cautioned.

Jayce was growing impatient. He desperately needed an ally, but the gray light of dawn was beginning to seep through the long hallway beside them. It was now, or not at all.

"Fine. Run off and snitch," he spat as he spun back to guessing the code. His fingers jabbed at the keys angrily while muttering the numbers. "Zero, zero, one, seven, eight. No. Zero, one, one, seven, eight? Did I already hit the zero twice?" He sighed for the hundredth time.

To his surprise, his sister had not run off. Heidyl lingered in the doorway like a shadow, watching her older brother labor over the key code. Biting her lower lip, a curious look clouded her face as her insides scuffled over what she should do.

Finally, she spoke into the darkness, "It's your birthday."

Jayce snorted a laugh. "Nope. You're way off, sis. Like, by a few months." He kept clacking at the keys.

"No. The code. It's your birthday. Try entering the date for August seventeenth."

Jayce paused. *Could it really be that simple? And of all people, and of all the important dates in the world, why* my *birthday?* He shrugged and gingerly tapped out the combination: zero, eight, one, seven.

Nothing happened.

Once again, he sighed. "Sorry. No go."

"Did you hit that enter key at the top?"

Now she was *really* beginning to get on his nerves. He had already been at this for many minutes. Who was she to simply appear and begin telling him what to do? To prove his point, he obliged and let his finger thump the shiny round button.

"See? It's the same as—"

Whoosh.

There was a slight rush of air as the hidden door gasped open. Jayce and Heidyl both stared into the gaping maw of the descending staircase. A blanket of silence smothered the room. Before he could change his mind, Jayce snatched up his backpack and crept down the steps, his flashlight beam stabbing into darkness below. Halfway down he turned the flashlight beam back up at his sister.

"You coming?"

Heidyl threw up her hand to shield her eyes from the piercing ray of light. She was still biting her lip in indecision. Without a word she pressed the door closed behind him and was gone.

"Typical," muttered Jayce and he continued his descent into the world below.

Part VI: The Trap

IT NEARLY KNOCKED HIM BACK TO EARTH. The stench was so thick it felt as though burning mud was coating his eyes, nose and mouth at once. Jayce tumbled out of the Tree Gate and collapsed onto the sticky grass below, gasping for air. He pulled his shirt collar over his nose, but it provided little relief. Jayce felt he would die of suffocation if he did not get away from the area immediately.

With burning tears gushing from his eyes, he scooped up his backpack and flashlight and sprinted forward. Two pale moons hanging like orbs suspended in an indigo sky partially illuminated an enormous black forest before him. He made for the trees with wild abandon, pumping his gangly teenage legs as fast as they possibly could go. He could gawk at the trees later. The physical exertion demanded fresh air to fill his lungs, but all he could pull in were putrid gasps that scorched his throat. The field was overgrown with thick greenery and weeds that tangled his feet, threatening to pull him to the ground with each stride. Huge rocks jutted up from the landscape in odd, twisted angles in at least a dozen places.

He ran past several of the glistening boulders before realizing with a newfound fear that they more closely resembled some breed of enormous animal. He jerked his head to the side while running past the nearest one and let his flashlight angle across the rough surface. Dread gripped his chest with its frosty claw. Scales!

By the time he returned his eyes to the path before him, it was too late. His foot caught on a ragged branch and Jayce was sent into a tumble. Momentum took over, hurtling him end over end across the landscape. The flashlight flung into the sky and spun through the air, sending strobes wildly into the night. Jayce's world abruptly stopped spinning when he collided with the huge trunk of a fallen tree. Stunned, he lay in silence holding his breath against the fear that gripped him as much as the stench that assaulted him.

Nothing stirred. There was no sound but the low groan of creaking trees in the forest nearby. Ever so slightly he allowed his head to swivel around, his eyes scanning the darkened scene for the flashlight. Fortunately, his pack had remained firmly strapped to his shoulders. A faint blue glow poked through the thick grasses several feet away. Knowing there would be little hope of surviving the night without that precious device, he inched his way toward the flashlight. Jayce cupped his palm over the face of the light to avoid detection, yet he still felt as if many pairs of eyes were studying him from beyond his field of view.

With great care he eased the lucent beam upward. His hands were shaking as he panned the horizon. The smell had lessened somewhat but was still very strong. He had to keep dragging in shallow breaths from beneath his clothes to keep his lungs from burning. The light cut through the gloom around him, sending long bending shadows into eerie movement patterns. In a moment, the brilliance of the LED bulbs fell across the great log that had broken his fall. He followed its length, which bent in a U-shaped curve around him. When he finally reached the end that was nearest to him, Jayce clapped a hand over his mouth and screamed into it. In a panic he scrambled backward as his light shown full into a mouth bristling with steel-sharp teeth, just inches from him. His breath came in great gasps and he gagged on the rancid air. Once again, he found his legs whirling beneath him as if they had a mind of their own. He no longer was running toward the woods, but back to the way he came. Maybe Heidyl was right. This plan of his seemed more foolish now than ever.

He had barely shaken the thought from his mind, when a dark figure burst directly into his path and latched onto him. A tangle of hair and a hard skull knocked Jayce in the mouth. The salty metallic taste of his own blood poured across his gums in an instant. A hand gripped the back of his shirt and the fabric tore. In a tangle of legs and limbs, Jayce thudded to the ground and rolled with the figure on top of him. He swung his arms wildly and felt one of his hands get wrapped in the folds of his assailant's clothing. Bringing his knees up he kicked and rocked his body until he was free and rolled to his feet, fists at the ready.

The slender form before him rose up on unsteady legs.

A frightened voice spoke, "Jayce? Is that you?"

"Heidyl!" His knees nearly buckled with relief. "What are you doing here? I thought you went back to bed!"

"I'm a diabetic, you dummy! I can't just rush off into another world without taking all this junk with me!" She held up a small backpack that contained syringes, sugar snacks, insulin vials and other odds and ends necessary for keeping her out of dangerous blood sugar levels. "Plus, I had to change out of my pajamas. You could have just waited five minutes!"

She bent to rest her hands on her knees and took great gasping breaths, trying to calm herself. But the stench surrounding them proved to be too much for her to say more. Jayce could see her forcing back the bile rising in her throat.

"The air. Can't breathe." She retched into the grass.

Though annoyed at his bleeding lip, Jayce was relieved to have his sister with him. Then, remembering the danger he was running from, took a moment to stop and listen. He squinted hard into the dark for any hit of movement. There seemed to be no sign of pursuit. *Maybe that thing was asleep,* he thought. Under the dim light of the dual moons, he turned to Heidyl who had recovered from her spell and motioned for her to remain quiet. They had to get out of here.

Picking up his flashlight for a third time that night, he grabbed his sister's hand and began threading the way through the beast-covered field. In the silence, Jayce's thoughts spun rapid fire through his head. *What are these things? Grayvyks! But Dad only called three of them. Why were there so many here now?*

Had he called more of them by mistake? I hope they have poor hearing. The memory of the huge mouthful of teeth he had just seen flashed across his mind and he shuddered. He prayed they would not wake up before they got back to the safe side of the portal.

Suddenly Heidyl froze. Her fingers dug into the flesh of Jayce's hand and he pulled up. Her feet had rooted to the ground and her eyes went wild with terror as she stared straight ahead. Jayce turned to see what had gripped her so and was startled to see that he was shining a beacon of light full into the face of another resting grayvyk. He quickly flipped off the switch, allowing near blackness to reclaim the scene.

Jayce had completely forgotten that she had never seen one before. Even though both he and their parents had tried to describe the creatures to her, all the talk in the world could never fully prepare one to come face to face with a real monster.

With a tug, Jayce pulled Heidyl past the great heap of a beast and around the serpentine body of another. In the moonlit dusky haze, he could just barely make out the strange silhouette of the Tree Gate with its great trunk and two odd limbs that stuck straight out from its middle.

He drew near to his sister's ear and mouthed the lowest whisper he could manage, "I think they're asleep."

Heidyl nodded and eased her grip on his aching fingers. She tried once again to catch her breath, but the acrid atmosphere clung viciously to her windpipe and sent her into another gagging fit. Heidyl had always been hyper sensitive to smells, but this was nothing like anything she had ever experienced. It was far worse than week old trash or the sulfur smell of rotting eggs in the garbage disposal. It was the perfume of utter rottenness mingled with death and was choking her beyond what she could bear. She stumbled backward several paces and tripped. Scrambling to get up, she pressed her hand against what looked like a large stump. The surface was rough and scaly and gave slightly when pressed. Instantly, she recognized it as the texture of flesh.

An open eyeball stared unblinking into the moonlit night. The stump-sized head was zippered around with scaly lips peeled back into a snarl showing rows of the longest teeth imaginable. She could hold back no longer. A scream tore from Heidyl's throat like a wailing siren and echoed against the great trees rimming the field around them.

In a flash, Jayce bounded up to her and roughly clapped a hand over her open mouth. The scream clipped off, reduced to a low muffled moan. "Quiet!" he hissed. "You'll wake them all!"

She struggled against him, her eyes darting around wildly before settling on the face of the beast beside them that had startled her so. Heidyl noticed something about the odd way it was positioned. She quickly relaxed, and began shaking her head, trying to speak. She twisted free from her brother's grasp.

"No," she gasped—a little too loudly. "No, I won't." She turned back to the enormous scaly face of the brute lying on the ground and gave it a hard shove with the sole of her boot. Jayce stiffened and prepared to run. The great head rolled to the side, and then, continued to roll end over end into a ditch. The headless body that remained behind lay still as a stone. The slick grass around it glistened with black blood.

"They're not asleep. They're all dead."

With a *click*, Jayce's flashlight came alive once again in his hand and he examined the fallen creature. The sinuous stump of a headless neck oozed black slime. The wound did not appear to have been inflicted by a sharp weapon. It looked more like the head had been *pulled* off, rather than cut. He allowed the light to play across the bodies of several other grayvyks who had met with similar fates. A rock the size of a minivan had been piled onto the head of one. Still another looked to have had both of its legs plucked from its body. Jayce squinted into the darkness and blew out a sigh. One grayvyk hung high from a nearby tree, its body skewered through the middle by a thick, broken branch.

"Well, that explains the smell," he said, remembering his encounter in the pantry hallway with the bucket of putrid black water. "I don't think Samuel could wash *this* away!"

He shrugged off the backpack and began rummaging through it. Holding the flashlight in his teeth, he plunged both hands in and pulled out several items. Heidyl, her nose tucked into her sweater, muffled out her concern, "Jayce, we need to get back. We have to tell Mom and Dad!"

Jayce, his mouth still occupied with the light, shook his head.

"Hurry, Jayce! Before the portal thing closes behind us!"

Impatiently, her brother pulled the light from his lips. "It's probably already closed by now. We've been in here for a while."

Heidyl felt the blood drain from her face, "What? How will we get back? We're trapped!" Waves of panic began to seep up from her toes. She felt the urge to run.

"Calm down. I've got *this!*" He proudly held up a rolled parchment and waggled it in the air as if it were the cure to all their troubles.

Heidyl stared blankly back at him, a little annoyed at being told to calm down. She shrugged. "What's that, a note from some dumb girl at Haizorr high school?"

Jayce rolled his eyes, "You know how Dad labels everything. Well, I remembered where the scroll was, and I borrowed the Open Gate scroll that works on this side of the portal. I wasn't just poking around in the secret room, I was also thinking ahead!" He beamed at his own pronouncement.

"Good. Then let's go use your silly magic words and get home!" She turned to go but Jayce caught her arm. His eyes shone with determination and his jawline was now set. He shook his head slowly in response. Heidyl felt her blood boil. She could not believe how stupid her brother was behaving! Was he blind to what surrounded them?

She motioned her arms across the landscape littered with the bodies of dead monsters. "Are you brainless? Don't you see how much danger we're in?"

Jayce smiled and mimicked her movements. "Don't you see how this changes everything?"

Heidyl huffed and folded her arms. "No. I don't!" The gagging sensation returned, and again she buried her face under the fold of her shirt so she could breathe.

"Because whoever did *this,* "he said as he kicked a loose pebble at the nearest grayvyk carcass, "is on *our* side."

"But you don't even know where you're going!" Heidyl pleaded desperately.

As if on cue, Jayce held up a tattered handful of scribbled notes and papers bound together in the folds of a well-worn notebook. He illuminated the cover with his light. There, in their father's unmistakably messy writing were the words *Haizorr Maps and Notes*.

"Like I said, Dad labels everything."

Without a word, Jayce turned to repack his bag. Heidyl stood rigid, glowering at him while the acrid air stung her eyes and nose. For a moment she considered trying to wrestle the pack from him but something else flamed inside her. She blinked. As unexpected as a bolt of lightning a tiny flicker of curiosity sprang to life inside her. She was surprised at how quickly it overruled her good sense. Standing in a private storm of indecision she thoughtfully chewed her lip. Jayce, satisfied that his gear was sufficiently organized zippered the pack, slung it over his shoulder and started back toward the distant tree line. Courage had given new fire to his stride. He even ventured a kick at one of the grayvyk corpses along his path—although he readied himself to run should it be roused. He did not look back to see if his sister was following.

He knew she would.

And she did.

IT FELT LIKE A SPLINTER IN HER BRAIN. She could not figure out why, but Jillian woke with a niggling sense of worry that persisted through her early morning routine. As dawn broke with an ashen sky, she set about trying to shake the feeling by busying herself with the mundane chores that Samuel used to perform with such ease. When that failed to shake the uneasiness, she attempted to steady herself with a cup of tea and a time of prayer by the window. Songbirds came and went in turn on the feeder outside, but she stared through them, lost in thought.

She did not know if she had sat for minutes or hours. The sullen sky made it impossible to tell if the sun had risen an inch or a thousand miles. The scuffling of feet behind her drew her back from the shroud of her quiet thoughts.

Thomas' strong hands gently massaged the stress knots that always seemed to form between his wife's shoulder blades. Closing her eyes she relished his gentle, strong touch. The stress she felt earlier seemed to melt and was nearly gone when Thomas spoke.

"Since when does our daughter like to take early morning walks on a Monday where she can sleep in?" His voice was rimmed with amusement.

Jill's eyes snapped open. "What do you mean?"

"She left us this note on the table. Says she went for a walk."

Jill snatched the note from her husband's fingers. Heidyl's normally graceful cursive had given way to a hastily written chicken-scratch note. The paper was torn from an old cookbook Jill usually kept on a shelf in the pantry. Warning bells began jangling in Jill's mind. The stress knots reformed themselves across her upper back.

Her brow furrowed as she studied the strange note. "It's a teaching staff development day at school. She never rolls out of bed until later on those days."

Thomas tried to soothe her once again, but it was too late. Motherly intuition had awakened. She took another sip of tea and began to pray.

THEY HAD BEEN WALKING FOR MILES. The twin moons had long since retired and were replaced by the fiery disc of a sun that dazzled the world around them.

With wide-eyed wonder, the brother and sister team took in each new scene with breathless excitement. Everything in Haizorr seemed like a glorious magnification of the mundane things of Earth. Mushrooms as big as woodsheds stuck out from behind tangles of knotted roots large enough to house an elephant. Blues were bolder, trees were taller, and yes, the grass was most definitely greener, they both had agreed on that point. Twice they thought they heard hoof beats and scampered to hide behind massive tree trunks for fear of pursuers, only to find dog-sized centipedes drumming the earth with their feet as they passed along the path ahead. An enormous butterfly with the wingspan that would rival that of an Earth eagle soared silently between the trees above them. Its shimmering wings shone through a color

127

spectrum so vibrant it stung their eyes. A trail of glittering dust trailed from the gossamer wings as it flew. Heidyl captured some of the stuff in her hands. It was like catching a rainbow. She smiled and showed it to her brother.

Their amazement quickly gave way to horror, however, as that same luminous butterfly was snatched from the sky by an enormous black winged bird. In the space of half of a second, the giant beak neatly clipped the glorious insect in half, sending one of its wings spiraling back to the ground like a downed helicopter. Both children dove for cover under a canopy of red and blue ferns as the great fowl winged overhead and out of sight. When the tense moment passed, they agreed that while fraught with great beauty, life on Haizorr required they apply greater caution to every new discovery, no matter how harmless it appeared.

Jayce regularly consulted his father's maps and scribbles. Years of research and expeditions had made for a valuable set of field notes. Thomas had been meticulous, if not messy, about landmarks and to his surprise Jayce was finding it quite easy to navigate the foreign land. Before long, they crested a rise that gave them a semi-panoramic view of both the path they had trodden and the way before them. The landscape was lush and vivid with sprays of color dotting the view where entire groves of flowering trees spilled out from the thick forest canopy. Both brother and sister turned in slow circles to drink in the breathtaking wonder about them. Several more enormous butterflies made their way through erratic flight patterns from flower to flower. It was like watching colors dance.

A near paradise surrounded them with the exception of a blackened smear of mountain range that stabbed upward at the sky like an accusing bony finger. A thick foggy shroud of smoky haze hovered about the distant peaks. Jayce held the map in front of him and swallowed. He hoped they would not need to travel in that direction, but his father's sketch clearly showed that was exactly where he had first found the scroll that had been the cause of all their recent troubles. Jayce felt in his heart of hearts that was where the scroll would be once again. It appeared that the newest entry on his father's map was the word *Blackynspyre* with a little arrow pointing to a crude dark tower set in a roughly sketched mountain range. He stirred the coals of courage inside himself. *If Dad can do it, so can I.*

Heidyl sat to rest a bit on the softest grass she had ever felt and began to marvel at the view behind them. "Can you believe how far we've come in such a short time?"

Jayce looked up from the map. He too had to marvel. "Yeah, you're right. We have covered a lot of ground."

"And I feel wonderful! I'm not even winded. Or thirsty. You?"

Jayce shook his head. Come to think of it, he felt pretty good himself. A hike like this on Earth would have at least made his feet hurt.

Out of habit, Heidyl unzipped her satchel and produced a small glucose meter. Carefully she pricked her finger and checked her blood for the third time since crossing into Haizorr. Jayce watched, expectantly. He had to admit, he was getting a little nervous for her sake. If she had a seizure or her blood sugars would not come down, he was not sure he could care for her properly out here. In a moment, the meter beeped. Jayce looked over at his sister, "High or low?"

"Eighty three. Perfect. Again." She smiled to herself. She felt wonderful and had not needed to treat herself for many hours. An exhilarating thought coursed through her mind; *Maybe I'm not sick here!*

"Good," Jayce replied, a little relieved. Then he mused, "It's weird. I'm not even hungry. I brought some snacks, but I don't even feel like touching them yet."

"You? Not hungry? Now that *is* weird!" she chuckled.

After a moment more of soaking in the sun's radiance Heidyl stood up, picked up a stone and threw it. "I don't even really need to rest, I just—" She froze mid-sentence. Both of their mouths hung open as they watched the projectile fly through the air and never seem to come down. A small puff of dust appeared at the point of impact some five hundred feet away.

"Did you see that?" Heidyl exclaimed. "I hardly even tried!"

But Jayce was already scooping up handfuls of stones. He drew back and let fly with a baseball sized rock. The air sizzled as it sliced through the sky and disappeared out of sight beyond the hills.

Jayce smiled at his sister, "You still throw like a girl."

"I do not!" she shouted and launched another stone.

The playful rivalry lasted until they ran out of stones, both small and great. The discovery of their increased strength in this world progressed from throwing to jumping and even to breaking things with their bare hands. Jayce's eyes nearly bugged out of his head after he broke a six-inch thick limb like a twig. "I like it here!" he grinned.

Heidyl mused, "I wonder how my gymnastics routines would look if I did them here."

Jayce laughed, "There aren't enough gold medals in the entire world for a performance like that, Superstar!"

Heidyl smiled at her brother's use of his affectionate nickname for her. They had not connected like this in a long time and it felt good. It also stirred a sense of longing inside. She frowned and looked down at her toes.

Jayce saw the sudden shift. "What's wrong?"

"Mom and Dad. They're going to worry."

Her brother shrugged. "Well, Mom will worry. Dad will probably just get worked up and think up a lecture or some punishment for me." He whipped a stone into the woods a hundred yards away. It neatly clipped off several branches like a bullet before lodging deep into the bark of a tree. "Besides, didn't Dad say time passed different here? They won't even notice we're gone."

Heidyl rested a hand on his shoulder. "Jayce, he loves you."

"Yeah," came the reply, but it lacked much conviction. He drew back and angrily threw another stone with more force than he thought possible. It seemed to sail into orbit before thudding into a distant knoll at the crest of the horizon. A great plume of dust announced the impact. Jayce squinted at the dirt cloud he had just created and noticed that it appeared to be growing. Heidyl spotted it too and lifted a hand to shield the sun for a better view. Great swirling puffs swelled and grew, spreading a haze to the left and right. A faint rumbling reached their ears from far below.

"Do you hear that, sis?"

"It sounds like more hoof beats. Do you think it's a bunch of those centipede things?"

Jayce strained his eyes to see into the swirling dust, but the sun's glare prevented any hope of a clear view into the thickening mass. "I don't know, but whatever it is, it's heading this way. Look!"

Brother and sister spun and tore down the hill in the other direction. The dust storm below was already at the base of the hill they were standing on. The ground shook with the beat of a thousand drums behind them. Though they were far faster on Haizorr than on Earth, the siblings quickly found themselves overtaken by a thronging mass of bluish creatures engaged in some sort of frantic stampede. The dust they kicked up from their hooves made it impossible to see them clearly, but Jayce could not help but notice their thickly muscled legs. They resembled large horses, but much larger than any breed he had ever seen. Their hairless bodies reflected the light as if made of blue glass. He could feel hot breath against his neck and knew he would be ridden down any second. Out of the corner of his eye he saw Heidyl hoisted from her feet by one of the beasts. She shrieked and was carried out of sight. He veered his course to aid her, but the hazy fog of the stampede obscured his vision. The last thing he saw before all went dark was an enormous tree trunk.

EMERALD LIGHT FILLED HIS VISION. Emerald, rimmed with shimmering blue as well. Jayce blinked to clear the haze, but his eyesight remained clouded and the colors wavered and danced like flame. He could feel swelling around one of his eyes–the same blackened eye that had finally started to heal. He blinked again, grimacing with pain. His face hurt, but the scene before him began clearing somewhat. Silhouettes of figures stood all around him. Mumbles of excitement seemed to spread through the group as the blue beings leaned toward one another, as if passing along good gossip. A rush of recollection filled his thoughts as he remembered his sister's abduction. Jayce gasped suddenly, trying to sit up.

The pain shot from the rear of his skull to his eye then back again, forcing him to drop his head back onto the mossy cushioned table he lay upon. The shock of it helped to further clear the disorientation.

"He is waking," came a voice above his head. It was a deep, yet airy voice that rose and fell in the middle like notes of a woodwind instrument. Someone started caressing his face with a cluster of soft blue feathers. As his senses cleared, he saw that the feathers were actually attached to a muscular blue arm, which connected to an enormous, feather-covered torso. Impossibly large wings were folded back against an equestrian body. Taut skin stretched over the muscular frame. The body was like a translucent sapphire and Jayce could actually see networks of vessels and nerves under its skin, illuminated with a pale light. The great beast leaned forward to observe him closer with its piercing azure eyes. Jayce noticed they did not blink.

Atop its shoulders an owl-like head swiveled and twitched. Two tufts of feathers stuck out from the top, giving the appearance of horns. Jayce felt as if he were being sized up like some sort of meal. The hooked beak parted, and it leaned in close to his face. Jayce started to throw up his arms to defend himself, but strong, feathered limbs held him fast. Jayce slammed his eyes shut and felt the pain of his recent injury flare up anew with the effort.

A low hiss burst from the open beak and Jayce felt a blast of steamy breath wash over his face. He flinched, waiting for its razor beak to tear into his neck or perhaps his eyeball. Instead, he noticed the creature's breath smelled sweet, like something utterly wholesome that had been baking in an oven all day. Its warmth was not unlike that of a campfire, filling his entire body with a pleasant heat. Jayce ventured a peek with his good eye but was met with a second blast of warm breath. This time, he felt the throbbing pain in his head and face begin to ebb. His eyes flashed open and he could actually see the swelling of his eye go down as his field of vision increased. His captors released their hold on him, and he gingerly touched his face. The pain had totally vanished.

The owl head bowed slightly, and a wind-deepened voice spoke.

"I have done all that can be done for your wounds, young one. The bruise, however, has a mind of its own and may remain for some time." The head bowed again, "My apologies, young Verity."

Jayce's tongue could not find the right words, so he simply sat up. The great beast drew back to its full height and the teenage boy found himself at eye-level to the being's massive abdominal muscles. He had to lean far back in order to see the bird-like face. This was perhaps the most beautiful creation he had ever seen. The sound of a dozen stamping hoofs drew his attention to the others around him that he had not even known were there.

He gazed in awestruck wonder at each of them standing in a semi-circle formation. They looked regal as they held high posture, standing shoulder to shoulder like pillars of elegant strength and beauty. For a moment Jayce wondered if perhaps this is how angels might appear. He realized his mouth had been hanging open and clapped it shut.

He then found his voice, "Am I dead?"

A mild commotion stirred at the back of the pack. Reedy voices cooed and clucked deeply, and the audience began to shift. Two of the steed bodies nearest to Jayce parted and Heidyl burst into the center of the ring, throwing her arms around her brother in a joyous embrace.

"You're okay!" She was nearly in tears as she squeezed him tighter still.

Her brother hugged her back, "I won't be if you keep choking me to death!" They both laughed. Drawing back he looked into his sister's glistening eyes. "What happened? Where are we?"

"You and trees are not a good mix, big brother," Heidyl teased. A low chorus of hooting noises and clucks purred from the crowd around them.

Jayce nodded toward the onlookers, "Who are they?"

In answer, the tallest blue body stamped its hooves and trotted forward a pace. By way of a formal introduction, it bowed gracefully and met Jayce's gaze with a steady royal stare. Jayce had to look away.

"I am Justhynial, lord of Sunnsothryn." His expansive wings unfurled, and he spread them wide. From tip to tip, the span would have touched both corners of their living room at home, Jayce noticed. Justhynial motioned to the gathering crowd with his solid arms, "And these are my children."

As one, the throng popped open their wings, stretching them skyward. Hardened blue bodies pulsed and thrummed with glowing threads of light beneath their glassy blue skin. Throwing their heads back they shot a screech to the heavens in what seemed like a family salute before returning their gaze forward. Justhynial puffed his feathers with pride.

With the pious display over, the great host continued, "The clarion call has sounded. He draws us north to Blackynspyre," he lowered his face and darkness flashed in his great pupils. "Though his intent for my family in that foul region is unclear to me."

Jayce glanced at the feathered appendages and found his voice once again, "But why not fly, wouldn't you get there faster?"

A low cluck rose from his throat, "You Verity types do cut to the point! Faster, yes. But at great cost. We are too easily seen and counted from a great distance away while in flight. We no longer use the northern skies." The great family lowered their heads as one, nodding in unison as if sharing an ancient, mournful memory.

Heidyl could sense their hosts had suffered a great pain in the past, and offered to change the subject, "Then why go there? Who is calling you?"

Lifting his noble head, Justhynial's voice slipped into a monotone, as if reciting something from ancient memory. "The One who calls is the One who calls. Be he calling one, or calling all, none resist the clarion call." A chorus of windy coos and bird-like heads bobbed up and down throughout the group. "I am sorry that our hasty travel has waylaid you, fair Liberty," said Justhynial, offering her an apologetic bow of his kingly head.

Heidyl blushed a bit. To have so magnificent a creature treat her with such high regard sent her insides squirming. She attempted to soothe the moment, "It's fine. We're actually headed that way, too!" Jayce shot her a look. He did not like her volunteering too much information to strangers. Even kind, wound-healing ones.

Feathers ruffled and hoof beats pawed the ground around them at the news. "You've been sounded to assemble as well?"

"Not exactly," Heidyl bubbled, "we're sort of heading there to try to—uh—fix something." Her eyes met her brother's and he gave her a cautionary shake of his head.

"Blackynspyre is broken beyond all repair, young one. Yet, as in all of the Liberty kind, I judge your heart and quest to be pure." He whistled out a sigh. "It is with stones in my own heart that I must lead my family there. We likely tread to our doom. But the caller calls whom he will."

Jayce was beginning to realize that perhaps these kindly creatures could be trusted. An idea struck him and he cleared his throat, "Maybe we could travel with you. We all seem to be headed the same direction anyhow.

We'd travel much faster that way."

The great blue noble shook his head from side to side. "My apologies, Verity. The called must journey each in his own way, and your feet must tread your own path. I sense we have lingered too long already."

A chill wind whistled through the trees about them, and the great limbs groaned and rocked. The herd stamped about nervously and their heads swiveled in all directions, searching for an unseen danger. "We must resume," spoke Justhynial. "But, if it is to Blackynspyre you must journey, then you cannot be found ill-equipped upon arrival." He chirped a low clear call into the throng beside him, and a much smaller member of the royal family trotted to the front of the line. The delicate curve of her soft wings and the exceptionally wide blue eyes radiated innocence and childlike purity. The father-king urged her forward. She stepped on light hoofs toward Heidyl and pulled a simple, silver bracelet from her own feathered arm. She fastened it to the young girl's wrist before skipping off with a chirp to rejoin the others.

Justhynial spoke again, "Through the millennia, they have all come bearing great quests. We have seen Hunters and Seekers, Cyphers and Guardians – but never have we met both a Verity and a Liberty! There may indeed be hope."

Heidyl examined the cool metal bracelet on her arm. It had almost no weight and was very plain. Its surface was polished smoother than a mirror and the light danced about as she turned her arm to admire the gift.

Justhynial assumed the tone of a teacher speaking with a student, "You have been given the Fydas. As true liberty must both free and protect, so you, Liberty, must do the same. Ponder this in your time of need, and you will have all that you need." Heidyl nodded, wide-eyed, trying to grasp the meaning of those words. She wanted to ask what he meant exactly, but the commanding finality in Justhynial's voice told her she should remain silent.

The great eyes then turned and fixed upon Jayce. Justhynial lifted a great hoof and brought it down to the ground with a thud. Jayce felt the ground beneath him tremble. "Your gift comes with a price. Verity always does."

With a low ripping sound, the earth beneath the hoof print began to peel back and a dark mass bubbled up, mounding and building upon itself.

When it stopped, there appeared an oozing black mound that smelled and looked like a putrid pile of waste. Jayce recoiled from the stench. This was his gift?

"Things are never what they seem. But this is not unknown to you, young Verity. A truth uncovered is not soon forgotten." The great head nodded toward the smelly pile. Green pus ran down the sides of it now, and Jayce could see what looked like fat white slugs feasting on the rancid slime. He choked back a gag. He knew what he had to do but did not want to do it. Jayce dragged his feet forward and knelt in front of the pile. A fat slug lost its footing and tumbled down the mass and thumped against Jayce's knee. He grimaced and inched away from it.

The great Justhynial lowered a command. "Dig."

Jayce did not move. The smell stung his eyes. He wanted the prize that must lay buried inside, but felt rendered powerless by the task before him.

"Dig," came the breathy whisper of the winged beast.

Slowly Jayce lifted his hands.

Several more clucking bird voices chimed, "Dig!"

The thin outer slime felt like a skin of mucus against his fingertips. Jayce closed his eyes tightly and held his breath.

"Dig!" The entire throng became a chorus of voices. Opening their wings, they became as a great cloud surrounding him, cheering him onward in his search. *"Dig. Dig! DIG!"*

He pressed his arms deep into the muck, felt it sucking against his flesh. It was at once hot as flame and yet icy cold. It felt full of brambles that stuck his hands. Or was it insects biting his flesh? He wanted to pull away. Slowly he inched his arms backward.

"DIG!" Hoofs began to paw the ground in time with the chanting. Jayce could feel his heart thumping in time with their stamping. Something beneath the mass wriggled against his wrist and he yelped in fear, but he pressed back in. The pounding hoof beats shook the earth all around him now. Dust choked the air. Still he willed his aching fingers to probe through the thick layers.

Suddenly the knuckles of his right hand brushed something hard. A

136

rush of excitement flooded Jayce's veins and he turned all of his attention to the spot with renewed vigor.

"Dig!"

With great effort he stretched open his fingertips. The weight of the pressing mass made it hard to flex the muscles of his hands. Sweat rolled from his brow as he strained into the task.

"Dig!" A blast of wind whirled dust all around him and ruffled his hair. Jayce kept his eyes scrunched shut. He could feel the slender object between his fingers now. The hoof beats sounded lower, more distant. A tumble of voices whispered one last time, *"Dig."*

With his last bit of strength, Jayce forced his hand to clench around the oblong object. He pulled backward with all of his might, his ears ringing with the effort. The muscles of his forearm went into spasm and he cried out in pain, but still would not let go. Bracing both feet hard against the ground he heaved against the weight. And then, he was free. The black slime released its crushing grasp and Jayce tumbled backward onto his seat.

Breathing heavily, he slowly opened his eyes. The disgusting pile that had once defied him had vanished. He looked at his wrists and arms. No trace of stains or dirt could be seen. They were as clean as could be. Even the smell had evaporated beyond all trace. Uncurling his aching fingers, he examined his hard-won gift.

A slender stone tapered and smooth at either end glistened in his palm. One half of it was a polished white, glimmering and reflecting the sunlight in a spectrum of color. The other half was mirrored exactly like the first, but completely black. It felt smooth and polished like obsidian, but seemed to absorb the light around it, rather than reflect.

Jayce turned the stone in his hands, studying it closely. Finely etched across the hardened surface was a single word: *Vyritas*. It was then that he noticed how quiet the woods had become. Looking about, he saw no trace of their blue companions. Only Heidyl remained. Her hands were pressed together, touching her smiling lips. Tears of relief streamed down her face. Another rush of wind pressed at them from above drawing their gazes skyward. Justhynial's great wings beat the air as he wheeled and hovered over them.

The owl eyes shone down, staring hard at Jayce. "Speak the truth with love on your lips, and victory shall be yours." Turning his gaze into Heidyl's wide eyes he added, "Fydas and Vyritas are strongest together." Then the great head swiveled toward the path below, observing his family herd as they thundered along the trail. In the next moment, his wise face suddenly darted upward toward the horizon, as if something had caught his attention. The feathers on his head rose as if in alarm while the telescopic eyes zeroed in to study some distant object. The enormous blue body looked too large to be hovering with such grace, but Justhynial did so with ease. He stared once again into Jayce's upturned face, "The deception approaches quickly. Flattering lies from their tails will yield great wounds. Stop their tongues to yield the healing." And with one great pump of blue feathers, their amazing new ally darted away. Flying low before diving beneath the treetops, Justhynial was gone.

A LONE CANDLE ILLUMINED HIS WORN FACE. Sitting cross-legged on the cold ground, he sat in shadow. The heavy brown cloak draped across his large frame made him appear more animal than human. The dim flame cast barely enough light to show little more than the parchment before him and his whispering lips that uttered words swollen with power.

"*Veni…ad meam…vocant…Justhynial.*"

He smiled beneath the thick hood drawn over his head. He imagined the great herd galloping toward him at this very moment with their shining blue muscles and hoofs flinging clods of dirt as they thundered along. In his mind's eye he pictured the great winged beasts taking to the sky, all in a flurry to answer his call.

It had been too long since their last encounter.

He would give them a proper greeting when they arrived.

138

DAWN SEEPED BENEATH THE WINDOW SHADE. The stale taste of potato chips and sugar felt like someone had painted his tongue with tar while he slept. Davey felt instantly thirsty. With groggy eyes, he rolled over to see if his friend was still asleep. Crumpled blankets on the cot were all that greeted him. *He's probably in the bathroom,* he thought.

When twenty minutes went by without a trace of Jayce's return, curiosity replaced Davey's sleepiness. Groaning, he swung his legs over the side of the bed, the floor cold on his feet. His bedroom was an utter mess. If clutter was any indication of fun, it looked like they certainly had enjoyed themselves. Davey rubbed his eyes and blinked, then sat staring in dim silence while they adjusted to the slowly growing light.

After a few moments, he decided he'd waited long enough. He rose to go to the bathroom to find Jayce but found the room empty. The house was still quiet. *Where could he be?* he wondered as he shuffled back to the bedroom. If he had not been looking for clues in the haphazard mess of his room, he never would have noticed Jayce's missing shoes and belongings. Frowning, he scanned the shadowy bedroom.

His eyes rested on a scribbled sheet of yellow notebook paper lying on the cot pillow: *Hey man, went for a walk. Back soon.*

Davey snorted a laugh at his friend's note. "Since when do you take early morning walks on a day off from school?"

He wadded up the paper to throw it away, but noticed the wastebasket was already overflowing with wrappers and used paper cups. Shrugging, he stuffed the paper into his sweatpants pocket and picked up a video game controller.

"Might as well make good use of my time while I wait."

THE LEVEL WAS SIMPLY UNBEATABLE. Davey had once again immersed himself in the world of virtual combat and strategy. The screen before him flashed and warbled as he navigated his character through numerous perils and magnificent monsters. At first, like always, the gaming was gloriously fun. Then, just as often, the entertainment was replaced with a slow building frustration. No matter how fast he mashed those buttons with his thumbs, he could no longer advance his character through the labyrinth alone.

Pressing the pause button, Davey roughly pulled on a crumpled sweatshirt he found under his bed and slid on his shoes. He needed some backup.

THE NEIGHBORHOOD WAS JUST WAKING UP. Somewhere, a couple of houses over, a zealous neighbor was already mowing the lawn. The birds had begun their overly loud morning conversations as Davey breathed in the crisp morning air and stretched his arms. Peering up and down the street there was no sign of Jayce, so he sat on the front step to wait.

As with most boys his age, waiting becomes tiresome quickly. Through the kitchen window, Davey heard his mother rummaging for a coffee cup. He poked his head back inside and asked her if he could go for a quick walk to find Jayce. With permission granted, he darted down the steps toward his friend's house, hoping that he would find him there.

The sharp knock on the front door startled Jillian's already tense nerves. She felt a wash of relief come over her, hoping that Heidyl had returned, but quickly dismissed the hope with a laugh. Why would she have knocked to be let into her own home? Still, it was early for visitors.

Thomas strode to the door to greet their guest. With a puzzled expression, he motioned for Davey to come in. Seeing no sign of his son, Thomas stepped onto the porch to find him. "So I take it you guys are swapping parents today?" he teased.

Davey stepped inside and stood awkwardly in the foyer, his eyes traveling around the great room. He never could quite get over how impressively large his friend's house was. Every corner appeared to hold some interesting artwork or intricate, foreign pattern. The very furniture seemed to have stories to tell of ancient, perhaps even heroic days. His eyes landed on Thomas and he realized then that he had been asked a question, but in his distraction had ignored his host. He blushed.

"Oh. Sorry. What did you say?"

Thomas cleared his throat and smiled. "It looks like you boys are swapping today. What happened, did your mom threaten you with chores and leave Jayce in charge?"

Davey shook his head. "I'm not sure what you mean. Is Jayce around? I haven't seen him for a while, and I thought he might have come home."

In the next room, Jillian felt her ears tingle at Davey's words. She sprang from her chair and entered the room, worry lines etching her face.

"How long has he been gone?" she asked, trying to hide the mild tremor in her voice.

Davey shrugged as he dug into his pocket, "I don't know. A couple of hours maybe? When I woke up his stuff was gone, and this note was on his bed." The boy laid the wadded yellow paper on the table. Thomas picked it up and after a moment handed it to his wife who carefully placed it on the table beside the hastily scrawled note that Heidyl had written earlier.

Davey watched the concerned glances being exchanged back and forth between the parents. "Is Jayce in trouble?"

Thomas clapped a hand onto the young boy's shoulder and gave it a good-natured squeeze. "I hope not."

THE TATTERED PAGES WERE HARD TO DECIPHER. Jayce had been trying to make heads or tails of his father's tangled mass of scribbled maps for the past twenty minutes. Earlier, from the top of the rise it had been easy to see which direction to go. The bony black finger of Blackynspyre standing stark against the sky was an easy target to follow. But now that they had traveled into the dense forest below, the path became unclear in a matter of moments.

"We need to find high ground," Jayce declared.

"We just left perfectly good high ground," retorted his sister as she sat down to wait. The excitement of the journey had already started giving way to some boredom now that they were tramping through the undergrowth. In her heart, Heidyl just wanted to get back home. She still did not fully understand her brother's plan, and suspected that he did not either. In the silence of waiting, anxiety about their predicament had resurfaced. She lifted a silent prayer into the sunlight that was filtering down upon her face through the thick branches of the trees above. In a moment she smiled.

"Found your high ground, big brother," she said in a singsong voice. Jayce snapped his attention from the shuffled papers to see Heidyl pointing upward to the nearest trabalisk tree. There were several low branches with footholds easily within reach. In minutes he scrabbled up the side of it, then straddling a wide branch he spread out the maps to survey the lush scene before him. This time he was determined to highlight certain landmarks to guide them. He decided upon an enormous boulder about a quarter mile ahead as their next destination, followed by a tight cluster of black trees beyond it. Jayce took out a pencil to scratch his own notes on one of the sheets among the pile of his father's papers.

Heidyl took these few moments to drink in the beauty of their surroundings and to keep praying. The gentle breeze made lovely *whooshing* sounds in the greenery above. Lying on her back in the soft carpet of emerald grasses and large leaves, she steadied her breathing and closed her eyes. How torn she felt inside! Intense longing for home and worries about her parents were at war with a sense of duty to her brother and the quest she had been thrust into. Absently she began to finger the smooth bracelet on her arm. The polished metal felt strangely warm to her touch rather than cold and hard. Her mind drifted back to her home and the safety and solitude of her own bed. She imagined the sheets and covers pulled up over her head, muffling out the intruding sounds of a troublesome day. For the first time in hours she breathed a sigh of relief.

Ping! A soft metallic sound broke the silence. Heidyl's eyes snapped open. All looked as it had before, but now a cloudy bluish haze rested over everything as if a very thin fog had settled about her.

Ping! She sat up this time, feeling alarmed. The surrounding forest had grown deathly quiet. She strained her senses to listen. Her own pulse was loud in her ears, and the leaves under her crunched and crackled as she shifted about. All distant sound seemed terribly muffled. The breeze in the trees still churned the branches, but she could not hear it. Heidyl thought she could hear her brother's voice calling, but it sounded so very far away.

Ping! Pa-ping! The odd noises were coming from just above her head. When she looked up, she saw her brother waving his arms wildly in the tree. He was shouting at her and pointing into the distance. Somehow the blue mist was muffling the sound as if he were a mere whisper in a dream. He threw a small broken twig at her to get her attention, but just before it hit her squarely on top of her head the projectile deflected suddenly and fell harmlessly to the ground.

Ping!

It was then that Heidyl noticed the bracelet on her arm. It was emitting a soft blue light that flowed and danced on her wrist like a wispy vapor. *Protection in the time of need!* Heidyl thought. *It must be some sort of shield.* She brought the glowing metal up to her face and whispered softly across its surface, "Thank you."

The next moment, the mist about her vanished and the sounds of the forest rushed back to her ears. Her bracelet—the Fydas—had returned to its normal metallic state. She was still admiring her gift when a sharp pain on the top of her head snapped her attention up to her brother. She rubbed the spot where the newly thrown branch had struck her.

"Ow!" She cried, "Cut that out!"

"Have you gone deaf? I've been hollering at you for two minutes now! I see someone coming up ahead!"

Alarm gripped Heidyl, "We should hide!"

"Too late for that," Jayce started as he began climbing down, "She's already heard us by now, thanks to your daydreaming!"

Heidyl was instantly defensive. "My daydreaming? You won't believe what just happened, it was incredible—" His sister stopped mid sentence, "Wait, did you say '*she*'?"

"Yeah, it looked like a little kid in a dress coming. I'm almost positive she saw me." Jayce jumped the last few feet to the ground, landing heavily beside Heidyl.

He had nearly finished cinching his pack, when a small, fair-skinned child stepped out from behind a nearby tree. The sudden appearance startled Heidyl, forcing her to stifle a cry.

"Wow, you sure do move quick!" Jayce said in astonishment.

Their visitor hid her face in the crook of her elbow in reply.

"The poor thing! She's crying." Heidyl rushed over to the young lady immediately. "Are you OK? Are you lost?"

The little redhead peeked her emerald eyes from behind a thin arm but gave no reply. She sniffed. Her freckled nose was running and Heidyl gingerly wiped it with her own sleeve. She tried to calm the frightened girl by changing the subject, "You have such a pretty dress!"

The lass said nothing; she seemed content to simply stare at Heidyl. The trickle of mucus from her nose began anew snaking a slick trail down to her lips. Heidyl reached up to wipe it off again with her sleeve and then drew her hand back sharply. A small, white bird peeked out from behind the visitor's fiery hair, perching unsteadily upon her shoulder. It bobbed and hopped from one foot to the other, in excitement or fear Heidyl could not decipher. Looking down she noticed the gnarled walking stick the young maiden had been carrying. It had curious markings and appeared to have been made by an artisan, not a little girl. How she had not seen it before was beyond her. She sat back to study the girl before her. "My, you sure are full of surprises."

"I think she's sick," chimed in Jayce. "Her nose is running like a faucet. Who knows what sort of germs live in this place?"

"She's just scared."

"Scared doesn't make you sick. Better to be careful."

Heidyl was getting annoyed with her brother's overprotective tone, "I'm not a child, Jayce. But she is, and she needs our help!"

The youngster's wide eyes stared, moving back and forth as the siblings quarreled. The thick slime was pooling over her upper lip now, threatening at any moment to drip into her mouth. The bird on her shoulder continued bobbing its head, shifting from side to side and swapping perches from one shoulder to the other.

Both brother and sister quibbled on like this for several moments until finally Heidyl had enough. Angrily she glared at Jayce and stood pointing at the dripping face of the young lady beside them. With a huff, she pulled down her sleeve and roughly reached over to begin wiping the oozing stream. It was at that same instant, however, that the child had decided to snake out a long, purple tongue to lick the muck from her own nose. Heidyl, in her haste did not see this detail.

But Jayce did.

In a flash he reached out an arm, batting his sister's hand away from the horribly long tongue. Heidyl whirled on him. Their visitor, fearing a blow to her face ducked her red head forward. This left the white dove wide open for an accidental backhanded swat from Heidyl as she pulled away angrily from her brother's protective gesture.

In a flutter, the feathered creature was knocked to the ground. Heidyl, feeling at once embarrassed, mortified, and not a little enraged rushed over to the little bird as it convulsed in the grass.

Jayce shouted, "Heidyl, no! Don't touch it!"

She was about to shout something utterly unkind to him when she stopped cold. The little innocent bird had ceased its spasm fit and was growing in size while black and white speckles danced and wiggled over its entire surface. In a moment a putrid, winged beast stood erect from the grass. Bulbous green eyes stared at her from above a gaping mouth, a long purple tongue lashing about like a maddened snake.

"Run!" hollered Jayce.

But the warning came too late. Long dark wings shot out impossibly fast from the fiend's body and tangled themselves about Heidyl like two strong arms. She screamed and was rewarded by a bony-claw with leathery skin being clapped over her mouth. The rough treatment had split Heidyl's lip and blood started dripping from her chin.

The visage of the young redheaded girl had undergone the same hideous transformation, as did the polished staff. A few writhing seconds later, the once innocent looking child and her walking stick had been replaced by two malformed foes. Jayce backed away slowly as their great green eyes surveyed him. They advanced toward him, the black tips of their wings dragging in the grass. The boy nearly stumbled over a thick branch as he backpedaled. Scooping it from the ground he brandished it before him like a weapon of war. He caught a glimpse of his sister struggling in the arms of her attacker and the vision filled him with crimson rage. He rushed forward with his makeshift club, swinging and screaming savagely. The first blow caught one creature in the neck, knocking it aside with a sickening thud. He swung around with all his might at the second beast. But it was ready for him. With impossible strength for such gaunt limbs, it caught the branch with a single winged arm before plucking it from an astonished Jayce.

By this time the other monstrosity had recovered from the blow and let out a piercing wail. Glancing back at Heidyl it noticed the blood dribbling down her chin. The great green eyes of the creature opened impossibly wider. Flapping excitedly, it flashed a great tongue before rushing toward her. The other, upon seeing its companion so keenly interested in Heidyl disengaged its tussle with Jayce, choosing to explore the blood as well.

Terror filled Heidyl as this new dread rushed upon her. She was already weary from struggling and the horrifying sight of the two bulb-eyed demons lapping their tongues at her face proved too much. Her legs went limp beneath her and her head began to swim. She felt her consciousness sliding away.

Adding to the chaos, the beast that was holding her began twirling her around away from the others. Like a screaming toddler fighting with other children over a toy, it wrenched her back hissing at the others as if to say, "Mine! Mine!"

Jayce felt like he was in a living nightmare. Desperate to help his sister, he quickly removed his pack in order to move faster and picked up the club once more. But remembering how easily the attackers had removed it from his grasp he dropped it and began a frantic search for a sizable stone instead. The stone! He thrust his hand into his pocket and pulled out the polished rock that Justhynial had given him.

"Speak the truth with love on your lips, and victory shall be yours," Jayce recalled the somber words spoken to him not long before.

But try as he might, he felt no love at the moment and could think of nothing to say. Rage flooded his senses and obscured his mind. The creatures flapped about his sister like vultures over fresh carrion. Her limp body flung this way and that like a rag doll. They seemed driven by madness. Or desperation.

Then, a surprising feeling arose from within him. It felt like sorrow and pity mixed together at once. An odd sense of clarity seemed to widen his vision and he could see that these were witless beasts, unable to devise such a cunning plan of deception on their own. Now that their backs were to him, he plainly observed marks and scars across their tattered wings and bony shoulders. All three appeared to have been beaten savagely at some point. He could not be sure with all of the scuffling, but he thought he saw an iron shackle rattling about each of their skinny ankles.

"They're just slaves in need of freedom," he mused aloud.

A warm surge and a flash burst from his right hand. The once black and white stone had sprouted a beam of solid blue light that tapered to a dangerous looking point at one end. Wisps of vapor wafted from its center, the beam crackled and sparked giving Jayce the sensation that it was very, very hot. Oddly, it felt no heavier than before, though it now looked as if it should have much more weight.

The marvelous weapon filled Jayce with courage. And just in time. The trio had Heidyl nearly to the ground by now. Though she had regained a sense of consciousness and had found some will to fight back, her flailing kicks at them had only managed to slow the creatures a little.

Their greedy tongues were dangerously close to her face now. The blood from her wound was trickling freely from the brawl and had an effect on the winged attackers similar to sharks in frenzy. It was lucky for her that she had just jerked her head back and away from the nearest lapping append-age for it was then that Jayce struck. She felt a flash of heat as a crackling blue light whizzed past her face and neatly clipped off the purple writhing tongue of the nearest attacker.

The resulting scream could have shattered thick glass as the offend-ing beast reeled back howling a throat-garbled cry of pain. Thick black blood fell from its mouth here and there as the creature danced about in agony. With a mind of its own, the severed purple tongue writhed on the grass like a snake and began slithering away from the scuffle toward the direction Jayce had just come. The other two, upon seeing this new development, hopped and flapped backwards from the scene like startled chickens.

Heidyl's body lay stone still in the grass. Her lifeless form brought dread full and heavy into Jayce's heart. He knelt beside his sister. To his great relief she was still breathing but she looked so pale. With his free hand he shook her shoulder. "Heidyl? Wake up!"

She lolled her head to the side with a groan. Her eyes fluttered open weakly at first. Then, as if remembering a nightmare, she shot bolt upright.

"Are they gone?"

Jayce looked around. The area had gone silent and he could see no sign of the bat-like monsters. "Yeah. I think it's safe."

In flood of relief she threw her arms around her brother and squeezed. "Thank you," was all she could manage to whisper over and over. She was having trouble breathing. Seconds later however, she went rigid and squeezed him quite hard. "Duck!" she shouted, and threw herself backwards shielding her face with her arms.

Rather than heed his sister, Jayce whirled around to face the new onslaught. Before he could even catch a mere glimpse of his attackers, Jayce received a crushing blow to his back that sent him tumbling across the ground. The evil trio had taken to the sky after being driven back, launching a cowardly but effective counter attack upon the children from the air. The wounded creature had plowed into Jayce from behind like a winged linebacker. The other two pounced upon him in the grass to hold him down, but it was not necessary. Jayce had been knocked unconscious.

The blue blaze of Vyritas winked out as the black and white stonesword fell from his grasp and settled harmlessly on the ground not far from where Heidyl lay. She rolled over and snatched it up, willing it to spring back to life and come to her aid, but it remained cold in her trembling hands. Its instructions had been given to Jayce, not to her. In the heat of the moment she could not recall what Justhynial had told him about how to use it. Stuffing the lifeless stone into her pants pocket she stood to confront the threat.

To her horror, she saw her brother lying the in the grass and the three wretched beasts exulting and shrieking around his body. The one without a tongue could only make a horrible gargling noise from its throat. Heidyl swayed unsteadily on her feet, trying to square off her stance in case they charged again. But they never did.

Quite suddenly, as if zapped by some remote signal, the trio went rigid and stood shoulder to shoulder at attention. Six bulging green eyes locked straight ahead. The creatures froze as if staring at something far and away.

As one, they struck their tails together. Their frames twitched and jumped, becoming shapeless piles of squirming black and white spots. Then the three bodies fused together forming one tall mass to stand before Heidyl.

Drayven's image now towered in the space before her. He wore a long cloak that draped down to his boot-covered ankles. Clothed in a mix of dark leathers crudely sewn together with rough sinew, he looked menacing, yet oddly artistic. Stringy, shoulder length hair clung to his scalp like long, slick worms. Broad shouldered and head held high he looked down at the girl with an air of superiority.

It was not his clothing or intimidating appearance that gave Heidyl much alarm. It was, however, his face that puzzled her greatly. If not for his pale skin and hollow cheeks he looked very much like her father. He had the same handsome nose and strong chin and held his head the same exact way Thomas did just before lecturing his children. She knew for certain it could not possibly be him, but the image of the man before her now could have easily passed for a distant relative. At worst he looked like a sullied, distorted version of her father, as if he were doing a poor job of copying him.

For a moment, silence stretched between them. Then the tall apparition spoke.

"Don't fear, little one." The voice echoed as if he was standing in a spacious room or hall.

Heidyl certainly did not expect those to be the first words to tumble out of a ghastly illusion. She wrinkled her brow in curiosity.

"I propose a simple trade," he continued, "You have something I need, and now I have something you need. Or, if you prefer, you stole something from me, and I have repaid in kind." He laughed then as if a funny memory had just struck him. "If we were to delve further back into your family history, the irony of this situation would be most suitable." His smile vanished, replaced by a mask of malice, "Fortunately, I hold no grudge."

Heidyl tried to interrupt and explain that she had no idea what he was talking about, but Drayven droned on as if he did not hear her at all. "The boy will be my honored guest. All I require in exchange for his life is the key to open one of the doors in my home."

Heidyl felt her scalp tingle. Her feet rooted to the ground. How did he know about the key she had around her neck? She glanced down to be sure it was still hidden beneath her shirt. She felt the weight of it dangling low beneath her throat and wondered if this was the very key he wanted. She was about to hand it to him and make the trade for her brother's life here and now. All she wanted was to go home and forget this nightmare. But the man spoke once more.

"You have the look of your mother, child. Bring her to me. She knows what to do."

The young girl stood staring at him with her mouth slack, a dumbfounded expression crossing her features. Confusion and fear rooted her like a statue, rendering her unable to move. She considered asking how he could possibly know her mother, but her tongue seemed to stick in her mouth. Her lack of response drew immediate displeasure and Lord Drayven's visage grew angry. Jayce, who had been lying quite still until this moment, began to stir on the ground beside Drayven's apparition. Noticing the movement, the image of the dark lord bent down to grab a fistful of the boy's hair and roughly tugged him to his feet. Jayce moaned, his face twisting in agony.

"Mind you, I will not wait forever!" shouted Drayven. "Go! Bring her to me at once!"

Then there was the jumbled mass of jiggling black and white spots all over again. The horrible shape of the man melted and reformed itself into a living cage that unfurled and enveloped Jayce. Heidyl gasped and staggered back a few steps. By this time, her brother had regained full consciousness and began throwing himself against the crude bars that held him prisoner. Thrash about as he may, the wild protests did little more than bruise him further. At once, the cage transformed again and four leathery wings sprouted from the top and sides of the enclosure. Flapping wildly, they beat the earth and the air with a deafening rhythm that lifted the massive prison off the ground with a lurch. The unnatural motion caused Jayce to lose his balance. Falling to his hands and knees on the base of the flying jail, he could see Heidyl getting smaller in the distance as he rose higher and higher above her.

He shouted over the thunder pounding black wings, "Heidyl! Get out of here! Use the scroll words! Find Dad!"

But she was already running.

PART VII: THE KEY

THOMAS FELT HIS PULSE QUICKEN. After assuring Davey that everything was fine and ushering him back out the door to go home, both parents searched the house and grounds for any sign of their children. Together, Thomas and Jillian shared a waning hope that Haizorr had not been their children's destination. Upon exploring the pantry, and finding the hidden keypad covered with flour and fingerprints, their fears were confirmed.

"Looks like they inherited your knack for code-cracking," Thomas declared, and he and Jillian flew down the secret stairway.

"And your knack for chasing trouble," Jillian retorted.

"Touché."

They searched the room for any sign of their children. Everything looked untouched, save one seemingly small detail. The crystal dial beside the wall portal, had been turned back to the open position. Thomas and Jillian both felt the clamping pressure of a parent's worry begin to squeeze their insides. It felt as if the air in the room had suddenly been sucked out. Jillian sat heavily on the remains of what was once their luxurious leather couch. Hot tears formed and marched down her cheeks. Then a look of horror covered her face like a pale sheet. She stood, visibly shaken.

"Her insulin! Her glucose tablets!" Jillian tore up the stairs two at a time in a fit of fear. She burst into the kitchen. Thomas could hear her rummaging through the refrigerator and the cupboard where they kept their daughter's medical supplies for treating her condition. Thomas felt his mind begin churning like a frothy sea. A dozen questions and just as many plans assailed him at once. His jaw ached and he realized he had been making a frightful crunching sound by grinding his teeth. In a moment, his wife's soft feet padded back down the stairs. She crossed the room in silence and fell back again on the broken couch like a limp rag. Momentary relief washed over her. Heidyl had at least remembered to bring the necessary medical supplies with her. But she was still gone. They were both gone!

Jillian's shoulders shuddered with a deep sob and Thomas sat beside her to wrap his strong arm about her slender form in comfort, pushing away his own fears in the attempt to settle hers. In the silence, they both shared the burgeoning desire to rescue their children.

"They're too young to be in there alone," whispered Jillian, wiping her eyes. "Why would they have even crossed over in the first place?"

He had no idea why, but with an air of hope Thomas offered, "They're smart kids, Jill. And they have each other. We'll find them. We have to."

And just like that it was decided. As if sharing a silent signal between them, the brave couple steeled themselves to the mission at hand and stood up at once.

They had barely taken a step toward the stairs, when an abrupt crash behind them nearly sent their already frayed nerves into spasms. As if shot from a circus cannon Heidyl tumbled through the portal wall and fell to the hard floor behind them in exhaustion. Her sprawled landing caused her to lose her grip, sending Jayce's backpack, her medical bag and an open, tattered roll of parchment paper scraping across the floor in all directions.

"Heidyl!" Jillian nearly burst with relief. Tears gushed from her in torrents as she rushed to gather her precious little girl into trembling arms. She looked expectantly toward the spot where she had emerged, waiting for her son to tumble through next.

"Where's Jayce?" she asked.

Heidyl gulped great gasps of air in between sobs. She had been running with all her might. Even the increased strength she possessed on Haizorr had limits, and Heidyl had pushed them to the maximum. But now that she was back on the Earth side of the Gate, her frail mortality was amplified even further. Her lip was scabbed with dried blood and perspiration matted her hair in tangled clumps dotted with twigs and bits of leaves. In a moment, Thomas knelt beside them and held them both in a strong embrace. Heidyl trembled with each breath as the safety of her parents washed over her with comfort.

But something was still not quite right. She could not stop shaking. Her vision was blurring, and her limbs felt like dead wood hanging from her body. She recognized the feeling instantly and managed to croak out the words, "I'm low." Her eyes could barely stay open, and she began to shake and spasm even more. Haizorr had granted her relief from the disease, but Earth brought it crashing back upon her body.

Alarm spread across her mother's face. "Quick, get her bag!" she shouted to Thomas. In a flash he grabbed her kit which had skidded under a desk, pulled out a tube of sugary gel and began squirting the pinkish stuff into his daughter's mouth. Fortunately, Heidyl was still able to swallow. Her body was greedy for sugar and she gulped it down involuntarily. After several tense moments, the shaking grew less and Heidyl grew more alert. Jillian checked her blood sugar levels several times to be sure they had climbed back into a safe range before allowing herself to breathe easy. As Heidyl's awareness returned, she became increasingly grumpy. Haizorr had been the first place she felt free from the awful disease, and the fact that it had come back with such vengeance upon her return upset her greatly. Thomas lovingly stroked her hair, gingerly picking the forest debris from it. Every few seconds he looked over his shoulder at the portal wall, then returned to the embrace. His heart began pounding harder as the seconds stretched into minutes. He knew the Gate would close again soon, if it had not already. At last he could stand the waiting no longer.

"Where is Jayce?" he asked.

When Heidyl had regained the strength enough to answer, she shook her head as if trying to clear the cobwebs of a bad dream. "They took him,

Dad."

Thomas felt ice and fire flood his veins simultaneously. "Who took him? Where?" A sinking pit in his stomach quickly formed.

"They were horrible. At first, we thought it was just a little girl, but then she turned into something." She scrunched her eyes shut against the ghastly recollection. Jillian nudged her to go on. Heidyl dropped her voice to a whisper, "Three monsters. They were trying to lick my face." She began crying again, "I thought they were going to eat me!" The effort had reopened the cut on her lip, and it began to ooze blood once again. Jillian cradled her daughter in her arms and tried to soothe her. She thought of how she used to cheerfully assure her children that there were no such things as monsters.

Those days had ended all too abruptly.

Thomas stood and stalked to the dial on the portal wall. Angrily he spun it into its closed position before pounding his fist against the wall. Both Heidyl and Jillian jumped at the sound, which seemed to create a sharp and ominous stillness in the room.

Then all three of them heard it. A slight scuffling noise, like canvas cloth being dragged across the floor. It was so muffled that none of them could immediately zero in on where it was coming from. Alarm gripped Thomas as he began scanning the room with a critical eye. The girls, kneeling on the floor, stilled their breath and stifled their sobs for fear that something else had come unbidden through the portal during the short while it had remained open. Instinctively, Thomas reached for his sidearm. But when his searching hand closed upon empty space, he cursed himself inwardly for leaving the weapon locked upstairs in the safe, rather than keeping it on his hip.

Another soft scrape drew Thomas' attention toward the corner of the room where the backpack had come to rest when Heidyl made her tumbling entrance to Earth just moments before. He motioned for his wife and daughter to remain quiet while he crept across the room like a panther stalking prey.

The backpack lay in a haphazard heap of straps and partially zipped pockets. Something inside, or under it, moved. Thomas stopped in his tracks. Whatever it was seemed like it was trapped or lost as it bumped and pushed the pack around. Slowly Thomas inched toward it and then pounced. He seized the bag with all the force of a man expecting an intense struggle. The thing seemed to be trapped inside one of the open pockets and had not the sense to simply escape back through the same point of entry. Rather than the wild thrashing he had expected, the creature inside just kept pushing and probing against the bottom seams of the pocket oblivious to the harsh shaking it had just received.

Jillian and Heidyl watched wide-eyed from their place across the room. They had not moved a muscle, but at this point allowed themselves to begin breathing again. Thomas' strong hands were clamping the backpack openings shut and they felt safer already. Their fears resurfaced when Thomas, overcome by curiosity, squatted down with the wiggling sack and peeled it open once more.

"Don't let it out, Thomas!" Jillian frantically cried out as both she and Heidyl scrambled to their feet.

He peered into the dark contents of the pouch and a bitter expression twisted across his face.

"*Trillych*." The word was a curse on his lips as he plunged his hand into the gaping mouth of the satchel. In his clenched fist he extracted what looked to Jillian like a long purple snake that flopped and coiled against itself, glistening with slick putrid slime.

Heidyl's eyes nearly popped from her head and a ragged gasp caught in her throat, "That's its tongue!" she cried, "I saw Jayce cut it off to save me!" She had no idea how it got into the backpack.

In disgust, Thomas crammed the writhing article back into one of the pockets and zippered it closed before dropping it back to the floor. Rather than wipe the sticky saliva from his hand, he balled his fist and held it in the air as if cradling something of importance. A ponderous look furrowed his brow and he mumbled, "Yeah, I'm almost positive it's the trillych." He spun to consult the great Book on the table and flipped the ancient pages back and forth a few times before stopping at a section full of sketches and descriptions of what appeared to be exotic animals and frightful fiends. His lips moved rapidly as he traced a finger across the worn surface, scanning the script. In triumph he tapped the page and looked back up at his daughter.

"After this I'll know for sure," he said, examining the congealing slime in the palm of his hand. Heidyl and Jillian wore puzzled expressions wondering what was running through his head. He rounded the table and stood before his daughter. "Trust me," he whispered. Then, with gentle care he dabbed a bit of the gooey saliva onto the tip of his finger and touched it to the open cut of her lip. At first Heidyl recoiled, giving her father an incredulous look. Then her expression changed to wonder. "The pain's gone!" she declared.

Thomas nodded. He observed the open gash close itself before his very eyes. The bleeding stanched completely, then in a moment, there was no evidence that there had ever been a wound, save the dried blood on her chin. "Definitely trillych," he announced. A puzzled expression crossed Heidyl's face as she ponderously poked her newly healed lip.

Her father explained, "They always travel in groups of three and together have the ability to morph into any object or creature they can imagine. If they get separated from one another they are useless. It would appear that this trillych tongue is still searching for the rest of its body." He shook his head, first in wonder, then in dismay, "But they don't just go about capturing people. They're not very bright and don't have good imaginations. Usually they just try to blend into their surroundings like a chameleon in order to hide from a threat." He paused, wrinkling his brow in thought. "They aren't naturally this aggressive. Someone had to have sent them."

Heidyl was still curiously poking at her lip. "The tall man in the cloak," she replied, slowly nodding her head. She widened her eyes, "Dad, he looked a lot like you! But I think that was probably some sort of trick."

"Who? You saw him?" He shot an anxious glance over to Jillian, who wore a blank expression on her pale face. The shock of the situation was making her lightheaded.

"No, they—the, um, trillych—changed into the shape of a man. I don't know who he was, but he seemed to know about you guys." The knapsack on the floor convulsed with movement once again. Heidyl glanced at it and shuddered. "If Jayce hadn't been given his weapon, I can't imagine what they would have done to me." She slid the smooth black and white Vyritas stone from her pocket and handed it to her father.

He turned it over and over in his hands, examining the gift and the curious etchings. He shrugged lightly, "Weapon? It's just a stone. Who gave you this?" he asked as he handed the item back to her. Returning it to her pocket, Heidyl gave a shrug of her own and answered, "Somehow Jayce was able to make it into a sword. I tried but couldn't figure it out. A huge horse-owl thing named Justhynial gave it to him. Oh, he was amazing, Dad!"

At the mention of the ancient name, the eyes of her mother and father became like saucers.

It was Jillian's turn to marvel. "You met Justhynial? How?"

To see her parents' expressions—mouths open, eyes wide—was almost comical to Heidyl. She could not help but glory in their awed silence for just a moment longer. Proudly she held up her wrist to show off her own present. "Yes, and he gave me this, too!" The precious bangle was a little loose and slid up her forearm a bit. Jillian reached over to trace the smooth metallic surface admiringly with her finger. Heidyl smiled broadly to see her own mother so intrigued by the trinket. "I'm still learning how to use it properly," she explained, "but I think I've got it mostly figured out. Sort of."

Finally, Thomas spoke the one question that had been needling both minds of her parents, "Why did you two ever cross over alone?"

A thick silence bordering on reverence filled the room. Somehow, Heidyl felt older and wiser in that moment. It seemed to her that the appropriate time to share her tale had come. In great detail, she recounted the full scale of events to her parents, covering everything she could remember from Jayce's explanation of his plan to fix his blunder to them tumbling out of the Tree Gate and discovering the slaughtered grayvyks. She smiled as she recounted the moment they had run with Justhynial's blue-bodied herd of winged giants. In rapt attention both mother and father leaned in toward her like children during campfire story hour. Clutching on to her every word, they listened eagerly for hopeful clues that would assure them of Jayce's safety.

When Heidyl had finished, Thomas felt a sting of guilt. "I told him it wasn't his fault! Why does he still feel the need to try to fix anything?"

Jillian smiled and gently elbowed his side, "He's more like you than you think, love."

When Heidyl described the dark lord's demand that Jillian must be brought to him, Thomas began working his jaw angrily. He mused aloud, "If he has figured out how to control the trillych like that, then why does he need a Cypher?"

Heidyl gave her father a puzzled expression. "A Cypher? What's that?"

Jillian took a turn explaining. "All of us have been given certain gifts and talents," she said as she moved to sit beside her daughter on the torn couch. "It's God's way of making us unique and more readily able to help one another."

Thomas too sat down with them and added, "But us marked ones have something extra special," he began. Reaching down to tap the coil shaped mark partly visible on Heidyl's ankle he continued, "We share a special endowment."

"What do you mean?" she asked.

"I'm what's known as a Seeker," her father replied. "Seekers are sort of like bloodhounds. We've been given the ability to find and discover great wonders of the known worlds." He motioned toward the wall of scrolls and the portal wall. "It's how we discovered entry into Haizorr." Then, pointing to Jillian, "Your mother is a Cypher."

Chiming in, Jillian gestured to herself. "We Cyphers are code breakers and possess a knack for unraveling mysteries and puzzles. It's why your father and I make such an incredible couple. He finds the lock, and I find the key." She gave Thomas a playful wink.

He blushed, then quipped, "I'm still trying to figure you out!"

"Seek and ye shall find," she teased.

Heidyl rolled her eyes but could not help but smile. Though at times she outwardly protested her parents' mushy affection toward one another, deep inside she loved them for it. She found hope and great comfort in knowing that true love did indeed exist.

"Justhynial called me a Liberty. Is that what my mark makes me?" Heidyl began to feel like a weight of great responsibility had been passed to her as she nervously twirled the bracelet on her wrist.

Jillian rested a motherly hand on Heidyl's knee, "No, love. God makes us who we are. Sometimes others just hold up a mirror so we can see it for ourselves." Heidyl looked again at the polished surface of her bracelet. Her hazy reflection stared back at her. She saw a tired, haggard face and felt nothing like anything special at the moment and wondered if Justhynial had been wrong about her.

When Heidyl looked up, she was surprised to see that her father was smiling at her. "Wow. A Liberty? Right in my own home!" he said. "Your gift is one of the Compassion gifts." When Thomas saw her confused expression he continued, "I read about it in The Book." He motioned toward the thick manuscript on the far desk. "It means that you possess special courage that enables you to overcome great odds when you sense others in need. You long to see captives set free, the oppressed be protected, that sort of thing."

Heidyl pondered that for a moment and wondered if maybe that was why she dove into Haizorr after her brother. She had been overcome by an urgent need to help him. Normally she would have avoided the portal altogether and just told her parents about it later.

Thomas continued the summary, "There are dozens of other marked ones out there as well; Guardians, Hunters, Seers—although I've never met any of them."

"What about Verity?" interrupted Heidyl, "Because that's what Justhynial mentioned about Jayce."

"Yes, that's another one of the classes, it has to do with those that search out truth and expose lies, but Jayce doesn't have a mark." Thomas stroked his chin in thought. "Justhynial may be wise, but he is not all knowing. Maybe it's just his potential that he sees in Jayce."

With the conversation turned back to Jayce, the sense of urgency returned to their situation. They needed a plan of attack. The grim demands from the dark lord of Blackynspyre rested heavily on them all. Thomas and Jillian knew that in order to save their only son, they might very well unleash an ancient evil that would destroy all things known to any of them. They had no intention of doing that, nor could they bear to lose Jayce to the dark wiles of an evil maniac.

Wanting desperately to help, Heidyl injected what little information she had left to offer to their situation. "The man mentioned needing a key to open a door." She fiddled with her necklace. "Do you think he means this?"

she said, removing the curiously marked key from around her neck to dangle it before her parents. In truth, that very basic thought had not occurred to either of them that he might actually have need of the enchanted tool. They simply assumed that he was looking for Jillian's decryption skills in order to read the key code page and the matching summon scroll that had been stolen.

They wondered how he could possibly have known that Jillian had ever possessed such a key. The only thing that made any sense to Thomas and Jillian was to believe that he was somehow trying to unleash and control the great Dragon. But could Heidyl's key really be what he is after? Could the simple trinket truly contain that much power? None of them knew for sure and Jillian had never tested the full force of the key.

Jillian reached out a hand and gently fingered the cool metal. "Great mysteries reside in many a simple thing," she sighed as a distant and pleasant memory stirred within her.

Heidyl noted the look in her mother's eyes. "Was this a gift to you from Justhynial?" she guessed.

Jillian blinked, amused at her daughter's perception.

"Yes," she smiled, fondly tracing the familiar etchings. "Which means that its power is probably greater than any of us may ever realize." She pressed the key back into Heidyl's hands. "Keep it well hidden."

All of this conjecture made Thomas' mind buzz. Attempting to take stock of their situation he counted the possible scenarios, but each seemed to have an equal portion of flawed logic. The key's riddle stated clearly that it would open any locked door, or maybe a portal, but only if motives were pure. He seriously doubted that Jayce's captor had any pure intentions with the ancient serpent. The summon scroll could call creatures, but could it control them? It certainly did not give Thomas any control over the three grayvyks or the Logarth he had summoned earlier. Or perhaps he had missed something?

Then, wondering aloud he said, "The portal scroll would open a door, but would it be wide enough for the entire beast to emerge?" He was pacing around the room trying to think.

Jillian added, "And the portal area has to be thinned first. He must have somehow figured that out, too."

Thomas nodded grimly. Their foe seemed to grow more cunning with each passing moment. "He must have discovered the hidden writing on the code page. That blasted Black Dragon of Dearth is his end game. I can feel it. I'd wager he thinks deciphering the code page will give him control over it. But if he has deciphered it enough to know about the Dragon, then why does he need Jillian? Or a key?"

Jillian's eyes widened, "He'll never control that monster. Not in a thousand Haizorr years!"

"This explains why the darchlytes have become so heavily involved." He patted the place on his chest where he kept the grayvyk claw he had been gifted. "They must somehow sense that their ancient enemy is near."

Heidyl sighed and suddenly drooped her shoulders. She was still grappling with the harsh and uncertain new reality she had been thrust into. "I wish Samuel were still here. I always feel safer with him around."

At the mention of the old caretaker's name, Thomas stiffened. He had not been able to push the thought aside that had he not been so hard on his friend, perhaps none of this ever would have happened.

Jillian noticed the worn look play across her husband's features. Reaching up, she caressed her daughter's hair to soothe her. "We all miss him," she said. "His wisdom and calm strength would be so helpful right now."

Thomas was still pacing. The thought of his last fiery conversation with Samuel assailed him with fresh barbs of guilt. "He had his reasons for leaving, but the problem before us now is that Jayce has been taken. We need to get moving."

With that he scooped up the writhing backpack and, much to her horror, dropped it into Heidyl's lap. "We need to teach you how to properly pack for a trip to Haizorr."

PART VIII: THE ALLY

THE CRUST OF BREAD SQUIRMED BESIDE HIM. Riddled with maggots and worms of unknown species, the festering lump of food held no appeal to the boy. Huddled in a dank, rock-hewn chamber he hugged his knees to his chest against the chill air. Some time ago a rough looking thug wearing little more than a filthy loincloth had tossed the morsel through the rusty twisted iron bars of his confinement cell and moved on down the corridor with a throaty grunt.

Jayce had tried a dozen times or more to wiggle the heavy door or jar it loose with a well-placed donkey kick, but each attempt ended with the same pain in his heel and hollow echoes of his struggle mocking him from the cavernous rock beyond his cell. In spite of the dire circumstance, he was trying his best to stay level headed and positive. This did not come easily or naturally for Jayce, especially after enduring the harrowing journey of being shuttled across the land in a flying trillych-morphed jail. He was at least grateful to be on solid ground once again. The flight through the Haizorr atmosphere had been anything but enjoyable. His captors had the most erratic flight pattern and jostled him and dropped altitude so frequently that Jayce was certain that death was imminent. He had screamed more times than he cared to admit.

On the rare stable moments of the voyage he was able to see clearly that their destination was the black, bony tower of Blackynspyre. Though that horrid place was his intended destination from the outset of his journey, he had hoped to arrive there of his own accord, rather than ferried to the wretched place like a caged dog by shape-shifting demons.

As they drew near to the ebony tower, Jayce was taken by how immense it was. The entire landscape appeared to be more like a fortress complete with rocky outbuildings; buttressed by walls covered in grotesque carvings with black sconces emitting grimy flames which seemingly created more shadows than they dispelled. He could not be sure from so high in the air, but it looked like great beasts lumbered about the premises as if slaving or pulling great loads.

The truly terrifying part of the journey had been the transition from his air prison to the one made of true stone and bars, which held him now. Without warning the trillych had tucked their leathery wings and simply dropped from the sky like a boulder. Jayce had hung weightless in the air for a moment before the wind resistance of his flailing arms and flapping clothing had mashed him against the far side of the makeshift bars. They were in an all-out dive toward a dark opening in the side of the murky spire. Jayce squinted and braced for impact. When the expected crash never came, he ventured the tiniest of peeks only to find he could see nothing. Alarmed, he popped both eyes open and strained into the inky scene. Utter darkness assailed his senses turning his mind in circles. They were still flying. Dank air whipped at his clothing and the leathery flapping wings echoed against cold stone. How the beasts could navigate the blackness of the fortress interior was beyond his grasp. Jayce tried hard to swallow back the bitter bile that roiled into his throat with every lurch and unexpected twist.

At last, the hellish ride ended with an abrupt scrape and rapid descent onto a gray stone floor. In the same moment his trillych captors separated, spinning out and away from him to resume their normal repulsive shapes. The abrupt dismantling of the flying prison pitched Jayce onto his side, rolling him across the dusty bedrock surface. It felt like he had been flung over the handlebars of a bicycle at top speed to land upon pavement. The tumble scraped holes in the knees of his pants and tore the skin from his palms. His world finally stopped spinning and Jayce lay in the darkness gasping to catch his breath and reckon with the pain in his limbs.

The dust he kicked up irritated his lungs and his coughs echoed against bare, hard walls. A flapping sound to his left brought his senses to sharp attention and he sat up straight. The hair on his arms prickled. Whining hisses came from somewhere to his right. He spun to face the new sound. In that moment horror gripped the boy's insides. He could hear the three beasts scuffling about in the black space around him, but he could see nothing. They were circling him. It occurred to Jayce that they could still see him perfectly and he raised his fists and arms up about his face to ward off any potential attack. He even let fly with several violent kicks into the black. If this were to be his end, he reasoned, then he would go down swinging.

In a moment, the atmosphere in the room shifted as if a door had opened and a new current of air with fouler scents wafted in. With a flurry of flaps and hisses, the malevolent trio retreated suddenly into the dark recesses of the room, leaving Jayce alone.

But he was not alone at all.

Something else had entered the area and was lumbering heavily across the room toward him. He could hear heavy breathing much like the grunts of an advancing bull. Alarm rushed over Jayce in the black room and he turned to run. But run to where? For all he knew he might gallop over the edge of a thousand-foot gorge or skewer himself by sprinting into a bristling wall of spikes. He could feel the ground beneath him tremble at the bulky advance of this new assailant. Jayce decided that he no longer cared what befell him if he ran.

He bolted into the blackness.

A second later he felt the ground beneath his feet simply drop away. In that awful heart stopping moment, Jayce knew he had made a terrible mistake. He was in a free fall and was gripped with the icy dread that his life may be at an end. In the next half breath, however, his feet scraped against the top of a second stone step and his knees buckled. His world violently tipped, and he tumbled down a short staircase before meeting another wall of stone. He shook his head to clear the disorientation. His thoughts felt clouded as if his brain had been stuffed with throbbing wool. He tried standing.

And then, the beast was upon him.

Several rough tentacles encircled his waist and wrapped themselves around his upper torso, pinning his arms to his sides. He was no longer able to defend himself. He was about to launch into a flurry of angry kicks when Jayce was hoisted off his feet as if he weighed nothing. Struggle was futile, but fear would not allow him to stop wriggling and flailing his legs against the monstrous foe that carried him back across the room through the large door through which it had come.

The door opened into a long hallway dimly lit with torches. The flames danced in deep purple hues spewing thick black smoke that stained the walls above their iron brackets. Shadows whipped across the surfaces like black snakes and Jayce strained his eyes to see through the murky gloom. He learned at once that the tentacles that were wrapped about him were not tentacles at all, but huge fingers of an enormous hand. A towering beast with a hog-snout carried him as if he were nothing more than a sack lunch. The terrible thought of being eaten alive crossed his mind just as Jayce caught a glimpse of sharp tusks jutting up and out from the drooling maw of his captor. He wanted to scream, but the crushing grip around his chest left him with just barely enough room to breathe.

At last the trudging monster stopped. The next moment Jayce was careening once again across a stone floor as the huge hand tossed him into the dark cell in which he now sat. The iron bars slammed shut behind him.

In the faded light Jayce could not recall if that had been minutes, hours or days ago. The gnawing pain in his stomach kept his mind from thinking clearly. He glanced once again at the rotting morsel of food that lay in the dust and considered eating it until a fat purple worm burrowed into its center, driving the thought from his mind. He made a face and turned away.

He ached all over and suddenly felt very tired. He scooted into a corner of the cell; being careful not to bump his sore head on the low rock ceiling before letting it fall back against the cold stone pillow. Despair threatened to choke out his hope as the dreadful reality of the situation crept into his mind; he was locked in prison in a land full of monsters.

JUST BEFORE HE HIT THE GROUND, Jayce's eyes snapped open. He was clutching his pounding chest as he panted in the darkness. The nap born of exhaustion and hunger had produced a horrible dream that startled him right back into the living nightmare he now found himself. Dreams of falling, flames and clawing limbs had stretched through his mind for what seemed like days. He was glad to be awake now, even if he was still under lock and key. Yet, the dream did have one pleasant moment in which a tall figure in a brown cloak had pressed against the iron bars and whispered, "Have courage," before tossing a loaf of fresh bread under the lowest crossbar of the prison door.

Jayce yawned and rubbed his aching eyes with sore hands. The tiny cell appeared just as before. There was no more or no less light, making it impossible to tell the time of day, or night it may have been. He shifted away from the corner and bumped his leg against something. Fearing that it was some loathsome rat, he kicked at it and sent it tumbling back toward the iron gate like a football. The boy squinted hard into the gray, studying the object for movement. The oblong mass resembled a boulder more than a living creature; still he approached it cautiously. Reaching out a wary hand he gingerly probed the surface. It had a firm texture that gave somewhat when pressed.

At that moment a familiar smell caressed his nostrils and started his mouth to watering.

"Bread!" Jayce nearly shouted the word into the gloom. Had it not been a dream then? He looked up at the gate to see if he could catch any trace of the cloaked visitor and noticed a tin cup had been placed beside one of the lower bars. It was full of water. Greedily he stuffed his cheeks with great mouthfuls of crumbling bread and washed it down with a long draught from the cup. The water had a somewhat metallic taste due to the vessel he drank from, and the bread was just shy of stale, but he did not complain. In fact, he felt like he had never been more thankful for food in his entire life.

But who had left it? Certainly, this could not have come from the pig-snouted thug who had rough-handled him into the cell, nor from Mr. Loincloth who had tried to feed him that maggot-laden crust earlier. Jayce reasoned that it must be another prisoner who had some sort of 'good-be-havior' privilege, enabled to have more freedom throughout the dungeon. The entry to his cell looked like a huge, black gaping mouth with metal teeth looming over him. Cautiously he inched closer to the ragged bars. The youth's curiosity had been piqued now that the bread had eased his hunger and he hoped for a glimpse of this benefactor. Perhaps he could even concoct an escape with help from this outsider.

Jayce opened his mouth to speak. A dry croak snagged in his throat and he coughed. Dust and grit had worked their way into his windpipe and the chill air seemed to have cemented them there. He drained the water from the cup and tried again.

"Hello? Are you there?" His own voice sounded hollow and small in this place. He tried again, "Thanks for the bread!" The cavern threw his voice around until it became no more than a soft and weak sounding warble. Jayce became annoyed at the feeble squawk that came from him. Mustering his courage, he shouted, "Hey! Anybody there?" This time a satisfying echo coursed through the various chambers and hallways adjoining the meager cell. Jayce smiled. That was much better. But he was not yet finished. He began to clank and rattle the empty tin cup against the bars, which made an awful ruckus. Pausing to listen for responses every now and again, he continued to clang and chatter into the black while courage seemed to swell inside him. The metallic clink of the cup made a terrific sound that sent Jayce into using it to keep time as he began to sing snatches of songs he learned in Sunday school at church when he was a young boy. He had no idea why those particular songs came to his mind at a time like this, but they did bring him a measure of comfort.

Without warning, a shadow passed before him and long bony fingers reached through the bars, snatching the mug from his grasp. The noise was clipped short. Jayce felt the air rush from his lungs and fear filled his next gasping breath. A towering cloaked figure stood above him. For the moment, the lad was happy to be behind bars and he scrambled backward to get out of arm's reach.

"It appears I've ensnared a songbird," issued a man's hollow voice from under a drawn hood. "One would think you were trying to rouse the dead with such clamor." The shrouded visitor pulled the drinking cup up toward his face, inspecting it as if it were foreign to him. Jayce thought he heard him sniff at the article like a bloodhound. "Though, in my palace the dead never sleep anyhow." With a mighty crunch, the man crumpled the metal vessel in his hand as if it were made of tissue paper before tossing it between the bars where it landed beside the half-eaten loaf of bread at Jayce's feet. "Have you been making friends?"

Jayce stared for a moment at the ball of twisted metal. His mouth hung open in a slack gape. He could think of no answer and was indeed afraid to even attempt one. Jayce allowed his eyes to dart upward to the figure standing on the free side of the bars. To his surprise, the man had pulled back his hood. A curious expression crossed the boy's features. He had not expected the man to have a face that was altogether human. There was no long pointy nose or mouth rimmed with needle sharp teeth. Sure enough the man was pale and very bony, with piercing eyes and an unpleasant, even malicious grin. But something about him looked familiar. It was most disquieting. Jayce squinted a little and cocked his head to the side, trying hard to stare through the trappings and hard edges that made the man before him appear so menacing.

Probing the furthest edges of his mind Jayce desperately tried to recall where or if he had seen him before. Then his eyes widened.

The picture on the stone bookshelf at home!

He knew this man!

"Uncle Dray?" The boy's voice was no more than the wispy tendril of a whisper. A fearful inquiry born of the slimmest of hopes.

Drayven stiffened. Then twisting his face into a grimace of disgust he roared at the boy, incensed at the affectionate use of his Earth name. Years of malice had hammered his heart into blackened stone, yet this youngster before him had cracked that impenetrable shell with two simple words. Jayce shrank further back into the cell, genuinely afraid.

After a moment the man seemed to calm. Forcing himself to breathe through his nostrils. Closing his eyes, he spoke with icy calm. "It's been a long time since anyone has called me that." Silence engulfed them in its folds like sodden wool and neither person moved for what seemed an eternity. Drayven stared at the ground swaying on his feet slowly. He seemed locked in distant thought. Jayce sat still on the cold stone wondering what the appropriate next course of action might be. For the present it seemed that silence was the best card to play.

Drayven snapped back from his reverie and bellowed quite suddenly into the black hall, "Jailer!" With a rough grunt and scuffling footsteps, the loincloth-clad ruffian came to stand beside its master. Drayven viciously slapped the beast, which was nearly twice his size, before carrying on as if merely swatting an annoying fly, "This is no way to treat family! Get him out of there at once!" But the snide way he said the word "family" made Jayce seriously doubt that he meant any sort of kindness by it.

The bumbling oaf produced a set of keys that rattled and jounced against the bars. Large grimy fingers fidgeted and quaked as they fumbled to find the right key. It was odd to watch so large a creature behave so timidly. Jayce had no doubt that the beast could squash Drayven's head like a cantaloupe if it wanted; yet here it was falling all over itself to appease the huffing bark of the man beside it. A darker, less pleasant thought made Jayce wonder what Drayven had done to instill such fear into creatures that otherwise should be counted worthy of dishing out their own fair share of fright.

At last the proper key struck home and the rusty lock grated and squealed in protest as the mechanism turned. Drayven shoved the hulking minion aside and jerked the door open with a gritty scrape. He stalked toward Jayce and stood towering over him for an awkward moment. Having lost sense of appropriate human manners in his years on Haizorr, and rather than offer his nephew a hand Drayven reached down to grab the boy by the shoulder. Before Jayce could blink, he had been painfully hoisted into a standing position. Lord Drayven examined the youth's ragged appearance with a disapproving eye. Without a word he spun on his heel to exit the cell, kicking aside the good morsel of bread as he passed. The open mouth of the prison cell yawned black at Jayce who stood in stunned reserve. What had just happened? Was he free to go? Dozens of questions clamoring for answers within his mind brought no clarity, but rather succeeded in making him wholly indecisive. He felt he should flee, but to where? A castle full of nightmares was hardly a place to wander about.

A large part of him also wished to follow Drayven. Jayce remembered his uncle only in snatches and scraps of distant memories. Though the rough man who had just freed him was hardly a shade of the man he had encountered as a young boy, Jayce recalled now how the infrequent visits and holidays with him had oddly ceased years ago. His father rarely spoke of Drayven and if he did, a great sadness came upon him, which reduced conversations about the man into moments of strained silence. Over time and left unspoken, the memories faded into oblivion. It was this same curious mystery that now tugged at Jayce's reluctant feet. He felt them move as if of their own accord and in a moment went padding down the dank corridor after the dark man for a most unusual family reunion.

THE STENCH WAS WORSE THAN EXPECTED. Heidyl had done her best to warn her parents of the strangling stink that awaited them the moment they passed through the Gate. The trio had taken precautions by wrapping dampened handkerchiefs about their mouths and noses, but the rank fester of rotting grayvyk flesh scorched their every breath. Haizorr's moons had sunk below the rim of the sky and the fiery crown of a crimson sun was inching its way above the opposite horizon. In the growing light Thomas beheld a great grayvyk graveyard through watering eyes. As a precaution, he had been sure to pack his revolver. The grasses were matted with black blood and entire sections of ground were torn in huge swaths where great beasts locked in combat had wrestled—and died. Forever these corpses would lie in their repose, for neither scavenging bird by day nor scrounging creature by night would dare feast on their poisoned flesh.

Thomas and Jillian knew this terrain as well as any other and normally would have charged across it, but so twisted was the land now that they were forced to take halting and wandering paths.

"What do you think happened here?" Jillian choked through the thick air. Thomas and Heidyl were both lost in their own deep theories as to what had occurred. Jillian scrambled over a great tree trunk then turned around to offer a helpful hand to her daughter as she too climbed across the obstacle. Thomas was about to puff out a doubt ridden response to his wife's question, when quite suddenly the tree trunk shifted and something like a growl or groan rumbled deep from within its core. The threesome jumped back in alarm, Thomas' hand flashed instantly to the weapon at his hip.

The bulk before them trembled and rolled slightly.

Thomas breathed a whisper that was both answer and awe, "Darchlytes!" Relaxing his hand away from his sidearm he stepped back to take in the immense giant that lay before him.

Jillian and Heidyl, standing on the other side of the bulk did the same. Great gashes covered the beast's body. Heidyl nearly tripped over a stray tree limb as she stepped backward. Her stomach lurched when she learned in startled dismay that it was actually one of the arms of the majestic darchlyte lying before her. Thomas felt a wave of sadness. "They've torn him apart." Jillian heard the cheerless tone in her husband's voice. Thomas held these impressive beings in high esteem. Something in their history resonated within him. Perhaps it was the deep sorrow emanating from their curse that filled him with empathy for their plight. Whatever the case, Thomas sighed heavily as he stepped lightly toward the face of the dying behemoth.

The first rays of sunlight trickling through the tree line washed pale across its great body. With what looked like great effort, it raised its remaining arm toward the sun gently rising on the horizon. Outstretched fingers of the great hand extended to their fullest reach as if trying to capture the great orb. The darchlyte turned somber eyes to yearn and plead with the sunrise. Thomas stared into them. He saw desperation and great anguish pooled within those deep-set ancient eyes. But he also saw a spark. Like a lone, brilliant butterfly flitting against a backdrop of darkened forest he could see it. Hope. Without realizing, the man rested a hand on the rough face before him in a gesture of comfort. "Don't fear, the curse will be broken someday," he whispered. Then, as if waking from a dream, the eyes flickered and blinked turning their royal cobalt stare away from the waxing sun toward Thomas' face.

In that moment, the man felt smaller than he had ever felt in his life. All of his own problems and worries seemed to melt away under such a gaze. Then, the darchlyte's eyes widened in recognition. With great trembling the heavy arm pulled in close to its body. Thomas felt something thump against his own chest. Looking down he saw a gigantic gnarled finger gently nudging the place where the grayvyk talon hung from its leather strap beneath his shirt. He looked up in astonishment. Could this be the very same darchlyte that had rescued him from the jaws of the grayvyk all those nights ago? Gazing into the fading azure eyes of the colossus he swallowed a hard lump that had gathered in his throat. Thomas watched the heavy eyelids shroud the final life-light of the darchlyte as the great arm slumped to the ground at his feet. He looked up at Jillian and Heidyl standing in a solemn embrace and shook his head.

For a silent moment they stood as the spreading daylight bathed them in a mixture of warmth and cool morning mist. The passing of a noble giant is no easy event to part from, but the urgency of the task before them prodded their hearts along. Thomas rounded the body of the fallen hero and joined his wife and daughter once more. In awed quiet they strode from the field of battle and into the waiting trabalisk wood. Thomas and Jillian had traversed these paths many times and knew the land well, but after a moment Jillian noticed they were heading in the wrong direction.

Clearing her throat to ease into breaking the silence she said, "Thomas. We should be heading in the direction toward Blackynspyre, shouldn't we?" She was afraid that the encounter with the slain darchlyte had clouded his senses a bit.

"Yes, according to Heidyl's account, that's where they would have taken Jayce," he replied as he turned along a less traveled route leading them into what at first seemed quite the opposite direction. A plan had begun taking shape in his mind and he was still not very good at communicating his thoughts.

"Then why take this passage? It seems it would take us much longer to arrive" she prodded gently, trying to be careful of her husband's feelings.

He stopped so abruptly in his tracks that the two women nearly collided with him. Thomas turned, taking one each of their hands in his he said, "Because we are in the middle of a war," then added, "and if we want to get Jayce back, we're going to need an army." He gave a knowing wink to Jillian then tenderly kissed her hand and then his daughter's before whirling about to continue onward. Jillian smiled, nodding to herself as she guessed where they were headed now.

With that the tiny war-band marched together, their steps swallowed by the somber silence of the thickening forest.

THE ANTEROOM WAS LIKE A TOMB. So thick was the stillness that Jayce kept touching and testing his ears to be sure they were working properly. Drayven had led him to the chamber with his long quick steps making it difficult to keep up with him through the darkened corridors. Upon halting, he indicated with a wave of his hand for Jayce to stand in the center of the room. Six bone-like pillars curved upward joining in an arc at the center apex of a dark purple ceiling. Thick tapestries clung in haphazard fashion to the high arches and seemed to absorb all sound. Deathly silence engulfed every scuffing footfall or sniffling nose that would have normally echoed wildly through such a chamber. The walls of the hexagonal room were covered in painted compositions of absurd and unnerving scenes; a goat being slain by a unicorn, another depicted a herd of sheep each with legs of a man, tumbling over a cliff edge to jagged rocks below, a third showed a singular enormous eye staring out from a black framed canvas—it blinked! Jayce startled and blinked back. The eye twitched and followed his movements. The boy hopped further backward in surprise, nudging hard against what felt like a child wearing a heavy robe.

The boy spun around to see a small person wrapped in brown rags and veils before him. "Oh! Excuse me," said Jayce. He was about to say how sorry he was but the little being clapped its hands over where its ears appeared to be and threw its head back as if in great pain. Lord Drayven raised a finger to his lips motioning for Jayce to remain silent. In a moment the frail figure recovered and stood once again facing the young man. Like a mummy he, or she, was wrapped head to toe in long filthy rags. All features were indistinguishable, save for the shape of a head, torso, and limbs. The shrouds were so thick and complete that Jayce doubted the poor creature could breathe or see through such smothering. When he looked up again, he saw the great eye in the painting now staring at Drayven, who was making motions with his arms as if trying to communicate without sound to the unblinking orb. It was a ghastly sight. At last when he had finished his odd bit of sign language, the veiled figure that stood in front of Jayce nodded its wrapped head vigorously as if answering a question that Jayce had never asked. It then turned and hobbled with great effort into a corner of the room, its tattered rags trailing like ghostly streamers. The watchful gaze of the enormous eyeball followed the small creature's every move with keen interest.

Presently, the wrapped figure returned with an armload of heavy clothing; a tunic, cloak and what appeared to be some form of heavy trousers. Impossibly thin arms held the bundle out to Jayce, who received them with a sheepish nod. The boy did not fully know what was happening and felt quite naked and unsure under the scrutiny of the others in the room—especially the eye. He stood motionless in the center of the chamber. The eye kept looking from him to Drayven and back again. The dark lord made more hand motions to the giant oculus, and once again the rag covered head bobbed up and down as if in reply. With a start, Jayce then realized that the eye on the wall was doing all of the seeing for the veil-clad body before him. The wire thin arms began to motion to Jayce for him to change out of his torn and soiled clothing. With pleading eyes, the youth looked up at his uncle who merely answered with a firm nod. Reluctantly Jayce dropped the bundle of new clothes and pulled off his shirt and then his jeans, noticing now for the first time just how tattered and grimy they had become.

Standing in his boxer shorts the chill air wafted over him and he reached down for the tunic at his feet. Before his hand ever touched the garment, he felt thin fingers encircle his arm and pull him back into a standing position. The ragged little being began roughly ushering him closer to the horrible looking eye on the wall. Jayce tried to pull away in protest, but the tiny fingers were like iron bands and the strength in the frail looking arms was deceiving. Held in that grip like a vise, Jayce was pushed closer and closer to the ever-widening eyeball. It surveyed his face and body, searching for what Jayce could not tell. As the framed oculus glared at the boy he clenched his fists, silently wishing they were full of gritty sand to throw. Little Rag Man, as Jayce was beginning to think of the creature handling him, turned him around so that his back was now facing the staring iris. He felt his skin crawl under the probing gaze and then after what seemed like an eternity, Little Rag Man released him.

Relieved, Jayce rushed back to the center of the room and began donning the tunic and trousers as quickly as he could. Little Rag Man, the Eye, and Drayven all seemed to be locked in their soundless communication once again. After a moment of the trio's arm-flapping and blinking, Little Rag Man slowly shook his head from side to side as if answering "no" to the dark master's query.

Drayven narrowed his eyes and then beckoned with his arm for Jayce to follow as he pushed open a heavy door that swung silently on its hinges. Jayce was all too eager to leave this horrible room, but not before getting in a parting shot. As he passed through, he grabbed the thick wood with both palms and slammed the massive door shut with all his might. The crash was tremendous, echoing like a cannon blast throughout the dark corridors and chambers of the fortress. Even Drayven startled a little, though he did his best to show no reaction. Jayce now stood facing the closed door with clenched fists and smiled to himself as he imagined Little Rag Man writhing in agony on the floor, covering his ears with his tiny rag-wrapped hands.

A thin smile spread across uncle Drayven's pale face. His cold gaze surveyed the boy before him. "It appears we have been sent an unblemished lamb." Once again, he spun away from the boy and stalked down another lengthy hall.

Jayce followed in the dark train of his uncle's flowing cloak.

There was simply no other place to go.

HEIDYL FELT LIKE SHE WAS SUFFOCATING. The heavy humid air in the dense forest was like trying to breathe through warm wet blankets. Her hair hung in tangles and kept swinging against her face like damp spaghetti strands. Stomping through wet underbrush had turned her pant legs sopping wet making each step feel heavier than the last. The moisture did not come from any rain cloud, as the sky was clear, and the sun gleamed its fiery heat from above. Rather, it emanated from the ground, billowing upwards in steaming mists to form great droplets that hung like crystal orbs in mid-air. As much as she loved her brother and wanted to see him again, this trek was already proving most miserable.

To make matters worse, her father had set an incredibly blistering pace. His ground-eating strides defied his heavy pack and Heidyl felt her own burden bear down on her back and shoulders as if the weight had doubled itself throughout the past hour. Her feet and lungs burned with the effort to keep up. If this trip had been on Earth, she certainly would have collapsed long before now, but this added vitality they all possessed while on Haizorr was certainly being tested to capacity. She had been doing her best to watch the uneven ground and trying not to slip. The mere thought of trying to rise again after taking a fall with her heavy pack was an unpleasant one. She looked up just in time to walk through a low swarm of lazy flies. They looked like small brown grapes with wings hanging in the air like a clump of miniature helicopters. She tried to duck past them and quite by accident inhaled one of the floating insects.

"Bleah!" she cried as she spat out the foul taste.

"Try not to swallow them," her father chortled from the head of the line. He did not try to hide his amusement.

Jillian playfully chided him, "Thomas, you should warn the poor girl." Although, there was a smile in her voice that belied her gentle rebuke. She turned to her daughter and with a knowing grin whispered, "You should have seen the fit he threw when he sniffed one of those dreadful buggies right up his nose!" Both mother and daughter laughed, but kept their mouths covered to keep from inhaling more flies.

The path they took clung closely to the banks of a meandering stream that seemed absolutely plagued with the offensive, fat-bodied flies. Thomas and Jillian had pulled their shirt collars up over their noses to avoid inhaling them. Heidyl chose to battle the horde with a stout switch she had broken off from a low bush. She found that the horrendous little pests made a delightful popping sound when smacked just right. In spite of the circumstances, the young girl was now actually having a bit of fun.

Heidyl was still swatting and spitting when she bumped into her father. He had drawn up quickly and his hand was upraised in a gesture for the company to stop. Thomas and Jillian were standing side by side staring intently at something in the woods. They had come to a dell of some sort and Heidyl stood on tiptoe to see above her parents' shoulders.

"We're here," said Thomas, his head on a slow swivel as he surveyed the area. Heidyl had moved beside him now and squinted her eyes trying to guess what her father could possibly be seeing. Other than a few meandering paths that crisscrossed, it appeared to be no more than a clearing that was covered in game trails. But, the longer she stared the more she observed a sort of obscure order to the place. Vines and branches that would have ordinarily been haphazardly strewn across the forest floor were gathered and arranged in piles and organized by size and type. Lines and shapes formed from various forest materials giving the impression of an intended design rather than the usual chaos one might expect from a forest. Someone, or something, had built a home here. A flicker of movement teased the fringes of her peripheral vision and she turned her head to follow it. Her eyes landed on a dark hollow place low in the trunk of an enormous moss-covered tree. Heidyl thought she detected a shadowy blur flash across the opening but could not be certain. She took a step forward to get a better look, but her father stuck out his arm blocking her path.

His voice was a low whisper, "Don't move any closer. They don't know you yet." Slowly, he removed his pack and rummaged through one of the pockets for something. He withdrew a granola bar and began tearing it open. The crinkling of the foil wrapper made an awful clamor and seemed like an assault against the misty silence of that solemn forest. He handed the snack to his daughter. "But I'm not hungry right now," she said, whispering a polite refusal. She wondered how her father could possibly be thinking she needed something to eat at a moment like this.

Thomas smiled, "Hold it in your open hand like this." He outstretched his arm toward the view before them. "It's customary to offer a gift to show them you mean no harm." Heidyl did as her father directed and whispered, "It's whose custom—?" She had hardly formed the question when a whistling wind and a flash of pale green streaked across the forest floor toward them. It passed in front of Heidyl and disappeared behind a mossy stump as quickly as it had appeared. Her mouth hung open as she stared at her now empty, open palm.

Jillian giggled at her daughter's startled expression. "Speedy little things, aren't they?"

Thomas had smiled also but now a troubled look crossed his brow, "Strange, that offering should have brought out more than just one of them."

A muffled munching and champing sound could be heard from behind the great stump. After a lingering moment, two long tufted ears inched out from behind the mossy stub. Heidyl's first thought was that some sort of lightning fast rabbit had just swiped a morsel from her hand. But then a face appeared. A wide head set with deep green eyes peered cautiously out. The skin was covered in wrinkles and wisps of white hair curled out from under a light green head covering. The creature's small mouth was thoughtfully chewing the granola bar that had been in Heidyl's hand just seconds ago.

Thomas knelt slowly and spread his arms wide. He smiled, nodding with an encouraging gesture toward the little person. Its cautious and curious eyes suddenly went wide with recognition and a great smile sprang across the wrinkly face. In a flash that made Heidyl jump back, the tiny being streaked forward covering the distance between them in half a blink and wrapped its short arms around her father's chest.

"Tommy Big! Biggy Tom!" The voice sounded at once both childlike and wizened. Layers of green robes embroidered with ornate leaves and flourishes covered the small body. A brown sash met the waist of a sort of tunic, giving a formal and altogether ancient look to the flowing ensemble. Heidyl wondered how the creature could move that fast while wearing such a getup.

Like a grandfather who had not seen his grandson in ages, the strange little person began to pat Thomas' face with his wrinkly three-fingered hands. "Beensa longtimes, lets me give lookabouts," he said as he pinched Thomas' cheeks, ruffled his hair and squinted into his eyes as if looking for a lost grain of sand. Then he laughed. "Olden timer! Squigglies drawn lotsa on your face. Looken crinkly as me!" He threw his head back howling with laughter. Heidyl was still too dumbstruck to think the joke was funny, but the wrinkled little character had such contagious laughter that she found herself giggling right along.

Jillian knelt to join her husband in the joyous greeting, which to Heidyl appeared to be more like a reunion of old friends. Her mother was met with similar hugs, pokes and pinches as her father was. "Jilly Big! Biggy Jill!" Another ribbing gaff was made about how old she was looking, and the laughter began all over again. Heidyl felt a bit awkward as the lone spectator but watching the long-tufted ears flap wildly with each cackle kept her busy laughing at the absurd little exchange. Observing her parents interact so intimately with such a fantastic being filled her with wonder. Just days ago, she would have argued that such things could not possibly exist. Yet here she stood, experiencing the impossible in an impossible world. She shook her head, smiling to herself at the thought. Heidyl paused when she realized that three pairs of eyes were now all looking at her. She blushed a little, feeling like a princess standing before three kneeling servants, though one of them was standing at full height. Thomas made a motion with his hand for her to kneel.

As she stooped down, her father made the introduction, "This is our daughter, Heidyl." The young girl forced an awkward smile. Her father continued, "Heidyl, I'd like you to meet Tor'Engryn, esteemed Elder of the noble race of Logarthiym." A wide smile split the wrinkly face and he did a sort of bow while hopping lightly forward to take Heidyl's face between his stubby hands. Tor'Engryn's smile vanished suddenly, replaced with a somber stare. Like two shining jade orbs, his eyes peered so deeply into Heidyl's that the young girl felt her own heart begin hammering hard. Her face grew flush with heat. The ancient Logarth was breathing slowly, deep in thought while pondering the young face before him. Heidyl smelled a rich, earthy aroma on his breath, as if the last meal of the Elder had been a plate of flowers and seeds—along with a granola bar.

Tor'Engryn leaned his timeworn face in close to Heidyl and sniffed, long and slow like he was sampling the scent of a spring bouquet. His eyes widened even more and he spoke in a soft solemn tone, "Thussem Jilly-seed. Power of the Great One running allsover you!" Like a miniature doctor he turned his head to press a long ear against Heidyl's heart. He listened there for a lingering moment. Heidyl cast a nervous glance to her mother. This greeting felt exceedingly unnatural to Heidyl and had obviously set her ill at ease. Jillian only smiled and nodded her head to her daughter, assuring her that things were quite all right.

"Grand thumper tells much," the aged Logarthiym pulled his head back with a smile. He then lightly fingered the bracelet on Heidyl's arm, giving her a knowing look. "Says there b'more to see in you than can be seen on you." Then he threw his little arms wide and did his best to wrap them around Heidyl in a jolly embrace. "Welly welcome innit my homesome! So gladsa meetcha, Heidyl Big. Biggly Heid!" His voice echoed off the great tree trunks surrounding them. Tor'Engryn then made a grand sweeping motion with his arm toward the glade before them as if gesturing to a vast kingdom. Heidyl looked up half expecting to hear heralding trumpets or perhaps spot several footmen come to carry their heavy bags for them. Instead, the scene was met with a few lazy flies meandering from fern to fern. A lone call of what sounded like an enormous crow echoed from the distance. The clearing was quite quiet. The noble Logarthiym Elder waved off the lusterless moment and laughed. "Youscan follows. Mine's a'ready cooked it and tastes greatly for you! Come!" He turned, beckoned them to accompany him, and then took off like an arrow shot from a bowstring. Leaves and dust were kicked up into swirls in his wake.

Heidyl blinked and her jaw dropped open. "I didn't even see him move!"

Thomas laughed and just shook his head. "Fast little folk. Come on, I know the way. His home is close by."

One by one they fell into step behind their new host, doing their best to hurry along. The brief rest had given their muscles the opportunity to stiffen up, and they were all feeling like clunky, rust-coated machines trying to get up to speed after sitting idle for too long. Heidyl thought she saw the faintest glimpse of their new host on the edge of the wood far beyond them, but it vanished like a pale green vapor. "Wow! He is so fast," Heidyl mused aloud.

Jillian smiled as they hiked along, "You should see the young ones move. They make Tor'Engryn look like he's standing still!"

"Amazing! Will we meet any of them here?"

Jillian's brow furrowed, "I don't know. I thought we would have seen many more by now." Then to Thomas, "Where do you think the rest of them are?"

Thomas had been wondering the same and was about to say as much when he caught glimpse of the aging Logarth waving to them from a large opening that had been cut into the base of a nearby tree. The ample trunk looked large enough to comfortably hold all of them and many more.

"Welly welcome! We needs mucha chats!" He motioned for them all to pass through the opening in the tree. Thomas needed to duck a bit, but the passage was roomy enough for each of them to enter without ever having to remove their bulky packs.

They stood in a dim corridor that slanted downward. It smelled of damp earth and moss, but also held a sweet aroma that made one feel hungry. Traces of roots and winding vines struck out from the walls about them, but the floor was smooth and hard packed. It did not feel entirely like a cave, as it had a warmth and soft glow to it. The trio slowly unburdened themselves and leaned their overfull backpacks against a large root that had tunneled itself out from a low place on the wall some ages ago.

Thomas rubbed and stretched his shoulders as he watched their host peer warily out the door before drawing a sort of camouflage curtain of woven vines and greenery behind them. Thomas looked about, "Where is your family?" he asked. His voice sounded muffled in the moss-covered hideout.

"They is all coop flown," Tor'Engryn whispered as he drew away from the curtain.

"You mean, they left? Where would they have gone?" Jillian sounded puzzled.

The elder Logarth raised a thick finger to his lips, signaling for silence. With another cautious glance toward the verdant drape, he motioned them to move further down into the passage.

"We needs mucha chats about."

THE SHADOWY HALLS FELT MILES LONG. When they finally stopped walking, Jayce was nearly out of breath. Drayven had stridden the dim passages very quickly on long, stalky legs; never stopping once, nor did he look over his shoulder so see if his nephew was still trailing him. Fearful that he would get lost in a twisted maze replete with dark and sinister things, Jayce was obliged to pad doggedly along. More than once he was sure he saw sets of eyes leering at him from the darkened corners and yawning black doorways as he passed. In fact, the entire time he felt a prickling tingle along his spine as if something was following him. He would never admit it, but it was similar to the feeling he got when running up the basement stairs at home, certain that he would be grabbed from behind at any moment.

Only, here in Blackynspyre, that was a very real possibility.

The tunic and robe he had been given were far from being a perfect fit and sagged after the effort of jogging. They were uncomfortably hot and scratchy. At length, he drew up beside his uncle. Though the man had a formidable look, Jayce knew he commanded this realm and so took a small measure of comfort in that. Drayven now stood still as stone before an entryway of ornately carved wooden double doors. His hands were pressed together, and his head was bowed. His thin lips moved forming words without sound and Jayce thought he might be praying. As he stood peering up at the tall man's face, Drayven's eyes snapped open and he cast a sidelong glance down at his nephew. The man smiled. Not a friendly smile, but a smug and knowing smile. He unclasped his hands then balled one into a fist, moving it slowly toward Jayce's face. With a sudden motion he flicked all five of his fingers toward the boy, as if flinging water droplets at him. The young man flinched, but nothing hit him save a cool sensation that started at the tip of his nose and wrapped itself around the back of his head like a mask. Jayce felt his vision blur for a moment. The room wavered, as though he were looking through the heated air just above a flame, and then it stopped.

"Release!" Drayven's dry voice commanded. At once the doors before them opened of their own accord and Jayce peered in, bracing himself in a half squint in preparation for another horror. Jayce received a pleasant shock, however, as his eyes were dazzled by an elegantly arrayed room. Lustrous candle stands of gold cast warm light from every corner. Plush, high backed chairs were arranged neatly around a long, polished dining table that was spread edge to edge with food. Fruit bowls, platters of meats and cheeses, gold and silver goblets set upon white linen table dressings covered every inch of that glorious table. Music strummed from a high arched harp in the corner. A slender maiden in a soft white robe deftly worked her delicate fingers across the strings. She glanced at Jayce and smiled, her piercing blue eyes were flecked with dancing green sparkles. She was so lovely that he blushed and looked away. He wondered how such beauty could be contained in such a place as Blackynspyre. Was she a prisoner just as he was? Or perhaps his uncle was not as wicked as he appeared. The wafting scent of the feast before him drove all questions from his mind. Jayce's stomach rumbled loudly, capturing Drayven's attention. The lad gave a sheepish grin before clutching his belly. With a good-natured smirk, his uncle ushered Jayce into the room and drew back a chair for him to sit. The dark man then took his position at the head of the table opposite his nephew.

"Hungry?" he asked.

"Starving!"

Jayce reached for the nearest plate of food and dug in.

Drayven folded his bony hands and watched his guest eat.

THE FOOD WAS SURPRISINGLY DELICIOUS. Heidyl and her parents knelt beside a low, circular wooden table that appeared to have been made from the cross section of a great tree. She had tried numbering its age rings several times but kept losing count somewhere around the three hundred mark. She still had many more rings to count, but also much more food to eat. Ultimately, she gave in to the feast before her. It took her some time to convince her parents that she did not need to test her blood sugar or take any insulin injections for the food she ate while traveling through Haizorr. But eventually, the family enjoyed a combined sense of relief at being disease-free, if even for a little while.

Every dish, bowl and utensil had been hand-made from carven wood. The craftsmanship was impeccable. Fine flowered details had been painstakingly engraved onto the handles of each spoon and the outer edges of cups. The candlelight danced across the table as Heidyl inspected the etched bowl before her. While admiring the handiwork, her eyes suddenly went wide. She had seen this dish, and several others very much like it in their kitchen at home! Pointing at the bowl she locked eyes with her mother, who gave her a nod and a wink.

Jillian leaning close to her daughter whispered, "The Logarthiym are a very generous race."

Amazement hit Heidyl then as she learned that her family had been eating food served from otherworldly platters and bowls for years at home and she had never known it. She laughed to herself, shaking her head in comical disbelief.

Their swift host spread the fare with lightning speed. Vegetables were peeled, mushrooms cut, soup bowls fully ladled and mugs poured to the brim before the weary travelers had scarcely taken their places along the table's edge. How the Logarth patron had spilled nothing during his preparations was a mystery and wonder to all.

With a quick hop, he pulled over a short wooden stool and plopped into it, clearly tired. "Mine sorry so! Long times a prepping makes waiting bellies angry. Use'ta be done in flashes. Yes, use'ta." His once happy face took a sad turn and he worked a sullen stare into the steaming bowl before him. "Tis why Tor'Engryn is the nutsy lone leaf on this tree." He sighed again. The candles seemed to droop a little and the room felt as if it had grown dim and somber. The muffled rattle of wooden soup spoons was the only sound now as the company poked quietly at their meal. The sudden turn in their host's demeanor stifled the air.

Finally, Thomas broke into the silence with the obvious question now on all of their minds. "Tor'Engryn—what happened here?" He rested a caring hand on his friend's small forearm.

The ancient face looked worn and tired as he peered up at him, but the sad eyes were looking far past him into some drear history. "We's all heard it. Sang in our hearts a thumper big whisper! From the babes up to th' brawny green scouts and war-makers, all Logarthiym ears spinnings round when the Call comes in." He stared back into his bowl with a weathered frown. "I still hears it. Pulls to my heartsoul to bits! Down deeps." He pressed a three-fingered hand to his chest as a lone tear squeezed from the corners of his doleful eyes splashing into the soup. He shook as a sob leapt from his throat. Tor'Engryn appeared utterly forlorn and consumed with grief. While languishing here in his tree-home, loneliness and despair had latched onto his heart and became his sole companions for some time. He seemed utterly and totally lost.

Thomas could feel the little arm trembling and then his own throat knotted. Jillian and Heidyl both felt hot stinging tears of empathy begin to cloud their vision. Jillian's voice wavered, "Where are they now?"

The Elder sobbed out a pitiful cry. "Only he knows!" He pressed his hands over his face to recompose himself, then dabbed at his wet eyes with the hem of his robe.

"Only who knows?" asked Jillian.

Taking a deep breath and steadying himself, Tor'Engryn assumed a reverent tone as if reciting an ancient proverb as though it should have already been known to them, *"The One who calls is the One who calls. Be he calling one, or calling all, none resist the clarion call."*

Heidyl's eyes went big as saucers. "That's exactly what Justhynial told Jayce and me!"

Tor'Engryn turned serious, wet eyes toward her. "Then they's all trotted to the Caller's drum as well."

A shuddering groan filled the room about them, starting from above and vibrating down through the twisted roots below the earthen floor. Heidyl started at the sound, but none of the others seemed fazed by the eerie rumble that drifted beneath their feet and then faded. With a breath of relief, she recalled the strange fact that she was dining within a tree and the wind above had picked up, swaying the forest about them into a sea of sighing timber. Jillian's eyes were moist. Thomas still had his reassuring arm about Tor'Engryn, but a ponderous frown tugged at the corners of his mouth as he tried to reason out what was happening.

"But, if all of you were called, why did you remain here?" Thomas asked gently.

The answer came behind the breath of a mournful whisper, "Because I is too slow." He closed his eyes against a rush of new tears.

Heidyl was barely able to contain her surprise at such a statement.

The amazing creature before her moved faster than anything she had ever heard of, yet was accused of being sluggish? She was about to express this incredulous thought, when Tor'Engryn stamped his little booted foot angrily upon the earth and pounded the table at the same time with a tiny fist.

"Curses and shamers! Blast to bits and crumbles be these stickly leggers! For a million suns have I been fast as a flink, only now do the feets fail!" He turned and spat on the floor in disgust. "At the first I flew with the glory group as we's all chasing the Call. But then they was going by gone. All the chieftains and lorders says it at once as they flew by and away through the big woods. Words to me was *'Stick to the home! The Caller waits for none! You keeps it safes for the Big Return.'*" He slapped the table again, and then angrily dried away a stray tear. "Then, all the entire was off like shots." Silence reclaimed the room, save for the rhythmic groans of the windswept tree. He sniffed again, "Alone."

Their appetites, though ravenous only moments ago, had dwindled and the food sat cold and untouched. At length, their saddened host allowed his grief to pass and began to move about the room, tidying up and consolidating the dishes. Though he did it with a deliberate slowness—which was far faster than any of them could move—to match his melancholy.

Tor'Engryn's pace slowed yet more and when there was a lull in his work, Jillian cleared her throat to ask, "What did the Caller sound like?"

The Elder faced a rough-hewn plank counter top, away from the group. With trembling hands, he scraped and cleaned bits of food from the plates and serving spoons into a wooden wash basin. His small, gray covered head lifted slightly, and his long ears twitched and swiveled from side to side as if searching for some distant snatch of sound. "Like a bell. It rings to bring and to warn. Heards like a voice, like the Biggy Tom. Was bossy. Sad. Spooky. A teensy angry, per'aps. Hard to says it all." He sighed longingly, "Oh wishes could I go chase it!" He stomped his foot again, and continued cleaning for a moment more before another thought gave him pause. "We the Logarths hears best than most with these sound wranglers," he said as he waggled and waved the great long ears for effect. "But you Biggy types, grab at chats and whispers with your hearts. Mebbe you's be wrangling the Call withouts ever knows it?"

Jillian sat upright at the thought. The possibility had never occurred to her that perhaps they had been unwittingly following the Call themselves. Was some unseen force drawing them to some unknown end as well? Had their hearts not burned within them, driving them onward? She did not care to admit it, but cold threads of alarm began weaving themselves through the unswept corners of her mind.

Thomas shook his head and stood abruptly, thumping his head against the low wooden ceiling. "No. We started this mission of our own choice." He rubbed the rapidly forming lump on the top of his skull. "Our son was taken by the Lord of Blackynspyre and we set out to get him back. We came here seeking aid in our quest, but it looks like we've come too late."

Jillian had a thought, "But what about Justhynial and his family? They have been our allies since the beginning."

"Mom, I told you before, they left too. They nearly trampled us while they were following the Call," said Heidyl fidgeting with her bracelet, which had already become an annoying little habit.

Thomas squinted his eyes as if trying to remember something. "Don't they have a watchtower? I think I remember Justhynial mentioning that years ago."

Jillian brightened, "Yes! The Westyr Guard! Though it will take us miles out of our way if I recall correctly."

Tor'Engryn's sad eyes remained downcast as the family discussed their next possible course of action. He sat as if made of stone, gripped by a grave despondence. Finally, he spoke, "You's finds not but a shell is old Westyr. Your road stays full of empty steps."

But Thomas had made up his mind. "We can't face the dark powers of Blackynspyre alone. The blue watchers of Westyr Guard are faithful to their cause against evil. Perhaps they have not been so easily called away." He gestured toward Heidyl as she absently traced the enchanted gift about her wrist with a thumb. "If we show them that Justhynial himself has aided us, then they could be easily swayed to join us."

Without another word he turned to begin gathering his pack. Heidyl sighed inwardly. The rest and meal had been a bright spot in the journey, and she felt saddened to have to resume the harsh trek through the savage lands of Haizorr so soon. She could already feel the dread weight of her backpack dragging at her shoulders before ever putting it on. Even though the added strength of Haizorr made the burden feel much lighter than it would have been on Earth, the thought of carrying anything heavy was unwelcome. Her heart was already overburdened with fear over the fate of her brother. But her father was resolute, and at the moment she could think of no better course to offer. Except for one.

"Come with us, Tor'Engryn!" The invitation sped from Heidyl's lips before she had the chance to fully think it through. All three of them looked at her in surprise. In a blurred rush, the green-clad Logarthiym ancient wrapped her in an embrace that was nearly a light speed tackle. Heidyl felt his body shaking under her hands. At first, she thought he was crying and wrought with sobs, but a cackling laughter began pouring from him as if a dam had burst. The stray tufty hairs on the tips of his flapping ears tickled against Heidyl's nose and chin, sparking a laughing fit of her own.

Thomas tried to look stern at his daughter's brazen suggestion, but the upturned corners of his mouth betrayed him.

"Well, we'd better get moving then," he said with a smirk.

HE SHOT LIKE GREEN LIGHTNING OVER THE PATH. Heidyl shook her head again in wonder. How could anyone possibly consider this dizzying display of pure speed as being slow? After gathering their packs and reloading provisions, the group had taken the narrow track into the darkling woods heading toward the Westyr Guard. Tor'Engryn tore up and down the forest paths about them with all the energy of a nuclear-powered humming bird. One moment he was giggling from behind a trabalisk tree far ahead only to be standing beside his human companions in the next half breath. It was hard to think of him as being ancient at all.

In one of the rare blinks that he was actually plodding beside Heidyl, she ventured the question, "Just how old are you, Tor'Engryn?"

The little face wrinkled in thought for a moment and he puffed out his cheeks. "Mine thinkers says meh'be seven or eight hundred moonsies," he looked up at Heidyl with a grin and held up his three-fingered hands, "but mine's finglers isn't enoughs ta' counts real big!" Then he tossed his head back and laughed at his own silly joke before shooting off again into the forest like a cannonball.

Heidyl and her parents laughed aloud. His antics were as exuberant as a caged puppy being loosed from its bonds and now free to romp. She considered his words and began working the math in her head. Assuming the word "moonsies" meant a monthly lunar cycle, she figured Tor'Engryn to be somewhere around sixty years old. When she voiced her findings to her mother, Jillian gently corrected her.

"If we were on Earth you'd be absolutely correct, but here in Haizorr the moon is full but once every year."

Heidyl's brow furrowed again while she reworked the math in her head. Then her jaw dropped open. "He can't possibly be over seven hundred years old!"

Jillian smiled at her daughter, recalling the first time she had come to grips with the extended fullness of time in Haizorr. "No," she said, "he is much older than that. Your father and I figure that one year on Haizorr is roughly equal in length to two Earth years. That is, if you measure years the same way in each place, and only if you are on that particular world. Somehow, time spent in one realm does not affect the time of the other." Heidyl squinted her eyes, fighting the confusion. The universe seemed to be making less and less sense to her the more she learned about it. How could one spend more time here than on Earth, only to return home and find that virtually no time had ever passed at all? Would she end up being older when she returned home, or younger? Then a darker thought crossed her mind; if a person dies in Haizorr, will they be dead on Earth, too? It all made her head hurt, and for a moment, she felt older.

After hiking for several hours, the familiar discomfort of burden straps across tired shoulders began to make themselves known to the company. Though considerably lighter here on Haizorr than on Earth, a burden was still a burden. Even their fleet footed Tor'Engryn started to pant a little and had begun asking for a short break before huffing down on a mossy stump beside them.

"You's see? This is the why! Mine leggers gots so wobblesore in jus' a couples hops. They's all leff me. Alls 'lone. So slow-some has I become!" He crossed his arms and puffed out a long sigh, the picture of forlorn loneliness and frustration. Heidyl sat beside him groaning a little as she sat. A thin trickle of sweat had made a grimy path from her temple to below her ear. She smiled at her new little friend and rested a light hand across his thin shoulders. He felt like a trembling child beneath her reassuring palm.

"Well, I think you are perfectly marvelous," she began, "and you have a friend right here." The little Logarth sniffed and leaned his head against her, once again tickling her nose with his twitching ears. He gave a half giggle at the compliment and patted her knee with a small, wrinkly hand. Smiling to herself, Heidyl mused at the emotional behavior of the little creature.

Thomas allowed for a brief stop, taking the moment to rehydrate and gather new bearings. He squinted against the heights of the thick forest, searching for any signs of their destination through the dense tree trunks. He knew it was close, but it had been so long since he and Jillian had ventured this obscure path, that doubt began needling his heart. As a father, the drive to rescue his son felt overpowering. It fueled his heart with a flame that would not rest until Jayce was safe at his side again. But this same desire, he feared, might cloud his judgment.

He could not allow himself to imagine what terrors Jayce may be facing at this very moment, or he might stray from the path of prudence and lose him forever. The wiles of Blackynspyre were too great for a band of three humans and an ancient Logarth to be much use against. In his gut, Thomas knew they needed help, and a lot of it in order to be successful. But the time it was taking to gather the help they needed was wearing away at his resolve. With every fiber inside, he longed to be the hero of the day; to blaze down the doors of that black tower, casting down all foes and carry his beloved son to safety.

It is perhaps the same dream shared by all good fathers.

JAYCE FELT HIS EYELIDS DROOP. The combination of a full stomach and delicate tones of harp music had begun to dull his senses. The fair glow of the candles had dimmed considerably until the corners of the room were just barely visible. His head felt stuffed with cotton, like he had nodded off and was just now returning from sleep to find his wits slightly garbled. Blinking against heavy lids, Jayce scanned the room with tired eyes. The harpist still gracefully plucked the golden chords, the food still steamed and glistened with juices and glazes, and his uncle sat across the table from him like a somber statue; eyes closed with hands folded as if in prayer.

Jayce sensed a buzzing sensation around his eye. Feeling almost like heat, and at the same time it gave a subtle vibration to his vision. It was nearly imperceptible at first, but now had grown into an annoyance. His field of view seemed to obscure and narrow, like a cloud of insects had swarmed into his periphery and hung there like a million jostling purple dots. He rubbed his eyes, and instantly felt more awake as the cloud lifted slightly. He took a moment and studied the man seated before him.

Drayven's face was sickly pale. If Jayce did not see his uncle's chest rise and fall with each breath, he would have assumed he was, or was very near, dead. Sallow skin and hollow cheekbones gave a haunting appearance that was punctuated by the high ridge of a sharp nose. The man was large, but not as hulking as Jayce had first perceived him to be. A good portion of his size could simply be attributed to his apparel. His frame was accented by the way he had tailored his clothing. Layers of animal hide cloaks, rough cut and folded one upon the other added mass and girth to his chest and shoulders. The wide black belt tightly cinched across Drayven's waist gave him the appearance of a bodybuilder's proportions. Cross-woven patterns of crude leather strips sewn with coarse animal sinew gave the outfit a wild, yet intelligently designed ensemble that spoke of skill—and menace.

All this Jayce took in within seconds but he was constantly drawn back to the face of his uncle. With his eyes lidded shut, the wild fire and furtive glances were shrouded, giving Jayce the opportunity to notice just how fully the man before him resembled his own father. The brotherly parallels were unmistakable. In fact, the longer he stared, the more he began to miss his family. A sudden sadness swelled in Jayce's chest, but he was surprised to find that it was not for himself or his present plight. He grieved for his uncle before him. How long had the wiles of Haizorr twisted and hammered at his mind to make him this way? Was there no hope left in him that he felt the only remaining course was to grasp for power? In that moment Jayce desperately wanted to help the man. For that is still what he was—a man. Not a monstrosity, or wizard infused with dark powers. A man. More than that, he was family.

Without realizing it, Jayce spoke this tender truth aloud, "You're not evil itself. You're just like me—a lost captive."

Drayven's waxy eyelids snapped open with surprise. His eyes were coal black and Jayce gasped. Then the wide black pupils that nearly covered his irises before shrank back to normal size. In that instant, Jayce noticed his uncle's eye color was slate blue, like his own. Like his father's. In the same moment the boy also noticed a change in the room about them. The once blazing candlelight had gone completely dim. In fact, there were no candles to be seen anywhere. A pale slant of dusky light from a high window slashed across the rough plank table before them. The platters of food and flowing goblets of drink were replaced with crude wooden and tin dishes. Moldy bread and tepid water now replaced the vision of steaming piles of meat and thirst-quenching fruit juices. He looked down at his own plate of food he had been eating from and nearly vomited. Worms and maggots now crawled in and out of a moldy hunk of hard cheese that he had been gnawing on. He had thought it was roasted turkey leg just moments ago! Bile rose into his throat, but Jayce fought it back down.

Another change he perceived was the beautiful harp music had ceased. His heart leapt within him in a moment of concern. The harpist! Was that beautiful young woman also held captive such as he was? He whipped his head around toward the corner where her lovely form had been gracefully sitting on a stool, bent over the golden harp. Straining against the dim light he frantically scanned the darkness for her gentle figure.

His blood froze.

Three sets of bulbous green eyes stared back at him from the corner where the rapturous damsel should have been. Jayce went pale at the sight, instantly recognizing his three original captors. The ghastly trillych trio was just coming out of its morphed deception in which each of them had been posed in turn as the harpist, the harp, and the stool. The one nearest him rattled its leathery wings in a threatening gesture and gaped a wide mouth at him.

Its tongue was missing.

A sudden movement from across the table drew Jayce's attention back to his uncle. Drayven was gesturing wildly with his arms and hands now. His lips moved rapidly, spitting out low whispers of a dark and ancient sounding tongue. With a shudder and a flick of his wrist he tried to reclaim the deception spell he had cast over the boy earlier. Jayce felt something like a mist hit him in the face again, and for a moment, the room resumed its former glow. The scent of fresh bread and roasted meat filled his nostrils once more and the gentle thrum of harp strings resumed a faint echo through the chamber. But something about it all was not quite right. Jayce could see through the deception now as if squinting through a screen. He shook his head and rubbed his eyes, and the farce faded like vapor, revealing the horrific truth about him.

Drayven stood to his feet and glowered at the boy. He redoubled the effort, twirling his arms and hands about and viciously spitting the vile curse across the table. Jayce shook his head and stopped him. "Uncle, please. Please, just—stop. I already know the truth." Lord Drayven lowered his arms in defeat. A string of spittle still clung to his bottom lip and he was breathing heavily. His fists clenched and unclenched as if deciding whether or not to strike the lad. Before he could lash out, Jayce punctured the steaming silence, "What happened to you, Uncle Dray?"

The question was born out of more than mere curiosity. It was deep concern mingled with pity and compassion for the obviously tortured man. The man who was, and still is, his uncle. His family. Drayven flinched, taken aback by the heartfelt inquiry. He opened his mouth as if to speak and when no words came, shut it again. For a long moment, the two kinsmen stared across the table at one another. Every few seconds the ghastly trillych troupe chirped out a short chorus of wheezy notes, awaiting its master's next command. But Drayven's ashen face remained set in a stoic unreadable stare. Jayce thought he saw a pinch of sadness or shame cross his uncle's features. No sooner had the vulnerable emotion presented itself than it faded. A wry smile curled a corner of his mouth upward and a cunning glint flashed in his eyes.

"There, there, little nephew," a note of condescension tinged Drayven's voice and Jayce bristled at being called *little*. "Do not fear for my plight." His features softened toward the boy and his shoulders slouched a bit as he sighed heavily. "It was not always this way," he said while gesturing about the darkened room. He narrowed his dark eyes for a moment as if weighing his thoughts. Then, his countenance brightened. "Congratulations. You have passed my little test. You are the first to have done so. I can see now that you are a man of truth and have no love of secrets."

Jayce felt his senses prick at the mention of secrets. In an instant he recalled the years of his father and mother hiding the secret portal to Haizorr. The thought of shelves of secret scrolls and secret riddles in a secret room that he and his sister had lived above for years in their home crept into his mind. He hated to admit it, but his uncle was right. He hated secrets. Try as he might to keep the assumption at bay, he could not help but feeling like he had been lied to for most of his life.

Drayven saw the boy's furrowed brow. Sensing that he had struck a nerve, he surged ahead. "Tell me, Jayce. Has your father told you anything about me?"

Jayce swallowed hard. He remembered only snippets of his uncle. Shrouded fragments from a childhood puzzle of memories were all he really had of the man. There were no family photos with him in it at all save the one hidden high on the bookshelf at home. And mention of his uncle's name had not been made in a very long time. "Not much. My dad told me that we sort of lost touch with you a long time ago."

At this news Drayven barked out a rough laugh, "That's rich! As if I simply went missing like some mangy stray cur!" His choppy laughter clapped against the cold stone walls, bouncing around the room in hard, dry echoes.

Perplexed by his uncle's reaction, Jayce stood to his feet and tried to interject. "That's not what he said—"

Drayven held up a hand and cut his explanation short. "Do you really believe that one just wanders about and falls into this place like it's some sort of ditch in the dark? No, boy, you find Haizorr by searching hard for it or by being introduced to this home for demons." His face darkened once more. "In my case, your dearest Daddy drove me right through the front door."

Jayce tilted his head. He still did not fully comprehend what he meant and was about to say as much when Drayven erupted. Slapping a gnarled hand on the tabletop hard enough for the filth-encrusted dishes to rattle in the dust, he shouted, "Humpty was pushed! He never fell off the wall! I was tricked into this place and abandoned here to die by my own brother!" A shudder ran through the man as waves of anger washed throughout his body. The effect of this confession seemed to drain him and after a moment he hung his head over the table. His long greasy tendrils of hair drooped and brushed against a crust of moldy bread.

Jayce stared at the man. He had no words to say either of comfort or in defense of his father. He knew that his father was no deviser of malicious schemes. Was he? Yes, there was the secret of this place that had been hidden from him and his sister all these years, but that was for their protection, was it not? A slow gathering cloud of doubt began shadowing the boy's tired mind. But why had he not been told more about his uncle? Mom and Dad had finally opened up about Haizorr, but little mention was ever made about Uncle Dray. Was there a shame they could not bear to tell? Or a danger?

"Sit, nephew." Drayven's voice crackled like dry leaves through the darkness. "Sit and hear the truth."

"THERE IT IS!" THOMAS SHOUTED. The tip of a burnished spire poked just above the tree line in the distance. It glowed like fire in the reflecting sunlight. The other travelers all converged on the spot where Thomas stood to get a better glimpse of that hopeful sight. Tor'Engryn had to be lifted up like a child so that he could see what his taller companions were rejoicing over.

The group quickened their pace and soon crested a rise in the wooded path that gained them a better view of the magnificent watchtower of the Westyr Guard. Though they had heard of its beauty, Thomas and Jillian marveled now at how incredible the craftsmanship of the line of Justhynial truly was. Since strong winged beasts designed it, the tower had been built to truly dizzying heights. Rising far above even the tallest trabalisk tree, it enabled a spectacular view of all Haizorr points. Polished stone flecked with streaks of gold and blue shimmered in the blazing sun. The eight-sided obelisk stood like a noble beacon of hope in a wild land.

There seemed to be no lower entrances or stairways at first glance. The lineage of Justhynial's family was a race built for flight, so the top of Westyr Guard tower was a perch that could only be reached on the wing. Near the top, eight turrets struck out from each side of the monolith allowing the feathered warriors to bear a watchful gaze in all directions. The top center of the monument was a flat platform where additional sentries could rest or change guard thus never leaving the post untended.

Heidyl strained her eyes against the bright sun, eagerly trying to peep through the trees to catch a glimpse of one of them in magnificent flight. She recalled her earlier encounter with the creatures and the memory still took her breath away. Never before had she seen anything that was both terrifying and beautiful and she hungered to experience it once more. She could only avert her eyes from the trail for a few seconds at a time, for the knotted roots threatened to snag her ankles and drag her down with each step. Eventually she gave up the skyward glances in exchange for sure footing. She would just have to wait.

In a moment, Thomas drew up sharply and threw up a hand signaling the party to stop. The meandering thread they were following ended abruptly against a wide path. It was well worn and ran ramrod straight through the woods. Gnarled limbs of aging trees framed the passage in a wild, yet graceful arch. Tentative steps drew the group from the woods and onto the road. "This is it," Thomas declared.

"This is what?" asked Heidyl.

"Westyr Pass, the ancient road to the tower. Justhynial's family carved it out ages ago. The going will be much easier now. We have maybe a quarter of a mile to go and—" he stopped.

"And?" Heidyl looked at him quizzically.

Her father touched a finger to his lips to indicate silence. He felt the hair on the back of his neck rise in alarm. He took several strides up the path away from them to get a better look.

Tor'Engryn swiveled his ears in all directions, and then froze like a deer in the face of danger. "Feels it," he said kneeling down to touch the ground. "Shakings."

Jillian and Heidyl exchanged worried glances as they too began to feel a slight tremor beneath the hard-packed earth. The mild vibrations began building in intensity and soon their teeth were rattling amidst a rising thunder. Jillian squinted her eyes and looked hard down the path toward the tower. A cloud of dust was forming, and she saw the faint outlines of galloping blue-bodied beasts rushing toward them. "They're coming to greet us!" she cheered.

The traveling companions felt awe and relief as they waited for the arrival of the procession. It would not take long, for they were charging at full speed. Several shrill cries could be heard from beyond the tree canopy indicating that a few were also in flight, wheeling above them in graceful circles.

As they eagerly stood in the road, Thomas felt a cold sense of dread wash over him. He should have been excited, so why then did his skin prickle with sudden apprehension? His mind put the pieces together in rapid succession. This advancing contingent was the Westyr Guard. They are feared across this land as being the fiercest of warriors. What if they are not charging to meet, but rather charging to confront them? They could have easily misread the presence of these strangers in their lands as a threat as much as a friendly encounter. The thundering hooves and shrieking war cries from above deafened Thomas' ears now. A great swarm of blue bodies pounding the earth was nearly upon them, showing no signs of slowing. Thomas glanced back over his shoulder and saw the others waving their arms and smiling to welcome the herd. Heidyl was nearly bursting with excitement at the prospect of a second meeting with the glorious family of Justhynial.

But something was not right. They were coming in too fast.

With only seconds to act, Thomas spun on his heels and charged at his family with desperate speed. "Get off the road!" he shouted at them above the roar. For a split second, he saw his wife's face pale as the realization of the danger struck her. Like a linebacker, he neatly tackled the trio at an angle that spun them all tumbling into the bushes. Ferns folded and twigs crackled around them. A deafening explosion of hoof beats assailed their ears a second later, followed by billowing dust that covered everything in fine brown particles. Heidyl coughed and scrambled to her feet first. Streaks of thundering blue whizzed by at alarming speed. Above them, the heavens were dotted with the soaring creatures keeping pace with the galloping herd below.

Heidyl shouted at the top of her lungs, "Wait! Stop!" She inched closer to the road's edge, but Jillian reached out a protective arm to hold her back. Then both mother and daughter joined in shouts of pleading commands for the magnificent beasts to halt.

Thomas, still disoriented from the dive into the thicket, shook the dust from his eyes and tried to clear his head. The mind-numbing barrage of beats made his ears buzz. He cleared his throat and shouted in his most commanding of voices, but it may as well have been an underwater whisper. The clamor simply carried away all efforts to call to the creatures. He stood beside his wife and daughter at the edge of the road and all three waved and jumped. They were in plain sight now. As if in a dream, one of the creatures swiveled a head to look directly at Thomas as it passed by. Thomas thought he sensed something in those eyes. Longing. Understanding. Inner conflict. And then, they were gone. The dust settled, the screeches and hoof beats dwindled away to a dull hum, and then nothing.

Tor'Engryn slumped backward on the ground rocking back and forth. With tears trickling from his eyes, he stuffed his fingers in his long ears. "They hears it! He be clanging the caller bell and they runs to him! Mine hearers! Oh, mine hearers!" He seemed to be in great discomfort and despair. Hope ebbed back to a distant place away from each of their hearts as a new reality struck.

There would be no help for them here.

JAYCE SAT IN STUNNED SILENCE. The words of Drayven poured forth in an endless torrent of accusation against his father.

Jayce knew—or at least thought he knew—that much of what his uncle declared had to be false. He searched the haggard face of his bitter uncle. Looking past the pallor and etched lines of timeworn anger, Jayce thought he saw something behind those black eyes. Sadness? Despair? Broken humanity, perhaps. Either way, there was more to the man than he had judged at the first. The wheels of his mind were spinning wildly now. If what Drayven had just told him were true, even if it were partly true, then Jayce's own father was directly responsible for the mess he was in at this very moment. The boy alternated clenching his fists and then his jaw. A tide of acidic anger bloomed within him.

Drayven regarded the boy across the table. His story had upset the lad. The inner conflict played across his face like an old-fashioned movie. Before it went much further, Drayven spoke, "Again, I apologize, nephew, for my theatrics earlier. I needed to know how able you were to perceive truth before I bared my soul to you." A shadow fell across his face as a new thought struck. "Perhaps it is better if I show you." He rose from the table so abruptly that the heavy wooden chair raked the stone floor with a deafening scrape. Jayce jumped, marveling again at how unpredictable his uncle truly was. The tall man then strode out of the room without a word.

For a moment, Jayce assumed that he was leaving to retrieve some article from another room. But when he did not return, Jayce began to squirm. The room around him seemed alive and gave the feeling as if it were closing in on him. His spine prickled and the sense of being watched by dozens of hidden eyes pressed a cold fear against his mind. Jayce realized that he felt oddly more comfortable with his crazy host than without him. With that, he rose just as abruptly from his own chair, and with a clatter ran from the room into the darkened hall to find his uncle.

After a time of frantic searching and running through what felt like a maze of horrors, Jayce caught up to Lord Drayven. The man's heavy boots pounded a marching beat against cold stone. The stale air in the corridors was heavy. Jayce remained out of breath the entire time, marveling more than once at how anyone was able to walk so fast. A moment later, dancing light could be seen leaking from an archway ahead. Impossibly, his uncle's pace quickened as if he could not wait to reach its source.

Drayven soon stood before the archway. Framed in dark purple light he remained motionless, regarding the room, waiting for his panting nephew to catch up with him. A strange smile played over his features. "Here we are, dear boy. What you are about to see, no other human eye has ever beheld. It is a great wonder." He leaned his face dangerously close to Jayce and hissed, "So show some reverence."

Jayce gulped like a fish, trying to slow his labored breathing. He nodded and the two stepped lightly into the room. It took a moment for his eyes to adjust to the strange lighting, but once they did, Jayce turned in slow circles gazing in terrified wonder about the immense chamber. Cauldrons of purple flame bathed the blackened cavern walls in a sickly light. The room smelled like a mixture of pungent incense and death. A leathery flapping noise sang out from a dark corner and Jayce jumped at the sound. Three sets of bulbous green eyes gawked at him from the black and he backpedaled a quick retreat. Quite suddenly the rough hands of his uncle grasped him from behind. The man's strong bony fingers dug into his shoulders and Jayce winced.

Drayven hissed, "Do not disturb the circle!"

Jayce twisted himself away from the man and looked down. His feet stood mere inches from a crudely drawn mark on the floor. Lord Drayven raised a long finger and pointed toward the center of the room, circling his arm as if outlining a distant shape. Jayce followed his uncle's indication with his eyes. Then he saw it. A round pattern of what looked like reddish-purple paint connected each of the five cauldrons in an arc. Tendrils of inky smoke coiled from each flame toward the center of the circle, giving the appearance of a five-pointed star within it. Jayce thought he recognized the symbol from some creepy book he had seen in the library. Though he had forgotten what the emblem was officially called, he knew it was usually associated with evil.

Squinting through the smoggy air, his vision traveled to the center of the room where a trickle of soot-black exhaust poured in from a small break in the blackened stone floor. All around the hole were spatters and streaks of some darkish liquid. Alarm spread through the boy's limbs and he pointed.

"Is that bl—", he began, but Drayven slapped his arm down.

"Quiet!" He spat angrily. Then a slow smile curled the edges of his thin mouth. "He knows we're here."

Jayce's eyes widened in shock as the floor before them rippled like liquid. He rubbed his eyes and blinked. It did not look like it could possibly be real. Yet the hardened stone wobbled and bobbed like gentle ocean waves at their feet. A chill swept across his back, though the room was quite warm. The volume of thick black smoke began increasing, making Jayce's eyes burn. He reached up to brush back stinging tears and froze. At that moment the floor violently erupted into sharp peaks and protrusions all over its surface scattering dust and smoke everywhere. They crested high and then retreated only to reappear again in various places around the floor. Like a wild animal trapped under a bed sheet, something was straining against the membrane to rip free. Jayce staggered backward again, stifling the urge to cry out and run.

Lord Drayven caught him roughly by the shirt. "Beautiful, isn't he?" His tone was an awed whisper. When Jayce did not immediately respond he glared at the boy. Jayce swallowed and offered a shaky nod. Drayven returned a wistful stare to the churning ground and continued, "He's trapped, you know. Just like me. We are one spirit."

Still held in his uncle's iron grasp, Jayce tried to appease the man by asking, "Who is he?"

He slackened his hold on the boy's shirt. "He possesses many names." He began rattling them off, "Darkwyrm. Flame of Evyntide. Harm of the North. The ancients called him Darchlyte's Bane, for it was they who somehow raised this barrier against him. Even after he gave them the power of the sun! Such ungrateful beasts." Forgetting his nephew, he turned his full attention to the roiling bedrock, balling his fists and bellowing, "But their time is at an end! I've found the Thin Place and the Black Dragon of Dearth will soon be free." The floor churned and rolled anew, like a frenzy of sharks tearing at the surface of the sea.

Drayven turned to Jayce like an excited child telling a secret, "He's promised that I will rule, and the Hunter will rightfully reign the Order of Classes!" Jayce stared back at the man. He did not know how to respond. It was becoming clear to him now that his uncle may have gone completely mad in this place. The real truth hit him then; Jayce's father was not villainous or a liar, as his uncle had painted him to be. The man who stood before him now had somehow bought into a story of his own mind. *A story spun by years of staring at a smoking hole in the ground*, thought Jayce. Drayven gently placed both hands on Jayce's shoulders and looked him in the face. His features softened and his eyes glassed wet. His voice trembled as he whispered, "He promised I'll see my daughter again."

Jayce blinked. "Daughter?" He could hardly recall having a cousin.

The boiling floor behind Drayven had settled back down to a slow simmer. A forlorn look flooded his features and he dropped his arms to hang limp at his sides. "Your father took her from me. Stole her." His face made a pitiful quiver as if he might cry, though his eyes were quite dry.

He bristled inwardly at the false accusation. He decided he had endured enough deception and lies about his father for one day. Without thinking, he coiled back and shoved Lord Drayven with every ounce of his impulsive, wiry teenage might. Though the man was much larger than Jayce, he had been caught off guard and the blow sent him backpedaling. His heel caught against an uneven crack in the stone and he landed hard on his rump—just inside the black circle. Like a sudden tempest, the area inside the circle swelled and sloshed about. It was as if a massive hornet nest had been disturbed by a well-aimed rock. The air in the room became charged with a buzzing energy. Drayven was scrambling to regain his balance, but the undulating surface kept his feet from finding purchase.

Jayce was off like a shot. He had no idea of where he could run specifically, but he knew he had to get out of this place. He stole one last glance over his shoulder, catching a glimpse of his uncle as the man finally rose to stand. Veins bulging from his neck and forehead, Drayven's face was the picture of dark rage. Jayce doubled his speed and darted for a darkened archway that he had not seen before. It probably led further into the shadowy twisted labyrinth, but he no longer cared. Escape or death were his only two options now.

Drayven was faster than he looked. His strides devoured the distance between them, and he had nearly reached the boy already. Jayce put on another fear-fueled burst of speed, charging at the opening with all the force he could muster. He was nearly there! In a few more steps he could even the odds a little and perhaps hide or—

And then the doorway vanished.

It did not close, or lock. It simply was not there anymore.

Where once a promise of escape had stood beckoning, there once again stood the three bug-eyed trillych in its place. Jayce was moving too fast to make any effective attempt at stopping, and he nearly bowled them over. The wicked trio had just barely enough time to disengage their tails to end their cruel mirage and scatter before Jayce sprinted full force into the stone wall they were hiding with their doorway delusion.

There was a sickening *crack* as skull met stone. White-hot lightning bolts split his mind and Jayce dropped to the dust in a heap.

SO, THIS IS DEATH, JAYCE THOUGHT. Thick darkness wrapped him in an inky black blanket, dulling each of his senses. He felt like he was riding atop a cold ocean wave, yet his body was unmoving and lifeless as buried bedrock. Extreme sensations of largeness and smallness, height and depth assailed him in dizzying spells. It was like a dream, but with far less control. There was no up or down. There was no sense of being anywhere. His mind bucked against that concept, assuring him that he *had* to be *somewhere* or else how would he be having any sensations at all? After several long moments, months, maybe years—he could not tell—he got the notion that he must be inside of a sort of holding tank for his soul. Jayce wondered if his next thoughts, if he could call them thoughts at all, would determine where he would spend eternity. With a colossal effort, he tried to *feel* a prayer toward heaven to push through the darkness. The effect seemed to calm his breathing a little.

Breathing! Jayce thought. *If I'm breathing, then I'm not dead!*

Relief brought a wash of feeling to his veins. Warmth spread over him and he thought he might even be able to wiggle his fingers. His senses increased one upon another now, like light switches being thrown on in a sequence. Jayce almost felt like laughing, until the pain switch was thrown, and white spidery lightning bolts flashed across the inside of his eyelids again. He gasped and felt his fists clench. He tried opening his eyes and instantly regretted it. In that moment he almost preferred that indeed he were dead.

Some time later, Jayce stumbled further into a foggy consciousness and could tell that he was lying down on a hard, dirty surface. He heard water dripping into a nearby puddle. The sound felt deafening. His nostrils stung and the air seemed to scrape against his lungs as he drew it in. He dared not cough for fear of his throbbing head. The cold masonry beneath him contrasted with the dank warm air. A drop of sweat traveling the side of his face tickled his skin. Jayce cautiously raised a hand to wipe it away. It was warm and sticky, like maple syrup. Or blood. Anxiety struck him as he remembered where he was in that moment. Adrenaline coursed through his veins anew, causing him to forget the pain. His eyes sprung open. Well, one eye did. The other remained mostly shut, clamped down by the weight of swelling. Jagged memory returned to Jayce and he groaned. *Why must it always be the same stupid eye?* he thought to himself. *I really need to stop running into things.*

A loud barking laugh erupted nearby. The shock of sound sent new shards of pain through Jayce's aching skull. "Our hero lives!" came the taunting sneer of Drayven. Jayce craned his neck around to see where his devious uncle was lurking, but before he could locate him, three sets of leathery wings and clawed feet sprang upon him from the darkness. The trillych sat on his chest and grabbed his arms, pinning him to the cold stone as two long purple tongues probed and slapped against his bleeding face like sticky worms. Jayce thrashed about with his full might but was still too weak to throw them off. He locked eyes with the one that sat on his chest. It had no tongue. Baring its sharp teeth at the boy menacingly, it vented its malice upon him. Hatred seeped from behind its huge green eyes.

And then, as if on a shared cue, the three assailants hopped off the boy and retreated. Simultaneously, the pain around his eye and in his head stopped. He flashed out an angry kick, catching one of the trillych in the rump as it scuttled away. It hissed but continued on its mad scamper. Had he been quicker, Jayce might have realized they were running toward an exit and followed before the iron-barred door clanked shut behind them. In disgust he jumped to his feet, feverishly wiping away the sticky spittle left behind on his forehead by their putrid tongues. He managed to look up just in time to avoid the low rock ceiling—and another concussion. The swelling had all but disappeared and his vision had cleared. He probed his face gingerly with his fingers, expecting to wince in pain, but found no sign of injury.

"Amazing little beasties, wouldn't you agree?" Drayven leered at the boy through the bars. A gloating smile was pasted upon his cracked lips. He held a curved dagger in his hand, the handle of which appeared to have been carved from the jawbone of an animal. He loomed like a cloaked specter, absently tapping the gleaming blade against the locking mechanism of the door.

Jayce eyed the chamber, which was little more than a prison cell roughly cut into the bedrock. He tried staring past his uncle and could just see hints of purple flame and acrid black smoke. It appeared his cell lay adjacent to the "dragon room" as he was starting to think of it. The boy paced slowly, keeping a fair distance from his uncle and that blasted knife. The floor was dotted with watery puddles in several places. Scratching his head, he tried to puzzle out exactly what had just happened to him.

"Trillych are mostly known for their shape-shifting and healing tongues, which you so rudely removed from one of them at your first encounter," Drayven grasped the razor's edge of the blade with his free hand and jerked his flesh across the steel. Blood poured from the wound like a faucet, but Drayven's face remained a grim gray stone. He continued, "But they have another trait far more potent than these." He held his hand aloft and the three fat bodied imps sprang toward him like starving puppies. They whined and foamed at the mouth. Mucus bubbled from their nostrils and their impossibly wide eyes grew impossibly wider. The two trillych with tongues lashed them about like wild whips while the third one gaped its maw wide like a baby bird begging its mother for food. Their cruel master teased them, toying with their desire by keeping his hand just beyond reach. At last when their frenzy had reached a fever pitch, he unclenched his fist and let them drink in his vitality.

Lord Drayven let his eyes close and a shudder rippled his body while his mind molded together with the three slaves. Jayce nearly wretched at the scene. He tried to pull his eyes from the gruesome feast but could not stop himself from staring. At length, Drayven's wound was fully healed and the suckling beasts retreated back into some darkened corner. For a while, he stood there like a wax statue. His sunken eyes twitched and bounced behind gray lids as if he were locked within a thrilling dream. He barely breathed.

The dark lord popped open his eyes. They were completely black. Not black like his eyes had become obsidian orbs, but more like they had turned into two endless pits in the man's head. They seemed to suck the light out of the room. Startled, Jayce jumped back, bumping his head against the low ceiling. Biting his lip, he squinted against the pain and hesitantly returned his gaze to his uncle's face. The dark pits were gone. His eyes had returned to their usual disagreeable state, but the room still somehow felt darker than it had just a moment before.

Drayven was smiling now. "It appears we're about to have a full family reunion!" He strode to the bars confidently and gripped them as if he were at the helm of a great ship. Jayce wondered if he was going to try to rip the iron portcullis from its very hinges.

"What are you going on about?" the boy shot back with defiance, but still edged further away from the cell door. He really was in no position to stir up further ire against him, but Jayce was starting to care less and less about being on his uncle's good side. This place was a living nightmare, and he reasoned that if he were to get himself kicked out—or perhaps killed—by being rude, at least he would be free of it.

Drayven was unfazed by his nephew's tone. "Poor, poor child," his voice was condescending, as if correcting a naughty two-year-old. "You should be more grateful to my little friends. After all, they just healed you, even though you hurt them so." Jayce folded his arms and stood in the center of the tiny room, glaring at his uncle. He knew the man was trying to goad him into some sort of reaction, but Jayce was determined not to give him the satisfaction.

Drayven continued, "There is no need for the silent treatment, nephew. I have just read your thoughts." Jayce wrinkled his brow, and tried clearing his head, in case the man had recently developed some sort of Jedi mind trick. "Blood is the source of life. It carries great power. That is why my trillych are so drawn to it." Drayven turned his face toward them and nodded approvingly into a dark corner across the large chamber where they languished. "It stores memories, and even willpower."

Jayce stared at Drayven's bony fist casually curled around one of the iron bars. The man's laceration had stanched, that was for certain, but Jayce wondered how that created any sort of link to his own mind. He once again scratched his head and then froze when his fingers met the sticky spot of his own freshly healed wound. His eyes widened and his stomach sank at the realization. Somehow, those vile triplets had transferred his private thoughts to the wicked lord of this realm. The thought weakened his knees.

Drayven smiled a sickening grin, "I told you my friends are remarkable."

Jayce shouted, "You'll get nothing from me!"

Lord Drayven laughed, tapping a finger to his temple. "I've already got all I need from you. You are my calling card and you've led them right to me, stupid boy. In exchange for your life, your parents will set my servant free." He turned to gaze at the smoking hole in the midst of the floor pentagram. A gentle rising and falling of the liquid-like floor gave the impression that something lay just beneath, breathing in deep slow rhythm. A longing sigh filled Drayven's chest and he whispered, "Soon, my friend." Upon turning back to the prison door to continue his gloating diatribe, the man was caught off guard. Jayce had edged close to the bars and spat directly in the man's face. But before he could retreat, the cobra-like hand of his uncle shot between the iron gap and caught the boy's collar. Jayce wrestled and pulled, but Drayven's arm possessed unnatural strength. Drawing him against the cold metal, he painfully forced the lad's face across the ragged gate. Jayce grunted against the pain, but the defiant flame in his eyes never diminished.

Staring into the face of Lord Drayven was not unlike meeting the grim reaper, but Jayce could not help but smirk at the spittle he had left trickling down the man's hard cheekbone.

Drayven's breath was a foul vapor when he spoke. "You'll get to meet him soon, too. Not to worry." With that he shoved the lad backward, propelling him across the room where he landed on his seat in a cold puddle.

"Get your rest, my spotless lamb." Drayven jeered as he strolled out of the smoky room like a cocky prizefighter.

Still sitting in the rank puddle, Jayce stared at his own reflection as it bobbed across the watery surface. He looked tired, and though his recent wounds were completely healed, his eye still remained purple and bruised.

Mostly spotless, you idiot, Jayce thought as he gingerly touched the spot. *I'm probably going to have this stupid black eye forever!*

PART IX: THE CALL

HE HUNG IN THE SKY, CIRCLING IN FRUSTRATION. Careful to remain low he snapped his wings through the air whipping the treetops into swirling currents. How long must he and his kin wait? Blackynspyre was mere moments away, yet he felt a great compulsion to stay his hand and keep his enormous family corralled in this dark corner of forest. For fear of detection he only allowed several of the lead scouts to fly at any given time. It was best to try to keep their true numbers hidden until the intentions of the mystery Caller be revealed.

The sunlight was failing when the Westyr Guard arrived in full force, swelling Justhynial's ranks even further. Their mettle must have been tested to its breaking point to withstand the Call for this long. From his vantage point in the sky, Justhynial's sharp eyes could see their steaming flanks and wind beaten wings. They were worn, but the Westyr Guard remained ever vigilant and battle ready. His great chest swelled with paternal pride at seeing them step so proudly and strong, even through exhaustion.

One of the guard captains spotted Justhynial and winged up from the ground force to meet him mid-air.

Justhynial's deep voice bellowed a greeting, "You've made haste, my son. Does the Call still burn within you?"

"Great Father," the captain began with a bow of his large feathered head, "we held our position as long as we could." His voice held a tone of shame. "We had nearly reached this very spot when the Call went silent." He panted, drawing in gulps of cool evening air.

"You've done well," Justhynial reassured. "None can withstand the Caller. You and your brothers and sisters resisted longer than perhaps any creature ever has. Your honor remains true."

The captain relaxed at the mention of retained honor and continued his report. "Early in our departure, we passed travelers on Westyr Pass."

"Flora or fauna?"

"Twin legged," the captain replied. "Human by the first glance, accompanied by one of the silly Logarthiym race." A look of disdain crossed his somber features at the mention of the overly gleeful creatures. The noble captain of the guard had little time or patience for the kind of frivolity for which the Logarthiym were famous.

Justhynial whistled a low hooting sound. "Ah, the young ones have acquired a friend! This will be good for them."

The wind shifted and the captain flapped his sturdy wings against the gust to steady his great blue body. "Nay, Father. There was but one young among them. A maiden, accompanied by two elder humans."

The great patron of the feathered highborn race gave pause at the news. A low cooing issued from his throat while he processed and pondered. At length he mused, "The Caller indeed be calling all. This explains the pause in your Call, my child. Whoever the Caller may be, is selecting the proper pawns for the great match. Haizorr is no natural home to humankind. If these humans you speak of have too been called, then they have heard it from beyond the walls of this realm."

Night slowly crept upon the vale like a seeping swamp and the shadows lengthened. Justhynial gazed lovingly across the great herd of his family below. They circled and stamped in the brambles preparing to bed down for the evening. The young had nestled against their mothers for warmth and the weary warriors huddled together in quiet, restful groups. Even the mid-air meeting that had begun in paling sunlight had grown dusky and cool.

Justhynial and his captain felt the night chill making their feathers grow stiff. Their breath gathered and swirled in steamy puffs about them.

"Good captain," Justhynial continued, "take your rest. You've earned it more than most. Guard your heart above all else, for I fear the worst lay ahead. I will stand watch for the night. On the morrow, you will take watch over the family. I've business to attend."

The captain bowed his regal feathered head before tucking his wings to his body. His massive form descended like a blue missile freshly launched into a plummeting dive. Just feet from the ground he snapped his blue pinions back open, gliding to a graceful stop. Justhynial smiled with pride at the skill his guard possessed.

They would need every ounce of it in the days to come.

HE STARED LONG AT THE EVENING SKY. His mind vacillated between exhaustion and frustration. Samuel missed his family. Not his birth family. No, they had exited the story of his life years ago. When Thomas and Jillian had first brought him into their world, Samuel had found his reason for living once again. They had helped him discover his true purpose. Being a man of high honor, yet few words, he regretted that he had oft overlooked telling them how much they meant to him.

And now, he had gone away from them.

Just like that, in a moment of indiscretion, raw emotion and impulsive behavior he had ruptured the balance of life. Perhaps it had only been a matter of time before it would happen anyhow. The three of them had been walking a tightrope of secrecy between Earth and Haizorr for far too long to think that any of them were beyond slipping.

As time would show, someone finally had.

A hot tear snaked its way through the wrinkles of his weathered face, moonlight dancing along the tiny rivulet in its travel. He brushed it aside with a large calloused hand.

He longed to watch those wonderful children grow up. To feel Thomas' strong hand clapping him on the shoulder after a hard day's work.

To hear Jillian's lovely voice lifted in song as she admired the flowers in bloom by the south gardens.

Samuel's insides boiled within him.

How could I have been so foolish to leave the Gate open?

Was this current course an equal folly?

He knew that in time he had to go back to them, but not yet. It was too soon. *Besides,* he reasoned within himself, *if I know Thomas, he has already begun looking for me. He'll find me. Seekers always find.* But with all his heart, Samuel hoped that he would not. He was not yet ready. Too much remained unfinished.

Throughout the night, the internal argument persisted, robbing the old caretaker from the sleep he desperately craved. Not only for the physical rest it would lend him, but also for the glorious respite it would have provided to his overworked brain. Slumber eluded him like a crafty old fox dancing just beyond a hunter's reach.

At last, the gray dawn and damp morning chill prodded the old man back up into a sitting position. Tired bones and stiff muscles creaked and popped in protest as he rose from the bare ground. Several days of roughing it through rugged country were beginning to take their toll on him.

Camping under open stars had always been a joy to him in younger years. Though his cantankerous mind was definitely still stronger than his matter, nowadays adventure seemed better suited to a younger body. He rolled up his bedding and hastily broke camp without breakfast. His joints loosened up as he busied about the setup he had arranged the night before. No fire had been made, so as to not draw unwanted attention. Samuel was not yet ready to be found.

The great fiery disk of a sun began peering through the misty trees. Urgency welled within him as he cinched the final straps of his pack. He really needed to be moving on.

Motion caught his peripheral vision and he startled. Appearing like a serene spirit from the mists that had formed between the damp tree trunks, Samuel's mount strode toward him. For the second morning in a row, the faithful creature had returned just as Samuel had risen from sleep. He shook his head at the display of impeccable timing. Taking an apple he had packed for the beast, he smiled as he patted the animal's side good-naturedly.

The great hoof pawed impatiently at the earth.

"You're ready, too, eh?"

He held the polished red fruit up for his ride to inspect. The great mouth swallowed the apple in one bite. Then, pausing mid chew, it tossed its head up and then back down as if signaling an answer to his question. Samuel chuckled as he swung his pack across the beast's strong back.

With practiced ease, even for an older gentleman such as he, Samuel swung up onto its back like a leather-skinned cowboy.

Without a word of command, the duo rode off, threading through the misty trees like a silent ghost rider. Their destination was clear, and the compass was already set for both of them. In a moment, the light-stepping through the bushes gathered fervor and pace. Soon, a thrashing gallop ensued, and Samuel gripped tighter to the thrumming body beneath him. Wind whipped his gray hair and his eyes watered, but he set his jaw firm to the unknown task that lay ahead.

Passion flamed anew within his heart and he felt the years melt away in a second. The beast beneath him lengthened stride and they flew along the ground. So. He felt it, too. As if they had both had been called to perform some great work.

And time was fleeting.

WESTYR GUARD TOWER FELT LIKE A COLD TOMB. Heidyl's tired eyes opened to stare at a high polished stone dome. She was disoriented at first. The eight-sided room had an impossibly high ceiling and her eyes struggled to adjust to the perspective. It was still dark, but the moonlight playing over the magnificent reflecting stones allowed her to see a little.

Thomas and Jillian had decided the night before that the family needed to pitch camp and regroup after their disappointing discovery of the empty tower and the mad charge of the Westyr Guard. They had reached the fortress too late in the day to embark any further unaided, and Haizorr nights could be treacherous with the realm's own special blend of nocturnal beasts prowling about. Heidyl was relieved at the decision to pitch camp. Though she wanted to rescue her brother more than anything, she had been anxious about what new monsters might lurk about them in the dark woods. She was grateful for the cover of the magnificent tower. The noble race that occupied this region seemed to affect the atmosphere. She felt safer now than at any other point in her journey through Haizorr. She allowed her eyes to close again and dozed nestled against her mother.

Upon first reaching the monolithic foundation, the company had halted in awe, each in turn leaning far back to gaze upward toward the precipice. Though each strained their eyes to the limit, the blazing spire was too tall to see from the low angle. Jillian fondly rested her hand against one of the massive stones that made up the groundwork of the structure. It was polished smooth as glass. How any beast, or group of beasts for that matter, could have placed it with such precision was astounding. After admiring the workmanship for a moment more, Thomas took to striding about the stone base looking for a possible entrance. Estimating that it would take him at least five minutes to walk about the perimeter, he instructed the company to rest.

Tor'Engryn spoke up with a wrinkly grin, "Mines allreddy dunsa dash abouts! There be a biggy door on the flipper-side! Follows mine." And then, he was gone. Presumably rocketing to the other side of the tower.

Thomas laughed and shook his head, amused. He had not even seen the little Logarth go in the first place but was glad the search for the night's lodging was already finished. He glanced up at the sinking sun and beckoned his wife and daughter to follow. Jillian's face looked grim and tired. Worry lines were wearing furrows across her face. Her husband waited for her to reach his side before walking further.

He grasped her slender hand with his. "We'll find him."

Jillian smiled weakly and nodded but did not reply. She knew he was worried about Jayce, too, but she was grateful for his strength and energy at a time like this. The unknown was tearing at her heart. A great mix of emotions had begun swelling within her like a tempest and Jillian felt if she voiced any of them, she would burst into tears. Absently, she reached a hand up to her neckline to steady her nerves by worrying at the key pendant that had always hung there.

A moment's panic struck when her probing fingers found it missing. The next second flooded her with instant relief as she recalled that she had given it to her daughter. Jillian stole a sideways glance at Heidyl who marched beside her in silence. There, twiddled between her daughter's fingers, the ancient key was receiving the usual treatment. Nervous rubbing.

Heidyl noticed her mother looking at her and gave a distracted sort of smile. "I'm nervous about Jayce, Mom."

Jillian swallowed back the lump in her own throat and took Heidyl's hand. "Me, too, sweetheart," was all she could manage before the lump returned. With all her might Jillian fought back the cascade of tears that she knew stood ready to follow. It would do none of them any good for her to come unglued just now. The family walked the rest of the way in silence, hand in hand.

Rounding the back of the structure, they found Tor'Engryn sitting lazily on a small rock that was propped against the foundation. Upon seeing them, he jumped to his feet and threw his arms up, waving them about emphatically. "What's tookcha so longstime? Mines allsreddy takes triple naps!" Despite the somber mood, all three family members smiled at the Logarthiym ancient's funny antics. In a flash he darted through a tall archway that had been built into the base of Westyr Guard tower.

The room should have been very dark. But the stones that made up the interior seemed to bend and reflect light in such a way that nearly every corner was visible and clear. The chamber was devoid of any furnishings or filigree, save one massive circular table in the center of the floor. There appeared to be perches of some sort sticking out from the walls at various intervals. They looked like great flat stone diving boards. It seemed as if this great hall were some sort of assembly room or meeting chamber for the guards to hold conference. The ceiling was indeed high enough for the winged creatures to fly about and hover should the need arise.

It was here that the small group pitched their camp; in the great hall of the noble Westyr Guard. After milling about for a few moments in awe and wonder at the vast interior, they set about preparing a simple evening meal from the stores of food that Tor'Engryn had provided for them.

Before long the evening chill crept across the room as the dual moons began casting their blue and green light over the land. The group huddled closer for warmth. Heidyl lay on her bedroll beside Jillian, resting her tired head on her mother's lap. Jillian stroked her daughter's hair, humming softly. If not for the worried turmoil in all of their hearts, it would have looked like a peaceful camping trip.

Thomas rose, peeking his head out through the great archway to do a quick perimeter check. He saw his walking stick still propped beside the door and retrieved it. Noting the edges of the moons starting to peek slightly above the treetops he frowned. *The darchlytes won't be able to stay in this area for much longer,* he thought. Satisfied that the area was clear, he returned to sit beside his wife and allowed his eyelids to droop a little. Jillian's humming was so lovely. Her voice comforted the company and they all began feeling the shroud of slumber grow heavy upon their eyes. Ancient Tor'Engryn had dropped his little head and appeared to be snoozing soundly even as he sat, a tiny wheezing snore whistled from his nose. Thomas smiled and shut his eyes.

HE WAS NOT SURE HOW LONG HE HAD SLEPT, but the moonbeams coming through the doorway had shifted enough to let him know it had been a while. The air was still, and night had fully settled over the land. Thomas did not recall lying down, or crawling into his bedroll, but somehow, he had done that as well. Lifting his head, he scanned watchful eyes over his sleeping family. In the dim light he was just able to make out the forms of Jillian and Heidyl lying huddled in a warm mass of blankets nearby. Their tousled hair and resting eyes made him smile. *At least they're safe,* he thought. He tried to avoid imagining the kind of night Jayce might be having at this moment.

Craning his neck a little higher he searched for a glimpse of their fleet footed companion. Where once the small form of Tor'Engryn had sat, a lone crumpled blanket and his tiny hand sewn rucksack lay on the stone floor. Thomas lie back wondering if the Logarthiym ever had to use the bathroom in the middle of the night like humans do sometimes. After several minutes, he decided that whatever Tor'Engryn had gone to do, should not have taken this long. He usually did everything at light speed. Thomas threw back his covers, allowing the night chill to wake him further. He was just standing to his full height when a strange flapping sound passed just above his head. A light gust of wind played in his hair.

"Gets you down!" The shrill voice of Tor'Engryn pierced the still air and Thomas' insides jumped. He ducked just in time as a projectile whistled past his ear thudding into what looked like a diving bird in the dusky light. The flapping sound stopped instantly, and the flying animal flopped to the ground by Thomas' feet with a light crunch. He crouched down to get a closer look at it but before he could bend his knees, the sound of a second set of wings filled the air above him. They beat the air rapidly, sounding like a very large humming bird. Again, the warning cry of the Logarthiym ancient sang out and another missile spun through the darkness, taking out the winged creature. It too spiraled to the hard ground, dead on impact.

By this time, Jillian and Heidyl had woken up. The commotion and strange surroundings immediately began disorienting both of them. Jillian looked up at her husband, standing rigidly in a defensive posture. The tension written on Thomas' face alarmed her. Heidyl sat up and rubbed her eyes. She was about to ask what was going on when a look of pain twisted her face. Heidyl screamed and began flailing about. "Get it off! Get it off of me!" She threw herself backward and rolled along the ground, shrieking in terror and pain.

Thomas was over her in a flash, but panic had flooded her veins, making his daughter strong. He tried to turn her over to see the thing that tormented her so, but one of her kicking legs caught him in the stomach sending him backward. Then the air about them seemed to come alive. A steady drone of humming and flapping filled the chamber, echoing against the domed ceiling. The room itself seemed to vibrate with the sound. Thomas squinted into the low light, barely able to make out the dancing shapes of several flying bodies. It was too dark for him to see clearly enough to fire his revolver at them, so he bent down to retrieve his sturdy walking stick from beside his bedroll. Then he got a clear view of the attackers.

Heidyl had suddenly calmed down and her mother managed to turn her over onto her stomach. In horror, Jillian let out a shriek. There, clinging just below her daughter's left shoulder blade was the largest insect any of them had ever seen. Long, hooked legs held it fast to Heidyl's clothing while its slick black and purple body squirmed and adjusted itself to keep from falling off. It was the size of a large lobster and its double sets of wings buzzed and twitched. The eyes rolled about like those of a huge dragonfly, regarding Thomas and Jillian as new threats. A long, curved proboscis stuck out from below those hideous green eyes and was now buried deep into Heidyl's shoulder. A bloodstain had formed on her clothes around the wound. Its ribbed thorax began to swell as it greedily sucked down the blood of her limp body.

Jillian raised a hand to strike the beast, but Tor'Engryn was on her in a flash. "No's touches it! Looksie!" Following his pointing stubby finger, she saw the object of his warning. There, like a tiny curved dagger, a dripping black stinger flashed in and out of the end of its abdomen. The malicious eyes wobbled and danced back and forth from Tor'Engryn to Jillian as it waved the stinger and rattled its veiny wings to ward them off. Heidyl moaned weakly and tried to move. In response, the insect tightened its grip, driving its feeding tube deeper. Tor'Engryn snarled and moved like lightning. The next instant the huge arthropod lay twitching on its back on the floor, black blood seeping from its broken body. The Logarth stood over it, triumphantly swinging his sling and stone faster than an airplane propeller. Jillian fretted over her daughter's pale from. Heidyl was barely conscious while her mother put pressure on the wound to halt the flowing blood.

A flurry of wings and buzzes dove upon them then from the ceiling. Tor'Engryn let loose with a volley of singing black stones that struck each target true. Black insects rained from the domed ceiling, each dropping dead with a small polished missile buried in its quivering flesh. His aim was unwavering and the speed at which he attacked had the effect of machine gun fire. Thomas busily swatted them with his walking staff holding back those that got through the perimeter of slinging stones. He struck savagely, defending his family with all the vengeance of a lion. Grunts and battle shouts echoed above the humming swarm as their numbers were cut down. Some of the winged horde had retreated through the stone archway, but most lay dead in tangles of twitching legs and tiny pools of ink-black blood. The light in the room had grown steadily as dawn reclaimed the night. The morning sun aided Thomas and Tor'Engryn as they hunted the dark corners to route out any stray insects cowering there.

They had just finished clearing the room of the last of the villainous bugs when Jillian called out, "Thomas! She's stopped breathing!" Cradling her daughter's head in her arms, Jillian was shaking.

Though weak from the fight Thomas was at her side in a flash, but not before his speedy comrade-in-arms. Tor'Engryn's face turned grave when he saw the spidery black veins begin to appear on Heidyl's neck. He urgently nudged Thomas, "Turns her flipside! The poker nevers came out!" Quite roughly, father and mother rolled Heidyl onto her stomach. Jillian pulled her daughter's shirt out of the way and gasped. A festering black wound bubbled just below her shoulder blade. Something like the end of a small black twig stuck out from its center. Black and purple streaks spiraled out from the savage bite, crisscrossing her back.

With deft fingers, the old Logarth pinched the end of the mouthparts left behind from the bite and slowly pulled. Thomas and Jillian stared wide-eyed holding their breath as the three-inch long proboscis was pulled from her flesh like a black skewer. The instant it was fully removed, Heidyl inhaled sharply. A barking coughing fit ensued, expelling a black substance from her mouth and lungs. She breathed shallow and slow, but at least she was breathing. Jillian stroked back a sweaty tendril of Heidyl's hair and shuddered a sob of relief.

Tor'Engryn sniffed at the slick item in his hand and grimaced. Throwing it to the ground in disgust, he spit to the side and issued some form of Logarthiym curse that neither Thomas nor Jillian could understand. "Hatefuls and gorbleshucks! Mine hates them all to bits!" Then, turning a compassionate eye toward the young girl he said, "Gotsa gets 'em healers. Soon she'll being weakers than a skinny plimpkin." Without another word, he dashed toward the open door and was gone.

Together, Thomas and Jillian beheld their wounded daughter. The blackened veins on her neck and back were fading, but very slowly. Heidyl's breathing was still shallow and her fingers twitched every few moments.

Thomas hung his head and breathed a ragged whisper, "We never should have brought her here." Jillian's silence was answer enough. She felt the bitter moment as if she too had been stung. Pain and despair threatened to choke out what little strength she had remaining.

Suddenly, Thomas smacked the heel of his hand against his forehead. "I'm an idiot!" Jillian jumped at the sudden outburst and stared at him with wide eyes while he jumped to his feet and began rummaging through his backpack like a whirlwind. Presently he withdrew a writhing plastic bag. "How could I have forgotten?" He indicated to Jillian to turn Heidyl over once more. Pulling the slick purple trillych tongue from the bag, Thomas applied it directly to the swollen bite on his daughter's back. Jillian pulled Heidyl's shirt back so he could reach the wound. Though she was repulsed by the thought of the hideous appendage pressed against her daughter's skin, Jillian knew it might just help to save her life. Sure enough, in the space of a few seconds, the wound closed, and color began returning to the site. Thomas stuffed the tongue back in the bag and sealed it away before helping Jillian return Heidyl to a resting position. Both felt completely helpless as they stared at their ailing daughter.

"She's still not breathing very well," Jillian's trembling voice declared into the stillness. Beads of perspiration were forming across Heidyl's forehead now, indication of a fever spreading through her body. Thomas closed his hands over that of his little girl. Her limp fingers felt cold and lifeless. With an aching heart he began uttering the desperate prayers of a father. Though faith should have kept him hopeful, immediate doubt assailed him. *Would God even bother with the prayers of a man like me?*

"This is all my fault," he sighed.

Jillian lightly rested a hand on his shoulder. "You could not have expected something like this." Her soothing voice should have stilled him, but it only added weight to his accusation. "Why would you say something like that?"

Thomas paused a moment, listening to his daughter's labored breathing whistle from her mouth like stale wind through dry leaves. Every wheezing breath seemed to say *your-fault—your-fault—your-fault.*

He shook his head at his own foolishness and whispered, "Because

I think I know who the previous owner of that summon scroll is." Thomas cleared his throat. "He's found our family. Now he has both scrolls." He paused, "And our son."

Heidyl moaned once in the stillness and both parents leaned in to her, willing her to mend. Praying for her eyes to flutter open. But her labored breathing returned, and she lay still on the hard stone.

After a moment, Thomas continued, "I used to have hope that when I found him, we'd just pick up where we left off. Maybe be able to put our differences aside. But then when we never saw any trace of him, I just resigned myself that he was probably long dead." He roughly kicked away one of the dead insects lying nearest to him. "I never would have guessed this to be his fate."

Jillian sat in stunned silence as a long-buried memory resurfaced. Her eyes went wide, "Wait. You mean to tell me you've found him? After all these years? On Haizorr of all places?"

"It's the only story that fits. I don't know who else it could have been. It has got to be him."

Jillian's mind instantly filled with a thousand questions. She reached for the one that sounded the least painful. "But, aren't you glad to know he's alive at least?" She forced her voice to be hopeful.

"If it's really him, then he's changed. He's nothing like us, at least, not anymore. Haizorr has been his prison and my foolish mistake has been his jailer."

Jillian was perplexed, "What do you mean? How would he even get to Haizorr in the first place?"

Thomas shuddered and reached for her hand. It was more to comfort himself than her, and he knew it. Guilt squeezed his chest and a nauseous wave flip-flopped his stomach. Thomas drew in a deep, shaky breath. He had withheld the truth from his wife and now after all these years, it was time for him to tell Jillian how he had lost his own brother to the horrific, wonderful world beyond.

Shame tinged his every word as he recounted the tale to his darling, trusting Jillian. He had kept the story buried deep within and veiled from her for so long he was not sure if he felt better or worse for the telling. But after a few moments, the hot tears streaming down Jillian's face revealed that he definitely felt worse.

When he was done with the painful confession, a great gulf of silence settled between them. Jillian had never been fond of Drayven. They had rarely seen him, and never heard from him even before he disappeared. On the very rare occasion when he did visit, his surly demeanor always left Jillian feeling relieved when the interaction ended. But the secret life her husband had lived now pained her greatly.

Long ago, when she had returned from her getaway with the kids on that fateful night to find her haggard husband tearing the house apart "looking for Drayven" it worried her greatly. To make it worse, the ruse he had lived by calling the police and even reporting it as a missing persons case—it was all so pointless! Yes, she understood all too well the gravity of the need for secrecy concerning Haizorr, but he had needlessly born this burden alone. Another vexing thought struck her then—*What about their niece?* Still more questions assailed her mind, but Jillian had wisely learned to commit first to listening and then turn to asking.

"I'm so sorry," he faltered, "I—I need to fix this. I've dug us into this hole, and I have to dig us out." He shifted his weight, preparing to stand.

She paused a moment, then frowned. "No. No you don't."

Before Thomas could protest, she took his face in her hands and looked hard into his glassy eyes. Her stare was so intense that Thomas averted his gaze. She turned his face to meet her own once again. "We do. *We* need to fix this." Through the hurt, through the lies, she pushed forgiveness and love to the surface and Jillian tried to reassure him, "Well, at least the search for Drayven is finally over." She smiled lightly.

Thomas marveled at the amazing woman before him and felt the low burning ember of hope fanning to life within him once more.

Heidyl's rasping voice punctured the somber silence. "Who is Drayven?" she croaked.

She was awake! Her parents huddled over her. Jillian showered her with thankful kisses. She was so weak, but for the moment seemed lucid.

The question hung in the air like a brooding storm cloud. Though her eyes were closed, Heidyl sensed her parents' discomfort at the inquiry.

As the silence ticked on, Jillian looked to her husband, caught his eyes in her disarming gaze and nodded. It was time to come clean with his children, too. Only by facing his dark demons and exposing them to the light could he fully move forward.

Thomas blew out a long sigh and looked down. "He's my brother."

Heidyl thought hard for a moment. "I have an uncle?" Her eyes were shut tightly and her breath was a rattling wheeze.

"You were too young to really remember him. Jayce might, but he was pretty young, too, when— " he faltered, visibly upset by the raw memory.

"There was an accident and your uncle Drayven was lost on the this side of the Gate," Jillian finished for him.

"I was so foolish! I didn't respect its power enough. I never should have shown him like that!" Thomas' voice quaked with anguish. Tears fell from his cheeks as his grief squeezed his insides once again, wringing him out before his wife and daughter. He felt ashamed and vulnerable, but at the same time, felt a wash of relief. For the first time in years, those who loved him were sharing his burden of shame. He poured out the story once more.

Heidyl felt her eyes sting with fresh tears feeling the forlorn shape of her father shake in silent sobs beside her. She placed a weak, clammy hand on his strong arm and gripped him as he wept through bitter tears. A strong cord formed between them in that sacred, truthful moment. Eventually, the wave passed and Thomas dried his eyes, clutching his wife and daughter in a warm embrace. He had to admit; it felt good to let the secret pain crawl out from the deep hiding places of his heart.

Heidyl gave his arm a final reassuring squeeze before sinking into dark oblivion once more.

A SCUFFLING SOUND BROUGHT THOMAS TO HIS FEET. In a flash, he snatched up the walking staff ready to defend. With a sigh of relief, he relaxed as Tor'Engryn reentered the chamber, carrying an armload of what looked like a tangle of thin vines with small red flowers running along their length. Dumping them at Heidyl's side he then busied himself gathering sticks and small rocks. At one point he touched her forehead and clucked his little tongue like an old grandparent fretting over a sick grandchild. "Gotsa keepsem warmer!" he muttered while deftly constructing a small fire ring before kindling a blaze.

Thomas and Jillian felt powerless while watching. The cure for lethal Haizorr insect bites was beyond their realm of knowledge to heal. They were at the full mercy of the wrinkly creature beside them whose silly ways and darting movements were puzzling to behold. Worry and trust waged silent war with one another. Thomas prayed for her, Jillian held her, and together they watched their only hope begin mashing the red flowers and vines into a paste before them. Taking great gobs of the sticky substance, Tor'Engryn smeared it all over the girl's face and neck. It stank and stung the eyes like many sliced onions.

Jillian's curious concern interrupted his work. "What are you putting on her?"

Tor'Engryn smiled as he took another finger full and wiped it across the girl's forehead. His voice was a whisper, "Tis Lambweed. Lotsa heal. Covers much." Tears were streaming down the face of the Logarth from the effects of the pungent plant and his little nose had begun to run. He sniffled but continued his work, all the while humming some sort of lullaby that was part of his race's history.

After a few more moments, Heidyl was covered in bright red sticky plant paste. It looked grotesque, like she wore a horrific Halloween mask. The smell was overpowering, but it seemed to be helping her already. Her breathing had steadied, becoming more even and full. Scooping up the remnants of the paste, Tor'Engryn dashed to the door and smeared it about the door frame as high up as his little stature allowed. He gestured to Thomas for help, who in turn spread the rest of the red goo as high as he could. When they had finished, it looked as if someone had splashed blood all over the doorway.

Wiping his little hands on the front of his already dirty clothes the Logarthiym elder whispered, "This b'keeps 'em away. When's they sees the reds, they's all passes over."

Thomas nodded in understanding, recalling a similar story. "Like the angel of death," he breathed.

Tor'Engryn laughed, "These be nots evens close to angels! Buggies be devils and hatewormers!" With that he turned and rushed back to the fire to check on Heidyl.

Thomas lingered in the doorway a moment longer. His eyes played over the waking forest while his heart continued its heavy prayer. Movement caught his eye in the far distance, and he stopped breathing. Staring hard into the mist he strained at the spot where he was sure something had just moved. There it was again! Like a tall shadow stealing from tree to tree, something moved with great speed but with movements so fluid it was like trying to watch water flow downstream. And then he recognized what he saw. Long limbs and towering bodies merged with the trabalisk grove beyond. The darchlyte herd was on the move.

Whether they were obeying the eternal curse of following the sun or had been summoned to do the Caller's bidding he did not know. Just then, Heidyl moaned and he turned from the doorway to look at her. Jillian knelt cradling her head in her lap, while Tor'Engryn sat perched like an intent bird staring at her and whispering hoarse Logarthiym prayers. When Thomas looked back to the misty shroud, the army of darchlytes had vanished.

He decided to sit beside the archway to keep guard. Through heavy eyelids he turned to watch the scene by the fire. There was little more for any of them to do than watch and pray. Profound exhaustion hit him like a wave then. The night-long battle and fretful vigil over his daughter had sapped his strength.

His head dropped backward against the smooth polished stone behind him and he drifted off to another time.

THE VISION REPLAYED IN HIS MIND. Though it was much more nightmare-like than a vision. He had been much younger then. They all were. Younger and more foolish.

Jillian had taken their children to visit her parents for a long weekend. They were still toddlers, but she wanted them to have the opportunity to know their grandparents, who lived several hours away. Christmas and birthday visits were simply not enough to build strong family ties.

Unable to join them due to work demands, Thomas had taken the opportunity to try reconnecting with his brother during a few of the off hours his schedule allowed. He hated being alone anyway, and he had hardly seen his sibling since Drayven had split up with his wife years before. On a whim, Thomas called him, announcing that he had already bought Drayven a first-class plane ticket and that it was leaving in three hours. It was bold and risky, but then, so was Thomas.

At first, Drayven was thoroughly miffed at his brother's lack of fore-thought. *What if I had a doctor appointment? Or a funeral to attend? You can't just order people's lives like this!* The truth was, he had no real excuse not to go and it bothered him being caught off guard. And manipulated. He liked being alone and was greatly annoyed that his exuberant twin brother had interrupted his personal schedule of solitude. Reluctantly, however, Drayven took the flight to see Thomas.

The visit had been going well for the most part. At first there were awkward handshakes and stiff hugs accompanied by a few *You-look-good* state-ments. Both realized the distance of time and space had done nothing to improve their kinship. As twins growing up, they shared a natural bond sim-ply because of their birth phenomenon. They did not always get along, but *twinship* had certainly given them plenty of common ground. In their younger years that had been enough. Matching outfits, Halloween costumes of su-perhero and sidekick (often ending in fights about who played the part of the hero), and toys for twins like tandem scooters or two seated strollers had been early unifiers for them. But as they aged, their personalities and interests had drifted dramatically.

This could not have become more evident than during an early camp-ing trip the boys took together one summer in Maine. The outdoor adventure began as one might expect with their combined excitement and exploration of the great wilderness. They ran through the woods of their campsite climb-ing trees and turning over rocks. The palpable joy took a nasty turn when late in the afternoon of the first day young Thomas heard a garbled scream. It was unlike anything he had ever heard before. Fearful that some harm had befallen his twin brother, he bounded through the brush ready to come to his aid. Instead what he found churned his stomach. There, crouched beside a broken log like a vulture, Drayven sat hunched over an injured rabbit. Mixed shrieks of terror and pain rose from the animal as Drayven tortured the poor creature. The worst thing about the scene was not the writhing rabbit on the ground, but the twisted grin curving the corners of Drayven's little mouth.

Thomas had run from the place, covering his ears and crying. The event seared itself into his mind. He never fully trusted his brother again after that horrible moment in the woods.

Through the years, Thomas took a shine to his studies, sports, and various clubs, while Drayven enjoyed heavy music and lonely chemistry experiments. Their shared bedroom also became increasingly divided. One side a walled shelf of trophies and collectibles, the other plastered with scandalous looking rock music posters and dirty laundry piles. Though he never said anything about them, Drayven often glared beneath his long hair at his brother's display of accomplishments. He did not hate his twin, but he did hate how vastly different they were and the fact that try as he might, second place was probably the best he would ever be able to achieve. Maybe.

His hidden jealousy grew unchecked inside until it seemed to Drayven that Thomas' sole mission in life was to always outshine his older brother. He reasoned to himself that though they were born just four minutes apart, the differences they shared were nearly as numerous as their similarities—and the list was always growing. Blessed with charisma, wit, and a touch of daring, Thomas was generally the party favorite. No one seemed to care or notice when Drayven was around.

Today, even as an adult with his sprawling mansion and valuable artifact collection, it felt like Thomas was just rubbing it in. Even the family photos of Jillian, Jayce and Heidyl smiling back at Drayven through gilded frames as he followed his brother from room to room seemed to mock his own failed attempt at building a family legacy.

Now Thomas began going on and on about how he and Jillian had recently found some new artifact that particularly excited him. At first, he had spoken about it in hushed tones describing how secret it was and that he should not be talking about it at all. But when Drayven pretended interest

Thomas became all the more eager to brag about it and his tongue grew looser. He kept babbling on about Jillian's incredible code breaking abilities and how she had deciphered some magical gateway something or other. At that point, Drayven puffed out a scoffing laugh. Thomas had always been a little over the top, but the story he told now had turned ludicrous. Believing none of it, Drayven kept rolling his eyes and shaking his head.

"C'mon, Dray! Just trust me on this! It'll blow your mind."

He hated that nickname but tolerated his brother enough not to correct him. "Not this time, Thomas. I'm not falling for it." He spun on his heel to leave the room and return to the coffee that he had left on the kitchen table. It was getting cold by now. He hated cold coffee.

Thomas furrowed his brow. He really wanted his twin to share in his recent triumph and introduce him to the fantastic. "Fine. I'll prove it." Thomas had then produced a long container from under his bed. The metallic rattling of the fasteners as he popped the latches gave Drayven a curious moment's pause, and he turned around to see what his foolish brother was doing now. In a moment, Thomas unrolled a small swatch of leather, revealing a crystal shard. He laid it on the floor and withdrew two scrolls from the metal box. He held up each one in turn saying, "One to let us in, and one to let us out."

Drayven laughed, "You're ridiculous." He turned to leave once more, but Thomas stopped him. He wanted so badly to mend the gap that had formed between them. Inwardly he hoped that letting him in on this fantastic discovery would change things between them. He had not had time to talk with Jillian about whether or not it was wise to do so just yet, but he hoped it would be okay.

"Look, I haven't seen you in years. This might be our last chance to hang out together just as brothers. I mean, it's a weekend that both of our wives and our kids are away at the same time."

"My wife left me two years ago, Thomas. And I happen to like being around my daughter." He frowned then, sighing between his teeth, "Whenever my ex-wife deems me worthy, that is."

"Sorry, I know." Thomas felt badly for bringing up his brother's pain so carelessly. "But you know what I mean, right? We are just two guys hanging out together now. Let's be kids again!"

"I don't ever want to be a kid again." Drayven looked around the messy bedroom. The clothes strewn everywhere, the bed lay in a tousled heap. He shook his head and laughed. "You're already halfway there. Look at this place! Jill goes away for one weekend and you revert to caveman mode!" He pointed to the rumpled sheets. "Are those chip crumbs—on the bed? You need to hire a housekeeper or caretaker or something."

Thomas waved off the comment, "I will soon." Then turning his attention back to the scrolls added, "And Jill doesn't need to know about any of our conversation or what I'm going to show you. Nobody does. Got it?"

Drayven mockingly drew an X across his chest. "Cross my heart, hope to die, stick a pencil in my eye." He decided then to play along, if only to get his brother to shut up and return to sanity.

Thomas gave him a stern look, "I mean it, Dray. No one."

Drayven held up both hands, "Okay, okay. Not a word."

Thomas unrolled one of the tattered scrolls on his bedroom floor and rotated the crystal shard beside it. When the crystal began to glow, his brother let out a mocking, "Oh, wow. You're right. Now I do feel like I'm nine years old!"

Ignoring him, Thomas whispered something toward the floor that Drayven could not quite make out. Then, picking up the scrolls he walked in a wide circle to the other side of the room. "Come here, big brother, I want to show you something." He beckoned with his hand.

"The smirk on your face tells me I probably shouldn't."

Thomas baited him, "Then come here and wipe it off me!"

His brother blinked at the unexpected challenge. "What is wrong with you?"

"Nothing. Except I'm better than you, and Mom loves me more."

"She does not. This is stupid." Again, he turned to leave.

Thomas smiled. His little joke was working better than he thought it might. "OK, you're right," Thomas shrugged, grinning and cocking an eyebrow at his brother. It was time to clinch the deal. "But I've got your phone." He held up the device waving it back and forth as if luring a fish. He had swiped it from the kitchen table on their way up to the bedroom without

Drayven noticing.

Drayven, reaching for his back pocket, looked shocked. "How did you...? Hey! Give that back!"

"Come take it."

The game had grown beyond annoying. Drayven was not known for his patience, and Thomas knew he had finally cornered him. He began swiping his fingers across the screen. He tapped the surface. "Interesting conversation. Who is Stacy? She's pretty!"

That did it. With a lunge, the elder twin launched himself at his brother. However, when his foot landed on the space beside the crystal, he pitched forward as if stepping into a swimming pool. In a second, he had vanished beneath the surface of the carpeted floor. Its surface bobbed up and down as if it were liquid.

Thomas laughed out loud, trying to imagine the look on his brother's face at this very moment. He imagined him on his hands and knees in the grassy field somewhere on the other side. After a few seconds, he decided to let him off the hook. Tucking the other scroll under his arm, he lay down at the edge of where he knew the portal rim to be and playfully lowered his twin's phone beneath the surface. He slowly eased his arm forward, waving the device in a teasing fashion. He expected his brother to angrily snatch it away.

Suddenly, a wet blast of icy wind struck his arm, wrenching the phone from his grip. In shock, Thomas recoiled then plunged his face beneath the entrance to see what was happening.

The scene burst upon him with fury. Rain and hailstones pelted his face, stinging his cheeks. A wild wind ripped across his hair pulling at his upper torso. He felt like it could drag him in at any moment, and he kicked wildly with his feet until he hooked his heel around the heavy base of the king-size bed to anchor himself to Earth.

Thomas struggled to make out what he was seeing. His senses could not determine which way was up or down. Huge tree branches rattled against the wind. Entire limbs snapped and disappeared from sight but were falling away from him. The rain seemed to be coming from behind him rather than from above. And that is when he saw his brother, hanging upside down from a thick limb about twenty feet away. He kept looking past his feet and yelling for help. Then the scene made sense. Thomas had accidentally opened the portal *above* the tops of the trees. His brother was not clinging to a tree branch but was actually wrapped around the top of its trunk. Drayven kept looking down trying to find the ground below.

Thomas had to act fast. He snapped his head back through the opening. Drayven looked up and caught sight of his brother just as he disappeared. "Thomas!" he shouted. "THOMAS!" Louder this time, but the wind tore the word from his lips dashing his cry for help against the bending trees.

Rope! I need rope! Thomas was running through the house and through the back door. The grounds shed door was padlocked, so he threw his weight against it, splintering through the aging wood. A coil of thickly braided red and black nylon rope lay across the hood of an old tractor. He snatched it up, dashing back across the yard to the house once again.

He tied one end to the iron leg of the bed frame and threw the entire length of rope into the center of the floor. It was sucked into the floor and pulled taut as the storm on the other side took hold. Thomas plunged back in.

The red and black cord was whipping about wildly but was long enough to reach his brother. Thomas tried to guide it toward him, but it was pointless. The storm winds were too violent; it would only be by chance that the rope would ever pass close enough to Drayven to rescue him.

"DRAY!" Thomas tried to shout above the howling wind, but to no avail. Drayven was looking around him in a panic, oblivious to the lifeline that was whipping all around him, just out of reach.

Snap! They both heard the sound and panic gripped both hearts as one. In despair Thomas continued trying to coax the rope to pass by his brother. Then, quite suddenly he felt a squeezing sensation around his ribs. It was as if a huge anaconda had just encircled him and was beginning its deathly constriction. *The portal is closing!* Thomas could feel the wind in his lungs being forced out. His head began to throb. With all his might he pushed backward, slowly inching his way back toward the safety of the upstairs bedroom.

All at once, both horror and hope filled him. He saw the rope in his brother's grasp, just as the tree began to buckle under its own colossal weight. He was falling, but he had the lifeline! The slack was being pulled as he fell backward with the windblown tree.

Just before Thomas was able to squeeze his head back through the portal opening in the floor, he heard Drayven's voice shouting, "Raiya! RAI-YAAA!"

In a flash, Thomas stood to his feet and began pulling the rope with all his might. He could feel the weight on the other end. Adrenaline took over and inch-by-inch he drew the cord closer. But seconds later, it felt as if his strength simply gave out. No matter how hard he pulled, he could not force the red and black strand any further through the portal entrance.

His hands were bleeding now, but he refused to give up. The sweat mingled with the blood on his fingers and his grip slipped, sending him sprawling backwards. He dashed to his feet to grab the rope again, but the slack remained. The gateway had closed about the strand, rooting it to the floor.

In desperation, he faced the closed portal and shouted, *"Dissere portas!"* To his relief, the nylon cordage dropped beneath the floor's surface again as the entry reopened. Gripping it as tightly as possible, he yanked with all his might. But there was no resistance, and he flew back once again, crashing into the nightstand table behind him. The portal had neatly clipped the end of the rope when it closed. He dove onto the floor, burying his head and shoulders into the storm below.

The tree that his twin had clung to no longer stood. A flash of lightning lit up the surrounding forest and the following crash of thunder nearly deafened him. He scanned the trees and nearby limbs for any sign of his brother.

Anguish rose up in his throat and he screamed it out through burning tears that seared his face.

Another thunderclap pounded the sky around him, rumbling an angry reply. *Gone! Gone! GONE!*

DRAYVEN, WHERE ARE YOU? Thomas shouted. Bolting upright he banged his elbow against the hard stone wall. A sheen of sweat covered his face and his dampened clothes clung to his body. His eyes stung. Had he been crying in his sleep? He became faintly aware of the person now crouching beside him. Jillian stared into his face and gently rubbed his shoulder. Eventually, Thomas felt his breathing still and his senses return. His wife said nothing, allowing only her presence to bring tender reassurance, and he was grateful for that. Just knowing for the first time he was not alone in this secret pain was all he needed for the moment.

He had pushed the memory of that horrible night to the fringes of his mind for years. He had never given up the hope that he would find his brother someday, but now the thought of what Drayven may have become was worse than if he had perished. Death he could understand. It was the close of a book. A reasonable end to the search. But the very notion that his own flesh and blood might be playing the part of an unspeakable evil was more than Thomas could bear. Sure, Drayven had a side to him that came off as angry. Even as a child he always seemed magnetically drawn to the darker side of things. *But isn't everybody?* Thomas was trying to clear his conscience. He could feel the accusing fingers of his mind pointing deep into his very soul. *This is your fault.*

Thomas lay back against the stone arch once more, still trying to steady his nerves. Jillian rested her hand on his chest and began to hum softly, trying to soothe him. They had been here before, especially in the days immediately following his brother's disappearance. That first night Thomas stayed awake all night, secretly opening and reopening the portal door, searching frantically for his brother on Haizorr while his wife and children slept peacefully on Earth. He learned a great deal about inter-world travel that night.

For starters, Haizorr and Earth had different time properties. Each minute that passed on this side of the Gate meant many minutes on the other side. Sometimes it seemed the reverse. Only when the doorway was open did time seem to lapse at the same pace. Once, when he had gone back to the shed to tie longer lengths of cord together in an attempt to reach the ground on Haizorr, he returned to find the sun shining where the storm had been howling just moments before. That was also the first time he could clearly see just how tall the trees of that forest actually were. They were hundreds of feet tall, and even tying all of his remaining ropes together would not nearly reach the forest floor. From his vantage point in the sky he scanned the ground, expecting to see the twisted and broken body of his sibling. Tree trunks and thick limbs lay scattered in massive piles like a bone yard, but there was no sign of the red-black nylon rope or his brother.

He tried opening the portal in different areas of the house in attempts to get to the ground level of the forest, but that only made things more confusing. In the living room it opened up on top of a mountain, in the bathroom it opened directly over a lake, and in the kitchen, it opened near the same tree where he and Jillian had first come through together. That gave him an idea. He figured out the exact position on the first floor directly under the bedroom where he and his brother had first opened the portal. He dropped the scroll and crystal and reopened the hole between worlds. His assumptions were correct. The Gate had opened in the same area in the sky above the forest, but considerably lower to the ground than before.

Thomas went to the basement to do the same and came out lower still. But not low enough to get to the ground without killing himself. Most of the trees had blown over, so climbing down was not possible.

It was sometime during that long night that Thomas decided to affix the crystal to the wall of stone that was positioned in the basement directly under the kitchen. It proved to be a safe spot to enter and exit, opening up at ground level within the trunk of the large tree with outstretched limbs, which also made it an easy to find landmark on the other side. He determined to make a grid map of the area and search systematically until he found his brother—alive or dead. He marked the words "Tree Gate" on the page and worked outward from that point into several directions. Over the years he had developed a fairly detailed map of the region.

His brother's disappearance into Haizorr presented another problem. It became a missing person's case on the Earth side of the Tree Gate. Thomas was left to decide between national—perhaps even global—security and telling the truth. Should he choose to come clean about inter-world portals, the Book, and deadly scrolls and where his brother *really* went would certainly spell disaster, or at the very least land him in an insane asylum. For the sake of the greater good, he decided he must leave out those details, leading the authorities to believe that Drayven had simply left Thomas' house without so much as a goodbye before vanishing. Which, he reasoned to himself, was not *entirely* untrue.

In the end, however, the authorities quickly ruled him out as a suspect. There was not enough motive or physical evidence to indicate him as such. He simply reported the case, gave his brother's physical description and that was nearly it. Most of the scrutiny was placed on the side of Drayven's ex-wife and former places of employment. With a long string of unpaid debts, bad deals, and other darker involvements Drayven apparently had a list of persons of greater interest than Thomas for the police to investigate. Despite his own guilt in the case, he marveled at how mundane and quickly routine the disappearance of his brother had become to the authorities. After just a few months, calls with leads and questions ceased and soon the case was all but forgotten.

The worst part of the story, however, was Drayven's daughter Raiya. Thomas had only seen her a handful of times when she was very young. It was during a weekend when he had a meeting with a museum curator about submitting one of his rare finds from the ancient Hittite Empire. The museum was just a few miles from his brother's home. Thomas had flown across the country and yet was still only able to spend a few hours with his brother and niece. Drayven's wife had left him about a year before, and he had weekend privileges to be with his little girl.

Raiya was a bundle of energy. Her tight red curls and jade eyes could disarm the toughest heart. Thomas liked her instantly. Sometime during that visit he found he wanted to be the best uncle ever.

Some uncle. I lost your dad and can't tell you where he is. Thomas' thoughts grew dark and loathing as he recalled making the phone call to his brother's ex-wife. The phone reception was bad, and he had to keep repeating the words "Drayven's gone missing," his own voice accusing him three times in a row over the broken connection.

The voice on the other end sounded cold and distant, almost as if she half expected something like this to happen eventually. Thomas knew the divorce had been painful. Drayven refused to talk about it. The tone of the phone call seemed to indicate relief more than sadness. As he hung up the phone, he knew he would never see his niece again, unless he somehow found her father.

That was over thirteen years ago. He had spent day after day plodding across the wild and untamed world of Haizorr searching. By some miracle he did find the cell phone that the storm had torn from his hand. It was damaged beyond repair, but it had filled Thomas with renewed hope. But that hope had waned thin with each passing year and each unsuccessful search. Given what he suspected now, he was not so sure he even wanted to find his brother anymore. *But I have to go to him,* he thought. *The stakes are too high not to try.*

For years he had anxiously yearned for the opportunity to explain the events of that frightful night to Drayven. This could be his chance to reconcile. But with so much time passed, he felt unsure whether a heartfelt reunion was even possible. Still he hoped, like he always hoped, that this would be the trip to end the nightmares.

THE FIRE BURNED LOW. Several times throughout the day both Thomas and Tor'Engryn took turns tending the flames and gathering firewood. The day had slogged by at a snail's pace. If not for the fact that Heidyl's condition seemed to improve hourly, the waiting would have driven the group to near madness. Out of habit and concern, Jillian checked Heidyl's blood sugar levels routinely; baffled each time at the normalcy that Haizorr had provided her.

The waning light brought with it a new dread to the already exhausted group: would the insects return tonight? Tor'Engryn was taking no chances and had begun cautiously retrieving his small black projectiles from the carcasses of the fallen attackers that littered the room. Each dead insect received a savage kick and a string of curses from the little man before he moved to the next.

A soft voice drifted across the still air, "Wh—what is all over my face?" Heidyl awoke slowly, her mind disoriented. Jillian, who had been dozing as she sat, snapped her head up at the sound.

"Oh Heidyl! Thank God!" She practically dove upon her daughter then, hugging her and weeping great tears of relief.

Thomas sprinted from his watch at the doorway to his wife's side and cradled Heidyl, uttering prayers of thanks and a few tears of his own. Tor'Engryn, sensing their need for a family moment, continued his work at a distance. Although he could not suppress a little smile of satisfaction and whispered, "Sees it? Mine toldya!"

Heidyl was very weak, and though she begged to peel off the stinking red mask of Lambweed from her face and bare limbs, Tor'Engryn would not allow it. He set to building up the fire again, insisting that she needed more warmth, though she could feel the sweat trickling down her back. Satisfied with the refreshed flames, he began pulling more rations to eat from his small sack and indicated for the group to sit and dine with him. Jillian helped Heidyl into a seated position and helped her drink a little. Thomas reluctantly sat near the warming fire, but his eyes remained fixed on the open doorway. The blood-red stains of Lambweed made it appear as a gaping mouth that framed the coming night.

Sensing his worry, Tor'Engryn nudged at him, "They's nots b'coming back, Tommy Big. Weed'll keeps 'em afar." Thomas nodded an absent reply, remaining deep in thought. Between the bugs and dwindling rations, he decided to lose his appetite for the evening.

"Be the sides," the little Logarth continued, "they's not forgets these!" He proudly held up one of his small black slinging stones for all to see. The firelight danced over its polished surface as he turned the small pebble fondly in the air. Jillian him gave a weak smile while Thomas, still feeling somber, grunted. Since Heidyl had been unconscious during most of the fight with the vicious insects, this was the first time she beheld one of the little rocks.

"What's that, Tor-Tor?" she asked. She had given him the nickname once while hiking and it endeared him to her. Tor'Engryn did not seem to mind it at all. He shuffled close to her and placed the stone gently into her open palm. Heidyl was surprised at how weightless the stone felt. It looked metallic and she expected it to be heavy like a lead musket ball.

Tor'Engryn spoke almost reverently, "Shatter shield. Scale buster. Itsa biggle tale." He looked up and smiled at Thomas, "Tommy Big tells it bester!"

When Thomas made no move to reply, Heidyl urged him. "Daddy, what is he talking about?"

He shrugged, "It's nothing, really." But Heidyl thought he looked a little embarrassed.

"Tis everything! Alls of it!" Tor'Engryn blurted in protest. "You tells it bester! Heidyl Big needsa chatsabouts." He sat down and folded his arms, scowling into the fire.

Heidyl held out the black stone to her father. "Tell me, Dad."

Thomas took it from her and began rubbing the smooth surface with his thumb, thinking of where to begin the tale. Like so many of his stories, this one too originated with The Book.

"Jill, feel free to jump in here, OK?" He tried deflecting to her, but she would have none of it and urged him to proceed. The orange glow of the fire gave her disarming smile a warm radiance that Thomas could not deny. A sheepish grin claimed his face and he nodded as he began.

"It always starts with the burning," he pointed to the area on his hip where his mark lay concealed by clothing. "Your mom," he said, gesturing across the flames, "felt hers going off, too. We both thought that was weird since it almost always begins with one of us first and then switches to the other."

Jillian nodded, staring as if entranced by the flames. Heidyl felt instant connection to the story at the mention of the mark she shared with her parents. She smiled as Tor'Engryn reclined against her. His sullen mood had vanished, and his eyes flashed with keen interest at the tale about to unfold.

Thomas continued, "We hadn't been to Haizorr in a while, and since time passes and crisscrosses so strangely between our worlds, we were eager to return so we would not miss any important events. It's a good thing we went back, because this ended up being a pretty big one."

Tor'Engryn was nodding, his eyes seemed to focus on something very far away in the dark but close to his heart. He shivered at the memory. "We's were one snitch-away froms gone be gones" he whispered into the night. He pressed his little body against Heidyl as if for comfort.

Thomas continued, "The Book was sort of sending us an alarm. It gives me the shivers to think about, but it's as if that thing is a living, breathing document."

Jillian interrupted, "Or perhaps just an open window between our worlds."

Thomas smiled at her, "Yeah, you're right. That sounds less sinister." He waved a hand in the air, "Well, whatever you call it, the Book led us to three words within its pages: Logarthiym, grave-hound, war." He swallowed, and the chamber fell silent save for the pop and crackle of campfire.

Heidyl noticed the little Logarth elder was trembling. She gently rested her arm around his quaking frame until he settled.

Jillian added a crucial detail, "Well, my love, that's where the talking Book ended for you. For me, it kept burning and calling. My head buzzed for a full two days more until I found the phrase 'black mine' within those pages."

"Oh yes, that's right!" Thomas then recalled the tale how they embarked into Haizorr the next day to see what the enigma meant.

THE BOOK HAD LEFT OUT A LOT OF DETAILS. Originally, they had thought that some sort of species war was taking place at a location called a 'black mine'. The husband and wife team had found the mine shortly after crossing over, but it ended up being nothing more than a ragged gash hidden in the side of a mountain. The mouth of the cave was studded with black stones that glinted in the fading sunlight. Thomas, fascinated as usual, bent down to retrieve a fist-sized stone to bring back to Earth to study. The Logarthiym camp was only a few miles from the spot, so they hurried to reach the safety of their friends before dark claimed the countryside.

What they found was anything but safe.

They could hear the shrieks and cries long before arriving. When they gained the hill, both travelers gasped at the utter chaos engulfing their vision. Logarthiym were dashing about like tiny blurs throughout their encampment.

From the tree-homes, shrill voices were shouting in alarm. A blaze had kindled and was consuming the side of one of the enormous trunks. The sound of tiny Logarth children wailing tore at both Thomas and Jillian's hearts.

But that was not the worst sound.

The high-pitched hunting shrieks of several grayvyks rattled the limbs of the trabalisk trees and turned their hearts to water. Squinting through the haze, the thrashing head of one of the huge reptiles could be seen tearing apart structure after structure in the once tranquil village. Several small bodies lay unmoving on the ground beneath its stomping claws. The peaceful, unarmed Logarthiym were under attack. The injustice of the scene was at once infuriating and crippling. The couple felt powerless to watch, and more powerless to intervene.

If not for their speed, all of the Logarthiym certainly would have perished. The quick-thinking little people had dashed about the surrounding woods and gathered lengths of vines. Through a massive coordinated effort, they darted and wove about the grayvyks, effectively entangling them and tying their serpentine bodies to the trunks of several trees. Though enraged, the knots and tangles that held them overwhelmed them. In a short time, a great chorus of victory sounded from the Logarthiym voices.

With the fire now under control and their attackers ensnared, the tiny people set about trying to destroy the beasts. Their efforts proved futile. The armor scaled skin and muscles were so hard that pointed sticks and rocks splintered and bounced off their hides. One brave Logarth scout dressed in green, brandished a torch and thrust it into the face of a nearby beast. It howled and snorted, but the flame did no real damage. After many more failed attempts, the tribe ran out of ideas and grew weary. It was decided during a brief conference of the elders, Tor'Engryn among them, to simply leave the wretched monsters to suffer and die from starvation. Though none of them knew how long that might possibly take.

The damage to the little village was extensive. Thomas and Jillian timidly stepped from their hiding place atop the knoll and approached the somber scene. Normally, their arrival would have been celebrated with jubilance, but grief painted a gray day for the Logarthiym. They greeted the couple but with sad eyes and heavy hearts. The stouter Logarths took courage from their deeds of fighting back and overcoming the enemy, but the mothers of frightened young remained hidden deep in the hollowed-out recesses of the trees.

Jillian knelt down to embrace her little friends and offer what comfort she could. Thomas conversed with the elders, in an effort to decipher what had prompted the attack. But there were no answers other than wagging heads and tiny shrugging shoulders.

Then, a distant howl froze the air around them. The green Logarth scout, Wista by name, ran to see if it had come from the new captives, but their mouths had been tied shut by coils of tough vines. They were silent, but a new fire jumped to life in their reptilian eyes at the distant call. Another, not far off, answered it. A moment later, the atmosphere rang with echoing calls and shrieks of a large grayvyk pack fast approaching. Like savage wolves declaring commencement of an evening feast.

Fear gripped the camp and tiny forms streaked and darted about. Calls for children, weapons, and vines sang out all around. The chaos rose, matching the feverish pitch of grayvyk screams. They were close now. Scouts that had climbed to perches in the trees began shouting as slinking silhouettes weaving through the distant woods came into view.

Thomas and Jillian were ushered to a safer part of the camp. But they both knew better. There was no safety here. Escape was not an option any longer, for they were surrounded. This was to be the Last Stand of the Logarthiym.

THE FIRST BEAST EXPLODED FROM THE BUSHES. Shrieks ripping from its gaping throat sent a few of the Logarthiym scurrying, but in seconds, four speedy warriors leaped into action tying it in a tight wrap of vines. The same thing happened with the next several grayvyks. Before long a pile of giant lizards lay writhing on the ground. Thomas and Jillian were so surprised at how well coordinated the Logarthiym effort was, that the hope of survival began to shine in their hearts. Indeed, the whole company felt it and began jeering and belting out war cries.

All about the ring of defense, grayvyks were tripped, tied and neatly wrapped in forest vines. The wood echoed with the shouts and howls of war. But the pile of vines was shrinking, while the stream of oncoming beasts did not diminish. At first, the creatures came one or two at a time, but then the pack switched tactics beginning to emerge in throngs. A group of a dozen or more burst into view from the left. Logarthiym surged to the spot to make their stand against it. A small band of the defenders acted as decoys to keep the grayvyks busy while the others surrounded them in vines. Two of the brave little fighters fell, never to rise again. At the same moment, a second burst of beasts crashed through the underbrush and into the fray from the right side. A second, smaller force of Logarth warriors rose to meet them, but the line of defense was shrinking. The grayvyk noose was tightening around the encampment, and the woods were flooded with a new wave of throaty howls. The defensive group was backpedaling into an ever-shrinking circle toward the center of the Logarthiym village.

By this time, Thomas had drawn his sidearm, a sturdy .357 revolver capable of taking down a bear if necessary. Jillian, brandishing a heavy staff, stood at his back to watch the rear. But, lacking the speed of their Logarthiym friends, the couple searched for a suitable tree to climb to safety. Angling for the nearest trabalisk, they circled its base to find sufficient footholds.

They felt it coming before they actually heard it. A steady rhythmic vibration in the ground that grew in pace and intensity. A grayvyk had broken through the ranks and was charging their way. Jillian was only six feet up the tree with Thomas waiting on the ground for her to find secure footing when the beast spotted them. Abruptly it sent up shrieks that made both of them wince in pain. There was no other place to run or hide, so Thomas took aim and let his gun belch lead and fire.

The first shot caught the rampaging grayvyk squarely in the chest. While the bullet did not penetrate the skin, the force of it gave the monster a brief pause. Just long enough for it to decide to get angry. Like a raging bull it clawed the ground and let out a snort that sounded like barbed wire scraping against slate. It charged a second time and Thomas unloaded two more rounds in rapid succession. The blasts punched against the beast's head this time, but the streamlined skull deflected them harmlessly into the air. The creature raged, but barely slowed. Panic seized Thomas' chest and he let the last three bullets fly with much less precision this time. He supposed one of them hit the mark, but it did not matter. He was out of ammunition, and the grayvyk was bearing down upon him too fast to clumsily reload the revolver.

Jillian had been screaming at the reptile the entire time. Her efforts to distract the creature were proving futile until she was able to throw her staff to the ground in front of the leaping marauder just before it reached her husband. The sturdy pole bounced awkwardly in its path. It paused for the briefest of seconds to regard her with an icy stare, but it was enough. Thomas was in a desperate search for something, *anything*, with which to defend himself. The short pause in the attack gave him just enough time to remember the object in the deep pocket of his cargo pants. He withdrew the black rock and threw it like a fastball pitch in a final desperate act of defense against the beast. A true David versus Goliath moment.

What happened next could only be described as miraculous. It was not a spectacular throw, and the rock did not explode or magically turn the grayvyk into stone. Instead, the point of impact where the black object struck the body of the beast suddenly resembled a cannon ball being fired at a sheet of aluminum foil. So complete was the devastation that the monster tumbled backwards and died instantly. It did not writhe or howl but dropped like a sack of dirt never to rise again. One minute a monster, the next, a harmless mound oozing black liquid.

Thomas and Jillian gaped in frozen shock for an instant, but the surrounding war prompted them back into action. Thomas climbed the tree to join his wife and hatch a plan.

"The black mine! The Book was showing us how to save the Logarthiym!" Jillian shouted above the din.

"But how? We'll never make it through the front lines! Grayvyks are everywhere and I only had the one stone!" Shrill howls racing through the forest punctuated his statement.

At that instant, a green blur darted through some nearby trees. The lone Logarthiym scout was frantically gathering the few remaining vines that could be found. The fighters at the battlefront were running dangerously low on the defensive materials and he was forced to search further and further away to retrieve them.

Jillian pointed, "He could do it!"

Together they began waving and shouting to get the little scout's attention, but he seemed to pay them no mind, and after a while disappeared from view entirely.

Presently, a tiny voice in Jillian's ear nearly toppled her from the tree with fright. "Howzit you boths be monkeying in my tree whiles we battles the scaly wagglers?" The same green clad scout, Wista, had seen the couple in the tree from the corner of his eye and had come upon them unawares. His haggard face and torn clothing were covered with a layer of sweaty grime. He wore a scowl on his face revealing disdain for these two "cow-hurds" as he called them, who chose to hide in the trees during a battle.

Thomas pointed to the ruined carcass of the wicked grayvyk he had just slain. "We've found a way to defeat them!" He explained to Wista about the black rock and described to him the location of the mine where more of the precious material could be found. The green scout looked dubious yet could not deny the defeated foe lying in a rumpled heap a short distance away. It had begun to stink already.

"Buts the viney ropes does the tricky! We's catches 'em like buzzers in a web!" Wista pointed to the heap of vines he had collected and left at the base of the tree.

"You are running out of them, and out of time!" Thomas shouted above the wails and screams that were drawing nearer. Indeed, the battle seemed to be turning more in the favor of the enemy, as the weary defense of the Logarthiym began to slow.

Jillian placed a gentle hand to the little scout's soiled face. "It may be your only hope," she pleaded. Disarmed by the beautiful woman's gesture,

Wista relented. "You's mightsa be k'rect. Mines be offsta raise a war bander! Hally-Toe!" He pumped a little fist in the air, leapt from the tree like a frog and shot through the ferns into the thick of battle.

Jillian looked at Thomas, "Now what?" she asked.

He shrugged. "We wait."

Together they climbed higher into the trabalisk tree and sat back against the trunk, covering their ears against the deafening roar below.

IT WAS A BAD TIME TO LOSE WARRIORS. The vines had all but run out, and some of the captured grayvyks had actually wriggled free of their restraints to rejoin the slaughter. New flames had kindled within the camp and now the defenders were torn between rescuing their families from burning homes and guarding them from hungry grayvyk jaws. Wista's team was badly needed.

The howling was absolutely maddening. So shrill and unrelenting was it that several Logarth warriors had dropped to their knees while cradling their heads. The cursed grayvyk song had ravaged their senses. Thomas and Jillian, though they stopped up their ears, were also feeling the effects. Their throbbing heads made their vision swim. A wild, desperate look came over Thomas as he scanned the distance, silently willing Wista to return. Jillian frantically scouted for a new, quieter hiding place. Anyplace that was away from the noise. There, in the distance, she saw it. A dark stand of trees removed from the battle a little way off. Like a siren, it beckoned her to run to its quiet haven. She lowered a foot down from her perch, determined to leave the high safety of the trabalisk.

Fortunately, Thomas saw the movement and yanked her back into the tree just as a cluster of slavering grayvyks gathered at its base. They had seen the movement and rushed in. Together they lunged and clamored like a frenzy of sharks snapping at a dangling fish. Jillian screamed, renewed fear breaking her trance long enough to pull her foot back underneath herself. Like rabid hounds the beasts leapt and snapped over and over again, missing the perch by mere inches. At this distance their rancid breath and battle screams felt like repeated punches to the stomach. It was as relentless and overwhelming as a tidal wave. Thomas felt his senses stretch to their limit. He retched once and then threw up, hitting one of the roaring grayvyks with vomit. Jillian closed her eyes tight and fought the urge to do the same. The offended grayvyk below glowered with renewed rage at the treed couple and unleashed a great bellow that sent a tremor through the trunk of the great tree.

Jillian's eyes went wide. With swimming vision, she looked to her husband. A fresh trickle of blood now oozed from his left ear, indicating new damage to his eardrum. A dull look had replaced his once twinkling eyes. It was the cloudy look of defeat. It drained her of all remaining hope and Jillian cried aloud, her groans joining the chorus of death raised by the grayvyks below.

And then, it stopped.

For a glorious second the uproar ceased long enough for them to breathe again. Something had captured the attention of their attackers and they were looking to the horizon, intent on some new target. Jillian heard it before Thomas, as his ears still rang, but a band of war cries sang out from the misty trees. And then, one shrill grayvyk yowl pierced the stillness. It was unmistakably the cry of a savage beast in pain.

Wista had returned!

The force reentered the fray with ferocity upon the unsuspecting beasts. Each Logarthiym warrior was well armed with small black stones stuffed inside satchels and pockets and clenched fists. They were unleashing them in a torrent upon the heads and hides of the invaders with great effect. Some sought out additional warriors to arm them with handfuls of the rocks to further the defending force. Still others created a sort of bucket brigade that ran to the black mine and back, replenishing the magnificent ammunition in a steady stream. One elder Logarth, none other than Tor'Engryn, had fashioned a makeshift sling from a strip of leather and pelted the enemy from great distance and with great accuracy.

The grayvyk force melted away like butter against the heat of the Logarthiym resistance. They were no match for the new weapon now wielded with such speed. When it was over, great mounds of reptilian bodies lay forever silent, broken by the miraculous turn in events.

THE SCENE WAS A BLEND OF VICTORY AND MISERY. Shouts of triumph rose to mingle with great droning sobs of loss. Lost homes, lost livelihoods, lost Logarthiym children. Thomas and Jillian haltingly climbed down from their tree of refuge and joined a ring of somber Logarthiym in the center of the forest village. Their small, ancient voices began weaving together into a song of lament and new life. They sung of the heroes that had been born that day, and heroes they had lost. The song spun to a wailing climax describing how the enemy had been thrown down with the aid of these otherworldly humans and the blessed black stones. It then died to a whisper and stillness reclaimed the swaying throng.

During the song, the ring of grieving Logarthiym had pressed close to Thomas and Jillian. Presently, Tor'Engryn weaved his way through the crowd and indicated for the couple to kneel. The elder Logarth pressed his small hands to each of their foreheads in a show of blessing.

"Tommy Big. Biggy Jill. We's loves you forevers."

THOMAS LOOKED DOWN. He had finished telling the tale around the fire, and his little Logarth friend stood clutching him with a strong embrace.

Tor'Engryn was crying grateful tears. "We's still loves you!"

Thomas smiled and patted the small creature's back. "We still love you, too, Tor'Engryn." He stretched his arms as wide as he could with the familiar family gesture. "This big!"

He stole a glance at Jillian and Heidyl. His wife beamed a proud smile back at him. Heidyl had drifted off to sleep and was resting peacefully against her mother. Her breathing was now steady and calm. Though remnants of Lambweed still clung to her skin, healthy color had returned to her features.

Tor'Engryn pulled back from his embrace to smile a wrinkly grin up at Thomas. "You's saved us from the gravy hounds. They's all be goneaways gone."

A shadow passed across Thomas' face.

"Not yet, Tor'Engryn. I believe the Caller has somehow brought them back. And he still has my son."

Though exhausted, sleep was slow in coming that night. The anticipation of what lay ahead kept nudging their senses alert. It seemed the Caller had roused all of their allies against them. Thomas and Jillian fought back

247

the despairing sighs lodging in their chests. Their rescue attempt for Jayce would be unaided.

All too soon, dusky beams of light trickled in through the open doorway to announce the arriving dawn.

It was time to press on.

PART X: THE DRAGON

HE COULD NOT TELL IF MORNING HAD YET COME. The purple flames licking the black walls cast the same eerie light as before. The windowless prison made it impossible to determine if the Haizorr sun had just risen, sunken low, or hung burning in the midday sky. Jayce felt a level of exhaustion beyond anything he had ever felt before. Each part of his body ached and groaned. The stone floor and walls of the cell offered little comfort.

An iron shackle now dangled painfully from his wrist—the result of his latest failed escape. One of Drayven's pitiful minions had been sent in to bring food and water to the boy, but Jayce had been waiting for just such an opportunity. The moment he heard the keys rattle home inside the lock, he crashed into the door with all of his might. The little creature, which vaguely resembled a mixture of a small man and a mangy rat, was sent sprawling. Metal dishes and clay jars of water smashed to the floor. Jayce sprinted from the open prison as fast as he could go, but the clamor had alerted an unseen sentry posted near the cell opening. Like a striking cobra, it shot out thick tentacles ensnaring Jayce in a knot of fleshy limbs before dragging him back to the cell all in the space of ten seconds. Jayce was pinned to the stone slab wall by the squid-like arms, allowing rat-man to run in and clamp the crude chain to the boy's wrist. Jayce was dumped onto the floor and the door slammed home with a ring of finality.

Outside the newly fastened chamber door he could hear the rat-man sniveling and scraping about, attempting to clean up the mess he had made. Jayce inched forward trying to peer through the small barred opening, but the chain held him just far enough out of reach for him to see anything clearly. There was a sudden rush of commotion that sent the dishes clattering to the floor a second time as the sentry coiled its tentacles about the rat-man's waist and threw him into an adjacent cell. The creature whimpered and chittered in protest, but to no avail. Failure was not tolerated in Blackynspyre.

DRAYVEN SMILED AT THE VISION. He lay alone in his chambers, the light of a purple candle dancing lazily across heavy drapes and ornate black furniture. Sleep was elusive. Rest had never come easy in this realm, but to-night he was especially restless. His mind's eye framed his plans playing out perfectly. As if watching a favorite childhood movie, he analyzed each detail, gloating inside at future victory. The boy served as perfect bait. He knew his pompous twin brother would never back down from a challenge, and this was working out much easier than he ever hoped. Avenging his own loss and releasing the Dark Servant at the same time proved a far better notion than he original thought.

Initially he had intended to post his trillych slaves at the Tree Gate entry to Haizorr and simply wait for Jillian to emerge. Capturing her would be easy. But the waiting would have been intolerable, for it might have been days or even years before she poked her code-breaking nose into this realm again.

It had taken him years to build the temple fortress of Blackynspyre around the Thin Place, as he called it. There were a number of these thin places throughout Haizorr. The casual passerby might dismiss them as a random chill up the spine or a tingling silence that made one feel watched or not alone. These spots were regions where the veil, or skin, between worlds of the overlapping universe was pulled so tightly that it thinned like stretched latex. One could almost see the other side if they spent any real time trying. The more Drayven prodded at such places, the more he came to realize the vast depth of wonder that Haizorr possessed. At first it served as a hope that he might escape back to Earth through one of these places. Then it became a power he longed to wield.

The day he stumbled over the Black Dragon's Thin Place was the day his life changed forever. He smiled now and closed his eyes as he remembered that frightening and delicious moment years ago.

IT HAD BEEN PERHAPS A WEEK OR MORE since his deceptive brother first deposited him into the stormy trabalisk grove. Drayven's heart had become a churning sea of wrath, sadness, and pain peppered with dark thoughts of revenge—and survival. As his time in wandering solitude grew, so did the feelings of retribution. In a matter of mere days his desire for vengeance swelled above his own desire to see his daughter again. Hungry, tired, and wrapped in anger he trudged over rocks and hills. He had no idea where he was. Drayven's search for towns and hints of civilization filled him with growing desperation. He would have been elated to stumble across a road or even a simple footpath. Instead, endless wilderness greeted him over each hilltop. Finally, drawn to a bare patch of scorched earth within a hollow grove, he lay down to rest and grind his teeth.

That is when he heard the great sobbing.

The sound was deep and rumbling, like boulders pouring down a mountainside. It shook the ground and froze Drayven's blood. Gooseflesh prickled the back of his neck as the lonely open space in the wood on which he lay now trembled slightly beneath him. After a moment it rose and fell in large slow waves like the heaving chest of a slumbering giant. The motion somehow soothed the tired man, and his wide eyes slowly closed.

We are so much alike, my lord.

Drayven shot upright. Had the ground just spoken to him? With wild eyes he scanned the rim of trees that lined the bare glen like looming sentries. The low breeze had stopped. Not a bird sung. Just deathly silence so

251

thick he could feel his ears buzzing. The ground beneath him continued to rise and fall steadily like a gentle earthen tide. Cautiously Drayven eased his ear to the ground, listening once more.

Fear not. I will bring you no harm, my lord.

The man's heart was hammering now. The voice was so deep and soothing he could feel it within his very soul. The assurance soothed his aching heart and he felt a presence both distant and familiar. It was like a thought, but deeper. Something too deep to have come from within his own mind. Instant and intense longing filled Drayven and he found himself wishing to be poured out upon the ground to be swallowed up in that gentle rumbling voice.

"Who are you?" He asked the question, unsure if his mouth was moving at all. He squeezed his eyes tighter. Yearning for a response Drayven pressed his ear against the hard ground. He needed that voice once more.

I am your salvation. And you are mine. We are one, my lord Drayven.

The man gasped at the mention of his name, "How do you know me?"

The voice responded in a low chuckle that sounded like a diesel engine. *I have known you since your first breath. I have called to you. Always calling you. At last, you have come to me.*

Drayven was silent for a long moment. He breathed in the words and searched his soul with them. Had he indeed been called to this moment? Was not the fact that he was here, at the end of himself in this barren land, proof that this was always his intended destination? Unbidden images and childhood memories began racing through his mind. Remnant thoughts of poor decisions and heaps of lifetime failures trickled through his aching heart like a stream. He saw his ruined marriage, plagued through by his own lustful pursuits. Failed opportunities and disastrous ends to friendships had been the food of his heart. Rage and aggression, ever his companions, always seemed to scrape beneath the surface ready to sabotage each situation.

Then he saw her. Raiya. His high-spirited, flame-haired daughter. Her jewel green eyes stared at him through the blackness of his soul. She was the one good thing in his life.

But she's gone.

The words came like an accusation. He had lost her and was power-less to reach her again.

No. You did not lose her, my son. Taken. He stole her from you.

The dam within Drayven's heart burst then. A ragged scream ripped from the depth of his heart and exploded from his throat. The surrounding forest seemed to groan along with him. The dark trabalisk trunks bent their weight in his direction like a group of mourners. Great sobs shook his body and he strained with the effort so greatly that his head throbbed while wave upon wave of angry lament crashed against his very being. Smashing his fists against the ground until they bled, he cried his full anguish into the dirt. The ground below him became a painful mud mixture of blood and tears. A monument to his own failed past.

At last his energy ran out and he lay still. Having spent his torment, he could do nothing more than gasp on the earth like a dying codfish. With rage out of the way, jealousy and guilt were free to roam his soul like raven-ous dogs, devouring what little was left of his will. In the end, he lay empty and trembling like a dead, dry leaf.

I am your salvation. The ground voice rumbled a low note.

Drayven whispered a reply, "Yes. And I am yours."

In that moment, a searing flash of pain bit into the space just above Drayven's left hip. A new scream shot from his throat and he thrashed about on the ground. It burned sharply and would not diminish, even as he slapped at the spot. Violently he tore at his clothing, certain that a scorpion or live coal had embedded itself into his flesh. To his shock, there was nothing there but empty, unblemished skin. Then, he gasped. Before his eyes a ragged purple spiral began forming in that empty space. It burned anew as if being drawn by a lava-hot claw, tracing in circular fashion from the inside of the spiral outward.

"What are you doing to me?" Drayven screamed in shock and terror. Writhing in pain, he clutched his burning hip.

Yesss...You are mine.

As sudden as the burning began, it stopped. A final thin wisp of smoke faded from the spot. He rubbed the area and winced expecting more pain, but the skin was cool to touch and looked like nothing more than a purplish tattoo. Exhausted, he slumped back to the ground.

He sighed heavily. "What must I do?"

Dig.

Drayven blinked. Unsure if he had deciphered clearly.

Dig! Sounds of stones splitting and earth rending beneath him startled the already bedraggled man. He looked about frantically for a tool of some sort; a flat rock or sturdy branch, perhaps.

Dig! Dig! Dig! Open the doorway! I am your salvation!

The ground shook so violently that Drayven had to steady himself on hands and knees to keep from being tossed onto his side. With nothing else to do, he began clawing at the hard-packed ground with his bloodied, bare hands. Bits of soil and gravel wedged themselves painfully under his fingernails. Rocks and roots scraped his fingertips raw.

Dig! Find me! I am here!

The Voice urged him onward whenever it appeared his strength or resolve were flagging. Hours flew by, even though each moment seemed an unending mix of anguish and anticipation. The trembling ground beneath him felt warmer to the touch the deeper he dug. After a time, he found a sprawling hard object buried under several inches of dirt. The more he scraped away, the more of the immense article he found. It seemed to go on without end. Blood dripped from his torn fingers. How much more of this could his body take?

Dig! You will see! Salvation!

His hands found a curved edge to the object and Drayven bent his focus on unearthing its rounded perimeter. Finally, numb from the backbreaking work, He collapsed to the hard earth of the dig site. He had fully uncovered a large, circular stone roughly sixty feet in diameter. Its surface was entirely flat, as if some enormous stonemason had neatly cut it. The man sitting slumped in the center of the great stone stared in horror at his ruined hands.

Yesss! You have found me. I will be your salvation.

"And I will be yours," Drayven replied with an exhausted sigh.

You ARE mine! The Voice insisted, the once friendly, soothing tone had vanished. *Say it. Seal it with blood.*

Too tired to protest, he pressed his red fingertips to the stone beneath him. "I am yours."

In return, he received a shock to his hands. A bolt of white-hot electric current streamed from the stone directly into them. Drayven tried to recoil but found he could not. His fingers were fused to the stone! An empty scream contorted his face. He squeezed his eyes shut and opened his mouth wide, but no sound escaped his lips. Brilliant arcs of white light shot upward through his fingertips into his arms. The air about him crackled and fizzled with intense heat. The powerful current whipped his body into the air like a flag for a moment before dropping him once again to the solid ground. Silence reclaimed the scene. A thin wisp of caustic vapor filled the air around his hands and then vanished.

Drayven groaned and rolled onto his back. The muscles of his arms alternately knotting in spasms and then relaxing. He was afraid to look at his hands. For a brief moment, he wondered how he was even still alive after the events of the day.

Slowly he opened his eyes and in surprise saw two waxing moons hanging in the sky above him. Night's chill had spread over the land and instantly he felt cold. Had he missed the passing of an entire day? Cautiously he wiggled his toes and flexed the muscles of his legs, searching for signs of lasting injury. For all he had been through, he was surprised at how whole he felt. Forcing his breathing to become a steady rhythm, he paused before tentatively flexing his fingers. He set his jaw against the anticipated pain. When he had successfully clenched and released both hands several times without any discomfort, he ventured a glance.

What he saw took his breath away. All trace of injured flesh had been replaced by fresh new skin! He turned them over and over, rubbing them together. Astounded, he looked closer noticing that they were no longer dirty. Supple, youthful skin now covered his once mangled hands. There was not so much as a hangnail.

The ground beneath him bounced and rumbled with a warm chuckle, like a father laughing at the innocent antics of a bemused child. *You see? I take care of my own.*

Drayven had nearly forgotten about the Voice. He felt at once comforted and fearful of its raw power.

Look upon me, child.

Slowly, Drayven obeyed. Rising up and pushing himself to his knees he stared at the smooth stone ground before him. At first, he saw nothing but hard surface.

Your blood price has thinned the veil.

A moment later the surface of the stone grew porous and translucent like a stretched canvas sheet. It rippled like waves of a pond set into motion where a fish swirls the top of the water. Large shapes and textures pressed beneath him and Drayven struggled to make out what he was seeing. Soon, a detectable pattern emerged. Something like polished circular stones knit together in heavy rows rubbed against the Thin Place. The realization struck him then. Not stones—scales! Massive reptilian scales set into dark, sinewy muscle. The entire surface of the ground writhed and bubbled as a coiling serpentine body pressed itself against the thin surface.

Then, in the space just beneath his knees a blood-red eye appeared. It was as large as a dinner plate and glowed with dark fire. Drayven was awestruck by the terror and beauty of the beast.

He stammered, "You're...you're a—dragon!"

No, my child. I am THE Dragon.

The eye seemed to burn a hole into his soul. He felt bare before the ageless serpent, though they were worlds apart. The man tried to pull away from the stare but found he could only remain rooted to it. He noticed the eye looked almost human and possessed a depth of intelligence far beyond his own. Then the vision began to fade. The ground felt firm under him again, and soon all motion ceased. Something like a fog lifted from Drayven's mind and he regained use of his senses. Standing in the center of the great stone he scratched his head.

"What just happened?" he wondered aloud.

Keep the space between us thin.

Drayven could still feel the voice of The Dragon in his head, but it was noticeably quieter now.

"I don't understand."

Blood.

He looked at his newly healed hands and frowned.

Yesss. Thin the veil, my child.

Without so much as a pocketknife on his person, he wondered how he could satisfy the Dragon's demand. The thought of bashing his hands with a rock to make them bleed seemed beyond stupid to him now. He was about to ask how he should proceed when the small voice in his mind spoke again.

Behold your servant.

A twig snapped at the edge of the woods. His skin prickled and he whirled around to face the direction it came from. To his utter surprise, a beautiful young woman wearing a soft white robe sat perched on a stool. Her graceful hand rested against the curve of an elegant harp. In her other hand she held out a cruel looking knife with a curved blade fused into a handle of bone. It was a stark contrast against the maiden's raw beauty.

Moonlight danced in her emerald-flecked blue eyes. She flashed a beckoning smile to the dumbstruck Drayven. Like a moth to flame he was drawn toward her.

"Who are you? How did you get here?" he asked.

The lovely woman only smiled. Making no indication of hearing him at all, she kept her arm outstretched for him to take the knife. Drayven examined the weapon. It was well balanced and felt strangely natural in his grip.

Thin the veil.

Obediently he returned to the center of the stone. He stared at the fresh, young skin of his open palm and then at the wicked blade. He hesitated at what he knew he must do.

Thin the veil! The Dragon persisted.

Though the voice felt little more than an urging in his mind, the desire to please the beast below and see its terrible beauty once more swelled inside him. Without thinking further, Drayven pressed the blade to his flesh and pulled. It was more painful than he had expected, and the act made him gasp. A thin torrent of blood began pouring from his hand and onto the stone. In the space where the droplets landed, the surface cleared like frosted windowpanes against a warm draft. The red glow of the eye reappeared and the surface of the Thin Place trembled once more. Relief washed over the man and he felt the Dragon's favor and presence again.

A soft whining sound like hungry puppies came from the tree line where the maiden had stood only a moment before. But in her place three ghoulish imps jumped up and down. Three sets of large green eyes fixed upon Drayven and long purple tongues drooped from toothed jaws like salivating dogs. Their noses dripped streams of putrid mucus. Dark leathery wings popped open and they beat the air impatiently.

Behold your servant. The voice repeated the phrase, but this time it sounded more like a command.

And then, they were upon him. Two of the creatures took to the air and the third hopped toward him, hissing as it went. The beasts on the wing collided with the man, knocking him to the ground. The shock of it all sent the bone handled knife skittering out of reach. The third creature joined the chaos and jumped onto his chest to clutch at his wounded arm.

Drayven punched and kicked, but in his weakened state he was no match for the trio. Though they were armed with sharp teeth and claws, they seemed more interested in subduing him than harming him. Eventually they wrestled his bleeding palm open and, to his surprise and disgust, began lapping up the blood with those horrible tongues. When the blood flow stanched, they hopped away from him as one and sat. Like obedient hounds awaiting the master's call, they stared at him with large lidless eyes.

The man was visibly shaken by the assault. A shudder passed through him as he stood up and wiped the offensive drool on his hand against his pants. As Drayven examined his palm, his eyes shot wide with amazement. The deep wound had healed once more. He glanced in the direction of the nearby trio.

I serves the masters good. Yes?

A new chorus of voices now filled his mind. The sound was like being in a tin room with a group of raucous children. Though they all were saying the same thing, each voice seemed to be in competition with the others for his full attention.

Trillych heals it good! Does he see? Does he need more? Is there more?

The little monsters began hopping up and down again, excited at the thought of blood once more. Their voices were grating inside his head and Drayven was unable to think clearly. In frustration he kicked at them and shouted. "Shut up!"

As one they hopped backwards before he had even executed his kick. Drayven blinked at their quickness. He wanted them out of his sight and began searching for the knife. As he walked toward the spot where it had landed, he paused briefly to scan the woods for any trace of the lovely woman who had been there before. Obviously, these wretched things must have scared her off, but he wanted to talk with her. She certainly was lovely.

When he turned back, he nearly jumped out of his skin. There she stood, no more than three feet away holding the knife out to him as before. Her blue eyes sparkled with a glint of green, and a demure grin curved her delicate red lips. Her other hand rested on the same harp, which leaned lightly against the stool. Drayven took an uneasy step backward. This slender woman could not possibly have carried the harp and stool to this spot in the space of three seconds without him hearing her. Surely the harp weighed as much as she did! He stepped back once more to regard the woman, but she followed. The harp and stool moved with her, as if gliding on a cushion of air. She continued to smile at him, arm outstretched. He noticed her nose was running quite badly.

"Are you feeling OK, miss?"

She continued to smile and stare, as if she had not heard him. She did not seem to mind the trickle of mucus running down her pretty face. Drayven shrugged and reached for the blade. Clumsily, he dropped it clattering to the stone below. He quickly bent to retrieve the weapon, but his finger struck the knifepoint and he recoiled, pressing against the new wound to halt the flow of blood.

"Ouch! Well, that was stupid. It seems I—" he began, but the face of the woman before him made him jump a second time. A long purple tongue now snaked from between her lips and she uttered a low whine.

Instinct and fear took over and Drayven struck out with his palms. This time he did not miss. The maiden tumbled backwards into the harp and both went sprawling to the ground, taking the stool with them. Their separation broke the trio's bond, revealing the true nature of the deception that Drayven had been seeing. Scrambling to regain their footing were the same three demonic figures once more. This time they bowed and scraped to the ground. Again, the tin room in his mind filled with a cacophony of three shrill voices.

Trillych is sorry! So sorry! We only serves the masters! Master says 'knife' and 'woman' and we obeys! Yes, you said so. We does it.

Drayven regarded the groveling beasts before him. Realizing that he held some strange power over them, he scooped up the knife and brandished it. The trillych scrabbled backwards, cowering and scraping low to the ground. He decided then that he quite liked this feeling. After being so vulnerable for so long, it was nice to have a sense of control once more.

"But I never actually *said* anything to you," Drayven wondered aloud. He examined the creatures more carefully. It was impossible to tell if they were staring back at him, as their eyes had no iris or pupil. Just large green spheres sticking out from their little heads. They were truly putrid to behold, and he hated them. One of the beasts turned its head, and Drayven noticed they possessed nothing that resembled ears. Not even a hole where an ear should be.

"Can you hear me?" he asked.

Silence.

The man shouted, receiving no response.

He tried thinking toward them. *Can you hear me?*

Instantly he regretted the thought. *Oh yes! Such a strong voice. Is he not strong? Trillych loves the voice of master! Is there more? Blood? More?*

Their voices jostled and bounced around in his head like sirens in all directions. He held up a hand and mentally commanded them to stop speaking.

Then the ground beneath his feet trembled slightly. His clash with the shape-shifting trillych made him nearly forget that he stood upon a thin sheet separating him from the Dragon's realm. Realizing that the eye of the Beast had been watching the entire exchange, he felt instant embarrassment.

A low rumble and the great voice from below returned. It was laughing. The Dragon chuckled in amusement at Drayven as if enjoying a spectacle at a clown circus. A wave of anger flashed hot across his face and he slapped the nearest trillych in a fit of frustration. The trio scattered away.

The Dragon was still laughing. *Now, now. That is no way to treat my servant.*

Drayven was not amused. "You said they are *my* servants!" He shouted in protest like an angry child.

Instantly he regretted the outburst. The ground beneath him punched straight up beneath his feet launching him skyward. He returned to hit hard ground. The spiral scar on his hip blazed with new fire and he screamed.

You are my servant! The Dragon boomed like thunder inside Drayven's head. Pain coursed through his entire body for a few seconds and then stopped as if switched off by a power button. The encounter left the man gasping once more on the hard ground.

The veil between worlds slowly returned to its previous hidden state, thickening like a wall of ice. Urgency filled the air, and the Dragon strove to deliver final instructions before its influence over the man became diminished.

Your blood-bond with them will not last long. Use it wisely each time.

Drayven could only assume the Dragon meant the trillych.

Keep the veil between us thin and I will teach you all things.

He groaned at the thought of having to use the knife on himself again, but the promise of fantastic knowledge fanned a hungry flame within. The Dragon's voice grew more faint with each passing second as the portal space thickened between them.

Only the blood of a spotless lamb can ever fully satisfy me.

"I will be your salvation."

Yesss. You are mine.

"I am yours."

Bring me the spotless lamb—

DRAYVEN WAS STILL SMILING when he opened his eyes again. Remembering that moment of pain and power always renewed his focus. Through the years, the knowledge he had received from the Black Dragon swelled his chest with great purpose.

Dark creatures both great and small had been sent to him to command. Instructions and recitations were downloaded to his mind during the moments when Drayven thinned the veil of the Thin Place with his blood. In this way he had built Blackynspyre as a sort of altar-fortress at first to honor the Dragon, but later it became an expression of his own sense of power.

The control he possessed over the dark beasts was intoxicating. He drove them without mercy, especially in the first few weeks after that initial encounter with the Dragon at the Thin Place. He ordered the trillych about incessantly, but their strength was limited. Soon drawn like moths to flame, larger creatures began trickling to the area and Drayven utilized their raw muscle to construct the stone chamber about the sacred site.

Drayven sat up in his chambers feeling alive with the promise of finally fulfilling his dream. *The stage is now set*, he thought. *I will free the Dragon and rule both realms by its side.* The notion made his fingertips tingle with excitement. With so much power under his command, Haizorr and Earth will have no choice but to bow to his reign. But more importantly, his brother will pay for his sins.

And Raiya will know the truth at last. He sighed. He knew deep within that his current state made him unfit to father her well—if at all. He did not even know her. Drayven imagined that she must be a teenager by now, perhaps even older than that. He did not know for sure. Perhaps it was the lack of knowing that made it all the worse. A mind imprisoned in solitude for so long yields painful imaginations.

And dark yearnings.

The spiral mark on his hip began to itch. The Dragon was calling to him again. All that remains is to fully tear open the papery veil of the Thin Place and release the Dark Servant.

Blackynspyre is complete.

The spotless lamb awaits.

And the one to open the portal is on her way.

Today is going to be a good day, he thought.

THE PATH HAD DISAPPEARED. After breaking camp, the family left Westyr Guard fortress following an ancient path that snaked through the woods toward the dark hills on the horizon. Tor'Engryn had found it after some time, and with great difficulty. He recounted how he thought the trail once belonged to the Aelder Gnomes who used it as a trade route when mining the black mountains. Strange markings and curious skill shrouded it from prying eyes, but it was easy to follow once one knew what to look for and it was relatively free from obstacles. For a while, hope returned to the group.

But now the passage had simply vanished. In its place a tangled swath of downed trees and overturned boulders appeared. The footpath was completely erased. The woods looked liked a row of bulldozers had plowed through side by side. Jillian dreaded trying to find it again. Her small measure of hope disappeared along with the trail and she sat down on a fallen log.

Her husband was not yet put off by the turn of events. While Tor'Engryn zipped up and down the edges of the destroyed tree line searching once more for the gnomic path, Thomas scrabbled to the top of an enormous boulder. He scratched his head while squatting atop the great stone trying to figure out what to do next.

With nothing more to do, Heidyl sat beside her mother and observed his behavior. Quite suddenly she burst out laughing, "Dad, you look just like a gorilla!"

Thomas, lost in thought, had not heard her and continued his apelike posture. Jillian, grateful for the distraction, allowed herself a light chuckle. A moment later Tor'Engryn came panting up to the two ladies, his face the picture of weary disappointment. He did not need to say anything for his drooping head and downcast eyes told them he had been unsuccessful in finding the Aelder Gnomes' secret mining path to their destination. Heidyl graciously patted his small back to comfort him.

"It's okay," she said, "we'll find the way."

A moment later, Thomas bolted to his feet. Shielding his hands around his eyes he squinted into the distance. He then turned to his waiting family, a look of triumph painted on his face.

"I know who did this!"

He practically bounded down the high boulder and jogged to a flat patch of bare earth. Kneeling, he traced deep impressions in the dirt with his fingers before jogging to another similar impression about thirty feet away. "This is a darchlyte path!" Motioning the others over he showed them the curious footprint of the legendary beast he held in such high regard.

"It looks more like a darchlyte rampage," said Jillian, referencing the destruction. "Wherever they were going, they were going in a hurry and did not care who knew about it."

Thomas held up a finger. "Ah, but we *do* know where they are going. Look!" The wide swath cut straight through the hillside and could be seen like a dark thread against the green-carpeted hills toward a dark, bony spur in the distance.

Heidyl's eyes widened. "They are heading to Blackynspyre!"

For a moment everyone stood staring, not wanting to voice what he or she now feared. If the Caller could draw the powerful darchlytes to move with such recklessness, could he even be stopped? Doubts about the mission to rescue Jayce surfaced anew.

Tor'Engryn spoke the fear into existence. "He calls them."

It was a painful admission that felt like sore defeat.

Jillian closed her eyes tight and sighed. "What do we do now?"

"We follow their path," Thomas replied.

"But what about the darchlytes? If they are under some control and are turned against us, we'll never stand a chance!"

"They've cleared the way for us," he replied. "Now we can reach the fortress by sundown." He was trying to sound optimistic.

Heidyl had been listening to the exchange and furrowed her brow, not understanding her father's meaning. Thomas, seeing her expression, explained. "Darchlytes are cursed to follow the sun. They shouldn't be back to this area until sunrise."

Jillian looked at the failing light and strode forward, jaw set. "Then we don't have any time to lose. Let's go find Jayce."

INKY NIGHT SLOWLY STOLE OVER THE HILLS. From his high vantage point he watched the tiny rescue party picking their way through the crushed route formed by the darchlytes. They looked so helpless against the backdrop of a wide, harsh Haizorr landscape. For a moment he smiled at their courage, but then frowned at their foolishness. They would not survive the war to come. The thin light of two full moons was just now visible above the planet's rim. The time had now fully come. Turning his attention back to the summon scroll and code page from The Book before him, he began the great and final Calling.

It was time to end this.

THEY REACHED BLACKYNSPYRE WITHOUT A PLAN. None of them had ever been inside, which was not yet even the chief of their worries. There were sure to be sentries posted everywhere and finding a way in unhindered would be difficult. That was all any of them knew.

They shed their packs in a dark thicket, opting to bring only the barest of essentials for more nimble movement. These were stuffed into a small day-pack carried by Thomas. Stealth and speed were their best allies at the moment. Like a group of spies peering through thick undergrowth, they sized up the high-walled fortress. It was much larger than any of them imagined. Of the group only Thomas had ever seen it before, and then only from a distance. The immensity of the task before them weighed heavy as they stared at the barred black gates.

Thick iron glistened back at them, reflecting blue and green moonlight. The door looked to weigh several tons. Even if it were unlocked, there would be no easy way to open it. Two large lumps lay on either side of the entry. At first, they appeared to be rock formations, but the pale light bouncing off rows of gleaming scales said otherwise. It appeared a pair of grayvyk sentries would be the first great hurdle to clear.

"What do we do now?" Heidyl whispered. Even through a hushed voice it was hard to hide the fear and despair she was feeling.

"We needsa diverter," came Tor'Engryn's tiny voice. But with all eyes fixed on him, he knew the task would fall on his shoulders, as he was clearly the fastest of the group. "Wells, may mine stickle leggings carries me to the win!" He gave each of them a parting hug and before any could object, he bolted from their hiding spot like a miniature missile.

Thomas, Jillian, and Heidyl each held their breath. Hearts raced as the moment of action was suddenly thrust upon them. Once those grayvyks were roused, there would be no turning back. Thomas smiled, marveling at the courage of the tiny Logarth barreling headlong toward the face of a sleeping monster many times his size. Tor'Engryn reached the dormant beasts in the space of a half-second, then promptly drew back and kicked the nearest grayvyk hard on the snout. When it did not move, he raced to the other and did the same. It too remained silent as a marble statue. Frustrated, Tor'Engryn hefted a rock and smacked it against one of them, hitting it squarely in the eye. The stone clattered harmlessly to the ground. With a stymied shrug, the Logarth Elder bolted back into the bushes to his friends.

"They's deeper sleepers!" He panted for a moment and then made a face while holding his nose. "Ands stinky! Phew!"

The rank stench hit all of them then. The familiar odor of grayvyk blood stung their eyes and nostrils. Heidyl stifled a gag. Jillian pointed to Tor'Engryn's black-stained feet. His animal skin boots were slick with dark, inky blood.

The Logarth looked down and chuckled, "Ha! Mine's bloodied his noses with a kick!"

"No, I don't think so," said Thomas scanning the scene. "I think they're both dead." Puzzled, the team squinted against the dim light at the two still figures by the gate.

Jillian noticed that one of their heads was twisted at an odd angle, but other than that they appeared to be napping. "How can that be? No one even—" she began but was cut off by a low groan that rumbled down to them from the treetops.

Everyone froze. Slowly all eyes turned upward to the nearest tree where the sound had come from. It differed from the surrounding trees in a subtle way that felt unnatural. It swayed rhythmically as though breathing. A large black bat swooped in and roosted upon it, scrabbling with sharp claws up the side to gain better height. Before it had climbed ten feet however, a limb-like arm snapped out swatting the annoying creature like a gnat. It tumbled to the ground like a crumpled piece of black paper.

As a collective gasp escaped the companions below, two sapphire eyes appeared in the midst of the tree's trunk and stared at them. This was no tree.

"Darchlytes!" Thomas barely managed to whisper through a fear-tightened throat. As if in reply, another low groan came from behind them. Jillian grasped her husband's shoulder and Thomas felt his daughter's hand slip into his. Even the brave Tor'Engryn clung to his leg like a frightened child. All sensed that their journey's end was upon them, but nothing happened. The darchlytes stood as if rooted to the ground, content for the moment to just stare at the puny humans and their Logarthiym friend.

After standing frozen for what felt like eternity, the tiny huddle cautiously brought their heads together to quietly discuss the next possible course of action.

Jillian spoke first. "Why are they just standing there?"

Heidyl shuddered, "I don't like their eyes. I feel like that one is looking right into my soul." She squeezed Thomas' hand harder.

"Well, we can't outrun them," said Thomas.

Tor'Engryn was miffed at the statement. "Speakings for you's self! Mine's stills can run around them circulars!"

Thomas was frowning, puzzled. "How is it that they are even here? Darchlytes are cursed to follow the sun."

Jillian pointed to the full moons in the sky, reminding him of the loophole in the curse. Then she shrugged, "Maybe it's the Caller's power over them?"

At the mention of the Caller, Tor'Engryn loudly began reciting the ancient poem of the Call, but Heidyl covered his mouth with her hand. "Be quiet, Tor-Tor! They'll hear you!"

Another distant groan punctured the stale night air and the group stilled their breathing once more.

As if a light flicked on inside her head, the answer came to Jillian's own question then. "They must be waiting for the Caller's next signal."

Looking around at the dark forms in the forest, it was clear now that they were all standing as if at attention. Their azure eyes alternately stared at the tiny band of spies and again at the black gate of Blackynspyre.

Thomas nodded in agreement with her as a new thought came to him. "Maybe he doesn't know we are here yet." Looking at the two dead grayvyk guards he continued, "And he doesn't have full control over them. It looks like the darchlytes still have a mind of their own. He called them here and they must have crushed his grayvyks out of pure instinct! Maybe even out of spite!" He chuckled.

Heidyl brightened a little at the prospect. "Then we still might have a chance to save Jayce," she said.

"I think you're right," said Jillian, smiling at her daughter.

"Let's get to it," Thomas said readjusting his pack.

Like a tribe of thieves, they stole across the cursed land. The light of twin moons glared over them, casting long running shadows in the hard-packed earth before the gate. They held their noses as they passed the reeking stench of dead grayvyks.

With a great shove, they all heaved against one of the massive iron-work doors to the fortress. To their great surprise, it swung inward as easily and as silently as a library door. One by one they slipped inside.

Thomas cast one more backward glance toward the trees before ducking into the pitch-black opening. A movement caught his eye. He could not be sure, but it appeared as though one of the darchlytes had raised a mighty arm in salute.

A surge of new hope filled his chest.

Then the deep dark of Blackynspyre swallowed it whole.

THREE BAT-LIKE SETS OF WINGS BEAT THE AIR. Drayven looked up from his ghastly iron throne at the trillych as they circled the large room preparing to land. These days the ruler of Blackynspyre could almost always be found in the Dragon Chamber. Sometimes he would take to sleeping in the great room, choosing to recline against the hard stone so as to remain close to the dark serpent below. It made for long, impatient nights. His bloodshot eyes and deep frown spoke of yet another sleepless evening tossing and turning upon stone.

The flying trillych hit the ground near his feet like three clumsy children, tumbling over one another. As one, they hopped upright and eagerly approached their master, jostling each other as if trying to tell some bit of exciting news first.

Drayven already knew some of what they had seen. He had tethered his mind to theirs earlier through yet another blood bond and sent them on watch about Blackynspyre. The bond had since worn thin and shadowy over the past few hours before winking out entirely. Drayven was too weary to make another bond with them and allow their grating voices back into his head. Still the servants were anxious to report and began their story by striking their tails together. The result was not unlike a strange sort of clunky stage performance. First, their bodies morphed into that of an old Logarthi-ym. They tried to mimic his quick movements but looked more stupid than anything. Drayven sighed and folded his arms. He knew this much already. Seeing they were losing their audience, the trillych quickly moved on shifting into rough shadowy shapes of Heidyl, then Thomas and finally, as if she were the climax of their story, Jillian. Like a game of charades, they did their best to mimic her opening and then entering a doorway.

Drayven smiled and nodded. Then frowned. "So, they've finally come," he said, thoughtfully rubbing his chin. "But how did they avoid capture? The sentries are all posted and alerted."

Sensing his puzzlement, the gross trio tried to continue the rest of their scrabbly performance by morphing into a treelike shape with long arms and blue eyes. Drayven, now distracted and annoyed, had already turned and waved them off. "Enough of that. Yes, yes. I've seen it all you stupid beasts!" He threw a bronze bowl at them to drive them off and the trillych scattered back into their natural forms, clambering into a dark corner to sulk.

"Let's let them come," he spoke his thoughts aloud to no one. Standing to his feet Drayven paced around the outer rim of the circle. The ever-ascending plume of black smoke rose skyward from its center. He never grew weary of staring at that glorious smoke. The twisting and roiling shapes it made were so serpentine and organic that it made him feel as though the Dragon had already entered the room. He turned his attention to the billowing column as if greeting a friend.

"They are here! Your freedom is at hand!" He spread his arms wide as if making a great pronouncement. When the ground of the portal did not stir, nor the Dragon's smoke grow as he had anticipated, Drayven lowered his arms. "Yes. I agree, let's not celebrate just yet. We need to do this properly." He turned his head to a dark corner beside the low prison cell that harbored Jayce. "Keeper!" he shouted. At once a hulking, tentacled beast glided out from the darkness like a surly octopus.

Drayven continued, "See to it that my guests arrive unharmed." Like a shade, the creature folded in upon itself before blending away into the darkness of a nearby corridor. Drayven then strode to a wall simply covered with shelves of pungent bottled liquids and racks of other weapons and oddities. Reaching past a cruel looking club fashioned with bony spikes he lifted the item he had been saving for years from its hanging place on the wall. He shook it to remove ages of collected dust.

"We need to do these things delicately," he said as he twisted the black and red nylon rope in his hands.

JAYCE NARROWED HIS EYES. From his confinement he had overheard enough of the crazed musings of his uncle to know that things were about to get ugly. He stiffened at Drayven's use of the word *guests*. It could only mean that his parents were here to get him out of this place. A wash of relief came over him but was quickly replaced by a dreadful fear. They had no idea what Drayven was capable of, or how powerful he was. He had to warn them. *But how?*

He examined the rusty shackle about his wrist. It was too tight and too thick to wriggle his hand free. Following the length of chain to its anchor point in the wall, Jayce searched for weakness. Surely years of neglect and moisture would have rusted some vulnerable spots into the metal. Using the edge of the iron cuff on his arm he tapped at the iron plate and bolt in the wall. To his surprise, the hard anchor shifted ever so slightly, and reddish-brown dust drifted down from the tiny new gap he had created. He attacked the spot with vigor. Careful not to clank the chain too loudly and alert his captor, he pried against the weakened area with the corner of his shackle. For a moment he wondered why the newfound strength he possessed in Haizorr did not make him powerful enough to just rip the thing out of the wall like a superhero. He then reasoned that the elements that make up this realm must also possess equal strength to some degree, otherwise the physics of the entire planet would not work. He was definitely stronger here, but rocks and chains were stronger still.

After a few moments, tiny bits of chipped rock and rust formed small dusty debris piles at his feet. He wiped the sweat from his brow and continued his frantic claw toward freedom.

The thought of protecting his family became his sole motivation now. Though Jayce wished to see his family again, he would die before seeing them become prisoner to a madman.

HEIDYL COULD SEE NOTHING. Dank air and the smell of some type of rancid incense added to the feeling of being smothered. She blinked, squinted and even rubbed her eyes, but the blackness was so complete she might as well have had no eyes at all. Moments ago, Tor'Engryn had climbed onto her out of fear, and she wore him in piggyback fashion, edging along the wall behind her parents through the darkness. To keep steady, Heidyl allowed her fingertips to brush along its rough surface. She hoped there were no spiders.

The silence in the passage was palpable. Every foot scuffle, sudden breath and rattling zipper was magnified by the close gloom. They inched this way for several long minutes before Thomas dared to pierce the darkness with the blinding beam of his military grade flashlight. Shielding their eyes and after blinking away the glare spots, the group took stock of their surroundings. It was much as they had imagined, just a long hallway with high ceilings and rough stone walls. The inside of the black gate was far behind them now. They were perhaps twenty yards from reaching the end of the passage where it appeared to branch into two different directions.

Thomas was about to suggest a possible route when Heidyl screamed. She clapped a shaking hand over her mouth, pointing with the other. Like a fox in the dark, a set of large canine eyes reflected the shine of the flashlight back at them. The eyes sparkled green, blinked once and winked out when the creature turned its body and slunk away. Its large form disappeared around the corner like a mist, leaving no sign that it had ever been there. Thomas held the brilliant beam steady on the spot where the beast had just been. He was surprised to find he had already drawn his weapon. For a fleeting moment he wondered if he should be using silver bullets.

They hung in that space, watching and listening for the beast to return. Their adrenaline levels had all been spiked by the encounter. Knowing they had to regain control and think clearly, Thomas willed his feet to move forward. As one, the group stepped lightly toward the end of the hall.

They reached the junction without incident, although painfully slowly. The prospect of being watched unnerved them all. They figured Blackynspyre would be crawling with a host of sinister creatures, but they did not expect to encounter one so silent. A full grayvyk assault seemed more appropriate, but the hound-like creature they encountered appeared to be content to merely observe them. *Maybe it was some sort of spy,* Thomas wondered as he cautiously peered around each corner. Nothing but more hallways and joining corridors greeted his view. A collective sigh escaped the group.

A choice had to be made. Going left led further into a black void with more darkness. The passage on the right was dimly lit with a twisted sconce spewing dark purple flames. The promise of light, no matter how poor, made that passage instantly more appealing. But in this place of maddening hallway mazes, a left turn into darkness could just as easily bring them to Jayce. Or to something else lurking in the dark.

"We have to split up," Thomas whispered.

Jillian had already been thinking along these lines, but Heidyl felt the icy cold fingers of fear run along her spine at the words. Tor'Engryn reflected the same feeling by tightening his grip on Heidyl's back.

"You take the gun, Jill." Thomas handed her the sidearm. It was not unfamiliar in her hands, as she had practiced with her husband on numerous occasions. In many ways, she was a better shot than he was, taking her time to aim and breathe. But she had never fired at a living creature before. She hoped she would not have to do so tonight.

Thomas continued, "I've got the only flashlight, so I'll take the left passage here," he said nodding toward the darkness. "You follow the lights. If you run into trouble, fire three shots. I'll find you. If you find Jayce, get him and get out of here as fast as you can."

The plan was flimsy at best, and they all knew it. There were too many holes and what-if's in their approach to make it sound, but time was running out. With no other options, no allies, and no second chances it was either find Jayce and escape or perish trying. They felt like four fools against the world. Uncomfortable silence grew between them.

Finally, Thomas roused enough courage to speak. "Hey," he said, spreading his arms as wide as he could. "I love you—this big!" Jillian and Heidyl leaned in, both drawing and giving strength through the familiar family embrace.

Tor'Engryn, still clinging to Heidyl's back like a child, patted Thomas' shoulder. "We finds Thomaseed. You will looksee!"

Thomas smiled back into the wrinkly face of their faithful Logarthiym companion. "Thanks, Tor. Take care of my girls."

"Betchya!" The aging Logarth waxed brave at Thomas' charge. Then hopping down from the piggyback position, he drew out his sling and a black stone. "They's hafta squash mine to bits beesfore they getsa Biggy Jill and Heidyl Big!" To add emphasis to the claim he spun the sling, making it buzz like a power saw. Thomas, Jillian and Heidyl all smiled at the courageous little fellow.

Casting the powerful light beam down the darkened mouth of the corridor, Thomas turned and strode into the black. Jillian and Heidyl watched him go until all trace of his flashlight vanished. Then turning their attention to the eerie purple glow at the end of their own direction, they crept toward it.

"I miss Dad already," came Heidyl's shaky whisper. "He's so brave."

273

Jillian reassured her daughter, "He sure is, love." Then she added, "But so are you." Clasping Heidyl's hand with her own and leading the way with the revolver gripped in the other, the two of them gained the end of the hallway to stand under the burning purple flames of the torch. Like the last junction, this one forked in two different directions, however at the end of both halls the same type of burning sconce sent up its own lazy torchlight.

Jillian shrugged. "Which way?" She asked her thought aloud.

Heidyl squinted into the dim and noticed the left passage had something that looked like a large pile of wet laundry lying on the floor. It moved. Not quickly, but more like a slug sliding across the stones. Instinct took over and Heidyl shoved her mother to the right.

"That way, Mom. Definitely that way!"

THE BEAM STABBED AT THE DARKNESS. Thomas had taken to running through the fortress now. Urgency tinged with fear pressed him on. He figured a jogging target would be harder to catch than a walking one and a fast pace would only help them find Jayce sooner. Every so often his flashlight shone against a set of eyes in the distance or illumined the silhouette of some creature cowering in the darkness. He took a measure of hope in that they seemed to recoil from the glimmering light. Stopping to listen, he noted no signs of pursuit. No slapping of chasing feet in the black, or heavy breathing of dark stalkers.

But he had a new problem. In his blind race through the maze, Thomas had failed to mark any pathways he had previously traveled. For all he knew, he could be running in circles and crossing paths with the same baddies over and again. Stooping down he snatched up a chunk of rock that years of neglect had broken off from a nearby wall. He quickly scratched an arrow at eye level pointing in his direction of travel with a number one next to it, indicating that this was the first mark he made. Dashing to the end of the corridor, he made a second mark, designated with a number two. Then he raced off again into a new black passage, brandishing his flashlight like a laser sword against foes before him.

HIS FINGERS WERE RAW AND BLEEDING. Jayce continued to pick and pry at the loosening metal rod embedded into the prison wall. The effort brought aches and pinching in his wrist from the shackle, but he could slide the rod in and out of the wall several inches now. It seemed some sort of pin or fastener on the far end of the rod was preventing it from coming free. He found that if he rammed the iron rod with a twisting motion more dust and rubble would pour from the hole he had made. While the effort was rewarding, it had become more painful each time.

At first, Jayce had been careful not to make a sound. Stopping after each subtle scrape or clank of chain, he would listen for any sign of his captors. Now, desperation mingled with pain and exhaustion had caused him to cease caring and he continued his work loudly. His cell became an echo chamber of grunting, rattling metal and grating thuds. The blood rushing in his ears and his heavy breathing blocked out the surrounding prison world. All of Haizorr seemed to vanish as Jayce laser-focused all effort upon gaining freedom.

He never heard the key twisting in the lock behind him.

PART XI: THE SACRIFICE

JILLIAN ALLOWED BRAVERY TO RISE WITHIN HER. Years of exploration, discovery and peril had taught her this skill. She had learned that fear is much like a stubborn weed. If left alone to flourish, then flourish it will. Ignoring it only grants room for unchecked growth. It is the courageous choices one makes that choke out the most resilient of fears. She knew she could never fully remove the fear for her family that she felt so close now, but she certainly could challenge it. Each step deeper into the death-ridden maze brought her closer to her captured son, and this built up her fortitude.

Heidyl, who trailed behind only slightly, was not yet possessed of this skill. More than once she had rubbed the cool metal of the Fydas bracelet on her arm with her thumb, wondering if its protective power would be able to shield them all from danger. Her quaking heart caused her to doubt if she would even have the presence of mind to activate it fast enough. Her skin prickled all over. Imagining eyes watching their every move, she felt they would be pounced upon at any moment.

Tor'Engryn had also allowed his nerves to grow taut. His bravado display from before had melted away and he now clasped Heidyl's hand like a fearful child. She found herself pulling him along like a reluctant toddler.

Thus, their progress moved all the slower. Every five steps or so, Heidyl cast a backwards stare into the dimness scanning for pursuers. So far, not a hint of anything had surfaced. The air felt still and close. No stray sound could be heard. Just the uneasy shuffle of a small band of wary intruders stiffly walking down the dark passage.

Adding to her own fear, Heidyl began worrying about her father. His was the darker road. In the past few days she had already lost her dear friend Samuel and then her brother. The added thought of possibly losing her father squeezed at her from inside. A rush of muddled emotions flooded her heart. She marveled again for the hundredth time how quickly she had been thrown into this crazy new reality. Just days ago, her main concerns were difficult math problems or perhaps petty arguments with the annoying kids at school. Things were so different now. She could feel the innocence of childhood melting away and a thick sadness mounded up as a lump in her chest. It settled over her heart like a heavy stone. Burning tears filled her eyes and tumbled down her cheeks. She sniffed.

A mother's heart knows so much. Even before the telltale sniffling, Jillian sensed the troubled spirit of her daughter and turned. Heidyl melted into her mother and allowed the sobs to pour out. Even the emotional little Logarthiym pressed his wrinkly face against Jillian's pants leg and cried. Although he was unsure as to why, this just felt like a moment given to tears.

Jillian tucked the handgun into the back of her waistband and began stroking Heidyl's long hair. She knew this feeling all too well and had expected her daughter to react this way at some point. Perhaps not while standing in the tomb-like throat of the vilest place imaginable, but feelings are cruel masters, rising unbidden at the most inopportune times.

For Jillian, this same overpowering sense had come long ago when she first came to grips with how very unsafe the world truly was. Shortly after giving birth to her precious children, her eyes were forced open to a new reality. She recalled reclining at home with Heidyl, barely a week old, wrapped in her arms as a sleeping bundle in a fuzzy pink blanket. This particular moment had been one of the perfect ones; the sort of framed memory that greeting cards and Christmas calendars are made of. She recalled the warm fire burning brightly in the nearby hearth casting its dancing orange glow upon her son who lay asleep on his father's lap on the couch beside where she sat. Jillian and Thomas shared a brief, sleepy smile of contentment when their eyes met.

And then the tears had come.

At first, they were tears of gratitude born of an overwhelming sense of blessing and joy. Then, like a drop of black ink into clear water, savagery injected its poison to mingle with the sweet moment. She gazed upon the tranquil face of the peaceful little girl she held and felt her defensive hackles raise. A torrent of thoughts poured into her mind then. With the deepest of senses that all good mothers know, she felt the crushing weight of the evils in the world. Not only those bound to Earth, but those of Haizorr and count- less others that would seek to harm and oppress the innocent. That moment became a vow to Jillian worn as a shielding coat of motherly mail woven by the strongest of loves to protect her little ones from evil. In her one arm lay cradled the perfect purity of a newborn baby, yet with the other she held back the darkness that sat crouched at the ready to destroy it.

And here, now years later, standing in the dark lair of the beast, she held her lovely, innocent Heidyl with the same resolve. *Isn't this the same battle I've always fought?* Jillian thought to herself. *Yes, but for the first time, we're both standing on the front lines.* She bravely swallowed back the lump in her throat, though she felt more powerless than ever to stay the tide of death they both presently swam in.

After a moment, Heidyl's tears stopped and her breathing steadied. The spell had passed, and she felt much clearer now. The burden lifted some- what and was replaced by a renewed sense of resolve to press on. Pulling back from the embrace, mother and daughter shared a knowing smile in the pale purple torchlight.

Then, a look of alarm erased the pleasant expressions. An odd buzz- ing sound that neither of them could place, like the whirring of a high-speed fan, broke the stillness nearby.

Tor'Engryn's sling was spinning like a turbine. "Gets you back!" he shouted into the dim light. His face was the picture of ferocity.

Heidyl and Jillian followed his warlike stare down the hall into a hulking silhouette. The huge creature gliding toward them filled the passage with its bulk. Despite its gargantuan size, it advanced with fluid movements upon a mass of wet tentacles as thick as tree trunks. Pale yellow eyes set deep in its sloped head stared blankly at the trio while it crept forward, unfazed by the warning of the tiny Logarth. With a shout, Tor'Engryn let the small black stone sing through the air. The powerful projectile struck the jail-keeper sentry amid one of its long tentacles. The blow nearly severed the appendage and the beast rumbled a painful cry. It slowed, but did not stop the advance, now dragging the useless limb behind it like a wet log. Another stone was laid to the sling and sent flying at the monster. With astonishing speed, the creature dodged, flattening itself into a side wall as if made of living putty. The black bullet harmlessly struck the far end of the hall with a loud crack.

Jillian shouted, "Run!" as she shoved her daughter the other way. Tor'Engryn, determined to keep his promise and protect the girls, refused to turn.

"You's getsyoo gone! Mines will keep it at the bay!" He was launching stone after stone now. Some hitting, but most missing their mark as the incredibly nimble beast dodged time and again.

After just fifty strides, Heidyl pulled up short. Jillian nearly toppled into her at the abrupt halt.

"What is it?" she asked, panting.

Heidyl pointed to a slick mass on the floor.

"There," she said. "That's the same slug thing I saw before. It's been following us!"

As if on cue, the blob-like creature ballooned up before them to many times its size, completely filling the corridor. Blocking their escape, it inched forward like an enormous piston. The sounds of Tor'Engryn's personal war with the octopus-like beast raged on, his sling humming. War shouts and low groaning filled the air behind the two women.

They were cut off.

"Get behind me," Jillian said as she shouldered past her daughter. Tugging the revolver from her belt she pointed its muzzle center mass of the blob's slow advance. Squeezing the trigger, the weapon thundered with ear splitting violence. The blinding flash and sudden kick of the powerful .357 nearly caused Jillian to lose her grip. Heidyl had failed to cover her ears and the echoing blast gave her an instant dull headache. The advancing blob wall shuddered a bit but kept its slow forward pace. Jillian fired twice more, but the bullets were simply absorbed into the spongy wet surface of the slimy creature. Mother and daughter backpedaled together through the darkness.

For a moment, Heidyl thought she must have gone deaf. She could no longer hear Tor'Engryn's rallying cries or singing sling. And then, in a flash he was at her side, cringing with his empty ammunition satchel and weapon, now useless, hanging at his side. She spun to confront the revisited terror behind her, but not before her mother had done the same. Jillian pushed Heidyl to the floor and took aim at the heavy beast behind them and fired again. She hit her mark and seeing the beast hesitate, took a bold step forward. Motherly rage and instinct kicked in then. Tor'Engryn had weakened it, now she would finish it off. Sighting in at one of the creature's large eyes she pressed the trigger with cold accuracy, flooding the tight corridor with light and thunder. The explosive agony of the creeping cephalopod drove it backwards a pace, but now the advancing blob was nearly on top of them from behind. The group shuffled away from it as one, Jillian at the lead.

After a few seconds the sentry stilled. Dark liquid poured from an empty eye socket while malice and palpable hate seethed from the remaining good eye glaring at Jillian. She kept the weapon trained on it and cocked the hammer. Sweat dampened her hands as adrenaline filled her fingers with unsteady tension.

The instant it lunged, she fired.

The bullet tore a ragged wound just below the good eye of the monster and painful rage bellowed from its throat. Flashing out a thick, rubbery tentacle it knocked Jillian to the ground. Another encircled her waist dragging her inward. The repeated *click, click, click* announced that the revolver in her hand was empty.

Picking her up as if she were a mere rag doll it drew her in for closer inspection. In a desperate fit, Jillian hurled the useless weapon at the creature's rubbery skin, but it clattered harmlessly to the ground. She pounded her fists against the coiling limb about her while she kicked her legs to get free. Like a gnat in a spider's clutch, she was no match for its strength and soon relented the struggle. Turning her attention back toward Heidyl she screamed.

"Find your father! Get out of here!"

But all she saw before being carried down the hall was the hideous, swollen blob now covering the very spot where Heidyl and Tor'Engryn had been standing just seconds before. Jillian felt her heart crumble. She tried screaming, but the constrictor-like tentacle about her squeezed the breath from her lungs.

Pain like no other flooded her soul.

Then the world went completely black.

DARKNESS SWALLOWED THEM WHOLE. Covered in blackened silence, they were unable to move. Above and on all sides a rolling mass of crushing weight twisted and squeezed upon them.

Everything had happened so fast. During the scuffle her mother had with the tentacled sentry, the startled cry of Tor'Engryn had reached Heidyl from behind. The ooze-beast had attached itself to his feet, sticking him fast. Like a cold heap of creeping death, it was inching its way up his tiny body. Without thinking, Heidyl dove in to protect him. Pulling him free, they tumbled to the ground with the Logarthiym in her protective embrace. Massive tentacles lashed about their heads on one side while the wall of solid slime pressed upon them from the other. The next thing she knew, her mother was being dragged away furiously kicking to work herself free. Helpless indecision had frozen Heidyl's limbs. With little more to do, she squeezed her eyes shut against the surrounding horrors and wrapped her arms tighter around Tor'Engryn like a shield.

Then all went silent.

Expecting to be battered to death by octopus limbs or smothered by the creeping sludge, Heidyl held her breath. The Logarthiym ancient in her arms lay still as a stone. She assumed he must have fainted. She could feel his little chest rising and falling like that of a sleeping child. His heart drumming like a hummingbird.

After several long breaths, his tiny voice pierced the ringing stillness.

"Heidyl Big. Opens your peepers. Looksee!"

Something like a blue haze clouded her vision. She squinted against it to clear the fog, but it remained. The area immediately about them was faintly illuminated by an aura of thin blue light, encircling them in a sphere.

"Bangles be praised! Itsa glows so pretty," Tor'Engryn said pointing to the glowing bracelet about her wrist.

Heidyl allowed her eyes to drift to the Fydas gift she wore. She had forgotten about it entirely. Wispy blue smoke rolled from its polished surface mingling with and adding to the shield about them.

"Protective thoughts," she murmured to herself. "I must have activated it without knowing it." Gazing at the swirling layer surrounding their huddle like a ball of clouds, Heidyl wondered at once how long it might last. Is it like a battery that diminishes in power as it is used? If the Fydas can read her mind, could then a single stray thought derail its protection? There were too many paths for her mind to take regarding their current plight, so she settled back and attempted to still her heart and trust that Justhynial knew what he was doing when he had given her this amazing gift.

"Sickly ickles," Tor'Engryn whispered in disgust. He had stood up and was peering closely into the blue smoke. Just beyond the protective layer, the goo folded and kneaded itself over and over again as it probed for a way to reach them through the shield. As if trapped within a frosted glass bubble, Heidyl and the little Logarth watched the miry glop slide over its surface. It was littered with all manner of debris. Rocks, small tree branches, and tiny bits of rags were embedded within the thick sludge. Something thudded against the protective wall and the slimy creature gave a slight shudder in response. Suddenly, a jumbled mass of skeletal remains came gliding into view. The moving mucus that had consumed the bones jostled and tumbled them against one another in a manner that made them look alive, though clearly whatever—or whomever—they once belonged to had perished long ago.

A very human looking skull tumbled into the mix and Heidyl squinted her eyes shut. Fear would do them no favors now. To strengthen her resolve she reached out and clasped Tor'Engryn's wrinkly little hand so she could better think thoughts about protecting him.

Just how long they sat like this, they did not know but it seemed an eternity. Every few moments Heidyl opened one eye to peek through the blue protective curtain scanning for any sign that the slime had moved away. The old bones were no longer visible, but the dark ooze still covered them like a thick wet blanket. Like a starfish trying to open a clam, it squeezed and probed their shell of protection for any sign of weakness. The vigil made them both weary, and Tor'Engryn could no longer fight the sleepy feeling that made his head swim. He sat down and wriggled his body closer to Heidyl like a child ready to nap. She too felt the familiar heavy-lidded sense of sleepiness steal over her. Each blink lasted longer than the previous. Her eyes closed and her head bobbed like a cork along rolling waves of exhaustion.

She had nearly slipped into slumber beside her companion when a startling worry snapped her back to full attention. *What if we are running out of air?* Heidyl thought. *Are we sleepy because our bodies are starving for oxygen?* Surely the thick squirming barrier of slime would be choking off their oxygen supply by now! She tried to reduce her breathing down to shallow sips of air. Though Heidyl tried not to fret, a host of fears came unbidden to her mind, battering against her resolve like a storm squall. Her heart pounded a sprinter's pace and she felt the air thicken about them. The perimeter of the bluish clouds seemed much closer now. The Fydas bracelet about her wrist no longer glowed as it had before, and the blue mist now clung so close to her face she could no longer see much past the end of her own nose. She reached for Tor'Engryn. He was still lying beside her, oblivious to the moment.

Stay calm! Don't be afraid. No fear. She willed herself to enlarge her faith in the protective power about them, but the more she strained to grasp it the more she felt it slip away. Wrapping her arms about her knees she buried her face. Rocking back and forth, she slowly and methodically began imagining anything that might remotely remind her of protection. Barbed-wire fences. Shields. Army tanks. A wall. Body armor. Scales. At that final thought, an image of a red-eyed dragon flashed into her mind with nightmarish ferocity and she jerked her head up with a gasp.

Moments later she found herself staring into the smiling face of Tor'Engryn. "You's beens all a slumbers," he whispered. His large eyes blinked hopefully at her, with his short arms he gestured behind him. "Look-see like slippy slimer goes away gone!"

Heidyl looked around in alarm. She was still disoriented and tried to make sense of her surroundings. The blue shield of Fydas had completely disappeared and she sat on the stone floor squinting into the dim purple atmosphere. The thin, wet sheen coating the ground and the walls around them reminded her of the slug trails she had once seen in her mother's gardens. The corridor was deathly quiet. Their attackers were gone.

And so was her mother.

"Mom!" Heidyl bolted to her feet. She drew in a great gulp of air and screamed for her, but the tomblike walls swallowed the cry.

"You shush that!" Tor'Engryn said, grabbing her arm. "More's 'll coming back, and mine bag's gone all hollow!" He held his satchel open to her, showing his lack of sling ammunition.

Feeling as helpless as a trapped mouse, Heidyl stood frozen to the spot. It suddenly felt like the very walls had hungry eyes. There was no place to hide and running in any direction was just as likely to get them captured as standing still. She forced herself to think, but no clear plan came. For several moments, they stood like forlorn statues. Then, a new feeling surged through Heidyl. Surprised by its ferocity, she looked down to find her hands clenched into angry fists. Her arms shook and she had never wanted to kick something more in her life. She was experiencing the other side of adrenaline. The fight side. Her teeth were grinding now, and heat flushed her face.

Heidyl, careful not to lose her wits to the urge to punch the wall and break something, quickly considered her options. Chasing the slime and octo-creature without weapons would certainly lead to disaster. Even with weapons they had still been overpowered. She could try to find her way out of here and get help, but the looming darchlyte sentries posted at Blackynspyre's gate might be called to crush her. Without a light, there was no sense going back to try finding her father in the dark passages. Only one option remained; the other lit passage. Heidyl reasoned that it may still lead them to Jayce, and she was sure that wherever he was being held captive, her mother would probably be there now as well.

Impatience finally got the best of the Logarthiym. He had been tapping his foot like a snare drum for several seconds before nudging Heidyl's leg. "Now's whatcha we does?" His voice warbled a little.

Heidyl knelt, taking her companion by his tiny shoulders. "Tor-Tor, go collect your lost stones," she said, nodding in the direction the battle had taken place. Then added with a wink, "Be fast."

The light danced in Tor'Engryn's eyes and he tore off to salvage as much missing ammo as possible. Heidyl smiled at how quickly he was to rally to the fight. Like a lighting fueled bird in search of insects, he darted back and forth across the floor plucking up his precious black rocks. In a few seconds he returned by her side.

Patting his satchel, he said, "Lotsa gone's, but I haves 'nuff.'"

"Good," she nodded. "I hope we don't, but we'll probably need them. So, be ready, okay?" She fondly patted his nodding head.

Together they turned and walked back the way they had come. In a moment they arrived at the junction. This time, however, Heidyl chose the one remaining route they had not yet explored. The floor was still slightly damp from the mucous trail made by the creature that had already come this way earlier.

Taking a deep breath, Heidyl took Tor'Engryn by the hand and strode slowly toward the purple torchlight at the other end of the long hall- way. She had never considered herself to be a particularly brave person, but right now, Heidyl wanted this whole ordeal to end. And rescue was the only path left for her to take.

At the first step forward, curious warmth radiated from the marked spiral spot on her ankle. She paused. The warm sensation dissipated. She cautiously took another forward step. It returned and grew stronger with the following stride. Fearing that it would begin to burn, she stopped to press her fingers against the spot. The flesh above her foot was still cool to the touch and seemed normal. Tor'Engryn cast her a curious glance.

"It's my mark," she whispered. "I think it's trying to tell me some- thing."

The old Logarth squinted and cocked his head, swiveling his ears downward as if listening for a cornered mouse. After a few seconds he shrugged, "Mine hears not a titch."

"No, it's not like that." Heidyl tapped the side of her head to explain. "It's more like I hear it in here."

Tor'Engryn turned his ears upward toward her and closed his eyes to listen once more. Shrugging again he declared, "Nopes. My thinksa there b'nothing at alls in your noggin."

Heidyl laughed. "You're probably right!" Again she patted him affectionately on the head, then nodded toward the hall. "Come on, we need to go this way, I know they are down there."

Together they walked in step, their feet scuffing lightly against the stone floor. Tor'Engryn fished a black stone from his pouch and made it ready in his sling. Heidyl fingered the Fydas bracelet on her wrist. The mark on her ankle resumed its buzzing warmth, guiding them forward like a compass in the gloom.

BANG! BANG! BANG! THREE SHOTS. Thomas had felt his pulse quicken when the sound of distant gunfire reached his ears. The heavy walls and meandering hallways made it impossible to know for sure from where the reports had come, but he broke off in a dead run anyway. The girls were in trouble. Whizzing past the marks he had scratched on the walls, he careened around the stone corners at breakneck speed, his boots flapping hard against the thick floors. The beam of the flashlight bounced wildly as he ran. Thomas was like a possessed madman racing through the dark.

"I'm coming!" He shouted over and over.

BANG!

Another shot! Thomas pulled up short to listen. It was a little closer now. He had closed the distance somewhat but a junction point gave him pause. *Which way?* His mind wheeled frantically. Then as if in reply, two more shots echoed to his left. *Was that six? Is she out of ammunition?* He sprang toward the sound. *How stupid to have split up like this!* Thomas' anger at the decision to separate fueled his sprint. The purplish glow of a sconce peeped from around the next bend. Knowing that Jillian and Heidyl had been following the lights, Thomas doubled his pace. He sped around the turn and halted.

A pulsating wall of dark slime covered the passage. Filling every crevice and crack it was impossible to see beyond. He thought he could hear faint commotion on the far side of the sludge.

"Jillian!" He shouted. "Heidyl!"

The oozing mass absorbed the cries to his family. Picking up a chunk of nearby debris, he threw it at the slime in desperate panic. The piece of rock was slurped into the churning wall like rippling quicksand. Slowly the dark muddy creature slid away from him against the wall, leaving a thin coating of mucous behind. Without a weapon, Thomas scanned the floor for something—*anything*—to penetrate the surface. A pile of haphazard bones provided him with a host of choices. First, he began throwing them, but the attempt was as futile as battling the ocean with pebbles. Finding an old bone resembling a femur, he hefted it like a baseball bat. Swinging wildly, he hacked and slashed at the slop. At first, splashes and sucking sounds gave the impression of progress, but the slime simply folded back in on itself to heal the gashes he made.

In frustration, Thomas gave it one more tremendous blow. The bone sunk deep and sticking fast refused to come free this time. He hefted with all his might until his hands were raw, but it was no use. Thomas watched the bony weapon sink sideways into the monstrous wall and disappear as if being ingested. He shouted again for his wife and daughter then stopped to listen. The sounds of struggle on the far side had subsided. He feared the worst.

There must be another way around this thing! Thomas whirled about scanning the black with his light. There! Down the passageway and to the left another door yawned a black hole at him. He bounded to the spot disappearing onto yet another path through the twisted maze of Blackynspyre.

SCRAPE, SCRAPE, SCRAPE! HE WAS NEARLY FREE. Jayce twisted and tugged at the rusted chain anchor. The pain biting into his wrist and the resulting trickles of blood fueled his fire. He rested his hands on his knees to catch his breath for the hundredth time.

"Just three more," he panted. "Three more yanks!" Taking a deep breath, he threw his strength against his bonds, wincing against the deepening cuts.

The metal rod slid forward several more inches from the effort. "One," he grunted. Repeating the same rhythm, he pulled again with new effort. The rusty spike slid again, this time slightly rattling side to side. "Two!" Sweat poured from his face now, but he felt hope renew. He began formulating his next steps. Once he broke free of the chain, he would lie in wait by the door with this stupid iron rod and knock his wicked uncle—or one of his minions—senseless and find his family.

Tightening the slack on the chain, he braced both feet against the prison slab wall. With colossal effort he pressed his legs against the wall so hard that he suspended his body completely off the ground. The blood rushed in his ears and his vision swam with red heat. His wrist felt as though someone were cutting off his hand with a dull blade.

Someone was screaming. Realizing it was his own voice rending in agony, he gave in to the cry with full effort. He did not care if it brought every beast in this accursed place. Let them come!

The metal groaned and grated against the stone as it reluctantly gave up its ancient hold on the wall. There was an audible crack as the small section of wall literally exploded, sending fragments of rock and rust across the room. The loose spike skittered across the prison cell, dragging the chain with it. Jayce fell violently to the floor and lay there as though dead. His vision swam as oxygen worked to refuel his starved muscles and pounding head. He drank several deep gulps of air before rolling his head to view the door.

He blinked.

It was open.

Had the force of his efforts burst open the cell door as well? He could scarcely believe his luck! But before he could scramble to his feet and make a getaway, a pair of heavy boots stepped into the doorway, blocking his view of freedom.

"Three." The acid tone of Drayven's voice finished the dazed boy's three-count toward freedom with sarcastic charm.

Jayce was incensed that his escape plan would end so abruptly. He tried to rise but was met with his uncle's foot pressed cruelly against his throat. He struggled but was too exhausted to put up any real fight.

"Come!" Drayven hissed over his shoulder and three sniveling rat-men dressed in filthy rags scraped and bowed themselves into the chamber. Each of them bent low, clearly avoiding the unpredictable reach of their malevolent master. "Clean him and take him to the Chamber." He gave the command as if discussing the fate of a mangy dog. His eyes looked disapprovingly over the boy. Drayven's frown deepened when he saw the boy's mangled wrist. He looked accusingly him. "You were supposed to be an unblemished lamb."

Whirling upon the nearest of his rodent slaves he caught the wretch by the scruff of the neck before it could scamper out of reach. It shrieked in pain and horror, covering its horrible face with gnarled hands. Drayven shouted into its large rat-like ear. "You! Make sure that wound is sufficiently dressed and completely covered. Do you hear me?"

"Yesss, Lord Drayven. Oh, so merciful and wise." The rat-man groveled fearful praise at its master. "It will be done! It will. So wise." Drayven grunted and released the poor creature to do his bidding, then stalked out of the rubble-strewn cell. Three more rat creatures carrying clean clothes, a washbasin and a rope entered the cell behind him.

Jayce was smoldering inside. He punched and kicked, bit and scratched but was no match for six desperate slaves. When one of them produced a curved blade from its belt and held the steel against the boy's pale neck, he subsided a bit and obliged the wound dressing and donned the clean clothes under the cold stare of their beady eyes.

The gang of rat creatures led Jayce bound from the tiny cell and into the massive smoke-filled Dragon Chamber. Lord Drayven watched them from his wicked throne-perch and pointed to the far side of the pentagram drawn on the floor. Two rough-sawn wooden posts, about six feet apart stuck up from their anchor points in the stone floor. A lone figure was tied to one of them with a red rope.

Though her back was to him, Jayce recognized her form immediately. "Mom!" He started to call out from the far side of the room. He received a savage punch to his ribs that buckled him to the side, and then a thickly calloused hand was covering his mouth. The clawed fingers pressed so tightly over his face he could scarcely breathe. Jayce stilled under the grip of the rat-men surrounding him. His eyes widened in horror at the scene unfolding before him.

The stone floor of the portal churned like an angry sea. The monster beneath was ready to surface from its thousand-year slumber. The never-ending stream of black smoke poured into the room from the tiny hole in the center of the floor filling the air with the choking presence of pure evil. The room seemed electrified and Jayce felt the prickly chill of wickedness come alive as Drayven rose from the dark throne and strode forward.

Jayce blinked back surprise. The man had changed his clothes. The menacing cloak and dark leathers had been exchanged for an old torn pair of jeans and a ratty sweater. A red and black rope slung casually across one shoulder. The somewhat normal appearance was disarming. Evidence of attempted mending appeared in the form of some rough stitching and mismatched patches over a few of the more obvious holes in his clothing. If not for his gaunt face and angry eyes, being dressed in the dated street attire made Drayven appear very much like his twin brother, Thomas. He stopped when he reached the woman tied to the post.

"Jillian." His voice was gentle. "Are you awake?"

When she did not stir, he lifted her chin with a bony finger. His sister-in-law's eyes fluttered and then opened.

Confusion crossed her features for a moment before recognition took over. "Drayven!" she gasped. Angrily she jerked her head away from his cold touch.

"Always the feisty one, aren't we?" Drayven gave a grim smile.

Jillian was hardly in a mood for games. "Where is my son, you snake? I know he is here. I can feel him." The buzzing sensation from the mark at the base of her skull let her know she was not wrong.

"He is near and safe. For the moment." He eased back and folded his arms across his chest; his eyes darted to the struggling boy behind her across the room. "I fully intend to reunite the family. There is but one simple matter I need you to help me attend to first." Holding up a scroll he unfurled the document for her to see. Jillian's eyes scanned the parchment and then looked past it to the Thin Place on the floor behind Drayven. She recognized the obvious signs of a massive portal on the brink of collapse. The veil between worlds was stretched to its breaking point as the Dragon's jagged limbs pried and strained against it from the other side. Smoke billowed from the hole that had already been torn in the fabric between realms.

"Do you have any idea what you have done?" Her voice was both incredulous and sorrowful.

Drayven smiled, "I've found my salvation!"

"No. Don't you see? You've doomed us all. If that portal falls without being properly opened, then it can never be closed! You'll rip a hole in the universe!"

"I fail to see how this is bad, *sister*." Drayven sighed and pressed his fingers to his head as if talking to a dull child. "Don't *you* see? I *want* it open forever."

It was Jillian's turn to insult. "You're delusional! The other side of that portal is Dearth! It's a cursed void-land that will suck every living thing into itself like a huge vacuum. You're toying with matches while dancing on dynamite."

Drayven's face twisted into a pleased grin. He waggled the parchment in front of her face again. "Then you'd best help me put out the blaze, eh?"

Jillian looked again at the scroll. It was the simple gate opening scroll that the grayvyk must have retrieved for him from their own secret study back on Earth. It still bore teeth marks from being carried in its mouth. She had used its powerful words so many times when entering Haizorr that she did not even need to decipher the phrases any longer. They were permanently etched into her mind.

Drayven leaned closer, "Once you enact this scroll and give me control over the Dragon, I will release you and your boy. You have my word."

Jillian furrowed her brow, "What are you talking about? You can't control the Dragon with that scroll. You need the other one you've been playing with. And even then, you'll never control it!" Inwardly she marveled at the man's foolishness. Was he so blinded by darkness that he could not read a simple scroll? Even Jayce had been able to enact it back on Earth.

Drayven's smug grin vanished. It was his turn to look confused. He drew back a pace to study the tattered sheet in his hand. Though he was marked as a Hunter, not a Cypher like Jillian, certainly he knew one stupid scroll from another. He refused to admit that the words looked like absolute gibberish to him. For the thousandth time he stared hard at the words, willing himself to understand them. And for the thousandth time, the inky markings swam like a million gnats before his vision. It was as if the scroll did not *want* to be read by him, convincing him all the more that he must read it. The effect was maddening.

Scowling, he decided to call her bluff. "Nice try," he puffed out a scoffing laugh. "You think you're so brainy, but I'm not a fool. Bring the Dragon to me!" He shoved the scroll into her face once more.

Exasperated, Jillian sighed, "I've already told you, Drayven. You've got the wrong scroll. This won't give you what you want!"

"There is no other!" he shouted back. His limbs trembled in fury now.

"You mean you lost it?"

Jillian's eyes widened as a new thought cut through the confusion. "If it wasn't you, then how did the darch—?" A sharp slap from Drayven cut her off. Her head snapped to the side from the blow and her eyes watered instantly.

"I'm done bantering. I've been more than reasonable." He snapped his fingers in the air and waved them about like an angry teacher commanding an unruly student. A moment after the gesture, the boy emerged from behind Drayven. Dressed in a clean tunic and bound with a rope, he ambled slowly—eyes downcast. He stopped just behind Drayven's right side.

"Jayce!" Jillian gasped and new tears flowed down her face. "Thank God you're all right!" She wanted to break her bonds and rush over to him more than anything in the world. She called his name again, but he did not so much as glance up at her. He looked sickly and the bruise about his eye looked fresh.

Her eyes turned to narrow slits and she bored her stare into Drayven, "What have you done to him?" Her tone was both accusation and threat.

"To my dear nephew?" He turned and snaked an arm across the boy's shoulders in a mock embrace. Jillian saw him recoil away from Drayven in fear and it boiled her blood. "I've done nothing. Nothing, that is, compared to what you will do to him if you don't do as I ask," Lord Drayven replied coolly.

Then, leaning dangerously close until the tip of his nose touched hers, a malicious command rode along his rancid breath.

"Now. Do it."

THE HUGE DOORS WERE LOCKED. Heidyl and Tor'Engryn pushed and pulled at them to no avail. The little Logarth even tried his sling against the heavy wood, but nothing worked.

Tor'Engryn groaned, "Nows to where we get?"

Heidyl was still feeling around the edges of the doors trying to find a gap. "I don't know. We can't go back, this is the only lit pathway."

The little man paced back and forth in a worried fit muttering his woes aloud while flapping his short arms in the air as if in a heated argument with no one but himself. He kept throwing angry glances at the doors as if the force of his hard stares were battering rams. He stopped suddenly, cocking his head to the side.

"Hangs on a titch—" his voice trailed off and he eased his face forward, pressing one eye against a spot on the door near one of the carved handles.

"What is it?" Heidyl asked, lowering herself beside him.

"Mine cansa see!" His voice was an excited whisper.

"See what?"

He pulled back with a wrinkly grin. "Itsa hee kole!"

Heidyl tilted her head, her brow wrinkling. With an exasperated sigh, the little man pulled her down to the spot so she could take a look. She squeezed her face against the musty smelling door and observed a tiny diamond shaped opening. Pale light from the other side greeted her probing eye.

"It's a key hole!" she exclaimed.

Tor'Engryn rolled his eyes, "Thatsa my alreddy said—a hee kole!" He beamed proudly at her for a moment and then began frantically patting his satchel and parts of his clothing. "Mine has gotsit somewheres," he had taken to muttering again.

Heidyl squinted through the hole again trying to make out the obscure shapes on the other side of the doors. The light was dim, but it appeared to be some sort of sitting or dining room. There were place settings with plates and cups arranged on a large table in the center. Her heart quickened a pace as she realized they must be getting close if they have reached a common use room such as this. She scanned the chamber again for any signs of movement; it would do them no good to burst into a room full of monsters just sitting down to eat.

"Foundsit!" Tor'Engryn triumphantly declared. He elbowed his way past Heidyl, holding a thin metallic object in his stubby fingers. Stuffing it into the key hole he began fidgeting with the rusty lock. The lock-pick scratched and twanged inside the ancient mechanism. The Logarthiym elder scrunched up his face with the effort, his little pink tongue sticking out of his mouth in concentration. "Allsmost. Alllllsmost," he coaxed. He was straining with the effort. Heidyl could faintly hear the squeaking sound of tiny gears grating against one another inside as the mechanism turned.

"Owsa!" Tor'Engryn exclaimed and jumped back. "Bit mine finglers!" He released the lock, clutching his hand in pain. The lock-pick he had just been using was glowing fiery red as if heated by a blacksmith's forge. It rattled in the hole once before falling to the floor with a clink. The unholy Blackynspyre lock appeared to have spat out the foreign object. Angrily, the Logarth spat back before uttering a string of indecipherable curses at the stubborn door.

Cautiously Heidyl peered through the keyhole to be sure there was no one on the other side toying with their entry. Satisfied that the room was still empty, she retrieved the metal pick, which was now cool to the touch.

"Yous takes full of care! Thatsa hurts lots," cautioned Tor'Engryn, still rubbing his sore fingers.

Heidyl was about to respond, when she noticed his eyes suddenly go wide. Like a deer in the woods, Tor'Engryn swiveled first one ear, then the other to face backwards behind him toward the long hall. His upheld burnt little hand indicated she remain silent. She strained her ears into the dim but heard nothing.

"Something's a sneaker," he whispered.

Turning slowly toward the long, empty passage Heidyl and Tor'Engryn stared into the low light. There was no sign of movement save the endless dancing shadows cast by the purple flame of the distant torchlight.

Then she heard it.

A light shuffle like something heavy being dragged across the floor. It came in starts and stops but growing louder each time. For a long moment the two held their breath, staring hard into the gloom. The sound eventually stopped, but now the purple flame mounted at the end of the passage wobbled and weaved back and forth every few seconds, as if in reaction to some large creature breathing upon it.

Then, as if struck by a sudden stiff wind the flame danced low for a split second, creating a long shadow momentarily shrouding the hall in darkness. When the purple fire returned to full strength, something large now appeared in the corridor. It flattened itself against a wall, quickly melting into the shadows. So camouflaged was the approach, that had they not been staring at it, neither observer would have noticed. Slowly it eased its way toward Heidyl and Tor'Engryn, dragging a long, useless tentacle on the ground behind it with a scuff.

"It's come back for us!" Heidyl gasped. She spun around toward the lock and tried digging at it with the small lock-pick.

Tor'Engryn instinctively reached for his sling and readied one of the few remaining black stones. Never taking his eyes off the slinking creature he whispered to her, "You's needsa hurry the up!"

Try as she might, Heidyl was unable to make the pick even touch the cursed lock. Similar to the poles of a magnet, an invisible force now pushed the metal in her hand away from the keyhole. No matter what angle she approached from, Heidyl could only manage to get within an inch or two of the lock before being pressed back. She glanced over her shoulder and instantly regretted it. The tentacled sentry had already closed half the distance of the passage. Tor'Engryn took three bold strides toward the beast and started his sling humming once more.

"Comes back for second helpers, eh? Getsa taste!" he shouted and let loose a volley of stones. The first hit the mark, sending the creature doubling back a pace with a painful moan. However, it dodged the next two projectiles, one of which sailed down to the end of the hall striking the torch with a clank. Dropping from its perch on the stand it winked out with a scatter of violet sparks on the stone floor below. Total darkness engulfed the far end of the corridor. The only remaining light now was the dancing flame above their own heads making them perfectly visible to the beast. Without a backlight, the approaching creature had become invisible to the defending Logarth. He tried aiming for the dragging sound of the advancing sentry, but his panicked breathing was like wind in his own sensitive ears. With only a few projectiles left, he had to use them wisely.

"Figgers its outward yets?" he called over his shoulder to Heidyl. He sent another black stone whistling into the darkness, the sharp snap of it striking the far wall indicating another miss.

She had given up on the lock-pick and had taken to pushing and kicking at the door once more, but it did not so much as rattle on its heavy hinges. "It's no use. It won't budge without its key." The curious mark on her ankle was pulsing now with something like hot and cold flashes. She had barely noticed the sensation in her state of panic, but now she could feel it was telling her something.

"Hurries the up!" Tor'Engryn shouted to her again.

The beast was very close now. Heidyl was certain she could hear its heavy breathing rasping at them from the blackened hall. The Logarthiym Elder's keen eye spotted a tentacle snaking forward as the creature reached the fringes of the light. "Oh no's you don'ts!" he cried and spun his sling once more. At this distance his target was harder to miss, and the precious black bullet struck true. A horrible howl rumbled the hall and the sentry retreated, but only just slightly.

Heidyl stood with her back to the doors now, watching her protector attempt to stand down the onslaught alone. Knowing it was merely a matter of seconds before they were taken captive—or worse—Heidyl fumbled with the Fydas. She concentrated and whispered prayers, but the shielding blue bubble never formed. Again, she thought of every protective thing she could imagine from porcupine quills to bank vaults. The bracelet remained a cold hunk of dead metal on her wrist, while her ankle buzzed and throbbed wildly.

She felt like she was missing something.

Then, like a bolt of lightning, it came to her.

"Mother's key!" she shouted. Fear had caused her to forget about it entirely. Her shaking hands flashed to the ribbon about her neck as she spun back toward the doors. But before she could attempt to push the key into the lock, its cryptic warning flashed to her memory: *Any lock may be opened, should motive be true. If the eye contain darkness; forever closed to you.*

A cascade of thoughts poured through her mind as she tried to measure her motive for opening this blasted door. *If I get this wrong, then we're done for! Why am I really opening this door?*

Escape.

Surely, that would be a pure motive. But Heidyl quickly dismissed the notion, realizing that fear was what really drove her desire for escape. *Fear is too selfish*, she thought.

Her mind suddenly drew a blank as the tiny Logarth appeared, trembling at her side. He had valiantly made his last stand, but it was not enough.

"Tommy Big!" he shouted. "Biggy Tom!" he cried aloud for help and cowered with his face buried into Heidyl's clothes.

That's it! Heidyl remembered the entire reason for her trip to Haizorr in the first place. *For my family! I'm doing this for Jayce! For Mom! I am a Liberty and I am here to set the captives free.*

The pulsing sensation about her marked ankle abruptly ceased. Found.

In a flash she stuffed the key into the lock and twisted. The bolt turned smoothly in its housing. Swinging the heavy doors open, she dragged Tor'Engryn through and latched them closed again behind them. A second later the lumbering beast crashed against the dark timbered doorway, rattling the thick doorposts like thunder from the other side. With thick tentacles whipping against the ancient entryway, the stalking sentry beat an angry staccato percussion upon the sealed doors.

Heidyl and Tor'Engryn slowly backed away, expecting them to splinter any second. But they held, the curse upon the doors was too great to be broken by physical force. Heidyl kissed the key she still held in her hand.

"Thanks, Mom," she whispered before tucking it safely back under her collar.

After a few moments, the pursuing beast grew weary of pounding at the impenetrable door. The thudding beats grew faint, then stopped altogether. Heidyl took a moment to quickly survey the room. Moonlight from a high window illumined a large dusty dining table set with old wood and metal dishes and a few cups. Something smelled dead. A hunk of cheese covered in a thick layer of furry green mold sat next to a dry lump of what looked like it may have been bread once upon a time. A colony of bloated maggots crawled freely in and out of each morsel. Heidyl felt her stomach turn.

Taking Tor'Engryn's hand she said, "Come on. Let's get out of here before that thing finds a new way in."

Darting through an exit at the far end of the room they both instantly felt their nostrils begin to burn.

Smoke.

They were getting close.

JILLIAN FELT HER HEART RACING. She was convinced more than ever that her brother-in-law was an absolute madman. The danger he had put upon them all was beyond his ability to grasp and now with her family thrust into his game, the burden settled hard like a stone upon her soul. The crushing weight of what to do threatened to pulverize her insides. She fought back tears of anger, frustration and pain all at once. Her mark buzzed so wildly at her head that clear thinking seemed impossible. There was no good choice to be made here.

"I'm sure the rest of your brood will be here shortly," cooed Drayven. "We can catch up on old times. Perhaps have a barbecue!" He laughed hysterically at his own jest, playfully jostling the boy at his side. Presently, he coughed once and straightened saying, "Now, Jill. The key. Open the portal."

Jillian looked at the face of her son. He looked terrified by the man holding him there. Her heart flamed and broke at Drayven's mention of the key. Last she knew, Heidyl had been wearing it about her neck ever since she had given it to her in the secret study of their home.

Home.

Earth.

How that place seemed so far away and foreign right now. She would give anything to have the family all gathered around the table for a meal together once more. They did not even need to be speaking to one another—just *together*. How had her blessed life come to this? Hot tears continued to course her cheeks. Desperate to know what happened to her daughter she cried, "You already have the key by now! Where is she, Drayven? Where is Heidyl? What have you done to her?"

For a moment, he looked genuinely perplexed. Then narrowing his eyes at her he said, "Don't play your little mind games with me. This has nothing to do with her. I don't care where your daughter is—she's no concern of mine."

Jillian was sobbing now. The change in subject and the pitiful emotional display disgusted the man. The urge to strike her again surged inside and he balled a fist until his knuckles were so white, they looked like pure bone. He paused and considered Jillian's tears a moment longer. Then, a wicked smile contorted his already twisted face as a new realization struck him.

"Oh, I see." He clucked his tongue in mock rebuke. "Did one of my little friends find her first?"

Jillian's head snapped up.

Seeing he had hit a nerve, Drayven grabbed the boy beside him and pressed the point further, "It's a horrid feeling, isn't it? Not knowing the fate of one's own child. It's enough to make you crazy!" His grin vanished. Leaning deathly close to Jillian's face he whispered, "*You* are the key, Jillian. I never needed some useless trinket. Just you." Then he added with a hiss, "Now, open the door! Unless you want to lose *this* one, too." Drayven tightened his grip about the boy's neck until his face twisted in pain.

Jillian's reddened eyes fluttered to the portal on the floor behind him. Its activity had increased dramatically over the past few moments. Parts of it were stretching so tightly that it appeared like a translucent membrane with something very large straining against it relentlessly from the other side. She fought for the focus to weigh her options. If she opened the portal, then she and her family and countless others would likely be destroyed by the beast. She doubted very much that the ancient Black Dragon would ever bow to Drayven's childish whims. But at least the portal would remain intact and might still be closed somehow. If she refused, could the Dragon eventually rip through if Drayven keeps thinning the veil? Should that happen, then the rift would grow uncontrollably. The land of Dearth would swallow this world and eventually other realms, including Earth.

In the end, there remained no good option.

Both paths were gambles with horrible odds.

The only hope she had was that Drayven seemed convinced that the only way for the Dragon to come through was for her to open the portal. The hole in the center of the room did not give her very much assurance, however. *Still*, she thought, *perhaps it will hold*. She made her choice then. Setting her jaw, she glared at Drayven.

Seeing her stony stare, Drayven sighed. "Tut-tut, Jill. Don't be so hesitant. Here, let's see if we can't loosen your tongue a bit." Without warning he spun and struck the boy beside him, crumpling him to the floor.

Heat flashed over Jillian and she screamed, "Stop it, Drayven!"

Ignoring her, he hoisted the lad back to his feet. When he stopped teetering, Drayven knocked him to the ground again. The boy lay on the cold stone quaking.

"I can do this all day, Jill."

Jillian closed her eyes and prayed for the nightmare to end. Through bitter tears she whispered to the boy on the floor, "We can't open that portal, Jayce. I'm so sorry. If we do, all is lost."

He did not stir, and Jillian wondered if he had heard her at all. He appeared to be in a state of shock. Then like a frightened mouse, the teenage body curled up, turning a fearful face toward them. He glanced at her through his shielding arms but offered no sign of recognition or relief. His eyes darted about like an animal trapped in a cage. Jillian saw a thick trail of mucus running from his nose.

"Jayce? Are you all right?" she pleaded.

Like a cobra, Drayven's hand flashed to the boy's neck once more and hefted him to his feet.

Jillian shrieked, "Enough! Can't you see? He's sick!"

Drayven only shook his head, chuckling cruelly as if the lone participant in a twisted game.

THE LIGHT AT THE END OF THE PASSAGE GREW. Muffled voices and shouts bounced about the walls. Like two wary deer, Heidyl and Tor'Engryn edged forward, each silently praying they would remain unseen. The evil atmosphere of Blackynspyre urging them forward with the dread of constant pursuit had given them no time to forge any sort of real strategy. They had spent much of the past few moments darting through the dim light with fearful glances cast over their shoulders.

As they approached the doorway, Heidyl heard the unmistakable sound of her mother's shout. It struck her heart like an icy hammer and despite her trepidation, she began trotting toward the sound like a loyal puppy. The Logarth at her side clutched at her hand pressing her to remain quiet as they gained one of the several entrances to the Dragon Chamber. Together they crouched low, peering around the stony opening. At first, the enormity of the room caught her attention. She remembered a similar feeling years before on a school trip to the state capitol. The huge domed foyer had made her head dizzy with its grand height and impossible architecture. Except where that building had made her heart soar, this place only made it cringe.

Then her eyes were drawn to the boiling floor. Like a pool of flowing stone, it danced and jumped erratically. Even Tor'Engryn, who was more accustomed to the fantastic curiosities of this realm than Heidyl, stood mouth agape at the odd display. His nose wrinkled in disgust at the steady stream of polluted smoke curling from its center. Stifling an exclamation, he tugged his companion to crouch even lower beside him. After another moment scanning the room, his trembling little arm now extended toward movement across the wide chamber.

Horror washed over Heidyl as she struggled to take in the scene before her. At first glance, it appeared as though her father stood beside her brother, holding him roughly by the scruff of the neck. For the briefest of seconds her heart brightened to see his familiar form. It did not take long, however, before she picked out several alarming differences. To begin with, her father would never behave so roughly toward any of his children. He was manhandling Jayce with utter contempt, shaking him like an old rug. Also, the sallow skin and dark angry eyes could not possibly belong to her dad. Her guts churned as she recognized the figure of her brother's kidnapper. With an air of superiority, he had drawn himself up and was speaking harshly to the unmistakably gentle form of her mother tied to a rough wooden post.

She was crying.

A well of desperate rage flooded Heidyl's soul in that moment. Without thinking, the girl rushed forward. She had barely taken two steps, however, when the sudden weight of Tor'Engryn clamping his body around her leg stopped her mid-stride. His quick eyes had seen something she had not. Startled, she drew back a pace, her eyes darting to a cluster of bodies to the left. So focused had she been on her captive family that she had not noticed the other band standing in the room. Fortunately, she had not gone far enough into the massive chamber to be noticed. Drawing back into the shadowy cover of the doorway, Heidyl and Tor'Engryn surveyed the second group.

Like a small company of rat-like soldiers, the rag-tag gang stood attentively watching their dark master's tirade against the helpless woman. Their hunched shoulders and defeated stares indicated sad lives of subservience. For a moment, Heidyl pitied them. As Drayven's voice railed throughout the room she could see them cower and wince as if bracing themselves against some unseen, painful lashing. She wondered why they did not rise up against him. They certainly looked strong enough. Their thick limbs and gnarled hands spoke of strength enough to overpower just one man. And there certainly were enough of them to do it. Then she noticed that in the grasp of several of those strong hands lay a rope. Presently, two of the troop straightened upright, seemingly locked in a struggle of sorts. One of them was pressing a hand over the mouth of another to silence it. Two more ratmen stepped closer to help subdue the writhing figure with several blows to its mid-section.

Heidyl's hand flew to her own mouth in shock as she recognized the face contorting with pain before it disappeared once more below the line of bent shoulders.

"Jayce?" she gasped, ready to run forward again. She took a halting step forward and froze.

The thin skin of the stone floor portal had suddenly begun rising to an impossible height. Like a tidal wave in the center of the room it climbed toward the rafters. It was so large that it completely blocked Heidyl's view of the scene before her. Something like a long black spike struck out from the hole at the peak of the mound, twisting and turning as if probing for something. Smoke bubbled up and swirled in the air around it.

The maniacal voice of Drayven fairly shrieked with glee from the other side of the room, "You see? He is coming! Salvation is here!"

PART XII: THE REVELATION

DRAYVEN FLEW INTO A CRAZED FIT. He fairly danced with excitement at the towering display of the Dragon manifesting itself so closely. He shook the shoulders of the boy beside him while pointing wildly at the huge mound in the room. "He's searching for the blood!" he shouted. "He's coming through!"

Jillian's eyes went wide both at her brother-in-law's behavior and at the sudden transformation of the portal. She could see the unmistakable shapes of scales and limbs pressing hard against the portal desperately trying to force a way into Haizorr. The blackened claw stood out like a wicked spire atop a wicked tower. *This is how it ends,* she thought. *That portal isn't going to hold much longer.* And yet, impossibly, it still did not yield even under the full brunt of the Dragon's force from the other side.

Drayven suddenly seemed frantic. "I know what to do!" He was shouting into the face of the frightened boy beside him now. "We never needed a Cypher to open the portal—just the blood of the spotless lamb!" He smacked his forehead with the heel of his hand as if uncovering some great mystery. "How could I not see it, even when the Dragon told me himself!" He shook his head in disbelief at his own perceived oversight, then turning to the lad he commanded, "Bring me the blade."

The teenage face only stared blankly back at Lord Drayven. The trail of mucus from the lad's nose had reached his lips and presently, a long purple tongue snaked out, licking it clean.

"Useless fools! The blade, the BLADE!" he bellowed and shoved the boy.

Too hard.

Tumbling backward, the façade was broken as the three trillych imps that had conjured the visage of Jayce separated to reveal their true forms. The mirage of rope, clothing, and body of a teenage boy all came apart from one another in a jostling show of black and white particles. Transfiguring back into the trio of sickly gargoyle-like creatures, the trillych now lay forlorn upon the floor. One of them craned its pencil-thin neck around to face its boggled eyes at Jillian.

She screamed.

"What—What have you done to Jayce?" Her mind felt as though it were splitting apart.

Ignoring her, Drayven rushed upon the trillych, scattering them into startled flight like a flock of gulls. In a few seconds, one of them wheeled about the room and scooped up the dark lord's dagger from his twisted throne and deposited it into his impatient hand, before flying into a far corner to cower with its gruesome siblings. Brandishing the blade, Drayven strode back toward Jillian and raised the bone-handled knife high. "I've no need of you any longer," he said bringing the edge down in a flash. Jillian flinched, trying to dodge the pending slice, but the ropes held her fast.

And then, she was free, her bonds neatly cut by the blow she thought was surely meant to end her life.

Still stunned by the swift turn of events, Jillian staggered back a pace. Catching her by the arm in his iron grip Drayven bellowed toward the pack of rat-men, "Bring him!" He cast a glance at the form within the stretched portal looming even higher than before and added "Hurry!" The band of slaves rushed to obey, roughly dragging the kicking lad with them. Drayven tossed one of them the red and black climbing rope he had been holding. "Tie him up," he ordered, gesturing to the two posts.

Jillian could stand it no longer. The sight of her lost son now alive and well yet being rough-handled before her eyes filled her to overflowing. She turned abruptly and delivered a savage kick to her captor, buckling him at knees. With his grasp loosened she tore away and rushed upon the rats, her lungs punching out a series of startling shouts. The simple beasts were caught off guard and plainly did not know what to do next. Two of them, seeing their master down rushed to his aid but were angrily cuffed away. The others nervously remained with their charge, but so oppressed were they that none of them had much heart left in the task. One creature seeing the chance to escape the hateful presence of its master simply scuttled away from the room, while still another stood and merely absorbed Jillian's angry blows. Eventually she reached her captive son. Wresting him away from the iron grip of the nearest rodent-slave Jillian clutched Jayce in an eager embrace. Her eyes were wet with tears. At the sight of his mother displaying such devotion to her son, Jayce could feel his own emotions welling up, but the situation was still too grim for him to lower his guard. A rush of movement caught his attention.

"Mom!" he gasped. "Run!" The tearful reunion was cut far too short by Drayven's quick recovery. Seizing Jillian by the hair he yanked her backward, throwing her to the ground behind him. Unable to regain her footing, Jillian stumbled back and fell striking her head hard against the cold floor. She lay unmoving. Jayce heard the loud crack of the impact and though his hands were bound, rushed forward to her aid. But the strong arm of his uncle was already upon him, tearing his tunic at the seams. Jayce writhed and kicked. Desperation had given strength to his limbs and Drayven struggled to restrain him.

Turning to his dumbfounded slaves Lord Drayven cut the air with a shout, "I said bind him! Or you will feel my blade!"

As if snapping out of dreamlike stupor, the remaining rat-men jumped to the task. A moment later, and after much scuffling, Jayce was bound fast, arms stretched wide between the twin anchored posts. With the dirty-work done, Drayven waved off the rat-men, sending them scampering into their various holes and caverns. The fearful slaves were all too eager to leave their vengeful master. Jayce, tired from the struggle, watched his mother as she lay quiet on the floor beside him. She was still breathing, but a small pool of blood darkened the stone beneath her head. Jayce thought he heard her moan softly.

He called to her, "Mom? Can you hear me? Mom!"

Her eyes fluttered once but did not open.

"She needs help! She's bleeding! Let me go!" Jayce roared at Drayven, now looming before him. His silhouetted form starkly outlined against the backdrop built by the Dragon's wiles in the world just beyond.

"Ah yes, blood. Then freedom. That's the way it works, boy." He shook his head again and chuckled to himself, "I still can't believe I didn't think of this before." Abruptly turning to the rising mound of the gathering portal behind him, he called out, "Patience has won! You see? Salvation!" He raised the knife aloft in salute to the Dragon before whirling back to face his captive nephew.

Brandishing the blade ceremoniously, he approached the boy.

"Wh—What are you doing?" Jayce stammered, shying away from Drayven's approach.

"It's nothing personal, you understand," said Drayven as he adjusted his grip on the weapon's bony hilt. "We just need to be free."

He raised the blade high.

"Uncle Dray! NO!"

Suddenly, a raspy shout tore into the air from the floor, halting Drayven's advance.

"Dissere—!"

Lying on the hard stone, Jillian had been a captive audience to the sacrificial drama playing out before her; watching the whole scene through half-closed eyelids. Only now had her consciousness returned enough for her to act. Wobbly and racked with pain, Jillian struggled to her knees, the angry gash on her skull still slick with blood. Her vision swam and she rocked unsteadily. Then raising an outstretched arm toward the strained portal, she did the one thing she could think of to save her son from being slain by her husband's crazed brother. Whether it would buy some time or doom them all she did not know.

Regardless, she opened the door.

"Dissere portas!"

The effort was all she could muster before slumping back to the floor, unconscious once again. At once, the sound of a thousand freight trains poured into the room. Smoke and intense heat thundered through the widening portal as if issuing from a massive cannon blast.

The Black Dragon was finally free.

THE GROUND SHOOK VIOLENTLY. Like an explosion beneath the bedrock, Blackynspyre's dark halls vibrated as if struck by a mountainous hammer. Thomas skidded to a halt as bits of dust and crumbling rock rained down upon him from the shaking ceiling. He could smell smoke coming from somewhere up ahead. Imaging the worst, he put on a burst of speed through the dark, allowing his nose to guide him. Upon rounding yet another corner he saw a lit doorway at the end of a long tunnel. The sight that greeted him upon gaining the entrance stole Thomas' breath.

He arrived through the slaves' service entrance granting him a view of all points of the large room. Plumes of smoke billowed up from a large writhing mass in the middle of the space. The floor looked liquid, like a black puddle filling a deep hole. Something large stirred surface, but the obscuring smoke made it impossible for him to clearly see what it was—though he had a strong guess. Near the rim of the spreading hole in the floor stood two figures. Thomas felt his heart clench at the sight of his twin brother. He wore the same clothes as the day he lost him, and it took him back to that painful day and the following years of fretful, fruitless searching. He had longed for a redemptive reunion, but it was clear now that today was not going to grant him any such opportunity. Drayven's drawn face and angular features now framed a set of deeply hungry eyes. Facing the emerging beast, a mixture of elation and fear had fastened themselves to Drayven's taut face. Deeply taken with the object of his dark desires now rising from the void, he had all but forgotten about Jayce still tied up behind him. He let the ceremonial knife clatter to the floor.

Like swarming bees, rage and horror filled Thomas at the sight of his son tethered and bruised, and his wife lying lifeless on the floor beside him. His teeth grinding, he clenched his fists readying himself to rush upon Drayven. *Now there will definitely be a reunion,* he thought. He took an angry step forward but the subtle movement of something green across the room to the right caught his eye. He stopped his advance, squinting through the gathering smoky gloom. There, cowering in the opening of another doorway he noted the huddled forms of Heidyl and Tor'Engryn. Abject terror was painted across both of their faces while they watched a living nightmare being birthed before their very eyes.

Thomas drew back a pace, an idea quickly forming in his mind. Taking advantage of the distractive chaos in the room, he flashed a quick signal with the red strobe of his flashlight toward his daughter's face. The effect worked and she waved in startled acknowledgment. Thomas saw a flicker of relief at his arrival touch her frightened features while Tor'Engryn fairly danced with delight at the welcome sight of his friend. Glancing again at the rapturous face of his distracted brother observing the Dragon's rise into Haizorr, Thomas motioned for them to run to him. The rapidly opening portal had become a bubbling cauldron of black. He could only hope that the tumult in the vast chamber was enough to keep Drayven from noticing the movements of his daughter and the nimble Logarth.

He need not worry about the Ancient one, for Tor'Engryn had flitted to his side in less than a second. Thomas held his breath as he watched Heidyl dart from cover to cover, working her way around the outer perimeter of the room until she fell into the waiting arms of her father. He fought the urge to hold her long. There was such little time.

Pulling back to look into her tear-stained face he asked, "Are you okay?"

She sniffed and nodded, rubbing her eyes with a sleeve.

"Good. Listen, we've got to get Mom and Jayce and get back to the Tree Gate as fast as possible." Shrugging off his pack he emptied its contents onto the stone floor. Amid the pile of supplies lay several scrolls. Snatching one of them up he then unzipped the pocket that held the severed trillych tongue. It still flopped and writhed like a lazy snake, although much slower than before. Thomas wondered if its healing properties were still intact. He handed it to Tor'Engryn who turned his face away in disgust.

"Itsa gross wiggler! Bleah!"

"I know," Thomas said, "but it may have the power to heal Biggy Jill. You've got to get it to her!" The Logarthiym Ancient looked doubtful, but nodded, doing his best to stifle the gagging urges he felt while holding the sticky tongue.

Another tremor shook the ground as the portal opened further. A low hissing sound filled the chamber, causing the hair on Heidyl's arms to prickle and raise.

"What should I do, Dad?" she asked, trying to push fear aside.

"You need to go with Tor'Engryn. Once Mom is clear, take that knife over there and free your brother," he said while pointing to the bone-handled blade lying on the floor beside Jayce. Heidyl's eyes went wide and she swallowed hard. Doubt and fear made her legs feel like lead.

Hugging her once more, he said, "I'll distract him so you can approach from behind. Trust me, I know my brother. Once he sees me, he'll be so fixed on my position, he probably won't even notice you. Now, hurry, before the Dragon is fully through the portal!"

With a brave nod she shuffled cautiously to the doorway. The room felt charged with dark electricity. Everything, including the air, felt dangerous. Fortunately, the smoke had thickened somewhat, adding further cover to their approach. Heidyl drew her shirt over her nose and mouth to prevent coughing. Thomas watched his daughter's catlike movements about the edges of the room. True to form, Drayven was still enthralled with the Dragon's birth into this realm. He cooed and called to it as though coaxing a tender child to emerge from a hiding place. He had not noticed the lightning-quick appearance of Tor'Engryn from behind as he crept beside Jayce toward the still form lying on the floor.

The ancient Logarth tenderly cradled Jillian's head in his small hands and began smearing the tongue about the wound. He whispered to her in his native language, watching her closely while still keeping a wary eye upon the back of Drayven should he whirl around unexpectedly. Jillian lay deathly still in Tor'Engryn's arms, her face drawn and pale. Worry creased the worn face of the Elder as he caressed the bruised head of his friend. Presently, the trillych tongue went limp and began to shrivel like a deflating purple balloon. Any healing properties it once held were now completely spent. Jillian did not move. Fighting fresh tears, Tor'Engryn tenderly kissed her forehead before shifting to a position to clasp both of her arms. Bracing his feet and heaving with all his might, he attempted to drag the much larger Jillian to safety. He could only move her body a few inches before he needed to rest.

The abrupt movement caught Jayce's attention. Thinking the little Logarth was another of his uncle's minions he shouted angrily.

"Hey! Get away from her!"

Startled, Tor'Engryn dropped Jillian's hands. He quickly motioned for Jayce to be quiet. Only then did Jayce realize his mistake. His eyes darted toward Drayven's back.

Thomas, watching from his vantage point across the room saw Drayven make a half turn toward Jayce. He had no choice now, he had to make his move!

Stepping into full view, Thomas shouted, "Drayven!"

Recognizing the voice, the wayward twin turned to face his brother. The perpetual scowl he wore slowly gave way to a smug grin. How he had longed for this moment. The upper hand was finally his and Drayven gave in to the urge to savor the dark satisfaction now flowing within him.

"Brother," he said licking his cracked lips. "How I've missed you these many years!"

Sarcasm dripped from his voice like acid and Thomas knew he must be careful not to play into his brother's deadly game. Everything hinged on Heidyl reaching Jillian and Jayce without detection. Careful not to draw attention to her, Thomas noted her advance through the corner of his eye. She had gained a blind spot to the rear of Drayven and was carefully picking her way closer to her captive brother. He was thankful—and surprised—that the portal was opening so slowly. How Drayven had ever gotten it to open he did not know, but he surmised that since it was so much larger than the Tree Gate, it must take longer to unfurl. Still, it would not take forever. Given the rate at which it seemed to be spreading apart, Thomas guessed they only had another minute or two. The guttural growls and shifting air growing from within the darkening center were a testament to that.

Jayce, now fully aware of the precarious rescue attempt at hand, held silent. For the hundredth time, he tested his wrists against the unrelenting ropes. Though his heart leaped within him to see his father once more, he dared not call out again for fear of drawing his uncle's attention to the Logarthiym ally busily caring for his mother. The relief he felt upon seeing his family's valiant mission to save him gave way to a seeping mixture of shame and guilt. They were all in the gravest of peril—all because of him. Jayce stifled a growing urge to call out his confession and love to his father. Instead, he locked his eyes on Thomas through the gathering smoke and prayed.

Like two rival gunslingers the brothers faced each other through the smoggy room. Thomas would have given anything to have his revolver at the present moment, not that he wished to harm his twin, but only for the leverage it would lend to him. Instead he held an old, flopping scroll in one hand and the flimsiest of hopes in his heart. Drayven, on the other hand, held his family hostage with a dragon. The odds were certainly not tipping fairly.

"Fitting, don't you think?" Drayven sneered. "You took all that was precious to me. And here I am to repay the favor." He gestured backward with his arm toward Jayce.

Tor'Engryn had nearly dragged Jillian clear of the area and Thomas could see Heidyl now crouching behind a heap of rubble about ten yards away from the spot where the knife lay on the floor. Thinking Drayven might turn around any second, Thomas jumped quickly back into the conversation. He took another bold step forward.

"I searched for you for years," Thomas explained. "You fell through the portal by accident. I had no idea—"

"You left me to die!" Drayven cut him off, jabbing an accusing finger at his twin. Then he added, "I find it very peculiar that a Seeker like you would only strive to find and steal my scroll rather than locate your own brother!"

Years of lonely bitterness had poisoned the man's mind. Thomas shook his head, trying to explain. "It doesn't work like that, Dray. I can't just turn it on or off."

Drayven shrugged, "It's no matter really. I've got what I want." He pointed to the portal. Its surface had quieted from a rolling boil to a simmering black pond. The gateway to Dearth had fully opened. He frowned for a moment, wondering why the Dragon had paused the grand entry from the void and into this world. *Maybe it's just enjoying the show,* thought Drayven.

Thomas regarded the deathly dark opening. It seemed to absorb all surrounding light touching it. He shied away from it a step. "Untie him, it's me you want."

Drayven snorted. "The Dragon needs a spotless lamb, Thomas. He told me that much himself. You and I are marked. The pure sacrifice is the only way we'll be free." He stared back into the black water, lost inside himself for a moment. For a few precious seconds Thomas thought he even looked a little sad.

Seeing a rare, vulnerable opportunity Thomas pressed him. "You don't want this," he said, nodding toward the portal. "Come back with me. I'll help you find your daughter, Drayven," he said softly. "We can do that together."

"Raiya's not a scroll, brother," Drayven sniffed. "You Seekers only care for trinkets and gadgets. I knew you'd come. Not for me, but for that scroll. A good Hunter always uses the right bait, Thomas." He looked up, grinning once again at his twin.

Thomas stiffened. "What do you mean?"

"I can't read those foolish parchments," said Drayven, waving his hand toward the one Thomas held. "That's a Cypher's gift."

The color drained from Thomas' face. "You mean you set this whole thing up?" Could this really have been nothing more than an elaborate plan concocted simply to draw him in? The shock of it all was maddening, but he had to keep his composure. He could now see Heidyl begin making her move behind Drayven to retrieve the knife. She padded across the dusty stones, silent as a cat.

Like delivering the punchline to his own savage joke, laughter rang out from Drayven. "I never needed your scrolls. Just someone who could open the door!" He jerked his arm backward again toward the place where Jillian had been lying, unaware that she was no longer there. "You've always been so predictable, Thomas. I knew you'd come for it someday. You led my grayvyks right to your door and now I've got the Cypher—and the spotless lamb!" With that he spun toward Jayce to drive his final point home.

And froze.

Heidyl had crept within a few feet of Jayce and stood poised to sever the red and black ropes that held him. But under the terrifying stare of Drayven, Heidyl was like a fragile doe caught in a beam of light. Her trembling hands clutched the knife awkwardly.

"Well, look what we have here! This just keeps getting better!" laughed Drayven making a step toward Heidyl. "Did you really bring the entire family to visit me, Thomas?" Turning his head, he flashed a grin back at his brother. "Poor little bunny," he said.

Thomas felt his insides turn to water. It was the same gut-twisting smile he had seen all those years before when they were children and Drayven had mercilessly tortured the tiny rabbit he had found in the woods where they camped.

Heidyl nimbly darted back and out of reach brandishing the blade to keep her uncle at bay. He turned his dark eyes back to the girl, his large pupils resembling those of a hungry hawk.

Thomas saw his chance then. Like a front line soldier he charged toward the turned back of his brother. If he could somehow distract him long enough for Heidyl to cut Jayce's bonds, they could make a run for it and leave this dreadful place. He had barely closed half the distance, however, when a thick black limb reached up from the portal floor to plant itself directly in his path. It landed with an echoing thud that shook the walls. Thomas pulled up sharply, unable to go any further. With the gaping black portal looming perilously close to his right, and the chamber wall to the left, he was forced to step back.

The foreleg of the beast was thicker than a tree trunk and ended in an array of glistening black claws as long as a man's arm. A second leg shot up from the dark hole and gripped the portal's rim on the far side of the room. Then a broad neck darker than the blackest night coiled up from the deep, bringing with it a massive serpentine head. Horns struck out atop its brow like a wicked crown set over large deeply set eyes that glowed like a furnace. Heaving its great bulk further into the room, two furled wings appeared, each one ending in a sickle-like hook at the joint. Its skin was darker than coal and absorbed the light around it like a black sponge. The monster's entire essence appeared to have been fashioned out of absolute darkness itself.

Drayven whirled around and found himself staring straight up into the fiery eyes of pure evil.

And the Black Dragon of Dearth stared straight through the man's soul.

DARK SILENCE CLAIMED THE ROOM. The presence of the Dragon was like that of many ancient kings filling the chamber with overwhelming authority. At once regal and terrifying the great head tilted to regard the room's inhabitants, swiveling eyes of flame upon each. This was no mindless beast, but a being possessed of superior intelligence. And great malice.

Though all felt tangible fear pass over them in that sweeping gaze, only Drayven knelt. The subservient display drew the attention of the Dragon and it loomed over the man, grinning with rows of teeth like black lances. Something like a liquid smoke leaked from between the spaces of its teeth to spatter onto the floor. The effect was like black acid scorching the stone surface.

"My Salvation!" Drayven cried out through a dry throat. "I've brought you the spotless lamb!" He bowed low, gesturing toward the boy beside him. Jayce was trembling in his bonds. With his arms stretched wide between the posts he felt stripped bare beneath the jaws of the Dragon hovering just a few feet above his head.

Thomas shouted, "Drayven, stop! This is not the way!"

Incensed that his brother should interrupt his long-awaited sacred moment, Drayven shot upright and screamed, "Silence! You have no say here! You took Raiya from me and now you will suffer the same." His voice climbed to an ear-splitting pitch and he shrieked, "This is your fault, brother—you made me what I am!" He shook with rage and sweat dampened his clothes. "Recognize this rope, Thomas?" he said, pointing to the red and black corded nylon rope lashed about Jayce's wrists. Thomas remembered it too well. It was the same rope from his rescue attempt years ago. The same strand that haunted his dreams at times, repeatedly accusing him of failure. Now it served as a mocking monument to his own foolishness.

"I tried to *save* you with that rope, Drayven," Thomas pleaded.

"And yet you will!" he retorted, licking his lips. His eyes had gone wild and were darting back and forth from dragon to brother.

Thomas knew then that his brother had traveled beyond the point of being reasoned with. Having performed this revenge plan of his so many times in the playground of a twisted mind, it had become a living part of the man. Thomas glanced down again at the brittle scroll clasped in his hand. Damp spots from his sweating palms had stained the surface, but he could still read the words clear enough. He swallowed hard. There would be but one chance now to save his son. The timing had to be perfect. The words had to be right. His hope had to be sure.

Drayven's speech amidst his masterful plan had bolstered his boldness and he stabbed a long finger at the towering Dragon and then turned it upon Jayce. "There! There is your spotless sacrifice!"

As if waiting for just such a cue, the gaping jaws spread wider. For a split second it leveled its gaze upon Jayce, as if sizing him up. The incinerating eyes flared brightly, and Jayce frantically pulled at the cords until his wrists bled. Then, like a cobra preparing to strike, the Black Dragon of Dearth drew itself back to full height while winding its great neck like a coiled spring. The jaws of the beast spread wide, unhinging at the joint to make room for the feast.

"*Permuatio locus transitus!*" Thomas' voice echoed about the chamber. The air directly surrounding him rippled and flashed as he enacted the transfer scroll in his shaking hand.

A half-second later, he was staring down the black cavernous throat of the Dragon. Instantly his wrists burned as the taut red and black rope bit into them, stretching his arms wide. Looking across the room to the very spot he stood just a flash before, he saw a bewildered—and free—Jayce. Thomas sighed in relief. The transfer scroll had succeeded.

Jayce staggered backward a pace and adjusted his balance to compensate for the sudden freedom. The sensation was like being locked in a tug-of-war match abruptly ending where the opponent had simply let go of the rope. His mind reeled, struggling to make sense of what had just happened. Taking stock of the new position in the room his eyes landed upon his father's bound figure before the Dragon. For a brief second, time seemed to stand still as father and son shared a glance.

Thomas was speaking to him. Though Jayce could not hear what he said, the familiar family gesture of arms outspread said everything. He mouthed the words, "I love you—this big."

A flash of shadow-black scales, and then he was gone.

The great mouth of the black beast had swallowed the man whole, leaving nothing behind save two neatly clipped ropes still tied to their sacrificial posts. They dangled lifelessly, now void of their captive, the coil of extra slack drooping lazily into the open portal below the Dragon's belly.

A chorus of three voices screamed as one. "No!"

The cry of sorrow from Jayce and Heidyl mingled with the cry of malicious outrage from Drayven. All three had witnessed the tragedy that consumed Thomas and each had raised a shout.

Instantly, tears leapt from Heidyl's eyes and she buried her face in her hands, trying to unsee that which could never again be unseen. Jayce felt as though he had been kicked in the stomach at the sight and thought he might never regain his breath. Tor'Engryn, who had dragged Jillian from the room and into a side passage, heard the anguish and could only guess at the horror. Jillian was making rapid recovery now, growing more awake each moment and he had to do his best to keep her still. The trillych tongue had spent its final healing properties upon her, and soon she would awake to the nightmare.

Drayven could not believe his eyes. His mouth hung open aghast at what had just happened. The Dragon had consumed the wrong sacrifice! Hot anger brought him to a boil. With untempered words he launched into a raging fit.

"You stupid beast!" he began, "You took the wrong one!"

Slowly, the great head swiveled toward the man, who was now ranting and raving like a spoiled child. His waving arms and stamping feet made him look like an insect compared to the great serpent.

"That's right, you old fool!" He was shaking his fists at the Dragon now. "I gift-wrapped a spotless sacrifice and you blindly gulped that unworthy wretch instead!" The Dragon cocked its head almost playfully at Drayven and leaned in close, eyeing the man as if he were a toad in the dirt. Scaly black lips parted again to reveal rows of razor-sharp teeth, Drayven took an uneasy step backward.

Hearing the railing accusation against his father, Jayce rose up in defense. He shouted from across the room through hot tears, "Shut your mouth, Drayven! Don't ever talk about my father! You're the unworthy one!" More than anything in the world he wanted to throttle him and choke the words out of the wicked man, but the portal and the Dragon blocked his path. Finding a chunk of rubble by his feet, he hurled it at Drayven with all his might. But his aim was not true and the stone caught the Dragon in the back of the neck before tumbling harmlessly into the abyss.

Eager to deflect the creature's attention, Drayven pointed, "You see? There! There is your insolent little sacrificial lamb!"

The smoldering eye looked upon the man with utter disdain. Then, in one swift motion, the Black Dragon raised a mammoth clawed hand and batted Drayven's body toward itself like a cat toying with a mouse. For a moment, shock painted the man's face before he was sent sprawling. He slid across the floor, frantically flailing his limbs for any sort of handhold to stop the momentum. He rolled uncontrollably toward the edge of the black portal and tumbled in. For a few precious seconds his strong hands held the rim of the gateway like a rock climber clinging to a cliff. But the land of Dearth sucked at him from below like a hot tar pit.

And then, Drayven was gone.

THE DRAGON WHIRLED UPON JAYCE. With the speed of an adder it struck at the place where he stood, but Jayce had been ready. Diving to the left he narrowly escaped the snapping jaws by a hairsbreadth. Missing its mark, the long snout of the Dragon collided with the wall instead. The room shook with the impact. Drawing back to strike again, the great serpent turned its body to fully face the boy. Slowly it drew curved claws together to hedge

318

Jayce in on either side. He backed against the wall, trapped.

There would be no missing this time.

Heidyl, still recovering from the shock of her father's disappearance rose unsteadily from her hiding place. The sudden fear that came with the emergence of the Dragon followed by the mind-boggling switch Thomas had made with Jayce had driven her to remain under cover for a time. Though she had been helpless to help her father, she was determined now to act on her brother's behalf. Tracks of tears ran down her dusty face, but she was desperate to distract the Dragon and spare Jayce. Knife in hand, she darted back to the edge of the portal and hacked at the beast's enormous foreleg.

It was a useless gesture, and the Dragon batted her away as if carelessly brushing off an annoying fly. Heidyl tumbled backward but quickly regained her footing. The knife flew from her grasp in the shuffle.

The black monster chose to ignore her, turning full attention back upon the boy trapped between its razor clutches. Its huge grinning mouth parted revealing many spear-like teeth. A black forked tongue flicked out from between the opening jaws while the neck coiled back again.

Heidyl screamed.

Jayce flattened himself against the hard stone at his back.

But before the creature could bring the great jaws to descend upon him, a hollow thud echoed from the chamber walls followed by a loud crash. A small pile of dislodged rubble from the domed ceiling rained down upon the Dragon's head. Confident that Jayce was still trapped between its iron-black talons, the beast paused to regard the source of the interruption. The pounding increased, as did the debris tumbling from the ceiling. A series of low groans seemed to reverberate up from the ground.

Then, a thunderous crash from a place high on the wall produced a gaping hole in the dome. Stone and debris flew into the room like a meteor shower. Another concussive blow and the hole widened, allowing a great ray of Haizorr sunlight to stream into the blackened chamber like a brilliant laser beam. The light struck the Dragon full in the face and it recoiled. Blinded by the brilliance, it raised both clawed hands to shield its hurting eyes.

Jayce saw his chance then and ran. Rounding the thin bridge of stone that rimmed the portal edge he bolted straight for his sister. They held each other tightly for a moment, but the room shook violently again and startled them apart.

"What's happening?" Heidyl gasped.

The ragged hole in the arching stone was widening still. In seconds it became a gaping cavern that reached from floor to ceiling. Several more sets of enormous gnarled hands were reaching in to rip and tear at the structure. Light poured through the rough opening, bathing the room and covering the Black Dragon in warm luminance. The beast convulsed as if in great pain.

Eyes wide, Jayce pointed, "The darchlytes have come!"

As if on cue, several of the tall tree-like creatures climbed through the large entryway they had made and immediately began attacking the Dragon. Though still much smaller than the black serpent, their savage blows and strong limbs made up for the difference and they greatly encumbered the beast for a time. But in the end, the initial assault sadly ended with the first three brave darchlytes being shaken off and raked into the abyss of Dearth by the steely black claws of the Dragon.

Then, as if unfolding a great black canopy, the Dragon unfurled its enormous wings like a shield against the offending light. Immediately, the room was shrouded once again in a darkness thicker than blackened ash. Another wave of attacking darchlytes had already reached the opening in the wall, and beyond them still more could be seen lumbering across the barren land to lay siege to Blackynspyre. The dark gate of the fortress lay torn to pieces outside, and the noble giants poured through the breach in somber silence. Their cerulean eyes flashed with blue heat as they advanced. The darchlyte race had not forgotten the treachery of the Black Dragon and were eager to dispatch the beast once and for all.

But the ancient serpent would not be taken so easily. The moment the next surge of darchlytes reached the opening, the Dragon struck. Black flame spewed from the gaping mouth of the monster in a torrent, spraying liquid death across the attackers like a fire hose. The weapon of the Dragon was no ordinary fire, but a wickedness born of the land of Dearth. Rather than burst into flames as one might expect, the poor creatures were disintegrated in black flashes of imploding smoke like miniature supernovas. The essence of each darchlyte was swallowed up by the black inferno and instantly transported to the void land itself, bound in the eternal prison of Dearth.

Though they could see still more of the darchlytes gaining entrance to the stone fortress, Jayce and Heidyl felt hope drain from their bodies. The blast from the serpent had been utterly devastating. How could anything stand against such a weapon? They decided then to turn full retreat, find Tor'Engryn and their mother and get back home. They had not gotten far when a piercing howl suddenly dropped them to their knees. Clapping their hands over their ears against the biting sound, brother and sister cowered together on the hard chamber floor. Through squinting eyes and clenched teeth, they looked with dread upon the source of the clamor.

The Black Dragon of Dearth stood with its neck extended and toothy maw gaping wide at the opening in the chamber. Its wicked voice shot like a cannon blast toward the sky outside. The most unholy scream imaginable tore from its throat to smother the world in blended tones of rage, agony, hatred, and fear. It was the sound of a thousand wars and a million anguished cries piercing the atmosphere like a column of blistering noise. After a long moment, the beast clapped its jaws shut with a punctuating snap, abruptly biting off the horrible roar. The onslaught of darchlytes had halted for the moment looking from one to another in bewilderment. The entire land was over swept with an eerie creeping silence that brought chills to the spine.

Jayce and Heidyl looked at each other with widened eyes and cautiously unstopped their ears, which were ringing horribly now. Soon the ringing was replaced by dozens, maybe hundreds of answering howls. Some distant, and others quite near.

"Grayvyks!" Jayce gasped, a little louder than he realized.

The Dragon, hearing the boy's mounting fear, swayed its horned head to stare at him with blazing eyes. Its teeth jutted out at all angles creating what only can be described as a smug sort of grin. The roar had been a rallying cry for all dark creatures to attend to the battle.

And attend they did.

Shrieks and grunts floated through the air at all angles. A gathering cacophony of growling, snarling and snorting was accompanied by the unmistakable rumble of many charging feet. The Dragon had assembled its rag tag army of darkness in the space of a single breath. Resuming its posture under the shadowy shield of its dark wings, the ancient serpent turned its attention back to the battlefield where his dark children had begun their defense of Blackynspyre. There was no organizing of ranks or orderly assembly of any kind. Just a savage display of chaotic destruction as a variety of dark creatures swarmed against the towering darchlytes like a colony of ravenous fire ants.

Tentacled sentries entangled the legs of their quarry to trip them, enormous white wolves with pink eyes and bright red mouths slashed and snapped, slithering blobs clung to the darchlyte warriors like slimy acid to burn away at their hardened skin.

But the grayvyks were the worst.

Howling as they went, the stampede of teeth and talons tore into the darchlyte ranks. The outer courtyard of Blackynspyre resembled an angry sea churning with flailing limbs and shimmering scales. With the added aid of the other dark forces, the charging lizards toppled darchlyte after darchlyte, driving them further back.

With the Dragon preoccupied by the battle outside, Jayce and Heidyl resumed their retreat toward the rear entry of the crumbling cavern. There was nothing more they could do here but leave the battle to the beasts. Before rounding the corner to where they had seen Tor'Engryn drag their mother to safety, they were surprised to find both of them standing hand in hand in a different doorway altogether. Jillian was smiling now, as if she had been spectator to their heroics for a long time. She appeared totally healed. Son and daughter sprinted across to the place where they stood. Tor'Engryn was grinning up at them as if pleased to no end. The woman held out her arm to welcome them both with an embrace.

"Mom! We've got to get out of here!" Jayce was saying. He leaned forward quickly to return the hug she offered, but Heidyl tugged at his shirt abruptly stopping him. He threw a confused look at his sister. Digging at her pocket she pressed the black and white stone into his palm. He rubbed at the word *Vyritas* inscribed along its polished surface with his thumb. He had totally forgotten about the gift he had been given, and the test he endured to receive it.

"As a Verity, it's your duty to discover the truth," she said, nodding her head forward. "Remember what Justhynial told us. *Flattering lies from their tails will yield great wounds.*"

Jayce studied the wondrous oval stone a moment before turning back to face them. Only then did he see what should have been plainly noted before. More than the forced plastic smiles on their faces or the hunk of rubble held awkwardly in the woman's outstretched hand, it was the telltale dripping noses. Jayce squinted to concentrate on their eyes and saw flecks of luminous green in place of eyes that should have been totally blue. He had seen these eyes before.

He leveled Vyritas at them and spoke plainly, "Deception is the chief tool of an enemy. You have no power over us!"

There was a crackle and flash of blue heat as Vyritas flamed to life. With their ruse exposed the trio separated and the triple mirages of Logarth, Jillian, and chunk of rock returned to their true vicious forms. Hissing and baring their teeth the trillych rushed to attack, but Jayce's arm, guided by the strength of Vyritas, dispatched them in three short swipes. Their bodies dropped to the floor and vanished in three puffs of black smoke, each returning to the barren land of Dearth. With its work done for the moment, Vyritas winked out to become a simple black and white stone once more.

"Nice work, big brother!" Heidyl rested a hand on Jayce's trembling shoulder.

"Thanks for the help," he said. Casting a look over his shoulder he saw the Dragon hauling its great bulk completely out of the portal behind them. Crawling toward the crumbling wall, it had taken a keen interest in the battle outside and began belching black fire into the fray. The Dragon's flame was indiscriminate, devouring darchlytes as well as its own wicked allies in blasts of disintegrating heat.

At the same instant, Tor'Engryn's battle cry echoed from the nearby archway, "Gets you back!"

When Jayce and Heidyl entered the hallway, they found him in a warrior's stance between Jillian's body and an approaching white wolf. With his stout legs firmly planted, the ancient little man brandished a makeshift war staff, spinning it and swinging it madly at the slavering beast. The enormous wolf's pink eyes shone in the dark and saliva dripped from the blood-red mouth. It had crept through the halls of Blackynspyre coming to the Dragon's call for aid and judging by the answering howls reverberating through the corridors, many more would be here soon. Consciousness was just now returning to Jillian, but she was still too disoriented to retreat or fight.

Without his slinging stones, Tor'Engryn held little hope of driving the creature back and defending his charge. It lunged at the little man repeatedly, red jaws snapping. Seeing her friend and mother in dire need, Heidyl felt a wash of courage flame inside her.

"Follow me!" she said to Jayce before launching into a sudden forward sprint. With her added Haizorr strength she vaulted into a handspring that carried her sailing over her mother's body on the floor. Her heart hammered a beat in her chest as she worked through the remaining moves of an improvised gymnastics routine. Planting her feet hard and springing to the side she propelled into another jump, twirling at an angle to avoid Tor'Engryn's spinning staff. As if lighter than air she bounded first from one wall then to the other before turning a full backwards flip to stick a perfect landing directly in front of the snout of the onrushing wolf.

Confused, the creature backed up a pace raising its hackles at the new threat. The beast was huge. Far larger than any Earth wolf. One bite from the dripping fangs would spell certain death. The distraction did not last for long. It lunged forward savagely and snapped at Heidyl's turned back. Instantly, the wolf regretted the decision for its lips and teeth smashed into an invisible barrier. The Fydas bracelet Heidyl wore glowed steadily upon her wrist. From within her protective bubble the world appeared a hazy blue and silence engulfed her.

Jayce, so stunned by his sister's display, had forgotten to follow her. He stood agape at her for a moment before catching her impatient expression. Jumping back into motion he ran forward. In passing, he encouraged Tor'Engryn and his staggering mother toward the other end of the hallway. Jayce could see the wolf slashing and biting at the invisible shield behind his sister, inflicting further damage upon its already bloodied lip.

"What do you want me to do?" he asked.

Heidyl shook her head and tapped her ear, indicating that the Fydas blocked out his voice. Then she pointed to the Vyritas stone still in his hand. Jayce nodded in understanding and Heidyl held out three fingers to indicate a countdown. One by one she lowered each finger until all that remained was a closed fist. Then, dodging to one side she squinted her eyes shut tight and willed the Fydas shield to stop. The white wolf surged forward as if on springs.

Directly into the flaming Vyritas blade.

Like the trillych, it was reduced to an imploding wisp of black smoke and was gone.

The halls were now flooding with the curling cries of wolves, gray-vyks, and a host of other unholy monsters. There could be no escape the way they had come.

Jayce and Heidyl raced to catch up to Tor'Engryn and Jillian who had just reentered the Dragon Chamber. The two were staring in terrified awe at the display of power being unleashed by the huge lizard.

Jillian, feeling much more revived, hooked an arm affectionately around Jayce. "Where's your father?"

Feeling him stiffen at the question, she knew instantly Thomas was gone. Turning to cast a sideways glance at Heidyl, her suspicions were confirmed by the grim look on her daughter's face. Swallowing back her own lump of grief, Jillian did her best to remain strong. The present danger facing them required she turn all efforts to her children now. They would grieve together later, but for the present they had to somehow get past the Dragon and worm their way to safety through the raging battle that had overtaken the cursed courtyard of Blackynspyre.

Like a small pack of silent mice, they stole across the expansive chamber, carefully hugging the wall to avoid the gaping portal. The Dragon was either oblivious to their approach or no longer cared as it roared and belched its own special blend of black death upon the courtyard battle outside. It stood half-in, half-out of the ruined chamber now, as it gained the upper hand against the darchlyte attack. Its tail whipped wildly about the room forcing the approaching group to dive for cover several times to avoid being sliced by the sickle-like end.

When they reached the opening, they were so near to one of the dark hind legs of the beast they could have reached out and touched it. For a moment Jayce entertained the thought of executing a surprise attack to the Dragon's exposed underbelly with the Vyritas blade and avenge his father, but the sheer size of the monster filled him with doubt. He was sure that if he tried, the Dragon would squash him with one well-placed step.

The noise from the battlefield was a deafening roar. Since there were no metal weapons such as swords or shields being used, it was an awful bestial clamor of thuds, snarls, shrieks and the terrible sound of dying animals. And the stench was horrific. Between the stinging black smoke and the pungent reek of grayvyk blood, the group of escapees found themselves scarcely able to breathe. Each of them covered their mouths with whatever bit of clothing they could to filter the air.

The group scanned the fray for a way through. Heidyl nudged her mother and pointed to the opening in the far wall where the darchlyte army had broken past Blackynspyre's outer defenses. It was open and unguarded, but the path to reach it was fraught with savagery. There was little hope that any of them would reach freedom unscathed. Just then, the ranks of ratmen, grayvyks and several white wolves burst into the room behind them in response to the Dragon's call. Plucking up their courage, the small band made the collective decision to run for it. Climbing over the chunks of rubble in their path, they emerged into the courtyard, just barely squeezing past the legs of the Dragon. They inched to the side, their backs to the undamaged part of the chamber's outer wall and crouched behind a large pile of debris.

A high-pitched call from above snapped their heads to the sky. Another answered it from somewhere else high over the dark Blackynspyre towers. The din of battle ceased for a moment and even the Dragon paused its hateful fire to squint through its winged canopy into the sunlit sky. Then something dropped from the air like a great blue meteor landing directly on the head of an unsuspecting grayvyk. There was a muffled shriek followed by a hollow thud that shook the earth. For a moment, uneasy peace muffled the sounds of war as each creature quietly assessed this new development. When the cloud of dust receded, all eyes turned upon the intruder with its large stamping hooves and blue upswept wings. Then the regal head of the captain of Justhynial's Westyr Guard lifted and let out a screeching battle cry before rising into the air again with great flapping wingbeats. The crumpled body of the grayvyk beneath it lay still in a shallow crater, crushed by the impact of the attack.

Looking to the sky, Jillian, Jayce, Heidyl and Tor'Engryn nearly cheered as the air began to fill with the soaring blue giants of Justhynial's family. Instantly, snarls and vicious howls rose from the ground below in a return challenge from the dark forces, while the remaining darchlytes groaned out a deep, hopeful greeting while raising their great balled fists in salute.

Then, the ancient father of the highborn race winged into the center of the lofty army. Justhynial's noble body glinted in the sun, the light reflecting from blue undulating muscles as his great wings pounded the surrounding air like a small hurricane. And there, upon his back a lone rider sat astride Justhynial as if riding a winged stallion. He wore a simple brown robe, his head hooded.

Raising a fist, the figure shouted in a clear, strong voice, "To battle! All who have come to answer the Call, the Caller now commands you all! To battle!"

Then the rider leaned forward, spurring Justhynial into a dive. As if following the head of an enormous spear, the remaining winged warriors flocked into a V-formation screeching a war cry as they descended like blue lightning into the fray.

Jillian felt her pulse quicken at seeing the cloaked rider sitting tall and confident atop the broad back of the noble Justhynial.

This was the Caller? But what of Drayven? Her mind buzzed with a thousand questions but arrived at no clear conclusion. Then, as if in answer to her internal mystery, the rider's hood flew back in the wind, revealing a strong, tanned, familiar face.

"Samuel!" She nearly wept with joy at seeing the old caretaker alive and well. Pointing skyward she nudged her children. Heidyl's eyes widened in disbelief and Jayce felt a wash of relief, as if a great burden had fallen from his heart.

If the old family caretaker had noticed his friends, he made no sign, but dove straight into the war below. Hurtling like a wild blue mortar he and Justhynial dropped from the atmosphere to land hooves first onto the back of an attacking grayvyk, crushing its spine in an instant. The serpent writhed for a stunned moment and then lay still. Samuel and Justhynial swept back into the sky just before a pack of white wolves could rush upon them in a counter-attack.

Almost as suddenly, a great ruckus erupted from the opening in the breached wall of Blackynspyre's outer courts. Hundreds of quick-marching stout soldiers poured onto the field like speedy ants. The diminutive army was equipped with sharp spears, slings and formidable war clubs—each weapon fashioned of black stone. In less than a breath the primitive warriors formed ranks and now stood at the ready. Tor'Engryn had to stop himself from clapping with glee at the arrival of the Logarthiym army. From across the field he caught the eye of Wista, who was leading one of the squads, and waved. Wista nodded, permitting himself a half smile in salute to the Elder Logarth before returning to his grim battle stance.

As if on silent command the war flared up once more, much louder than it had been previously. Logarthiym slings hummed like tiny propellers sending black stones hurtling through the air like whistling bullets. The rhythmic thump of the pouncing Westyr Guard crushing the enemy below was like the sound of war drums driving the pace of battle. The arrival of so many reinforcements had given gusto to the tired limbs of the darchlytes and they began to sing a deep thrumming song in unison as they pounded back the attacking beasts. Mixed with the heroic chants came horrific screams of grayvyks, sentries, wolves, rat-men, and a host of other dark creatures as they fell in battle.

The Dragon's eyes kindled wild with new fire. Turning all attention to the greatest threat now raining down from above, the toothed jaws parted and unleashed a thick barrage of black fire into the air. Entire groups of Justhynial's family were reduced to ash as the Dragon swept a steady stream of black fire across the sky like a flamethrower into a cloud of bees. At once the noble defenders swooped and wheeled through the sky attempting to dodge the scorching blasts. Many opted for the higher cover of clouds, which temporarily took them away from the battle below. A few of the brave Westyr Guard continued to fight using a low flight pattern in hopes the Dragon would not strike for fear of hitting its own allies on the field. They were sadly mistaken as the evil, uncaring heart of the flaming monster sought victory at any cost. The Black Dragon of Dearth spared no beast, spewing its dark fire upon them all, devouring friend and foe alike in great clouds of acrid smoke. Those that evaded the burning stream were caught by jumping grayvyks or dragged down by the long tentacles of sentries.

One winged warrior on an attack run was met with the snarling jaws of a leaping grayvyk, its teeth catching her wing at the joint. For a few seconds the momentum brought the reptile into the air, but eventually both tumbled end for end onto the ground in a flurry of scales and hooves. The scene was a chaotic dance of flapping, kicking and biting. Unable to fly, the winged maiden dodged nimbly on her strong blue legs and struck the grayvyk with several well-placed kicks. But her wing, now dangling useless at her side, slowed her defenses. The fight attracted several more of the fiendish lizards that were now beginning to circle like sharks.

Nearby, a small contingent of Logarthiym warriors had locked in a tussle with a pack of white wolves. Wista, clad in green and leading the charge while thumping head after head of the canines with his black stone war club, looked up in time to see one of Justhynial's regal daughters bravely making her last stand. With a throaty cry Wista rallied several of his troops to her aid. They darted in like arrows, catching the assaulting grayvyks from behind. Their black stone weapons hacked back the howling serpents until they reached the exhausted victim. Her tattered wing bled badly and appeared to already be festering with infection from the bite she sustained. Wista raised his fingers to his lips and blasted three loud whistles. In an instant three more Logarthiym soldiers appeared, each carrying a small leather satchel filled with bandages and herbal forest medicines. Together they cleaned and bound the wounds with their lightning quick fingers. The warriors stood their ground in a semicircular array while the healers did their work.

With the support from above cut off, the battle fell to the Logarthiym and darchlyte ground troops. Side by side, towering giants and tiny speedy soldiers both drove back the enemy. Inch by inch they gained ground, though each group sustained heavy loss. The spewing flames had ceased for a time, and the group drew nearer to the Dragon's crumbling lair. The forces swelled to a gathering throng, surging forward into a building wave.

And the Dragon let them come.

With a hooked-tooth grin the black beast stifled the fire, letting it kindle long and hot. Taking a half-step back, the serpent feigned a halting retreat. The movement rallied the advancing army as they sensed imminent victory. Biding time for a few seconds more the cunning serpent allowed the darchlytes and Logarthiym to cluster together as they regrouped. Within moments they would all be within striking distance of its hateful black fire. The Dragon drew back its head, preparing to unleash the final killing blow that would consume all of the ground forces at once.

Then, like a bolt of lightning, Samuel and Justhynial struck. Using the Haizorr sun as a screen, they plunged like a blue stone launched from a sling. The bold duo dove straight between the massive eyes of the monster, striking it hard in the forehead with all four battle-hardened hooves. The force of it rattled Samuel's teeth in his head and Justhynial grunted in pain before launching off again straight behind the Dragon. The attack had the desired effect and the black head spun around spewing dark flame wildly into the air at the retreating silhouettes in the sky.

The distraction was long enough.

At once the darchlytes were upon the Dragon. Thumping, entangling and pulling at the massive creature. The tiny Logarthiym slung hundreds of black stones from below and drove their black tipped arrows and spears into the Dragon's legs and feet. With the Black Dragon so encumbered, the Westyr Guard returned their air assault upon the remaining grayvyks, sentries, rat-men and wolves, keeping them at bay from the backs of their allies.

Jillian saw their chance then.

Grabbing the hand of each of her children she pulled them along into a run. Their eyes focused on the gap in the far wall that was now open and unguarded. Together they dodged and weaved forward through spinning slings and great stomping feet. Tor'Engryn, so swept in the moment of seeing his family once more, joined the Logarthiym ranks. With the help of a comrade he refilled his satchel with black rocks and began pelting every enemy target in range, his raspy voice echoing triumphant hoots with each successful hit.

Jayce felt a longing urge to join the fight, and he gripped the Vyritas stone tightly in his fist. However, he could not abandon his family and chose to continue running the escape route through the chaos. Jillian spurred them forward, calling out cautions and warnings. Heidyl nimbly dodged the surging beasts. Leaping and twisting with gymnastic precision she cleared hurdle after hurdle through their hasty retreat. She threw a cautious glance back to see if they had cleared the danger. The Dragon was utterly overwhelmed by the tenacious darchlyte army. The moment one was bitten, raked off or dissolved to ash, another would replace its fallen comrade. Heidyl's gaze drifted upward into the face of the serpent.

Ice flooded her veins.

The gleaming furnace eyes of the Black Dragon of Dearth met her own. Locking onto her like a laser beam, the beast stared hard at the tiny girl below. The intensity of its gaze melted her heart and she felt as if her soul were laid bare before the world. Flashes of cold and heat ran up her spine and her heart squeezed in her chest like pangs of guilt mixed with intense empty hunger. Heidyl did not even realize that her legs had stopped running. The raging world about her drifted into a foggy silence and she felt like a cork bobbing along lazy waves toward shore. The Dragon, though fighting off wave after wave of onrushing armies, never broke the magnetic connection with the young girl. Without realizing her actions, Heidyl began a slow march of trance-like steps back toward the waiting beast.

Jillian, still dashing madly along with Jayce, felt a tingle in the mark at the back of her skull. Instantly, she drew up short causing her son to do the same. Out of breath she cast about, frantically scanning the swirling pandemonium. Collisions, snarls, screams. The tumult of war was dizzying.

"Where is she?" Jillian cried above the din. "Where's Heidyl?"

Stammering in alarm, Jayce shouted, "I don't know! She—she was right behind me!"

Both mother and brother screamed her name.

Then Jillian saw her daughter.

She was staggering slowly back into the thick of the swarm. Her slight frame and delicate limbs a picture of beauty and innocence cast against the ugly backdrop of battle.

"Heidyl! No!" Jillian screamed with all her might, but the young girl continued her slow plod toward the death-dark serpent.

"We've got to stop her!" Jayce yelled and tore after her. Jillian did not argue and sprinted along with him, dodging and weaving through the same gauntlet of evil they had just run seconds before.

Heidyl was within grasp of the Dragon's claws now and the wicked serpent reached for her with a powerfully muscled foreleg. But before the pitch-black fingers could close about her a stream of shrieking Westyr Guard, with Samuel in the lead astride Justhynial, flew in the Dragon's face. A flurry of flapping and stamping caused the beast to recoil, and the brief hold it had created over Heidyl was broken. As if waking from a dream and into a nightmare, she screamed and turned again to run, but not before she was caught in the arms of Jillian and Jayce as they rushed to meet her.

With an angry swat the Dragon batted away the blue assailants, sending a few of them tumbling, but most drew back just out of reach, preparing for a second attack. Samuel could see the scampering bodies of the family below and began directing the noble Guard to their aid. But now the Dragon had recovered fully and lunged at their fleeing forms.

Jillian felt the shadow of the beast hovering over them before she actually saw it.

Samuel shouted, "Jillian! Look out!"

He nudged Justhynial forward to aid his friends, but too late. The black hand of death was already upon them.

Heidyl and Jayce both looked up in time to see the massive claws block out the sun above before it descended upon their heads as if crushing mere insects.

The air went out of Samuel's lungs then as the overwhelming sense of his failure to protect them struck his heart like a sledgehammer. Too stunned for anything else, he did the only logical thing left to do. Allowing the hot rage to race through his veins and with the authority of the Caller he gave the forceful command, "To the Dragon! The Dragon! Bring it down! Slay the Beast of Blackynspyre! This is the Caller's charge to all, heed me now and answer the call!"

And with that, Samuel belted out a painful cry that was at once grief and searing vengeance. An instant tidal wave of renewed fight swept through the armies and they turned as one upon the dark winged serpent. Screeches, thrumming groans and a chorus of war cries went up in unison. But before they could execute the final attack, the Dragon lifted its talons aloft revealing the three cowering forms of Jillian, Jayce, and Heidyl in its blackened palm.

Gasping at the sight, Samuel pulled up Justhynial and they hovered mid-air. Momentary relief crossed the elder man's features. They were alive!

Heidyl knelt on the scaly skin with her eyes closed while an almost imperceptible translucent globe surrounded the family in a protective bubble. The Dragon's claws held them as if palming a glass ball as the Fydas shield kept the crushing fingers from coming any closer. Jillian knelt beside her daughter, whispering reassurances to help Heidyl concentrate while Jayce stood defiantly beside them, ready to defend. They were protected for the moment from the crushing grip yet remained lofty prisoners within that same dreadful grasp.

The hateful eyes of the Dragon flared at the hovering Samuel and Justhynial, then glanced downward. It flicked a long black tongue at the advancing line of its attackers before lifting the captive family higher into the air as if preparing to hurl them to the scarred earth far below. The sudden motion jostled the little family and sent Jayce to his knees to join his mother and sister. At once, the old caretaker understood the wicked intent of the cunning black serpent. The cards had shifted, and the Dragon now held the winning hand. Its scaly lips curved, forming a wicked obsidian grin.

"Hold!" Samuel's strong voice rang out and the armies below halted their forward march. Justhynial's wingbeats drifted them slowly backward in the air. "Cease the attack! The Caller commands you all, draw back!" As one, the darchlytes, Logarthiym and floating Westyr Guard began putting distance between themselves and the Black Dragon of Dearth. Slowly they faded all the way back to the outer walls of Blackynspyre, unhindered by the few remaining dark creatures of the Dragon's failed army of evil.

All stood in simmering silence and stared at the shadowy beast, which now oozed smug confidence. The darchlytes and Logarthiym, feeling robbed of their chance to settle ancient scores, seethed and gritted their teeth. The righteous Westyr Guard circled the battlegrounds in slow aerial patrols, ready to streak back into the conflict at the slightest indication from

Samuel, the Caller.

Thick stillness clung in the air.

The Dragon pulled the huddled family closer to its coal-black face and sneered. With burning eyes, it regarded each kneeling figure before finally locking stares with Jayce, who was the only one staring back at the serpent.

You do well to kneel before me, little one.

Jayce heard the Dragon's pompous voice in his head and felt his heart begin hammering in his chest. He glanced over to his crouching mother and sister. They made no sign of hearing the Dragon at all and continued their group effort of keeping the shield about them secure. Heidyl squinted her eyes shut to better concentrate. Jillian wrapped comforting arms about her daughter to keep her steady. The blue mist rising about them from the glowing Fydas bracelet told him they were safe, for now. Jayce turned wide eyes back upon the Dragon.

A grinding chuckle filled the boy's mind. *Why act so surprised? You have heard my voice many times.*

A sudden sea of guilt sloshed through his stomach like molten lead and he knew it to be true. Jayce knew that this indeed was the very same voice shared by all his doubts, evil desires and wicked cravings that called to him more often than he cared to admit. The voice poured through every corridor of his mind, filling it like a boiling liquid until he felt he could scarcely breathe.

Are we really so different, you and I? Both of us born of the darkness. You, blackened on the inside, and me on the outside. I cannot hide my true nature, it is who I am. But you—you try so hard to cover the truth of yourself. You may have fooled them, the Dragon nodded to his mother and sister, *but I am not duped by your charade.*

He did not want to, but Jayce suddenly shed hot shameful tears down his cheeks as though he were newly exposed of a litany of heinous crimes. It was all so very true. He was wicked inside. His own foolishness had led them to this awful place. His doubts and deceptions had brought him and his family to the very gates of Hell. And now, because of it, his family was captured, and his father was gone forever.

Yes, child. It was you who killed him, not I. The voice hissed like a swirling sandstorm in his mind.

He had killed his own father! A painful groan rose within Jayce. It seemed to come from the soles of his feet, turning him inside out as it gained intensity. He suddenly felt the surprising and powerful urge to have it all end.

I can make it all go away, the Dragon soothed. *Will you help me?*

Jayce looked up again, wiping his nose on a dirty sleeve. To his surprise the Dragon was holding a heavy chain in its other clawed hand. The thick links ran in a long sequence to a securely fastened collar about the serpent's neck. The other end traveled down in lengthy coils before disappearing beneath the bubbling surface of the open portal behind the Dragon. Jayce wondered how he had not noticed the fetters before. At the same moment, he felt a curious sensation about his own ribs and shoulders as if he were being dragged down by a strong magnet. He was shocked to see a thick black chain appear, wrapping about his chest like a metal python. The weight was crushing.

We are so alike, are we not? Both captive. Both longing for our freedom. The beast had put on the most pitiful face that Jayce thought it might actually begin to cry. Then the Black Dragon's features twisted again as it cast a scornful glance at the darchlyte army positioned along the rim of the walls. *They did this to me. They bound me and cast me into Dearth. They took away my home. Haizorr is rightfully mine.*

The fiery pupils of the Black Dragon flamed and danced anew.

Obviously, your father was an unworthy sacrifice. But you are the spotless lamb that will right this whole mess!

Jayce looked down again at his own heavy chains. The links were too thick to even try struggling against. There was no lock or release mechanism to be found. Just thick, grimy chains. Sighing heavily against the constricting weight he looked around. The world about him had faded into chalky shadows. He no longer felt the closeness of his sister and mother just inches away. He was alone as ever, kneeling in the palm of a death he somehow knew he deserved.

The Dragon's words both confirmed his suspicions about his own wicked heart, but also felt strangely confusing. It hurt to think of it, but at the Dragon's mention of his father, Jayce felt something stir deep inside. Like a pinprick to his heart. With it, a new flood of thoughts cascaded through his mind then, each one sweeping away a little more of the heavy cloud of doubt that fogged his senses.

"But wasn't Dad the one who left everything behind to risk coming after me?" Jayce whispered, unsure if he was making any sound at all.

At once the Dragon's hissing voice burst into his mind like a crackling radio trying to interrupt this new flow of thoughts. *He hid so many secrets from you. He never trusted you.*

"He tried to shield me from the dangers of this world."

He sought only to keep the wonders of Haizorr for himself.

Jayce shook his head, "Dad gave up everything for me!"

He's a liar!

Jayce was standing now. He did not recall when he had risen but he felt some of his strength return like a swelling tide. The mirage of chains about his torso and the Dragon's neck were no longer visible. The grimy shroud of deception slowly lifted like mist over a foggy lake burned off by the rising sun.

And then, in that moment, Jayce knew who he was supposed to be. A Verity. A lover of truth. He wrapped the thought about himself like a suit of armor. Confidence surged within like warm golden light filling his veins.

"No!" he shouted in the face of the Dragon, and the black beast flinched.

Jayce looked down at the stone in his hand. *Vyritas.* The clean markings across the black and white surface called out to him. Justhynial's charge floated to the forefront of his mind then—*Speak the truth with love on your lips, and victory shall be yours.* Taking a deep breath, he steadied himself.

"I am no spotless lamb," he began, "but Dad's sacrifice for me was perfect." His voice rose steadily with each word, "He has only ever loved me, and that kind of love will always crush serpents like you!"

With that, the Vyritas blade flashed to life with brilliant fire. Then hefting it high above his head, Jayce drove the sword point down between his feet where it bit deeply into the black palm of the Dragon's open hand.

There was a space of silence as the boy waited for a reaction. But none came. The flaming sword crackled and burned, buried up to the hilt deep into the Dragon's sizzling flesh, yet the beast did not so much as sniff.

Jayce looked up with wide eyes, the familiar tingle of fear creeping back along his spine. Had he been mistaken? The scaly face held the same smug look as it had just moments before, and he sensed that death must surely come now.

But the fiery eyes of the Dragon widened suddenly as if the doors of two blazing forges had been flung fully open. Then, the world tipped violently as Jayce, Jillian, and Heidyl found themselves hurtling through the air. The Black Dragon of Dearth flailed its thick onyx arms while frantically clawing at its great chest and throwing its head back as if in great pain. The abrupt change shattered Heidyl's concentration, and she lost control of the Fydas shield. Mother, daughter, and son now tumbled like rag dolls on the wind. Seeing the three humans flung aloft by the Dragon's hysterics, several swift Westyr Guard warriors swooped in like great falcons. Jillian and Heidyl were safely born up along the broad backs of two of Justhynial's blue sons. Jayce, however, lost his grip on the winged creature that broke his fall and took a harrowing tumble downward before being caught in the strong arms of a waiting darchlyte below.

All eyes were upon the Dragon.

The great beast was convulsing now and filling the air with ear split-ting screams that rattled the soul. The fragmented forces of the dark army simply did not know what to do. Some, seeing their master in need, crept closer to see what may be done. Still others saw the chance to escape the cruel dark dictator and fled, melting into the forest beyond the broken Blackynspy-re walls. The Dragon threw itself on the ground and thrashed about, its great bulk crushing a handful of hapless grayvyks. After the flailing black tail and kicking legs sent several more creatures flying, the few remnants of the Drag-on's tattered army fled entirely.

The Dragon was alone.

From across the yard, Jayce stood mouth agape and eyes wide at the raging display. Even from this distance the ground rumbled and shook under his feet from the serpent's death throes. The captain of the Westyr Guard edged beside the boy, nudging his shoulder.

"Well done, lad!" he said, tipping his regal, owl-like head in a con-gratulatory salute.

Jayce shrugged and gave an incredulous look at the simple black and white stone in his hand. "But I hardly did anything! I couldn't have caused that much damage." The sound of a collapsing fortress wall from one of the Dragon's savage kicks snapped his head back up.

A great cloud of dust now engulfed the entire area, shrouding the dying beast in gray cloudy swirls. Then, above the billow the heavy black wings opened and beat down upon the earth with tremendous force, slowly lifting the shrieking serpent into the air. But like a mad dog leashed to a tree, the Black Dragon's rising body halted abruptly. With a final herculean effort, the black wings strained, the beast screamed, and ink black liquid poured from its open jaws. Having spent the last of its strength, the Dragon suddenly went limp and descended back to the rubble with a reverberating thud.

Stone silence spread across the field.

All creatures in the entire array of armies held their breath, daring to hope. When the murky dust finally cleared, there lay the object of all their troubles. Like a crumpled insect, the bulky serpent lay on its side, crushing a tattered wing beneath its twisted body. The great forked tongue lolled lazily from its mouth and the fire that once blazed red in its eyes had winked out.

"Dead!" came a distant, elated cry that sounded very much like Tor'Engryn. The tiny voice was like a small explosion puncturing the thick silence. "Blackyn-Beastie is dead!" he chanted.

The throaty cry of hundreds of victorious warriors followed the pronouncement. Logarthiym fighters clapped each other on the back, others dropped their weapons and slumped to the ground in relief or fatigue. Darchlyte giants thrummed out deep satisfied tones. The winged Westyr Guard circled and swooped in aerial displays of victory before lighting upon the torn battlefield below. Justhynial's graceful wings brought Samuel back to Jillian and Heidyl where they shared a silent embrace. Jillian's trembling shoulders spoke volumes as she melted into the old caretaker's strong arms. Samuel's sighing heart gave mixed beats of both relief and loss.

It was a good and terrible moment.

All across the broken field the sounds of celebration shifted as the living turned to the grim task of caring for their fallen and wounded comrades. Longtime friends and companions being sought out among the debris of war brought reunions that were somber and tearful. Logarthiym healers darted about the field with their herbs and bandages. Some were revived, but many were beyond aid and succumbed to the ravages of the Dragon's war.

JAYCE WATCHED ALL OF THIS THROUGH HOLLOW EYES as he found himself inexplicably drawn to the lifeless body of the Dragon. He had all but forgotten his sister and mother and friend while he threaded his way through the sad aftermath of the fight. As he drew near, the carcass of the black beast loomed like a dark mountain before him. He paused when he was near enough to touch the monster's open claw that lay palm up on the ground. He stared at the hole he had made in the black hand. Jayce had driven the Vyritas blade as deep as he could into the monster, yet the wound looked like a mere pinprick compared to the size of the beast. *Maybe I hit a nerve or something.* He shook his head in wonder before allowing his eyes to survey the lifeless scaly body. He felt a lonely ache swell in his heart.

He had not noticed the silent group of darchlyte warriors slip in and begin forming a semi-circle about him. Fanning out like stoic pillars, their group swelled until it was large enough to surround the Dragon's body. Heidyl and Jillian had followed the line of giants to stand there now beside Jayce. And then the sadness came. Grief twined itself with exhaustion and the family wept until they were spent of tears. Though the Black Dragon had perished, it did nothing to amend the terrible loss of so great a husband, father, and friend.

Then, like a silent company of giant pallbearers, the somber darchlytes began to drag the beast's broken body back toward the yawning mouth of the portal. The thought that this hideous, scaled corpse now served as Thomas' burial casket sickened Jillian and the children. They all knew he deserved so much better. Still the heaving procession went on, pulling and pushing the lifeless body until it reached the edge of the swirling black doorway to Dearth. The weeping family members marched in step with the slow advance. Samuel and Tor'Engryn had joined them, further adding their own tears to the makeshift funeral.

They were surprised to find that the black opening had grown much wider that it had been. Normally a portal would close on its own after a time, but not so with the greedy door to Dearth. It was alive with spreading evil. The two ceremonial posts and dangling ropes were still there but the sides of the room and much of the roof had been swallowed by the expanding hole. A chill of alarm rippled through the entire company. After seeing the widening gate the darchlytes hurried their work, eager to rid the planet of the foul monster. Three of the strongest looking darchlytes dragged the tip of the Dragon's tail to the rim and unceremoniously dropped it in. They grimaced as they did so, turning their heads away in disgust as if depositing garbage into a reeking cesspool.

At that very moment, two things happened. First, the void of Dearth began drawing the Dragon inward, pulling at its tail as if the portal were the mouth of a giant vacuum and the empty land beneath was hungry to reclaim its own.

Next, the chest of the Dragon rose and fell.

Jayce noticed it first and felt his own chest tighten with stabbing dread. *That thing's still alive!* he thought.

The tail was nearly half submerged now before the scaly armor covering the Dragon's chest rose and fell again several more times in a row. It appeared as if the black heart beneath were regaining strength. Jillian and Heidyl both noticed it this time. Jayce took a half step back and readied Vyritas in his shaking fist. Heidyl's trembling hand began caressing the Fydas about her wrist.

"Hurry! It's reviving!" Jillian shouted her encouragement to the laboring darchlytes, who began doubling their efforts. The rubble along the ground was catching at the scales, making progress painfully slow. It was helpful that the beast had landed on its side, but the tattered wings kept snagging on boulders and protruding debris. Again, the chest rose and fell in jerking motions like muscle spasms beneath the blackened skin of the Dragon.

Jayce kept looking from the beast's quivering chest back to its eye, silently willing that the hideous fiery orbs would remain closed.

And then, there was a sort of scraping, tearing sound. A second later a small blue spike appeared between the largest seam in the scales at the center of the Dragon's chest. It withdrew only to reappear several more times in quick succession.

Recognizing the curved talon, Jayce shouted, "It's Dad!"

A moment later Thomas' arm reappeared through a hole in the scaly chest, his hand tightly gripping the sharp claw of the keen grayvyk. There was a moment's elation from his family, but then sudden panic. The Dragon's body had reached a tipping point over the lip of the portal. The thick tail and lower legs had been swallowed back into Dearth and the procession was gaining momentum.

Jillian shouted once more, "Wait! Don't let it go in yet!"

There was a rumbling humming sound of confusion from the darchlytes who had not seen the small arm of the man clawing his way to freedom. They looked from one to another and slowed up a bit but did not stop their toil.

"I command you, stop! Hold the beast!" Samuel's booming voice cut through the murmurs and the darchlytes instantly obeyed the Caller's order. Strong hands gripped various parts of the sliding Dragon and they planted their giant feet. Progress slowed, but Dearth's void still sucked at the bottom half of the serpent, drawing it inward inch by inch. Again, Thomas' arm flicked in and out, frantically sawing and widening the scaly hole with the sharp talon. He was making headway, but not fast enough.

"Hurry, Thomas!" Jillian cried clinging hard to one of the black limbs and digging in her heels.

Like a slow-moving train, the lifeless frame was dragged ever deeper. Though the darchlyte army pulled with their collective might they were gradually losing this tug-of-war against the undertow of the swelling portal. Thomas hung only a few feet from the edge of darkness, slicing away desperately. At once, Jayce, Heidyl and Samuel rushed forward to help. With no second to spare, Thomas wriggled his shoulders out of the hole while the others frantically grabbed at his wrists and clothing, which were slick with black liquid. He came free with a sudden jolt that sent them all tumbling backward. Seeing the man lying safely on the ground, the darchlytes released their steely grip. A moment later the remaining parts of the entire beast were sucked back down into the hungry maw of the dark portal.

The Black Dragon of Dearth was no more.

FOR A MOMENT NO ONE MOVED. Thomas lay on his back panting while his family and lifelong friend stared at him, wondering at his condition. The darchlytes stood as great pillars around the black portal, staring into the abyss as if making sure their work with the Dragon was indeed done. Slowly, more filed in to stand shoulder to shoulder until they formed a tight ring around the gaping hole.

Jayce was the first to stir. Throwing himself upon his father's chest he began to weep. Heidyl joined her brother while Jillian cradled Thomas' head in her lap, her grateful tears splashing on his grimy face. He reached up a dirty hand and touched her face.

"Found," he said wearily.

Jayce could hold back no longer, "Dad, I'm so sorry. I almost ruined everything!" He squeezed his father's chest as if he would never let go. "I do love you, Dad. I do! I love you—this big!" And he held the embrace even harder.

Heidyl added her tears to the reunion and pulled back to tenderly kiss her father on the cheek. Thomas, breathing the free air once again, felt his strength returning and sat up, clutching his wife and children close. For a long moment he squeezed his eyes tightly while drinking in the scent and feel of them. Samuel extended a strong arm helping him to his feet. He looked ragged and somehow thinner than he had before entering the Dragon's belly. His legs felt wobbly and he fought back a passing wave of nausea.

Scanning the haggard scene and noting the unmistakable signs of a bloody battle, Thomas asked, "How long have I been gone?"

Jillian tucked herself under his arm and half shrugged, "Hard to say, really. I was unconscious for a while." She looked at the Haizorr sun now lazily trailing lower in the sky. "The battle must have lasted for hours but it only feels like minutes."

"Minutes?" Thomas looked shocked and swayed unsteadily on his feet for a moment. Jillian leaned hard against him to keep him standing. With the toe of his boot he thoughtfully nudged the grayvyk claw on the ground where he had dropped it earlier. "I've been digging my way out of that horrible place for three days."

"Three days!" Jayce and Heidyl exclaimed at once.

Jillian felt her heart squeeze in her chest at the thought of her husband alone and suffering for so long. She knew this realm had its own strange time properties, and she imagined that what he experienced must have been agonizing.

Samuel nodded grimly, "Perhaps you passed through the very gates of Dearth." Turning to the nearest warrior he ordered a water skin and food be brought to Thomas, who gratefully accepted them.

After refreshing himself for a moment he reflected on the terrible darkness he had endured. He nodded slowly. "It was awful," he said flatly while bending down to retrieve the blue talon that had saved him. He had no idea how anyone could survive something like being swallowed by a beast, but this was different. The moment the Dragon's jaws had clapped shut over him, it felt like he was thrust into a new dimension. He had expected teeth or at the least, suffocation, but instead putrid darkness engulfed him and terrible howls of grief and pain assailed his ears. At one point he realized that one of the screams was his own as he fell through an endless chasm of black despair. He nearly forgot why he had switched places with his own son until a faint blue glow from under his shirt drew his attention. The talon! Sudden hope surged anew in his veins and he willed himself to stop falling. In that instant the rules changed somehow, and he was able to stand. Amid the deepest dark and terror filled pit he found the strength to claw upward to light and freedom.

Jillian's gentle touch on his arm shook him from the dark thoughts and he smiled at her. He never thought he would see such beauty again. It felt like he was seeing her for the first time. As he slowly recollected his wits, another thought struck him, "Where's my brother?" He looked around, scanning the gathering crowd. "Where's Drayven?"

Jayce did not want to, but he pointed at the black churning gate to Dearth. "He fell in, Dad. He's gone. I think the Dragon pushed him in." Despite the level of treachery his uncle had paid him, Jayce felt his eyes mist over. He was, after all, still family.

343

Together they walked around the wide ring of swaying darchlytes toward the sacrificial posts anchored to the floor beside the portal. A low, somber note rose and fell from the tall warriors like an ancient song rolling across the waves of an ancient sea.

"What are they doing?" Heidyl asked no one in particular. She spoke in a hushed whisper, although unsure why.

"It's hard to know for certain," Samuel replied while rubbing a patch of white stubble on his chin. "They are a mysterious race with ages of history. It sounds like a lament of some sort."

At that moment, a gust of wind kicked up the dust about them and the great blue body of Justhynial descended nearby.

"It is the Song of Sealing," he offered in his reedy, bird-like voice. "They are closing the black gate of this place forever." Even as he spoke, they all could see the rim of the portal receding like a great puddle slowly drying up. The Song was both sad and beautiful. Everyone stood very still, transfixed by the deeply stirring melody.

After a moment, Thomas threaded his way back to stand between the rough posts. He thoughtfully touched the ends of the ropes that had once held him there and marveled at how neatly the bonds had been severed by the sharp teeth of the Dragon. He looked down at his bare wrists and wondered why the knotted ends were not still tied to them. He could not recall ever removing them. His eyes trailed along the red and black corded rope and he shook his head—his own rope from his own shed! Kneeling, he reached to retrieve the excess that had drooped over the edge of the portal. When he tugged, he was surprised to find the rope was taut, as if snagged on the other end. Though still exhausted from the ordeal in the Dragon's belly he hauled at the rope, hand over hand. Like a fisherman, he could feel something moving on the submerged side. By now, Samuel had noticed Thomas struggling and knelt to help his friend.

A few more of the Westyr Guard had landed nearby and several stout Logarth warriors gathered around the portal rim. The wary eye of Justhynial watched the two men struggle and he hooted a simple admonition, "Caution, my friends." With that warning uttered from their leader, the nearest Westyr Guard made ready and lowered their muscular bodies into battle stances.

If not for the buzzing sensation around the mark on Thomas' hip he would have dropped the rope, but rather he found his heart filled with a strange hope urging him onward. Inching backward he called over his shoulder to Samuel, "Don't let go!"

Together the two friends drew the length of rope fully back to the surface. When the bony hand of Drayven finally appeared clinging to the lifeline there was a series of gasps and groans from the onlookers. A few Logarthiym warriors spat a curse and began spinning their slings. The nearest darchlytes balled their massive fists ready to crush the wily offender who had unleashed their nemesis. Slowly they dragged Drayven up over the edge where he lay on the cold broken floor as if a dead man.

Thomas carefully rolled his brother's tired body over and shook him gently. "Drayven?"

Pale eyelids fluttered open in the man's gaunt face. Instantly they widened in recognition and wonder. In a flash Drayven's arms flew up and wrapped around Thomas. The crowd surged forward as one, ready to tear apart the fallen lord of Blackynspyre but Thomas held up a hand to stop their advance.

Drayven was weeping.

His shoulders shuddered with wave after wave of powerful sobs as he embraced his twin. His voice poured out unintelligible expressions of guilt and shame and loss while Thomas held him there as if comforting a repentant child. Despite their previous desire for revenge, Jillian, Jayce and Heidyl felt a shared pity for the man who had wronged them all so grievously.

After several moments, Thomas helped Drayven to his feet and shared the water skin with him. Like Thomas, he too felt as if he had passed a great length of time in the depths of Dearth. He would not speak of it and chose to keep his eyes lowered. He was a guilty criminal now and dared not hope for a welcome. All suspected he must have seen the broken body of the Dragon tumble past him as it descended back into the empty land of Dearth. The crumbled castle, the fallen army, the closing portal—all of them now lasting monuments to the utter failure of his dark aspirations. Two of the burliest Westyr Guard trotted up, taking their posts on either side of Drayven. Their stern presence made it quite clear that the man was under arrest.

With slumped shoulders and downcast stare, it was evident that the fight had gone out of him. Drayven was the picture of utter defeat.

The darchlytes continued their haunting song while the others stood quietly outside the ring allowing them to work undisturbed. The melody rose and fell while the portal ebbed away, and the ground became solid once more. As the last note of the Song of Sealing faded into a hollow echo that drifted across the nearby mountains, the dreaded gateway finally closed. The onlookers collectively breathed a deep sigh. A cool breeze swept across the group then as if Haizorr itself were joining their expression of relief.

Thomas looked to the setting sun and wondered why the darchlytes were not running after it like they had for centuries. The moons on the far lip of the horizon had begun their waning phases, yet like ominous statues the old warriors stood watching the burning orb settle into its resting place for the night. The moment it disappeared a low comforting rumble escaped through their weary voices. Then their strong, tense limbs visibly relaxed as if resting for the first time in a millennium.

Thomas smiled to himself as the glorious truth became plain.

The curse of the Black Dragon of Dearth was broken.

PART XIII: THE MARK

THE TREE GATE WAS A MOST WELCOME SIGHT. Its wide limbs outstretched like open arms calling for an embrace. After taking several days to recover from the grueling ordeal they had been through, the five Earth natives were ready to return home. Along the way, Tor'Engryn had insisted they spend as much time as possible in his forest dwelling at the newly bustling Logarthiym village where he fretted over their wounds and nutritional needs like a mother hen. He had done his job well and the travelers felt stronger and more able-bodied than they had in quite a long time. After a series of hugs and tearful farewells, the Logarth Elder finally released them on their way but not without extracting a promise from them for a soon return.

The family's journey home, though several days long, was buoyed by renewed provisions and a sense of victory that kept their steps light and their conversations lively. To ensure their safety, Justhynial had sent a small band of Westyr Guard warriors to keep watch over them. Throughout the day they silently wheeled in the sky above or trotted beside them on the trail when darkness fell. As they traveled, each family member relayed his or her own experiences in the journey through Haizorr.

The travelers stopped to setup camp for the final leg of the trip home. Eventually, the question that had been nagging at Thomas, Jillian and the children since beginning the quest finally arose. That evening, while preparing their makeshift shelters and dinner, Thomas could stand it no longer and turned to Samuel, "Okay, tell me. How is it that you became the Caller?"

"I was wondering when you might ask," Samuel chuckled.

The others, overhearing the topic of the conversation, drifted closer to have their curiosity itch scratched. Samuel turned aside and began pawing through his pack to produce a tattered scroll and a torn page from the Book. Thomas accepted them and frowned as he examined them closer.

"Wait. *You* took them?"

Samuel nodded grimly. "Had to," he said.

"What do you mean, you *had to?*"

Samuel looked his friend in the eye. "Thomas, you're a Seeker. And you're good at it."

Thomas shrugged, "So?"

"You're also stubborn. I know you well enough to know that you were going to go chasing after that grayvyk that stole the portal scroll all by yourself."

Thomas shifted uncomfortably and bit his lip. Samuel was right, and he knew it.

Samuel continued, "I suspected there would be grayvyks watching the Tree Gate now that they'd found it, so I used the creature summon scroll and code page to call the darchlytes to clear the path." His voice lowered, "I was only trying to protect you and the family."

Thomas nodded, recalling the reeking graveyard they had encountered upon entering Haizorr.

Samuel continued, "Then I set about trying to destroy the page and the scroll to rid the realms of their danger once and for all."

Thomas was stunned, "You what?"

The older man nodded. "During the night I tried burning them, soaking them in water—even tried tearing them to pieces. Nothing worked. Believe me, I tried everything. There was obviously something more at hand that went far beyond me."

The camp became quiet then. Nightfall sounds stole across the landscape as the cool evening mist settled in. The rhythmic thumping of Westyr Guard hooves could be heard just beyond the line of sight as they made their own camp nearby and began a steady vigil of night watch patrols.

The old caretaker's hands had taken to building a fire ring, carefully arranging stones before mounding a frame of sticks and tinder. He struck a weather-proof match and kindled a small blaze that drew everyone closer to its promise of warmth.

"Eventually it occurred to me that perhaps the scroll and code page could only be destroyed while on Haizorr," Samuel continued, rubbing his hands over the fire to warm them, "So I crossed over."

"Why didn't you just tell me?" Thomas asked. He tried to understand the logic behind his friend's actions but only found himself growing more confused and agitated.

Samuel rose to his feet, "Because you fired me, remember? You were so hot under the collar you'd not hear any of it." Both men stood toe to toe for a minute before Samuel relaxed and sat down on a stump. He sighed loudly, "Besides, I had no choice."

Thomas threw him a confused look and started protesting in a long string of questions to go along with his usual routine of excited pacing. Samuel simply ignored him and began rolling up his left sleeve all the way to the armpit. It was just about when Thomas began declaring that Samuel indeed did have a choice that the older gentleman raised his bare arm above his head, exposing the underside of his strong triceps. Thomas closed his mouth and stared at the unmistakable purplish spiral on the underside of his friend's upraised arm.

Samuel was marked.

"I'm a Guardian, Thomas. I throw counter punches. I just do what I do. When I entered Haizorr right in the middle of that raging grayvyk-darch-lyte battle my mark burned with intense fire." The old man thoughtfully rubbed at the spot on his arm, "It was calling me to war against the Dragon." He grabbed the creature summon scroll from Thomas and held it up for emphasis, "So war I did." Then he handed it back.

Thomas was dumbfounded. How had he not known? After all these years of working together, never once did Samuel mention his marking. But as he stood there staring and thinking about it, the more sense it made that he bore the mark of a Guardian. Samuel was ever present with words of caution and wisdom and had always insisted on the upkeep of their home and maintaining the security systems. He also tried to recall if he had ever seen Samuel wear a short-sleeved shirt. Try as he might, he could not remember the man ever working the garden or property in anything other than his usual button-downs with long sleeves. Samuel did not even go swimming during the times they would vacation together. Thomas just assumed he was very conservative and did not wish to remove his shirt.

Sharing the burden of being marked was something to which Thomas could relate. He stepped closer to his friend and rested a hand on his strong shoulder.

"I'm sorry," both men said at once.

And that was the last anyone spoke of it. Samuel's hard choice had been the right one in the end. All the next day as the family trekked the final miles of the trip home, they continued sharing with one another the various aspects of their own adventures. There was so much to tell! As each spoke, the bond between them grew stronger and respect for one another's strengths deepened. Thomas and Jillian silently ground their teeth as they listened to Jayce describe the ill treatment he had received at the hands of Drayven. The fact that Justhynial had taken the man into custody was the only thing that eased their parental uneasiness.

Thomas' thoughts drifted often to his brother during the quiet moments of their trek home. The man had seemed genuinely repentant and eager to make restitution to the land he had once sought to conquer. The Dragon's betrayal of his trust coupled with his harrowing dangle inside the open mouth of Dearth had apparently altered Drayven somewhere deep inside. Only time would prove that theory now. He was to be taken to serve at Westyr Guard tower until Justhynial determined his sentence and rehabilitation complete. As the strong blue arms of his captors led him away, Drayven had begged Thomas to find and look after his daughter for him until he returned. Thomas assured his twin that he would try.

Now, all of that seemed like a lifetime ago as the family gathered around the Tree Gate. Most of the grayvyk bodies near the portal's entrance had been hauled away by the good natured darchlytes who were toiling hard to restore balance to Haizorr. They had mourned their dead and even now strode about the clearing to purge the area of any lasting signs of the battle that had occurred in this place. The smell was already noticeably better. Thomas thought it strange to see the once mysterious race of giants walking about in full daylight, humming like great bumblebees. Moving now with grace and ease, the burden of the curse no longer creased their brows. The small group of humans watched in silent awe for several more moments before clasping hands around the great Tree.

Thomas spoke the riddle with a knowing smile.

"From East to West the span is wide, with love cross to the other side. Should the Harm descend across the land, may Death's own sting be in thy hand."

With the powerful words spoken, the Tree Gate began its transformation. The low ripping sound followed by the trunk twisting and unfurling before them was a most welcome sight. With their task complete, the circling Westyr Guard above screeched a farewell and disappeared into the lofty mists as the hidden room on the Earth side of the Gate slowly became visible. Though familiar, it looked oddly foreign after spending so many days in Haizorr—like returning to an old elementary school one graduated from years before.

"That's how you did it!" Jayce said, eyes wide with an enlightened gleam. He was staring up at the two great outstretched limbs of the Tree Gate pointing East and West like an ancient compass.

"Did what?" Thomas asked.

"The riddle! It's like a prophecy talking about you—about us! That's how you beat the Dragon!" Pulling out the Vyritas stone from his pocket, he continued, "At first I thought that maybe somehow I had done it." He looked a tiny bit disappointed.

Thomas thought for a moment, then nodding said, "You played your part, Jayce. You confronted darkness with truth." He put an arm around his son's shoulders and squeezed. "We all did."

Heidyl asked, "But how did you survive inside the Dragon for so long?" She shuddered at the memory of watching her father being swallowed by the terrible toothy monster.

A shadow passed across Thomas' face. The belly of the Beast was a most haunting place. He knew it would likely plague his thoughts and dreams for years. "I really don't know exactly," he answered. "Something guided me through that horrible realm, like a light in my soul leading me to stand in front of the blackest, most vile thing I'd ever seen. It was—"

He paused and took a deep breath to steady his thoughts. Whatever he had seen had shaken him to the core.

After a moment Thomas continued, "I'm not sure how, but I knew it was the Dragon's heart." He absently fiddled with the keen grayvyk claw dangling once again under his shirt. Nodding his head toward the tree he went on, "The Tree Gate prophecy just kept playing through my mind. When I spoke the words aloud in that moment, I felt incredible strength rush through my body and into my arms, so I struck." He shrugged, "I just acted on faith and hope."

"And love," said Jillian reaching for his hand. "It was love."

"Yes," he said, "and love."

Thomas looked upon his family and a grateful feeling filled his chest. Yes. He certainly did love them. Sharing a glance with each one he marveled inwardly at the ordeal the family had endured together. They all had been altered somewhere deep inside. But Jayce had visibly changed. His eyes lingered a moment longer on his son. Where once resided a sullen despondence, courage and confidence now radiated from the boy's face.

And something more.

As the sunbeams streamed through the branches above and played across his cheek, the ragged bruise around Jayce's eye seemed to have lost its irregular pattern. It had obviously faded during the healing process, but now an unmistakable spiral shape had begun to form just below the skin. Thomas grinned at his son.

The Tree Gate finished its last stage of opening, and one by one each family member passed through. The colors and scents of Haizorr winked out as they returned to the old familiar sights and smells of home. Everything was just as it had been when they left, but each familiar shape now dripped with a sort of freshness that had not been there before. For a while, none spoke. Looking from one to the other each shared the unmistakable sense that they were standing together at the doorway to something new.

EPILOGUE

THE CHURCH FOYER BUZZED WITH CHATTER. Strong summer sunbeams poured through the high-arched windows to bathe the room in warm light. After services, this high level of commotion persisted as friends reconnected, children played, and families moved in a slow distracted progression toward their parked cars. Thomas, Jillian and Samuel were excitedly speaking with a new couple who had recently moved to the area. From where Jayce and Heidyl stood with their friends at the far side of the foyer, the greeting seemed more like a reunion than a friendly welcome to strangers.

Heidyl elbowed Jayce and whispered in his ear, "I'll bet they're marked. Mom and Dad always act like that when they find something important."

It was true. In the months that had followed the return through the Tree Gate, the family had embarked on several journeys together. With school out for summer vacation, they were able spend a great deal of time planning new family adventures. Thomas and Jillian had kept the expeditions simple in order to help their children hone their newfound skills and learn to avoid danger. A few times they had traveled across, returning to Haizorr for artifact collection or to study the environment. They even paid a visit to the Logarthiym village where the elated Tor'Engryn greeted them with an excited whirlwind of speedy sprints. But most of the time had been spent on the Earth side searching for people who shared their gifts. Jayce suspected that the latter search was more personal for his father but kept the matter to himself.

As he watched them, Jayce could not help but notice how his mother's hand kept reaching up to fidget with the spot at the back of her head as she spoke with the people she had just met. He nodded his agreement with his sister.

"What do you think they are?" he asked.

Heidyl frowned and thought for a moment as she scanned the two newcomers. "Hard to say. Seekers maybe?" she replied, then shrugged, "What are you asking me for? You're the one who's the Verity, remember?"

"Yeah, but I'm not a fortuneteller."

At that moment a beeping alarm sounded from Heidyl's pocket. She sighed with annoyance as the glucose monitor she wore signaled her blood sugar was low. Popping a few sugar candies into her mouth, she wistfully longed for another trip to Haizorr where she could be free from the condition—at least for a little while. The thought brightened her somewhat and she smiled.

Jayce's best friend, Davey, had been watching the brother and sister interaction from nearby. Not to be ignored he burst into their privacy with typical good nature, "What are you little hens clucking about?" Then he playfully jostled and elbowed them, planting himself to stand between the two.

They smiled and Heidyl made a face at him, then flapped her arms like wings. Clucking like a chicken she said, "Buh-GAWK!" All three friends shared a laugh. Her distraction worked and the subject changed.

Jayce felt badly about keeping secrets from Davey. Lately it felt like all he did was try to find new ways of inventing curious diversions to avoid lying to his best friend about his mysterious second life. In many ways he felt closer to Heidyl now than anyone else in the world. She was quickly becoming the one person with whom he felt he could be completely transparent. While he still loved hanging out with Davey, he always felt like he was hiding a truth that was written on his face.

In fact, that was exactly the case.

Suddenly Davey gasped and clutched his chest looking as though he had just been struck by a mini heart attack. Gripping Jayce by the arm he whispered hoarsely, "There she is!"

Following his wide-eyed stare, Jayce saw the object of Davey's affections walking toward them. Davey had gone white as a sheet and he looked like he might swoon. Heidyl rolled her eyes at how silly he was behaving. The young woman's red hair shone in the sunlight as she approached. The intensity in her emerald green eyes was made more so by her confident stride. She stopped several feet from them and smiled. Davey's mouth hung open like a fly trap until Jayce nudged him with his elbow. It snapped shut with an audible *clop*.

Heidyl was the first to show any sort of civil gesture. Holding out her hand she said, "Hi. I'm Heidyl." The new girl shook hands with her and was about to speak when Jayce interrupted.

"Aren't you the new girl in Algebra class?" he said.

Davey was nodding as if answering for her.

"Yeah, we moved here just before the school year ended," she said. Then, regarding Davey, added, "Is he okay?"

Heidyl smirked, "Oh, this is Davey. He's just madly in—"

"Tongue tied," said Jayce, rescuing his friend from further embarrassment. Nodding toward the couple his parents were speaking with across the room he asked, "Those your folks?"

The group was laughing together now at some joke his father had made. Yes, it certainly did seem more like a reunion of old friends than a first-time encounter. *Come to think of it,* Jayce wondered, *Mom and Dad did act a bit more eager to get to church today than usual.*

The redhead turned to see where he had indicated. As she did, Jayce noticed her absently scratching at a spot on her shoulder. Her fingers had flipped up the cuff of her short sleeve revealing the purplish edges of a spiral marking. Jayce smiled.

"No. Those are my foster parents. My mom died a few years back in a car accident and I haven't seen my dad since I was a toddler," she replied in a matter-of-fact tone. A cold acceptance clouded her face for a moment. She went on, "I don't know why exactly, but we sort of felt like moving here was a good place to make a fresh start."

The foster couple made eye contact with her and she waved to them. The chatting adults then began making their way through the sea of people to the group of teens.

When they reached them, Jillian spoke, "Well, we were going to introduce you guys, but it looks like you've already met."

"Not officially," said the red-haired girl extending her hand to Jayce, "I'm Raiya."

As Jayce accepted her greeting, a strange feeling crept over him. He blinked his eyes trying to clear it. Raiya grinned, then winked at him.

Thomas chimed in, "We wanted to surprise you guys."

Davey was still nodding and staring at Raiya.

Jillian looked at him and asked, "Are you feeling all right?"

Heidyl smirked and piped up again, still trying to get in her joke, "He's just madly—"

"Davey," said the nodding boy, "I'm—Davey." He stuck out his hand awkwardly as if striking a deal with a car salesman.

Raiya grinned and shook it. "Yeah, I know. I've seen you in Algebra. Nice to meet you, Davey." The boy fairly melted.

With the greetings passed around and after a short spell of small talk and a promise to "get our families together soon", it was time for Raiya to leave. Before turning to go, she raised an amber eyebrow and pointed to Heidyl's bare ankle and then up at Jayce. "Nice tattoos," she said with a smirk then spun back to catch up with her foster folks.

Heidyl gasped and looked stunned for a moment. Turning to her brother she asked, "She knows?"

Jayce absently rubbed the spiral mark around his eye that had been nothing more than a bruise just weeks before. It had stopped buzzing the instant he shook hands with Raiya. He was nodding.

"Oh yeah, she knows."

Davey was still admiring Raiya as she disappeared between the cars in the parking lot. "Knows? Knows what?" He had noticed the strange, familiar glance she and Jayce had shared earlier. A twinge of jealousy cropped up inside the boy.

Caught up in the moment, Jayce and Heidyl had completely forgotten that he was still standing there with them. Heidyl gulped and hoped she had not carelessly given away any of their family's secret.

Eager to quickly divert attention away from their marks, Jayce gave his friend a good-natured clap on the back and nodded toward Raiya's departing vehicle.

"It's okay, buddy. She's family."

Found.

HAIZORR MAPS AND NOTES

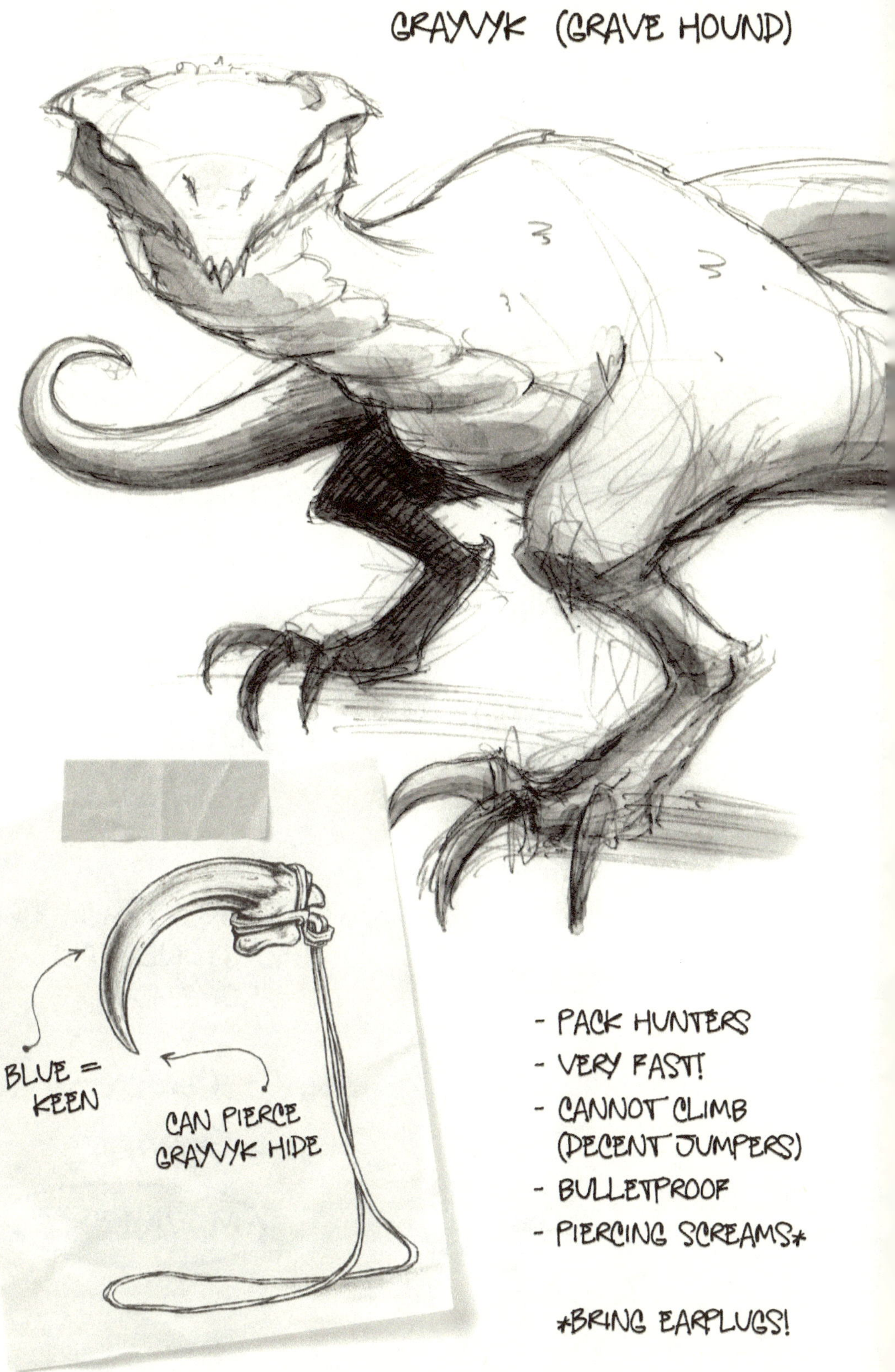

GRAYVYK (GRAVE HOUND)

BLUE =
KEEN

CAN PIERCE
GRAYVYK HIDE

- PACK HUNTERS
- VERY FAST!
- CANNOT CLIMB
  (DECENT JUMPERS)
- BULLETPROOF
- PIERCING SCREAMS*

*BRING EARPLUGS!

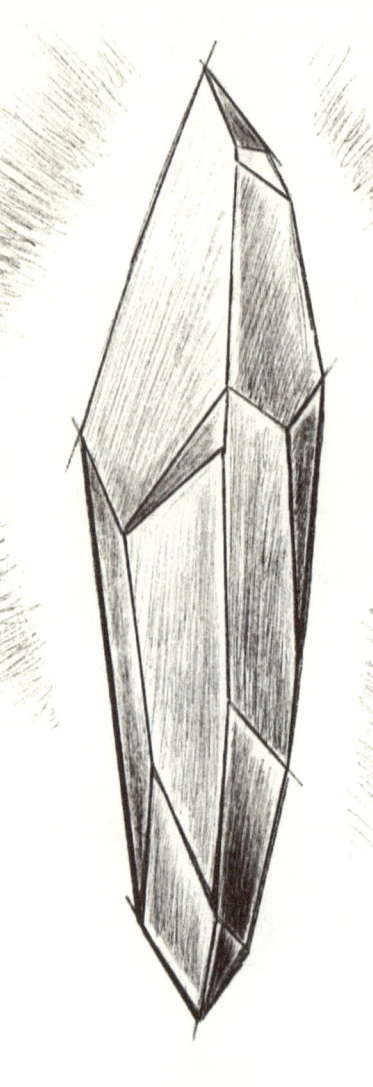

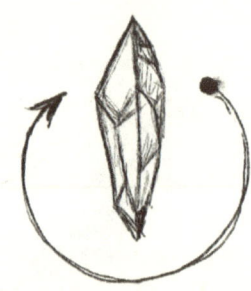

"DISSERE PORTAS"

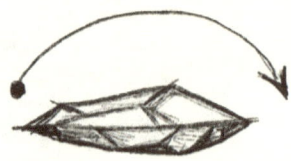

"SIGNATE PORTAE"
(STOPS THE THINNING)

GREEN
DOES NOT
MEAN GO!

*NEED TO ATTACH TO
THE STONE WALL
SOMEHOW:

- ~~GLUE?~~

- ~~VELCRO?~~

- MAGNETS?

SUMMON
PORTAL

LOGARTH (LOGARTHIYM)

"WISTA"
- GREEN SCOUT
- TOP SPEED?
- LOYAL
- BRAVE

"SHATTER
SHIELD...
SCALE
BUSTER!"

BLACK ROCK MINE
- NEAR VILLAGE

PROPERTIES
- LIGHT WEIGHT
- MALLEABLE
- DEVASTATING!

*KEEP SEEING THIS IN MY NIGHTMARES -
...IT MUST MEAN SOMETHING... BUT WHAT?

SURGICALLY REMOVABLE?
(WOULD I WANT TO?)

* DOES IT GIVE ABILITY
OR JUST CONFIRM IT?

THE
MARK

- ROUGHLY 2" WIDE
- BORN WITH OR APPEARS
  AT RANDOM
- HEREDITARY?
- LOCATIONS VARY
  (*SEE DIAGRAM)

INDICATORS:
  - ITCHING
  - BURNING
  - BUZZING
  - TINGLING
  - PAIN / THROB
  - ???

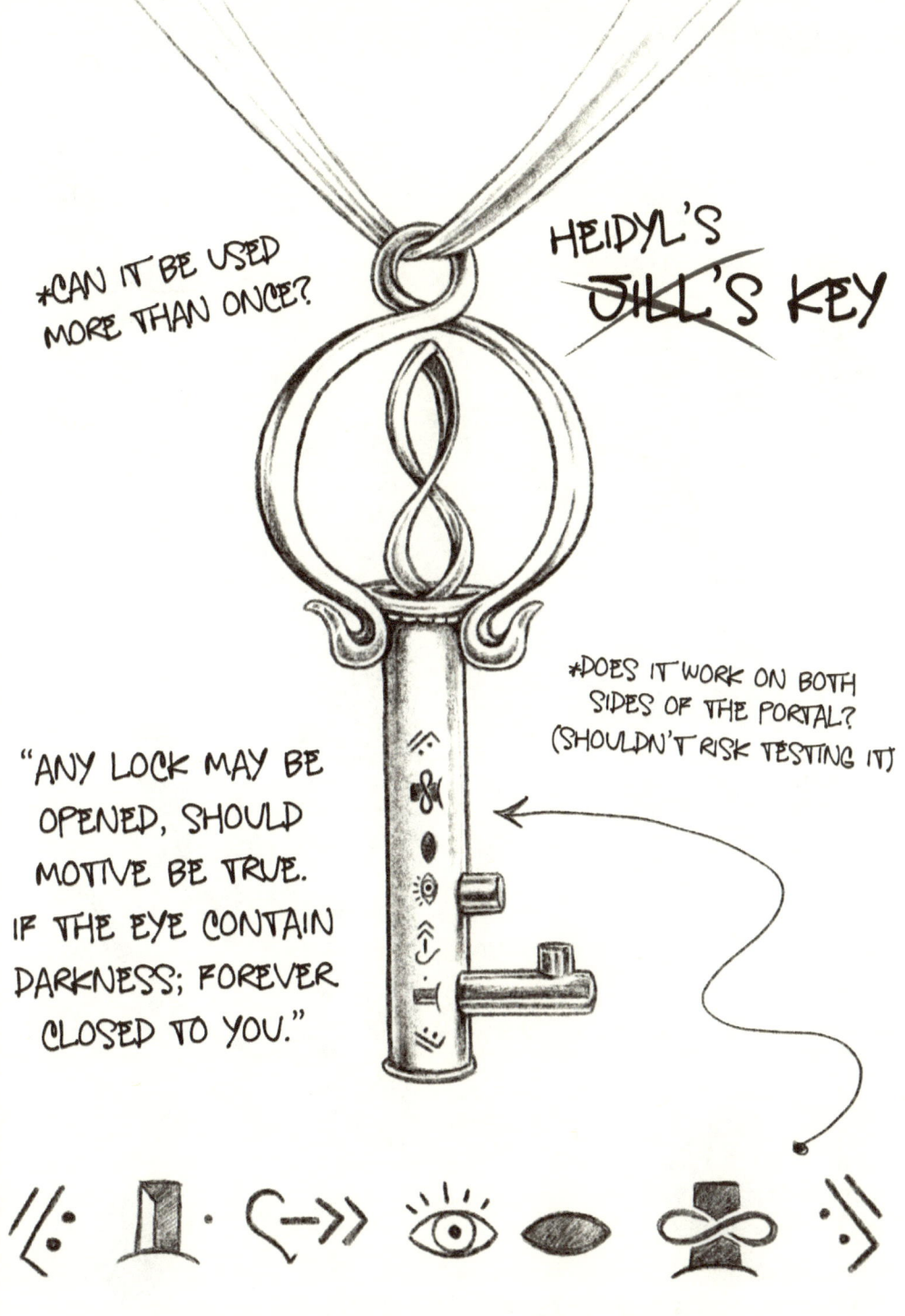

*ROUGHLY COPIED FROM "THE BOOK"

CURSE of the DARCHLYTE

IF ONE CROSSED OVER,
WOULD THEY BE CURSED HERE, TOO?

*HOW WOULD THEY EVER KEEP UP WITH OUR SUN?
(TWIN MOONS SEEM TO ALTER THE ROTATION SPEED OF HAIZORR)

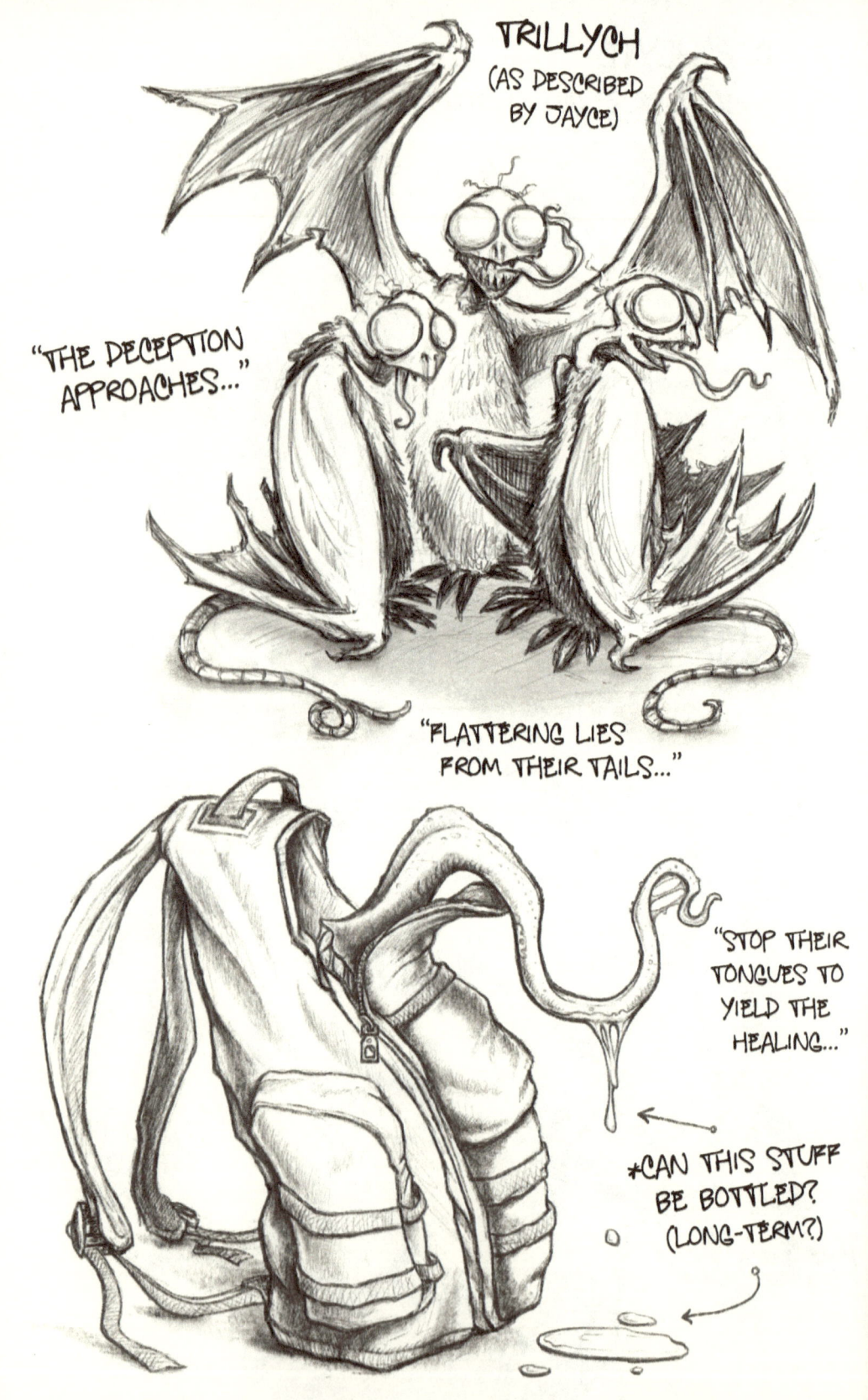

FYDAS

*WILL IT WORK IN
BOTH REALMS?

SPEAK THE TRUTH WITH LOVE ON YOUR LIPS...

VYRITAS

...AND VICTORY SHALL BE YOURS.

"DIG. DIG! DIG!"

SUMMON
CREATURE

*BE CAREFUL!

LITTLE RAG MAN
(AS DESCRIBED BY JAYCE)

- IS IT A SYMBIOTIC CREATURE?
- MIND SEEMS TETHERED TO GIANT EYE

*WHERE DID IT GO?

BLACKYNSPYRE SENTRY
(AS DESCRIBED BY JILLIAN & HEIDYL)

- AGILE / SILENT
- JAILKEEPER / CHIEF MINION
- CAN CAMOUFLAGE ITSELF!

*TENTACLES STRONG ENOUGH TO LIFT A HUMAN!

FRAMED OCULUS
(AS DESCRIBED BY JAYCE)

"I WOULD HAVE GIVEN ANYTHING JUST TO HAVE HAD
A FISTFUL OF SAND IN THAT MOMENT!"
— JAYCE

WHITE WOLF

- LARGER THAN ANY EARTH WOLF!

- CAN SEE IN TOTAL DARKNESS

- PACK HUNTERS AND SOLO STALKERS!

RAT-MEN

COMMON SLAVES / SERVANTS

WHY SO MANY SCROLLS ?!

WHO (WHAT?) MADE THEM?

WHY **MY** FAMILY?

WHY?!

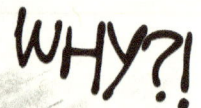

THINGS ARE NOT WHAT THEY SEEM, SO...

(dragon)

BE EXTRA CAREFUL BECAUSE...

MARK LOCATIONS AND KNOWN* CLASSES:

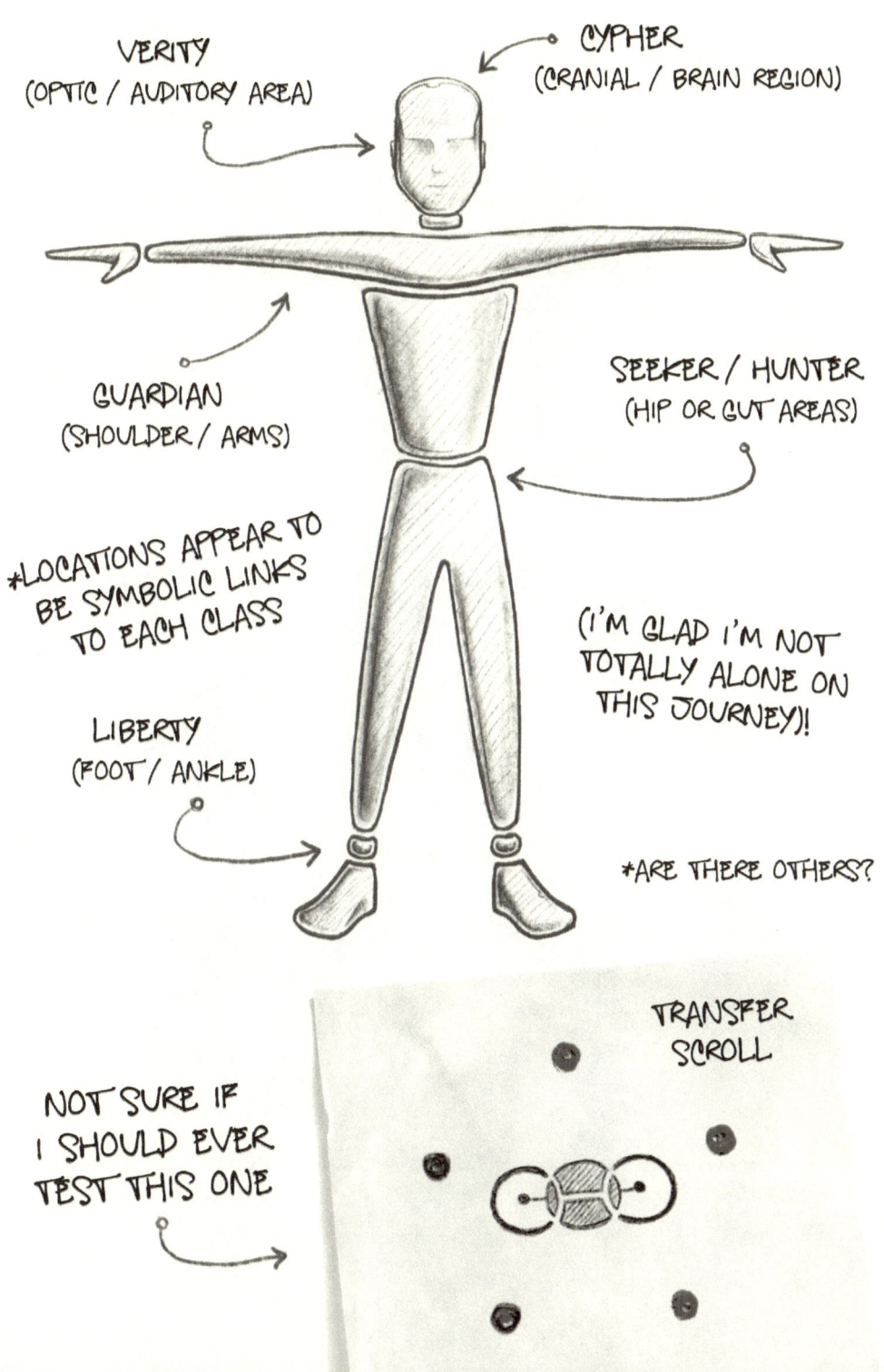

VERITY
(OPTIC / AUDITORY AREA)

CYPHER
(CRANIAL / BRAIN REGION)

GUARDIAN
(SHOULDER / ARMS)

SEEKER / HUNTER
(HIP OR GUT AREAS)

*LOCATIONS APPEAR TO
BE SYMBOLIC LINKS
TO EACH CLASS

(I'M GLAD I'M NOT
TOTALLY ALONE ON
THIS JOURNEY)!

LIBERTY
(FOOT / ANKLE)

*ARE THERE OTHERS?

TRANSFER
SCROLL

NOT SURE IF
I SHOULD EVER
TEST THIS ONE

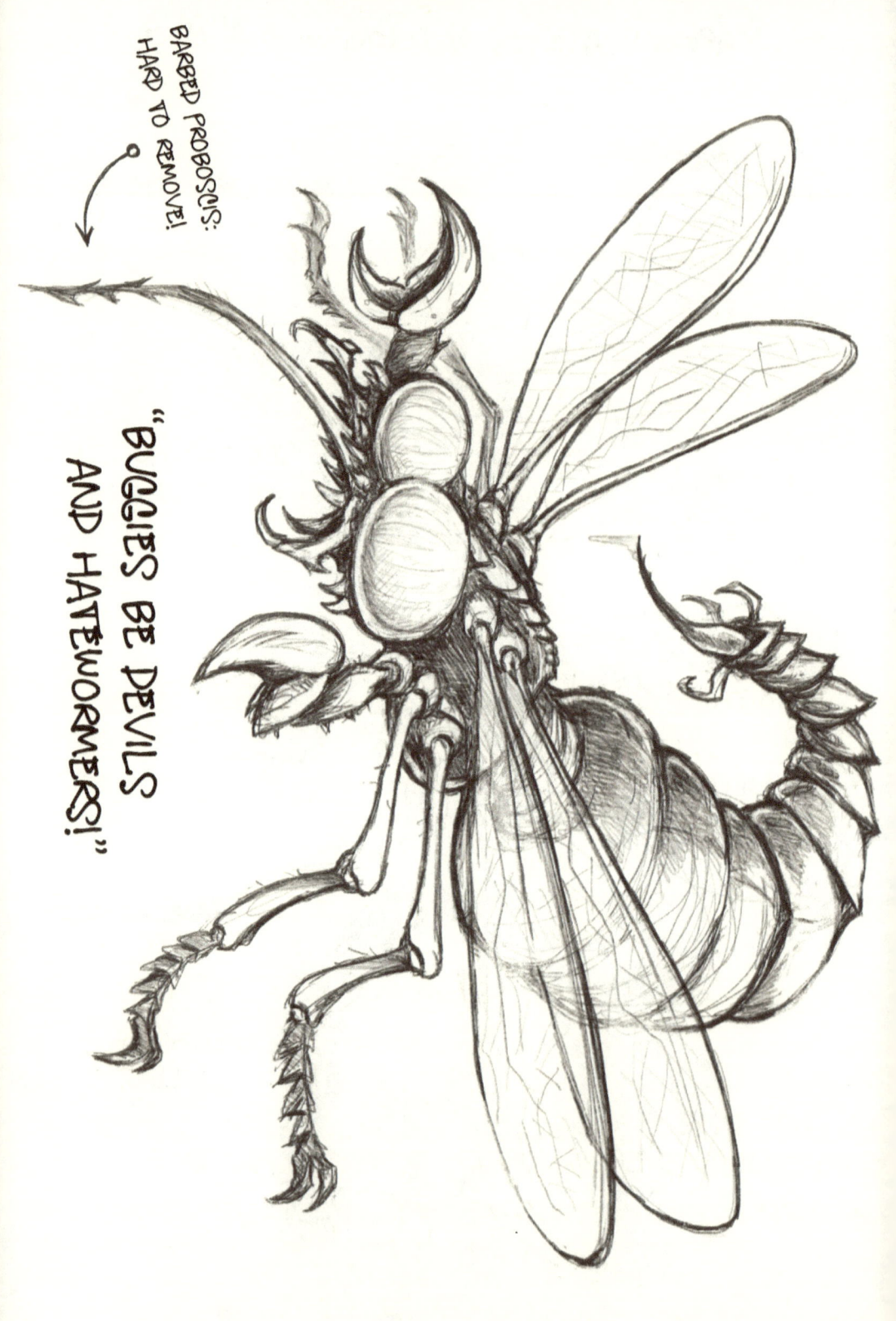

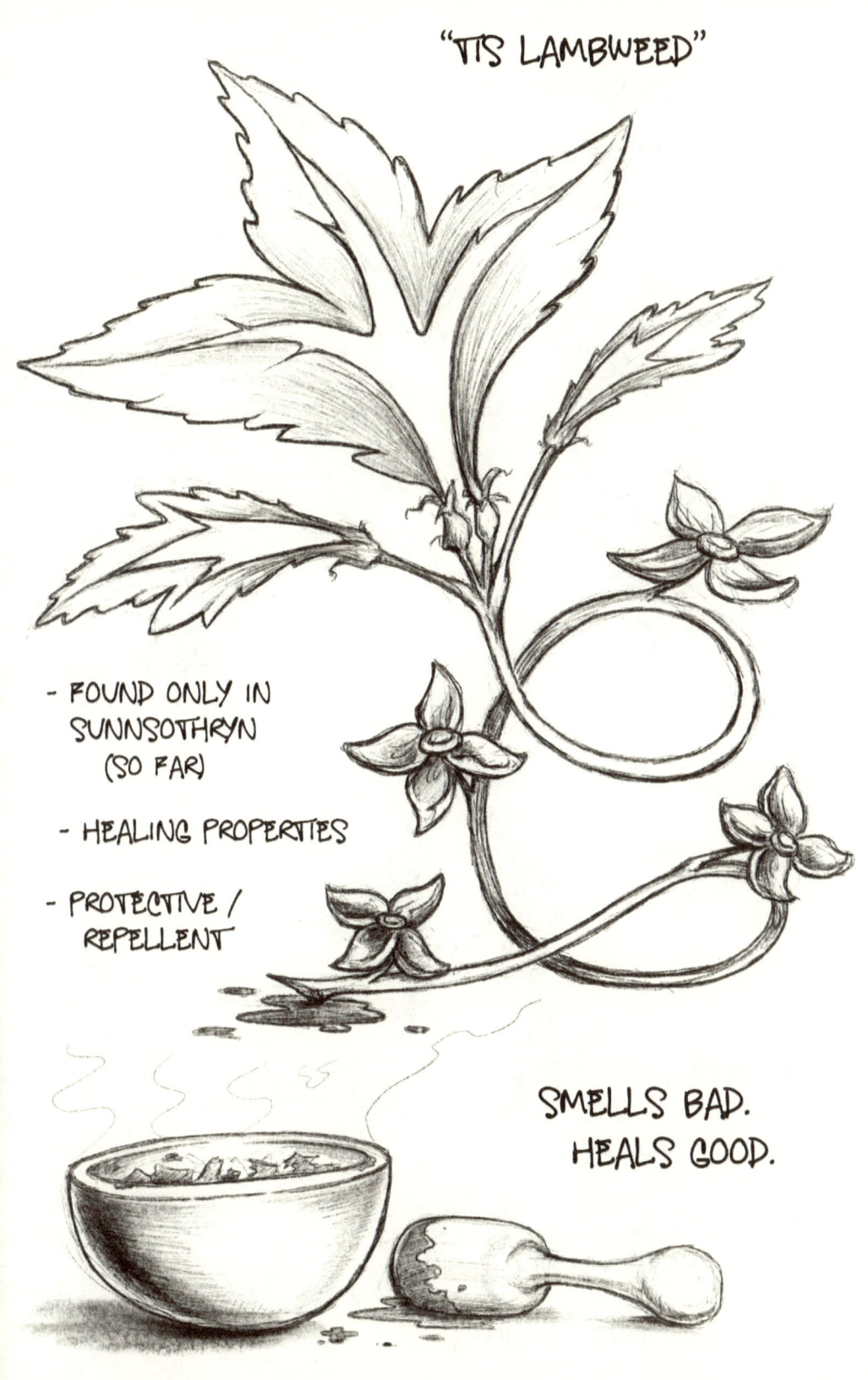

"TIS LAMBWEED"

- FOUND ONLY IN
  SUNNSOTHRYN
  (SO FAR)

- HEALING PROPERTIES

- PROTECTIVE /
  REPELLENT

SMELLS BAD.
HEALS GOOD.

JUSTHYNIAL
(LORD OF SUNNSOTHRYN)

- FIRST OF A
NOBLE FAMILY LINE
#HIGHLY REVERED!

- COMMANDER-IN-CHIEF
OF THE WESTYR GUARD

- GIVER OF MIGHTY GIFTS!

TRANSLUCENT
BLUE SKIN

(HOW OLD IS HE?)

POWERFUL HOOVES!

THE ONE WHO CALLS
        IS THE ONE WHO CALLS —
        BE HE CALLING ONE,
        OR CALLING ALL —

NONE RESIST THE CLARION CALL.

FOUND.

AUTHOR'S NOTE

Scroll Seekers: The Black Dragon of Dearth began as a tale told to my eldest son during a long car trip home after a camp out.

"Daddy?" he asked.

"Yes, son?"

"Can you tell me a story?"

So it began.

Worlds and characters long hidden within my heart bubbled forth for hours as the minivan weaved along bumpy back roads through wooded terrain. He loved the story so much that he begged me to tell it again when we arrived at the house so his younger sister could hear. While unpacking my suitcases, and my two oldest children now sitting wide-eyed on the floor, I recounted the story. When I had finished, they extracted a promise from me to enshrine the tale within the pages of a book.

That which you now hold is my promise fulfilled.

Keep seeking,

Jason D. McIntosh